# Lilly – D
# Royal Gesh of Seairland

## Book 1 – The Ring of Yishi

## By: Al-Li Sone

**ISBN:** 978-1-0697331-0-8

**Cover design, Illustrations, and Editing:** Created by the author using AI-assisted tools, including collaboration with ChatGPT, an AI developed by OpenAI.

**Printed in Canada**
**First Edition**

For more information, visit: **LillyDSeries.com**

## Acknowledgments

Wow—so many people to thank.

First, my mom. Thanks for putting up with me all these years (a medal might be in order). And let's not forget my dad—I learned a lot from that guy. He was a true lover of the outdoors, no question about it.

Then all the people who have passed through my life, each one teaching me something—kindness, patience, acceptance, non-judgment. How does one thank all those people?

And then there are my kids. They had to put up with my craziness. Yeah, I'm the crazy parent in their eyes.

If you think about it, we're just the sum of everything we've learned from every person—and every living thing—we've ever encountered. So... do I thank the entire universe? Maybe I should.

Some friends deserve thanks just for listening—whether it was rambling about this book or engaging in deep conversations about interconnection and world peace. Honestly, they should be thanked here as well.

In the end, here's to the people who haven't given up on humanity. You're the ones who keep the light on, who give us all hope.

Thank you.

*"Any sufficiently advanced technology
is indistinguishable from magic."*

*— Arthur C. Clarke, Clarke's Third Law*


*"Feelings come and go like
clouds in a windy sky.
Conscious breathing is my anchor."*

*— Thich Nhat Hanh*

<u>**Oath of the Royal Khem**</u>
<u>**Gesh of Seairland**</u>

May we, as the Royal Khem Gesh of Seairland, Live and serve as one, with the land, the sun, and the water, In sacred connection. We vow to act with integrity, in selfless duty, as protectors of all life, guardians of the life force, champions of bravery, advocates for peace, and defenders against all hostility. From this day forward, until our final breath.

# Chapter 1
### The Sky Falls Sideways

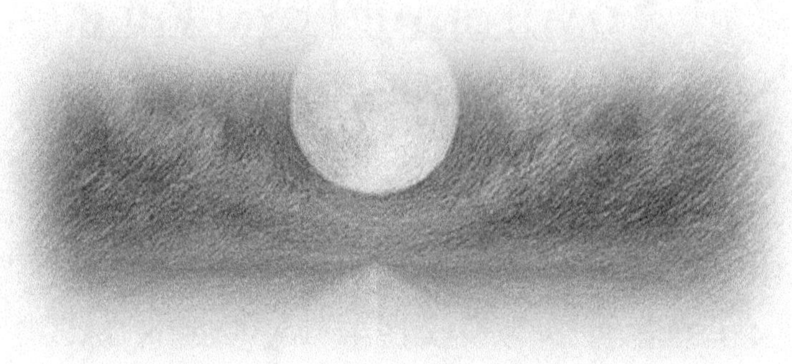

It is nighttime. The moon has squeezed out the sun.

A small car slices through blackness. One working headlight.

Inside, Mr. Dubois grips the wheel with one hand and his wife's fingers with the other. Pajama pants. Slippers.

Her contractions come like earthquakes—fast, mean, and rising.

Mrs. Dubois glances over at her husband with blazing green eyes. "She likes pineapple ham pizza."

"She who?" he says, not liking the answer before it comes.

"Our daughter," she huffs, wincing. "Don't forget."

He doesn't answer. He's too busy trying not to crash—or cry. *The hospital's still thirty minutes away. We're not making it.* He thinks, not saying out loud.

Instead, he jokes, "You sure? That's your favorite. How can anyone else on earth be that weird?"

She doesn't laugh.

Outside, the storm decides now's a good time to lose its mind. Rain begins to pound the windshield like it's trying to erase the car.

Then— fiery eyes of fire set deep in the darkest of dark. Charging towards them.

"Is that…a dog…or …a…machine?!"

**BOOM.**

The blackness slams them from the side. Metal crunches. Glass shatters. The world flips end over end.

When they land, miraculously upright, steam hisses from the hood.

Mr. Dubois' mind is still doing somersaults. He scans the wet ooze of night for a darker shape, expecting the next strike. His face is etched with confusion and concern. "Wha…?" His words fail to escape.

His wife presses both hands to her belly, teeth clenched.

"It's time," she gasps.

"No. No, no — here?!"

Her face tightens. She nods once. "Get something cool. Moss. Please."

"Moss?" He mutters in disbelief. He is still frantically searching the darkness for something of indefinite shape, but of definite intention."

"For her hand," she whispers. "You have to. Go."

"But—".

She grabs his shirt, pulls him close, and kisses him hard. "Go. Now."

He catches her green eyes. Sends his best smile back and opens the door. Rain stabs his skin. One slipper sinks in mud. He stumbles into the woods, arms up, heart pounding, on full alert.

# Chapter 2
## The Cry in the Car

Branches scrape his arms as he charges into the forest.
No flashlight.
No plan. Just fear and moss on his mind.
He skids to the base of a tree and digs. Fingers scrape something cold, damp, and maybe moss-adjacent.
Close enough.
He turns back toward the car—
**Whirrrrrr.**
Light bursts overhead, washing the woods in an eerie white.
His legs buckle.
Total confusion.
He drops.
Then, he is out cold.

From somewhere behind him—
A baby cries.
This wakes him.
He groans, scrambles to his feet, moss still in hand.
Back on the road, the car sits cracked and crooked.

Figures hover in the light. One shape floats—his wife—limbs limp, rising like smoke.

She is rising into …what?! That can't be a …spacecraft!?

"LEE!" he screams.

The light shuts off. Just—click.

Everything goes black …again.


He wakes again, face in the mud, still clutching moss.

A wail cuts through the silence.

He sprints to the car. No sign of her. Just twisted metal—and a baby.

He swings open the back door. There, wrapped in his wife's housecoat, is a furious, red-faced newborn.

On her palm, a glowing red mark burned into her hand—the same shape as her mother's necklace.

He scoops the baby up, rainwater running down both their faces.

"Lilly," he whispers.

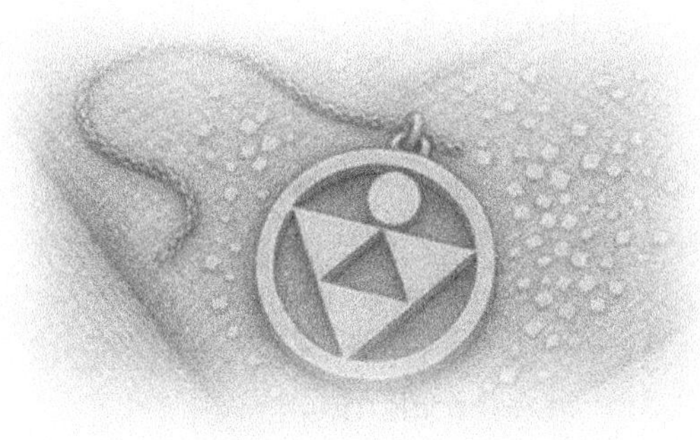

# Chapter 3
## The Ant Hill and the Chipmunk

**12 years (and 1 day) later**

Kids bunch in clumps as cars pull up, grab a kid or two, then drive off. Behind them, a big log building rises with pride.

A freshly painted sign hangs above the porch: **Camp Whatatwoda.**

Most kids are talking loudly, swapping hugs and back slaps before vanishing into the arms of waiting parents. The cool kids.

Most—but not all.

One girl stands alone, leaning against a pine tree.

The hood of her gray sweatshirt hides most of her face. Stray wisps of brown hair slip out underneath.

Her jeans are dirty. Last clean pair gone days ago. It's camp. Why bother?

She doesn't hear anyone.

Doesn't look at anyone.

Her earbuds are turned nearly to max—blasting a pretty good song.

Her head's down, watching ants.

They weave through the pine needles between her tattered sneakers. Busy. Clever.

She likes that.

A tug on her sleeve pulls her out of the moment.

Lilly sighs, yanks both earbuds free, and looks up—eyes as green as forest moss.

Way too close, a skinny face looms, topped with oversized glasses. The lenses make the kid's eyes look like a cartoon chipmunk. "Hey, Lilly, I said! Maybe you didn't hear me 'cause of your music. Is it a good song? Have I heard it? Is it a good group? I don't know much about music, but I'd probably like it if you like it."

It all comes out in one hyper breath.

No, it's not a chipmunk.

It's Stanley Nivel. Definitely … NOT … one of the cool kids.

"Ah… hey… hi, Stan," Lilly says, trying to smile.

A thin thread of snot swings from his nose. It moves in and out with each breath like a slow-motion yo-yo. Hopefully, he doesn't catch it with his tongue.

"You're taking the van too, hey? My parents are working, so they can't pick me up. You're good at archery—you beat them all! Last year they had buses, this year it's vans. I asked around, and they said you don't have a boyfriend. I don't have a girlfriend. Maybe you could teach me archery? Do you like the vans? I like the vans. Great suspension. I like the new smell. Maybe we'll be in the same van?"

His chipmunk eyes blink at her like he's expecting vows.

Lilly leans back, trying to escape the giant lenses—

But the tree behind her won't budge.

"I guess I like the new vans," she says slowly, not sure which question is the least dangerous.

Stanley beams like she just asked him to the prom. His whole face lights up as he snorts the snot back in. At least he didn't lick it.

**"Hey Snivel!"**
The shout booms across the camp yard.
Lilly looks up.
The crowd of kids parts like wheat in a storm. Everyone backs up a full arm's length—no, a gorilla's arm's length.
A big girl stomps toward them. Built like a pro football player and twice as mean. She charges straight at Stanley like a primate spotting a banana. She grabs his shirt—banana peel and all—
—and lifts him clean off the ground.

# Chapter 4

All bodily movement freezes on Stan. It's that predator-prey thing—and Stan's the prey. The only thing moving is a fresh dribble of snot inching down his lip. His eyes are stuck wide open.

"Hey… um… hi… um, Olga," he stammers.

"You were supposed to give me your dessert today, you little snot drizzle!" Olga snarls. Her face is all curdled up like a pudgy orangutan. Her eyes are dried raisins buried in curdled pudding. She shoves her beady glare right up to Stanley's glasses.

"Leave him alone, Bartlutt!" Lilly blurts out as she pushes herself off the tree and takes a stance, feet apart.

"Mind your beez-wax, *Dumbois*!" Olga spits, her eyes flicking down to Lilly's shoes. "What—get those from the second-hand store? Your crazy drunk daddy too broke to buy you new ones? Or was he too busy hunting aliens?"

"What? Same old recycled garbage?" Lilly snaps. "Let him go already!"

Stanley and his snot, dangle like a broken puppet, legs twitching, eyes bugged. Only a wet gurgle escapes his mouth. A perfect snot bubble forms from his nose.

The crowd begins to close in, circling like wild dogs smelling blood.

"Or what, *Dumbois*?" Olga growls. "You gonna kill me like your father killed your mother?"

"Oh, good one! You've used *that* before, too." Lilly's fists clench into tight little weapons. "Pick on someone your size!" *Ok. That one might have scared her.*

"What?" Olga laughs, loud and ugly. "You mean *your* size? You're about as puny as snot-face Snivelly here! Beat it, you annoying little fly."

She swings a backhand the size of a baseball mitt straight into the side of Lilly's head.

*CRACK.*

Stars explode in Lilly's vision. The trees and kids around her wobble like jelly. Her ears ring. Her jaw throbs. But her anger burns hotter. *Note to self: Duck next time.*

She plants her feet in the pine needles, squares her shoulders, and lunges.

She slams into Olga like a battering ram.

There's an *oomph!*

Probably from Stan, who drops like a sack of laundry the moment Olga loosens her grip. But Olga? She doesn't move an inch.

Lilly barely registers the blur of motion before—

*WHAM.*

The last thing she sees is a rock of a fist flying toward her face.

*Note to self: Duck faster next time.*

Then everything goes black.

# Chapter 5

## Something Hungry This Way Comes

A deer's face twists in panic.

He runs through the forest, legs flailing, head snapping back to check.

Nothing. Just trees. Just shadows.

But the forest explodes behind him. Branches snap. Small trees burst apart. Rotten logs blast into splinters. The ground shakes beneath him.

Boom. Boom. Boom.

Still nothing in sight. Is it some invisible predator, or the forest attacking?

The forest itself feels alive, angry, hungry.

The deer bolts in every direction, but the madness follows. There's no hiding. No escape. Only one chance.

The field.

He sees it—sunlight through the trees. A soft golden glow at the edge. He pushes toward it, faster, lungs burning.

The branches claw at his face, scratch his eyes.

He stumbles on a rock and launches forward like a bowling ball with sticks. He lands hard, scrambles up, and bolts across the clearing.

A breath later— BOOM!

The exact patch of grass erupts behind him. Dust billows into the sky. On that very spot, nothing seen mutates into something. The sunlight wavers. The air ripples. A shadow emerges from the haze. Then, becomes a monster, an alien machine.

It's massive. Dog-like. Carved from ancient darkness. Black scales glint like armor. It's three times the size of a bear. Legs thicker than tree trunks. Its red eyes glow like hot coals. On its back—

A rider.

He's huge. Swollen. Like a troll in a human suit. His skin is pale and pocked, like rotten oatmeal. His twisted face sits under a horned headdress. Flies buzz. A club dangles from one hand. A bone-colored armband grips his thick forearm. Smells like yesterday's trash after a heatwave.

He scans the yard, hunting.

Chicken coop.

Garden.

Gravel driveway. Small house. Garage.

A sign on the garage reads 32 Oak Drive.

Near the garage, a man bends over a machine, back turned—

The rider's gaze clings to the man's back, heavy and unnatural—enough to make any soul shiver.

Then the rider decides, turns, and taps the armband.

BOOM!

The beast launches. It clears the chicken fence in one bound.

Mid-air, metal beast, and ugly person vanish.

BOOM!

The chickens scatter, by some unseen force.

Where a chicken once stood, only a puff of feathers remains.

BOOM!

Another tremor, inside the chicken pen.

BOOM! Outside the chicken fence.

The ground dents—one heavy step after another—heading for the trees.

Then—silence.

One less chicken in the coop.

Feathers spiral down through the stillness.

Only the faint hum of machinery drifts from the garage.

Like nothing ever happened.

# Chapter 6

### A Pause Before... More Pain

A long white van pulls off at 32 Oak Drive. The tires shift from pavement hum to the bone-crunching grind of gravel.

Dust billows as the van rolls to a stop.

It just sits there—like a giant white bug that's landed. The windows vibrate with bass from a stereo cranked way too high. Green and red letters stretch across the side: **CAMP WHATATWODA.**

**BANG.**

The sliding door slams open.

Blaring music spits Lilly Dubois out like a white animal coughing up a furball.

She lands on both feet and yanks her backpack higher.

Her hood's up again.

There's blood splattered across her sweatshirt—her blood, of course. Maybe Stan's snot is too.

Gushing nosebleeds paint everything and take forever to stop.

One eye looks like a red plum jammed in the socket—already turning weird colors.

**BOOM. BOOM. BOOM.**

The bass slams into the trees. Into the ground. Into her toes. The door slams shut.

The van launches off, coughing dust and exhaust as the music fades.

Lilly waves after it. "Bye!" she calls into the dust. "Let's do this again sometime."

No one answers.

She stands at the edge of a gravel drive that vanishes into towering pine trees.

Her backpack drops with a soft thud. She pulls back her hood and wrangles her hair into a ponytail. "Hmph. I'm not puny. I'm height efficient," she mutters to the trees.

Off comes the sweatshirt—she ties it around her waist to hide the blood.

Her Camp Whatatwoda shirt is still clean enough.

At least it's not soaked in nose blood and Stan snot.

She runs her tongue along her bottom lip, checking the swelling.

Sighs. Shakes her head. Feels like a bicycle pump pumped her lip up too much. Nah …who will notice?

Then she slings the backpack over one shoulder and starts up the gravel driveway.

The air smells sweet—pine, dust, and wildflowers.
The gravel path bends gently.
Then the trees break open to the sky.
There's her house.
And just like that, the weight drops back onto her shoulders.
The knot in her stomach tightens.
Same as always. Welcome to the house of crazy.

# Chapter 7



It's just a one-level box. Big enough for a small family to start.

Way too small when you want to avoid someone living there. A few shingles are missing. The front door hangs from one hinge, like it gave up halfway through summer.

She's almost there when she hears a **whirring** off to the side.

The garage. It's one car door is open.

Her dad's hunched over something shiny inside. He's wearing a white one-piece coverall that isn't white anymore. It sags in all the wrong spots, stained with grease and oil. He looks like a marshmallow that fell in the dirt. Then the campfire. Then the dirt again.

Lilly sighs, eyes the sky, then exhales. "Maybe he won't notice," she mutters. "Yeah, right."

She squares her shoulders. Grits through the pain in her lip. Then walks toward him. "Hey, Dad!" she shouts over the whirring.

No response.

She taps his shoulder.

"Hey, Dad!"

The dirty marshmallow jolts upright—

—and spins around wearing what looks like a metal praying mantis on his head.

It's a homemade helmet: a kitchen strainer strapped on with goggles fused where his eyes should be. So much for straining the spaghetti tonight.

Lilly forces a smile. It pulls at her swollen lip.

The goggles zoom in—way too close.

His hair sticks out in black straw tufts under the strainer.

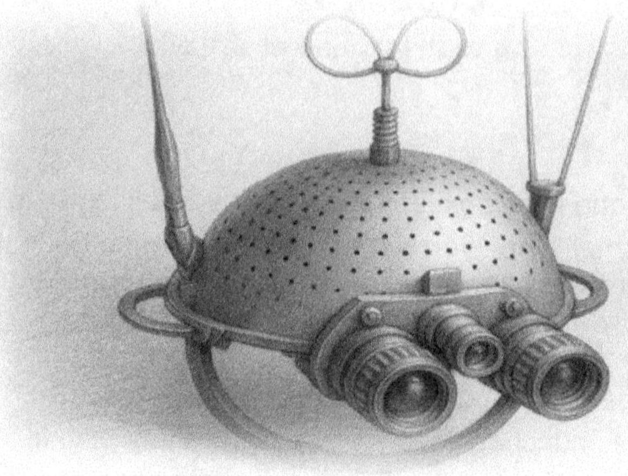

The lenses whirr into focus.

His hands grip her shoulders. "The aliens got you! I sent you to camp to keep you safe, and they found you anyway!"

"No, Dad. I'm fine."

"Were they blue? Or grey?" He scans the woods like an ambush is coming.

"It wasn't aliens."

"Are you okay?" He hugs her like he'll never let go again.

"I'm okay. I fell. That's all." Yeah, it's a lie.  But it's one of those that comes without being struck by lightning.

He peels off the contraption and sighs. His face is smeared with grease. His beard's a scruffy storm. His eyes—shadowed and red-rimmed. "But they're back," he mutters. "EMP readings are spiking. Thermal and UV scans caught something—too fast to record!" He gestures to a pile of wires.

Somewhere under it is probably Lilly's old computer screen. Who needs a big one anyway? Lilly has a small one now; she keeps it hidden under her mattress.

"Okay, Dad," Lilly says, keeping her voice calm. Stay mellow, avoid mayhem. Simple math.

"You need to be careful. Stay close to the house." His eyes sweep the woods again.

"Okay, Dad," she echoes gently. "Have you eaten? Used anything from the garden? Eggs from the coop?" She asks. *A meal a day ...keeps the crazy away.*

He straps the helmet back on. Twists a dial. The goggles come back to life with a soft whirr. Lilly squeezes his arm. "Dad. Have you eaten? Can I make you something?"

The goggles flick to her for a second—then back to the trees.

"Ah... yes... no... I mean... I'm fine. Be careful, okay, Lill? They're close today. I can feel it. I think the aliens have been in your garden." He stares past the coop now. "Maybe even the coop, too." He's spent most of her life guarding this property from imaginary enemies, aliens.

"Okay, Dad," she says again—this time to his back. She gives one last smile and heads into the house. Lilly has always wondered if imaginary friends would be a better option.

# Chapter 8
### Birthday Ghosts

Lilly enters through the back door into the kitchen.

It doesn't look anything like how she left it before camp. The sink is overflowing with dishes—her dad's dishes, undone and crusted over. *Oh, goody, lots of dirty dishes to do. Maybe later.*

On the counter, a whiskey bottle lies on its side, empty but for a puddle leaking underneath. Half-eaten meals surround it like forgotten, half-started projects.

The bottle reminds her of what Olga Bartlutt spat about her dad. Her chest tightens, like someone squeezing ice around her ribs.

In the living room, there's only one photo on the wall. It was taken twelve years ago. Her dad's holding a bundled-up baby—her, probably wrapped by some nurse who also snapped the photo. He doesn't look happy. He looks like someone who just lost everything.

Lilly bites her lip. Her throat thickens.

"Happy birthday, Lilly," she whispers—to the baby and herself.

Then she walks down the hall to her bedroom.

Lilly's room isn't exactly clean, but she knows where everything is…mostly.

It's full of stuff she finds interesting—forest treasures and adventure gear.

Weird stones, hollow wasp nests, giant pinecones, perfect acorns. One shelf holds a full snake skin she found last month. In one corner, five walking sticks lean like old friends. Because a good stick? Always useful.

Her gear is scavenged—yard sales, dumps, or saved-up allowance. Rope. Flashlights. Backpack frame. All ready.

She dumps out her camp bag.

Crumpled clothes and a few sports medals spill into the laundry pile.

An odor follows them.

She throws her head back. "Whew!" Coughs. Waves it away.

Medals can wait. Let the biohazard subside.

She grabs cleaner jeans and a shirt with less camp sweat. Adds a belt—because it helps hold the gear, and gear is life.

She starts scanning her shelves.

Fingers brush ropes. She picks the better one and stuffs it into the empty pack.

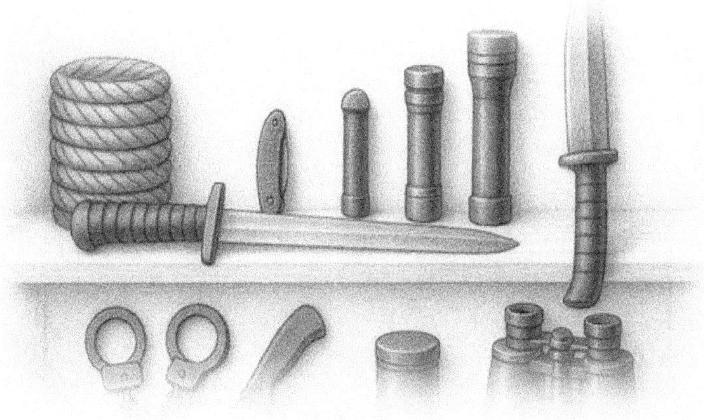

Her hand hovers over a real sword she got at a yard sale. "Naw," she mutters. She clips her favorite pocketknife to her belt. Spots the machete behind the flashlights. "Too big." Magnifying glass? "Not today."

Hands on hips. Mouth twisted. Thinking. "Where are you…" It's the curse of her organized chaos—stuff disappears like it's hiding from her.

She skips the BB pellets. Sees her five steak knives. Shakes her head. "Not today." That's for knife throwing. Today's mission feels different…dangerous. "Where are you…" More frustrated now.

Then, "Oh yeah!" She checks her nightstand. There it is—right between her flashlight and beat-up binoculars.

She picks up the small two-way radio and flips it on.

**Static crackles.**

She presses the side button.

"Hey, Zap-man, are you there?"

There's a pause.

Then—**crackle.**

# Chapter 9
### Radio Contact

"Hey Lilly-D! Back from your luxury resort vacation?" says a metallic-sounding voice.

Lilly smirks at the radio. "Shut up."

It's Zak Petterson. Her best friend.

"Wanna meet at the fort?" she asks. "Remember, we were finishing the elevator before dinner?"

"Yup. Meet you there. Standard procedure," Zak replies through the tiny speaker.

Another pause.

"But… the elevator's already up and running," he adds, super casual.

"No way! Does it work?"

"Of course it works!" His voice jumps out of the speaker—proud and just a little smug.

"I wish I could've helped," Lilly says, her voice softer.

"Hmmpf! Channel two in 21 seconds. Fort in five," Zak replies in full military mode.

"Geek," Lilly laughs into the radio.

"Shrimp!" bounces back.
She grins from ear to ear.
Swings her backpack over one shoulder.
Then stops.
Her eyes land on the machete.
"Hmmm…better to be prepared," she mutters, and tosses it in. I mean, hey, if a pocket knife is handy, why not a machete?

# Chapter 10
## Forest Escape

Lilly slips out the back door and breaks into a jog. She passes the garage like it's radioactive.

No sign of him.

She might make it—

"Wait! Where are you going?"

The voice hits like a tripwire.

Lilly freezes. Regret drops onto her like a bucket of cold water. Her stomach writhes like ants just woke up inside her.

Her father steps out from behind a stack of electronics. The strainer's gone, but his marshmallow suit remains—sagging and stained. "The aliens are here!" he blurts. "It's not safe in the forest today!"

"Dad… I'm fine," Lilly says, but her voice cracks. "I'm … just going to the fort. To meet Zak. Like always." She scans his face, begging for some scrap of reason.

"No! That's when they get you!" His hands shake. "They're watching!"

Something sharp turns in Lilly's gut. "All I have is the forest!" she shouts. "It's the only place that wants me. You don't! Mom doesn't!"

He blinks. Tries to speak—

She cuts him off. "There are no aliens, Dad! Not yesterday. Not ever!"

"They're out there!" he yells, voice rising.

"What do you care?" Her throat aches. "Did you even remember yesterday was my birthday?"

He stills. His panic melts into confusion.

"No. You didn't. Again!" Anger flares like fire licking dry wood. "You don't care about me! Just your imaginary aliens!"

He flinches, like being slapped.

"Aliens didn't take Mom!" she cries. "She left! Because she didn't want either of us!"

His mouth opens, but nothing comes out.

"She didn't want you because you're crazy! Drunk! That's what they say at school! They laugh at me! You're a joke!"

He sinks onto the step like the air's been knocked from him. "You …have …every right to believe that."

Lilly grips her backpack. Her other hand curls into a fist.

"I lost her, too," he whispers.

Tears blur her eyes. "Did you k… did you hurt my mother?" She couldn't say the words.

His face stills, like he's waited years for that question.

"That's what they decided," he says. "Not what happened."

"But you didn't. Right?"

"No, Lilly. I didn't. And that truth is heavier than a lie."

"Then why does everyone think you did?"

He hesitates. "Because… I didn't stop them."

"But… but…why?"

He looks away. "Some things are easier to live with than explain."

"You mean, you just …let everyone …think…!?" Twelve years of craziness and abuse for nothing. "I hate you." The words spill out of her mouth. The first time.

He doesn't blink. "That's not what you're saying."

"You let them think you're a murderer. You lied."

"I didn't want you growing up hunted, Lilly."

She steps back. "You let me grow up haunted. I hate you!" The second time saying it, didn't feel any better.

His mouth moves like a fish pulled from water—no sound.

She stands there one last moment.

Then she runs.

Bolts for the forest—for the only peace she knows.

"Lilly!" his voice cracks behind her. "Wait!"

But she doesn't. She runs—from something she can never outrun, fire in her chest.

# Chapter 11

## Bob the Tree Therapist

**W**hen she hits the lawn, it almost feels like she's left everything behind.

She slows to a walk past the chicken coop and garden.

A wall of green rises ahead—dense, tangled branches reaching like they're whispering secrets.

Lilly slips through a hidden gap only she and Zak know.

The forest inhales her. Quiet. Calm.

It wraps her up like a favorite blanket.

The rustling leaves drown out her father's frantic voice. The smell of moss and pine chases off the grease and metal stench of home.

She stops. Wipes away tears. The weight in her chest stays.

*Note to self: Acting angry equals saying crap you regret.*

A breath in. A breath out.

"Hello. I'm back," she whispers, like the forest might understand.

Here, school bullies can't follow.

The chaos at home can't touch.

The forest doesn't stare.

Doesn't shout.

Doesn't forget her birthday.

It just… is.

In the middle of all that green and stillness, something in her finally unclenches.

The air smells like wildflowers, pine, and cedar shavings—nature's healing spa.

She moves deeper, slipping past pine trunks too wide to hug.

Oak and maple trees lean in—older than her dad, older than almost anything.

No warblers. No woodpeckers. Just the wind.

Sunlight cuts through the leaves in bright beams, dancing across the moss.

Then she sees him.

"Hey Bob," she says softly.

Bob is a gigantic tree. Three times thicker than the others. One of those ancient, mystical types that could probably write a novel if it had Wi-Fi.

She wraps her arms around his trunk. Her fingers don't even come close.

"Good to see you again," she mumbles into the bark.

She steps back, craning her neck to look up.

"Is everything okay today?"

Silence.

"Little quiet out here, don't you think?"

Still nothing.

"Strong and silent, huh?" she says with a crooked smile. "Yeah.

We've got that in common."

She slings her backpack higher and heads down the trail.

Waves without looking.

"See you soon, Bob."

Bob thinks she's cool.

# Chapter 12

Lilly follows the trail between ancient pines.

A brook murmurs nearby.

Ferns brush her knees like soft green fur.

"Hello, everyone," she says.

The ferns think she's cool, too.

Past the stream, the biggest tree looms. Hidden in its canopy is the fort. You'd miss it unless you knew exactly where to look.

**Thwak!**

An arrow slams into a plywood target—nowhere near the bullseye.

Lilly jumps. "Zak! Hold your fire! Human being approaching!"

Her backpack crackles. "You're supposed to radio in after talking to Bob," Zak says through static.

"I got distracted! Usual craziness."

High above, Zak leans over the railing—dark brown skin, glasses gleaming.

"Looks like you finally remembered the way," he calls. Her radio echoes the same line.

"Bob was extra chatty," Lilly says.

She steps toward the nailed ladder.

"Wait—stop! Don't use the ladder!"

Her radio pings: "Please use our new-advanced-technology, vertically-escalating-platform!"

A motor hums. A wooden platform lowers from the treetop.

Lilly raises an eyebrow. "You added a motor?"

"You've been gone two weeks! What else was I supposed to do?" Zak yells back.

She steps on. As the platform rises, a low branch swipes at her face.

She draws her machete and slices it clean through. "Good call on the machete," she mutters to herself.

Zak blinks down at her. "You're kinda scary, you know that?"

At the top, she steps off. Zak stands nearby—pencil in his curls, worry behind his glasses. He is clutching the bow as if it were a teddy bear, and he just had a nightmare. He is staring at Lilly's machete.

"What?" she says. "Branch problem solved." Sliding her machete into her backpack.

Zak's eyes bounce from her backpack to her face.

"You hit something stupid again?"

"It was an accident?" *Maybe he will believe that.*

"Let me guess—Olga Fartbutt?"

"She was going after Stanley. Again."

Zak sighs. "Lill, you're not going to win by picking fights with people twice your size."

"You weren't complaining when she came after you for being an orphan. Or for winning the science fair. Again."

Zak tries not to smile. "Well… we're friends. You help a friend."

"Exactly," Lilly says. "Someone's gotta stop the Fartbutts of the world."

They stare at each other a beat too long.

Then Zak grins. "If that's true, you really should learn to duck." Lilly smirks. "I was thinking the same thing."

Lilly grabs the arrows from the wall and takes the bow from Zak.

She steps to the edge of the fort and sticks the arrows into the floorboards. The bow feels right in her hands.

Everything is just too quiet. That uneasy feeling creeps back.

"There's something out there," she says.

Zak stays well back from the edge. "Sure. There are trees and more trees. Also—how are you standing that close?"

"Shhh!" Lilly hisses. She stares out at a forest holding its breath.

Zak squints through his glasses. "What? I don't—"

"I…just …feel it," Lilly mutters. "It's an intuition thing."

"Yeah…OK." Zak scratches his head but keeps looking.

Silence. Only the leaves stir.

"So... why are we whispering?" Zak asks.

Lilly doesn't answer that. "Something's off. I'm not imagining it."

She knows what he's thinking—camp stress, her dad, maybe she's just a little loony. Whatever. What else is new?

She grabs an arrow, breathes, and releases.

**Thwak.** Edge of the bullseye.

Zak's mouth drops. "How do you do that?"

"What?" she says, blinking.

"You're scary-good. I can't even hit the wood."
Lilly shrugs. "Try using the bow instead of throwing them."
"Ha! Ha!" Zak snorts.
**Thwak.** Another. Dead center.

Lilly isn't even watching. Her eyes are scanning again.
"Still looking for ghosts?" Zak teases.
**Thwak.** Third arrow. Bullseye.
"Strange all right," Zak mutters. "All three hit the bullseye."
"Oh yeah? You're just strange," Lilly grins.

# Chapter 13

The fort is basic but clever—just like Zak.

Plywood floor, gear hooks, shelves, and a table made of scrap wood.

A porch opens into the trees. A zipline cable stretches into the shadows.

"I fixed the power problem," Zak says proudly. "Water generator charges a battery now—lights run off that. No power-outs."

"That's brilliant," Lilly says. "And thanks for using normal words."

Zak lights up. "Oh—wait! I have something for you!"

He bolts to a shelf and hands her a tiny brown package. "Happy birthday."

"What? You didn't have to…"

She unwraps it fast.

Inside is a brass compass. Old. Solid. Beautiful.

"It's the real kind," Zak says. "Button on the side."

She presses it. The lid clicks open. A delicate needle spins, hunting north.

Her heart swells—then stumbles. What she said to her father echoes in her head.

Zak's smile fades. "You don't like it?"

"I do," she says quickly. "It's amazing."

She lowers her gaze. "I messed up with my dad."

Zak sits beside her. "He forgot again?"

Lilly just shrugs. Silence is answer enough.

Zak exhales. "I'm sorry."

She wipes at her eyes, maybe more than necessary. "Hey, I do like it. Seriously."

Zak's smile returns.

They sit quietly.

Lilly shifts her focus to something else, anything else.

Somewhere in the forest, a breeze lifts the leaves.

"It just feels strange." She mutters, staring between the leaves of nearby trees.

# Chapter 14

## Gone Without a Sound

Zak leans back, thinking. "Talk about strange—did you hear about the Nelsons' goat vanishing three nights ago?"

He hangs the bow. "Got out of a fenced pen. Then locked the gate behind itself."

Lilly shrugs. "Maybe it's good with locks."

Zak stares. "Seriously?"

"Someone probably left the gate open. Goat got out. Someone else shut it later."

"Maybe," Zak mutters. "But the Wilsons' labs disappeared too. Both of them."

Lilly straightens. "Labs always come back."

"And the Bates lost their dog last night. Posters are already up."

Lilly grabs Zak's arm. "We need to go."

Zak blinks. "Wait. That look—your Fart-Butt face. You're about to do something reckless!"

Lilly yanks her rope down. "Something might be messing with our chicken coop. I didn't take it seriously. I do now."

She bolts to the zipline.

Zak sputters. "Are we really—?!"

Too late. Lilly's feet hit the ground running.

"Wait!" Zak scrambles down the fireman pole like it's made of molasses.

Lilly bounces from root to root, barely touching ground. She doesn't even say hi to Bob.

Zak chases, panting. "Just… tell me what's going on!"

Her machete bobs in her pack as she barrels ahead.

"No! Wait! Breathe!" Zak collapses, hands on knees. "Since when… does Lilly-D… rush out of the forest?"

She circles back. "Are you gonna live?"

Zak nods like a broken bobblehead. "Totally… just… testing oxygen limits."

She snorts. "My dad thinks something's getting into the chicken coop."

Zak's eyes widen. "Aliens?"

Lilly glares. "Other people lost animals too. And the forest— it's off."

She waves at the silence. "No birds. No squirrels. No sound."

Zak wipes his glasses and squints into the trees.

**Snap.**

A twig breaks, close.

Lilly freezes.

Zak stiffens beside her. "What was that?"

# Chapter 15



"Shhh!" Lilly hushes. Something in the forest catches her eye.

"What now?" Zak rasps, leaning in like she's about to whisper top-secret info.

Lilly doesn't blink. "Don't… move. Look over there, to my right." She blindly feels for his face and gently turns it. "It's just fifty paces out. See it? The ripple?"

"ooom…blub…blub ooom," Zak mumbles—her fingers must be squishing his mouth.

She loosens her grip but stays focused.

Zak adjusts his glasses. "I see… nothing." Then softens into a concerned look. "Maybe it's an air ripple? Happens when the sun warms damp woods."

Silence presses in like a held breath.

"It comes and goes," Zak adds.

Lilly finally turns to him.

His brown eyes meet hers. "Sooo… could you ease up, Machete Warrior?" His glance flicks to her hand.

She follows his gaze—knuckles white on the machete. "Ah… right…" she mutters, like the blade got there on its own. She slides it back into her pack.

Whatever shimmer she saw is gone.

She blinks hard. Still nothing.

She bursts into sunlight—and halts.

Not where the trail ends. Right in front of the chicken coop.

The coop, garden, and fencing—they built it all.

The coop sits on stilts. That was her idea, to keep predators out.

The pen's right there. Empty.

No chickens.

Zak stumbles out behind her, wheezing.

She eyes him. "Are you going to live?"

He nods, breathless.

She lets him catch his breath. "Okay. I know I'm not making sense."

He nods again, like Yep, no argument.

She tries again. "Something's been lurking. It's scaring everything off. Pets are disappearing. So are animals."

She gestures to the trees. "It's feeding. And no one's seen it."

Zak frowns. "Maybe it's a clever animal. Like a fox."

"A fox can't drag off two labradors."

"Hmm… true."

"I'm thinking something bigger. Like a lion."

Zak squawks. "This isn't the jungle!" He laughs—until he realizes she's not joking.

"This isn't like Tommy Tillman, is it?" he asks. "The time you said drop whatever I was doing because you needed my help. You said he was kidnapped and we searched all day—then found him napping in his raspberry bushes?"

Lilly winces. "Nobody told me five-year-olds nap in bushes." She shakes it off. "Come on. Let's check the chickens."

She circles the fence and heads for the front. Her eyes sweep the pen.

Feathers everywhere.

The pen is empty.

"Ladies? Where are you?" Lilly calls into the empty pen. She frowns at Zak. "They're usually out."

"Maybe it's a chicken holiday," Zak jokes.

"Seriously?"

# Chapter 16

Chicken Chickens

She opens the people's door. At first—empty roosts.
Then her eyes adjust.
Multiple pairs of eyes cling together in the shadows.

"What? Don't be scared. It's me."
They don't move. Complete silence.
"They're here!" she shouts to Zak.
She turns back. "Hi, ladies. Let's do roll call."
She counts them off.
They stay frozen, like kids caught smoking.
"Jenny? Amelia? Tabby...?"
Nothing. They don't say anything back.
Her heart climbs. She reaches the end—too soon.
"Where's Gertrude? Where's Amanda?"
A fist tightens in her chest.

She checks every corner, ducking low.
Two missing.
She closes the coop door—
Zak isn't there.
Her heart stutters.
"Zak?!"

# Chapter 17
## The Track

"Here!" Zak calls from the other side of the coop.

Lilly bolts over.

Zak's frozen, staring at the ground.

"So… uh… what do you have there, Zap-man?" she tries.

He points. "You need to see this."

She crouches. The track is huge—wider than her shoulders.

"That'd be one big lion," Zak mutters.

"More like a wolf. But …way too big."

They look at the fence.

"It had to leap that," Zak whispers.

A nervous hush settles over the trees.

"It went that way," Lilly says, nodding to the woods.

Zak tenses. "Oh no. What are you thinking, Lilly-D?"

"Just going to see where it entered the forest."

Zak raises a hand. "Shouldn't we call someone?"

"And say what? A dog the size of a small car left prints?"

She tightens her pack. "We find more proof first."

Zak stammers. "F-F-Follow it? What if we find it?"

Lilly's already at the gate. "Aren't you curious?"

"My caution overrides my curiosity when we might get eaten," Zak says.

She grabs his arm. "We're just looking."

Then, she meets his eyes. "Are you in or not?"

Zak groans. "Oh man. Don't look at me that way."

# Chapter 18
## The Snare

"Alright. Okay. I'm in," Zak grumbles. "Let's go. Do your thing."

"My thing?" Lilly arches a brow.

"You know—your tracking mumbo jumbo."

"Maybe you should try learning to track something without a battery."

"I've got you for that." Zak shrugs. "And you're good at it."

Lilly grunts and moves to the forest edge. "Another print… something's off."

Zak stays close, head swiveling.

She steps into the trees. "Whatever it is—it's been here before."

"M-More than once?" Zak squeaks.

Lilly crouches by the crushed ferns. "Step for step. Every time."

Zak peers at the ground. "Like… fern circles?"

"Exactly. Something's trying to hide its path."

Zak swallows. "What animal would do that?"

"One that doesn't want to be found," Lilly says, scanning the trees.

Then her eyes light up. "Ooooh, this is a good one." She drops her pack and digs out her rope.

Zak flinches. "You want me to… lasso it?"

"No, silly. A snare."

"But… I've never made a snare in my life."

"You can today. You're a brain on legs." She thrusts the rope at him.

Zak grins and grabs it. "Compliments help."

Lilly slices a sapling clean with her machete. Shing!

Zak jumps. Eyeing the machete. "Your dad won't let you keep this thing as a pet! You know that, right?"

Her smile fades a little at the mention of her dad.

Zak catches the change and quietly gets to work.

In minutes, he finishes.

"This should do the trick," he says proudly, standing back to admire his work.

"Nice job, Zap-man," Lilly smirks.

Zak puffs out his chest.

# Chapter 19
## The Pack

Lilly opens her mouth to speak—
Then freezes.
Something buzzes in her feet.
She glances down.
The forest floor trembles beneath her like her dad's old electric foot massager.
Zak inches closer, sensing it too.
A low rumble grows—from the direction of the chicken coop.
The ground starts to shake.
Boom. Boom. Boom.
A thunderous rhythm rolls through the earth.
Lilly drops. "Get down!"
She hits the fern's belly-first, vanishing into the underbrush.
Zak disappears too, leaves rustling as he dives nearby.

The pounding gets louder.
Faster.
The earth heaves beneath them.
Then she remembers.
The pack!
She left it on the trail.
Her breath catches.
"Zak! The pack!" she hisses.
One arm shoots up above the ferns—
Snatch.
Back down.
Boom. Boom. Boom.
The sound crashes through the forest like war drums.
But nothing is visible.

Lilly's instinct says, *stay hidden*.
But her curiosity says, *look*.
She peeks up—slow as sunrise.
The bushes at the forest edge explode outward.
Something massive pushes through—
Yet there's nothing to see.
Air slams through the clearing.
Ferns flatten like grass under a boot.
BOOM—
Then silence.

# Chapter 20


Snap!
The snare rope whips upward, jerking tight.
It quivers, suspended in midair.
A shimmer flickers.
Then thickens.
Haze becomes static—
Static becomes shape.
Lilly stops breathing.
A black-scaled monster flickers into view.
It's the size of a car.
Jaws clamped around a limp deer.
Glowing red eyes.
Razor tail twitching.
A machine.
Built to kill.
The beast turns, annoyed—
Then—
FZZZHT!
A laser blasts from its eyes, slicing through the rope.

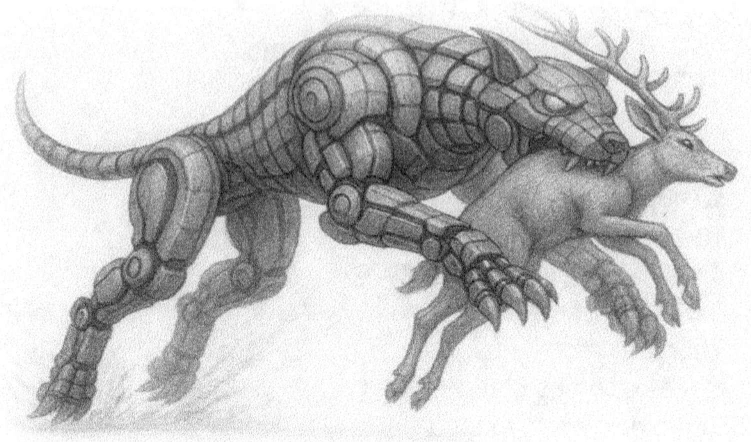

The deer flops.
The snare burns to ash.
Lilly can't move. Can't blink.
Then—
The monster turns its head.
Straight toward her.
Her body goes rigid.
No breath. No escape.
"Don't see us! Don't see us!" Lilly mutters under her breath.
Yeah, right, like that is going to help.
Then—
WHOOSH!
It leaps.
Straight over her.
Boom. Boom. Boom.
Leaves blast around her.
A stench of rot and scorched plastic fills her nose.
The machine crashes through trees—

Then flickers—
and vanishes.

Only crushed ferns and broken branches remain.

Zak's voice explodes out of the silence: "THAT. WAS. AWESOME!"

Lilly rises slowly, legs shaking. "What do you mean... awesome?"

Zak bounces on the spot, wide-eyed. "That was a cognitive AI platform with adaptive terrain response! A fully autonomous predator!"

She blinks. "You need help."

He grins and holds up her compass.

The needle spins wildly.

"EMF," he says. "That thing? It's a machine!"

Lilly's breath finally returns.

But her nerves haven't.

# Chapter 21
## Not a Chicken

Lilly watches Zak like he might start foaming at the mouth.

He's pacing, arms waving. "Self-thinking! Military-grade! Cloaking tech!"

"You mean it clucks?" Lilly deadpans.

Zak flings his hands. "Cloak! Not cluck! It's not a chicken, Lilly-D!"

She stares, blinking.

He exhales. "It can turn invisible."

Realization dawns. "Why didn't you say that?" Her eyes narrow. "Wait—can that even happen?"

Zak looks personally offended. "We *just* saw it. Kind of." He frowns, redoing the logic in his head. "It must bend light. That could explain the EMF surge."

Lilly blinks at the forest. "Okay... invisible robot. Sure. That's a thing now."

Then her eyes sharpen. "But why would a cloaked, military machine be stealing pets?"

Zak opens his mouth. Nothing comes out.

"Exactly," Lilly mutters, hoisting her pack. "We follow it."

"What?!" Zak chokes. "Follow it? Are you in need of professional help?"

"Possibly," Lilly shrugs. "But so are you, if you're still here."

She snags the compass from his hand, watching the needle spin. "This'll spike if we get close."

Zak stares after her as she strides off like it's just another Friday.

"I can't believe I'm doing this," he mutters, scrambling after her.

# Chapter 22
## The Signal

They move quietly. Step. Pause. Scan.

The trail is there—crushed ferns, snapped twigs, even a gash carved into a tree trunk.

Then Lilly sniffs the air. "Smoke. You smell that?"

Zak nods fast. "Steak? Burgers?"

"Or someone's dog," Lilly mutters.

Zak's face twists. "Ew—wait, you think we're close?"

"Not sure," she says. "But yeah... we're getting there."

Suddenly—

**Whirrrr.**

A mechanical sound slices through the trees behind them.

"Get down!" Lilly hisses.

They drop as a shimmering whoosh above the canopy. Not the thundering beast from before—this one *flies*.

Then—

**KABOOM!**

A blast shakes the forest. Leaves whip around them.

**KABOOM!** A second.

**KABOOM!** A third.

Zak flails beside her like a flipped beetle, glasses askew.

"Did you hear that?!" he gasps.

Lilly starts to answer—

Then—

**"...come in… Phi-Guya… this is Ist-San Seri. Repeat—Ist-San Seri requesting exfila. Gatiar compromised. Enemy on site. Target is in imminent danger. I repeat: Target in danger."**

Zak shoots upright. "Was that—?"

Lilly yanks out the radio from her backpack, dials the volume up.

Static.

She stares at it, heart pounding.

"That shimmer. The sound. A crash," she mutters. "She's out there."

Zak gulps. "You want …to *find* her?"

"She needs help."

He glances at the forest, then at her. "Fine. But if I get eaten by a killer robot dog, I'm haunting you."

Lilly smirks and tosses him the radio. "Let's go help Ist-San."

Together, they step deeper into the unknown.

# Chapter 23

## Wreck in the Woods

The forest has changed.

Not just from broken trees and crushed brush—they've seen that before. This is deeper. Quieter. Like, even the trees are holding their breath.

Lilly creeps forward, machete in hand, eyes scanning.

Zak trails behind, radio clutched like a lifeline. "Are we… sure about this?" he whispers.

"No," Lilly says, never breaking stride. "But we're doing it anyway." This is Lilly's superpowers, in full use.

They push through a curtain of leaves—and freeze.

Ahead, the trees give way to a clearing carved into the forest like a wound. Smoke drifts up in lazy spirals. Saplings lie scorched and flattened.

The ground is torn and shattered.

At the center lies the wreck. A sleek white shape, half-buried in the dirt. Its nose is jammed into a tree. Its tail bent up like a flag of surrender.

It looks like a rocket—compact, dented, and scarred. A deep gash down one side reveals flickering lights and torn wires. A faint hum rises from inside.

Lilly steps closer, hand still on her machete.

Zak follows, voice low. "It's like… something out of a sci-fi movie. Only …real."

Then—a sound. A cough.

Lilly spins.

Near the edge of the wreck, half-hidden in brush, lies a figure.

A helmet flickers on and off. A scorched armor pack. Black bodysuit smeared with shiny blood. One leg tangled in glowing wires.

Lilly drops to her knees. "Hey! Hey—can you hear me?"

The woman stirs. Her lips part. "Run… hide… they're coming," she whispers.

Lilly doesn't listen. She checks for wounds.

A head injury. Blood at the ear. Leg injury. The woman slumps. Her chest moves—but barely.

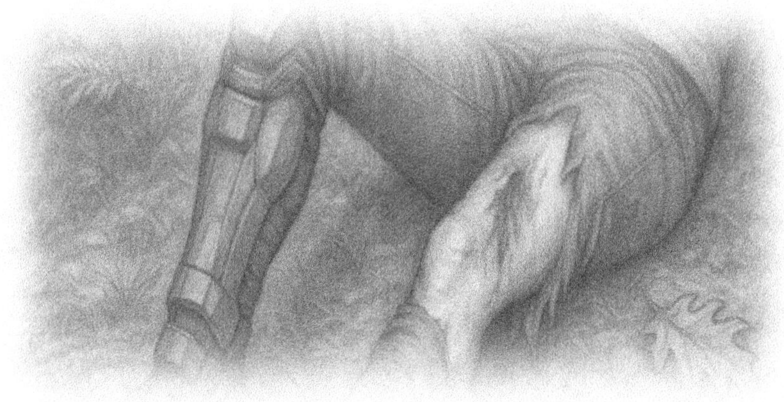

Zak hovers nearby. "Is she—?"

"She's alive," Lilly says. "But we need to get her out. Fast."

A branch cracks in the distance.

Lilly's eyes sharpen. "Before they find her."

Shing! One machete swipe, and the wires snap.

The pilot tries to stand, but her leg gives out. She collapses back to the forest floor.

"No! Here, we wait. They will find us faster." The soldier gasps out. Her eyes close. Silence.

Lilly is not certain if the soldier means the animal-eating dog machine or those coming to help.

Lilly checks her pulse—weak, but there.

Her face is bruised. Long black hair clings to her skin. Her brow twitches, like she's trapped in a bad dream. She is wearing a white armband trimmed in gold, looking both ancient and advanced technology.

Zak crouches. "Is she… our military?"

Lilly doesn't answer. She doesn't know. But something about the woman pulls at her—familiar, not in face or gear, but deeper. Her skin prickles. Her instincts are faster than her thoughts.

"She's breathing," Lilly says. "That's enough… maybe. I think we're supposed to …keep trauma victims awake?" It is more question than a statement.

Zak nods, then glances toward the woods. "You think that thing's still hunting her?"

Lilly tightens her grip on the machete. "If it can smell prey—yeah." She leans in. "Hello! Can you hear me?" She gives the woman a gentle shake. "Stay awake."

Nothing. Just shallow breaths.

Lilly tries again.

Still nothing.

The silence stretches. The forest whispers like it's hiding secrets.

Then—

The woman stirs. Her lips part. Her eyes open—a sliver. Like waking in a room too bright.

Lilly exhales.

Zak falls back in surprise.

The woman's eyes dart between them—confused, sharp, ready to fight.

"Hey—hey, it's okay," Lilly says, raising both hands. "You crashed. We found you. You're safe."

"Crashed…" the woman rasps. Her voice is dry, cracked.

"You were calling for help," Zak adds, holding up the radio. "We heard your signal."

That seems to land. She blinks slowly, then sits up with a grunt. Her hand searches behind her—finds the black, club-like object on the ground—and grabs it tight.

"Whoa—careful. Your leg's messed up," Lilly warns, reaching to steady her.

The woman's hand shoots out and grabs Lilly's wrist—iron-strong.

Lilly flinches but doesn't pull away. "You're okay. I promise. Just… breathe."

The grip eases.

"Lilly," the woman croaks. "Zak."

Lilly's eyes go wide. "Wait—how do you know our names?"

Zak waves stiffly. "Hi."

The woman gives a shallow nod. "Ist-San Seri."

"Ist-San," Lilly repeats. "Is that your name?"

# Chapter 24

### The Silver Threat

"Rank," she corrects. "Seri, name. Ist-san Rank. Royal Gesh. Assigned to this vector. Aro Two. Mission: compromised."

Zak's mouth falls open. "She's a soldier. Like… one of our soldiers."

Seri coughs and leans back against the tree. "Soldier. Not from here." Her eyes sweep the forest—checking exits, hiding spots, threats.

Lilly tilts her head. "What was chasing you?"

Seri hesitates.

Then: "Canker Abduction Unit."

"What's a Canker?" Zak asks.

Seri looks at him. Then glances out into the forest. "A problem."

"Is it that big dog thing?"

"No. That's a diablopero. Worse than the Cankers. They brought it into your forest."

Lilly feels it before she hears it.

A tremor in the forest. A breeze with no wind.

"Can I do anything to help until someone gets here, Seri?" she asks, heart speeding.

Seri gives a faint smile and shakes her head.

Lilly still wants to do something. "Water?" she offers, pulling a bottle from the backpack, her eyes searching for any movement between the trees.

Zak's compass—lying beside him—starts to spin.

Lilly passes the bottle—then freezes.

A glint of shininess.

A metal spider.

It steps onto Seri's leg. The body is the size of a golf ball. Legs long, jointed like pencils. Gleaming silver.

Not alive. A machine. Creeping. Silent. Deadly.

Lilly moves without thinking. Her hand strikes.

The spider sails into the nearest tree with a thud. It slides down—twitching.

She leaps up and stomps.

**Crunch!**

Metal snaps under her shoe. She presses harder. Then lifts her foot.

It's done.

Twitch. Still.

Zak stares. "What the…? What is it?"

Behind her, a sound.

Lilly turns.

Seri's grinning through the pain.

"I got it," Lilly says, breathless.

"You sure did," Seri replies, chuckling, then wincing.

Lilly slaps a hand over her mouth. "It was dangerous, right?" Her eyes sweep the forest. "Are there more?"

"It's …okay," Seri says gently. "There was only one. It can't hurt me now." She pats the ground beside her.

Lilly exhales—and sits.

# Chapter 25

Seri's eyes flutter—heavy, fighting to stay open. "I am …proud …of you," she whispers. Her voice carries that same soft, motherly tone.

More words that don't make sense to Lilly.

Then Seri's arm drops.

The black club slips from her fingers and tumbles gently, landing between her and Lilly.

Seri's eyes shift—first to Lilly, then to the club. She catches the flicker of interest in Lilly's gaze.

"It's called …a vok," Seri says softly, nodding toward it.

Lilly studies the object. It looks solid—like it's carved from black metal. Smooth and sleek, like one of her dad's precision tools. But more complex.

Interlocking rings taper together into one seamless cylinder.

One end is slightly thicker. Carvings run down its length— symbols, not letters:

# пЮѦ ю Ƨɦѧ ѧжƗ ӃжƗ

They remind Lilly of something she once saw in a book—not Egyptian, but older.

"It's a weapon and a defensive tool. Both," Seri murmurs.

"Wow! I'd love to see the inside of that!" Zak blurts, nearly bouncing. "Is it a prototype? Military grade? You guys are testing out new gear, aren't you?"

Lilly gives him a sharp look—half warning, half concern. "Zak."

Zak slumps back like a scolded kid, lips pressed tight.

Seri doesn't seem to hear Zak. Her eyes stay fixed on Lilly. With a grimace, she drags herself upright.

"You have to listen," she says. "There isn't much time."

Lilly reaches to steady her. "Save your energy."

Seri shakes her head. "No. It's already decided."

# Chapter 26

What was Hidden from Lilly

"All these years… I wasn't sure. Until today."

Lilly turns slowly.

"You saw me, didn't you? In the forest. You saw me as a shimmer."

Lilly's thoughts swam in weirdness. "That's not normal?"

Seri shook her head no. Her eyes locked on Lilly's. "Just you."

"Lilly's far from normal. Trust me!" Zak leans in, perhaps cracking a joke, because if not, the truth would be hard to take in.

Lilly and Seri both ignore Zak.

A connection between them. Something that has to be said.

Seri hesitates—then speaks. "Twelve years ago, the Cankers came. Your mother… she gave herself up to save you."

Lilly reels back. "No—what? No. That's not right."

"She made a deal," Seri whispers. "Her life… for yours. She believed you were the one and kept it secret."

Lilly's breath catches. Her body stills. She's not ready—but it hits anyway.

Lilly shakes her head. "You're confused. You don't know me."

Seri's eyes lock on hers. "I've been your guardian since that night."

Lilly's mouth opens. Nothing comes out.

"I know you are Lilly Edelweiss Dubois. Your father is Mike Dubois. He barely sees you—buried in obsessions. You escape into the forest. You defend the defenseless. You move like the wind. You fire arrows like you breathe. You—"

Seri coughs. This one hurts. "You call your … best friend Zap-Man. Zakary Albert Peterson. He lives in a foster home. He's twelve. Brilliant. Loyal."

Blood slips from her lip. Her voice falters.

Lilly leans in, wiping it away with the hem of her shirt.

Seri's hand catches hers—just for a moment. "I expected he was eventually going to figure it out and come after you and the ring."

Then—

Her eyes widen in horror.

Not at Lilly.

At something behind her.

# Chapter 27

Lilly snaps around.

A person is right there—moving through the forest, being all stealthy like. A leathery, hairless head.

For a second, Lilly's brain stalls: *Canker*—but the word sticks.

He slithers between the trees like a snake closing in on prey.

Seri's the prey.

His lipless mouth peels into a jagged grin. Yellowed teeth. His tongue slides over them like he's tasting leftovers from his last kill.

Shock turns to horror.

He's already paces away, aiming a black club—just like Seri's—at Seri.

Instinct ignites.

Lilly throws herself between them.

Her hand seizes Seri's vok from the forest floor.

She doesn't think.

She *knows.*

The vok thrums in her grip. Warmth floods her hand. Lightning rockets through her veins. A wave of certainty surges through her: *This is protection. This is power. This is life.*

As if guided by something unseen, she swings the vok and points it at the attacker.

Snake Face's grin dies—like water circling a drain.

**Flash!**

A burst erupts from the vok's end.

It blasts him across the forest. His body locks, spasms, eyes rolling back—then slams down to the ground.

**Whomp!** Echoes among the trees.

Lilly jumps up and races to the attacker, ready to strike again.

It is the smell that catches her first. It is like the waft of the school garbage bins on a hot summer day.

The Canker lies crumpled. Twisted. A hiss escapes his mouth—then silence.

She spins around to see if there are others—nothing.

Other direction—nothing, not a sound even.

She drops down to stay out of sight of whatever is coming next.

The air reeks of smoke, scorched earth, and burned wood.

Lilly's ears ring.

Lilly blinks through the haze and crawls back, knees thudding against sticks, stones, and leaves.

Zak has leapt over Seri, as if to shield her from harm.

"Are you okay?" Lilly gasps.

Zak gives a weak thumb-up. "Peachy."

Lilly and Zak's eyes lock. They exchange a 'holy cow!" moment.

Lilly slumps to the ground, breath heaving. Her fingers won't let go of the vok. Her eyes won't either.

Finally, she looks up. She glances back to the crumpled person she just…what…shot?!? "Is he d…" She couldn't say it.

But Seri didn't answer. Her face is pure shock. Her eyes bulge. Her mouth hangs open. She stares at Lilly—then the vok—then back again. "You!… *You!*…" Seri stammers, stuck in a loop.

"Sorry… I just reacted," Lilly says, voice shaky. Her stomach twists. "Is he going to live?" She asks.

"I *knew* it! I knew it!" Seri nearly shouts. Then gasps—clutching her chest.

"Seri!" Lilly reaches out.

Seri raises a hand to stop her. She steadies her breath. "We're running …out of time." She holds out her palm. "Please give me …the vok."

Lilly hesitates. So much doesn't make sense. But the vok… it *feels* like —hers. Not in a greedy way—but in a way that *belongs.*

Seri's hand stays out. Calm. Steady. "Please," she says again—soft and firm, like a mother.

Lilly nods and passes it over.

Seri touches her armband.

A soft beep.

She looks up, breath ragged. "Mensch Morder sent the Cankers here to kill you," she says. "There's no time to explain."

Then—

**Zap!**

The vok touches Lilly's arm. A sting. A jolt.

Everything changes.

# Chapter 28

## The Oath of the Royal Khem Gesh

$B$efore Lilly can move—before she even sees it coming—a surge punches through her.

A shock. A heat.

It feels like a swarm of bumblebees hits her all at once.

Pain explodes—then vanishes.

She throws herself backward, bracing for another blast.

But it doesn't come.

Seri slumps, sadness carved into her face. "I'm sorry," she rasps. "We're out of time. They're here… to capture you. And steal the Ring of Yishi."

Lilly clutches her arm, heart racing. "O… o… o… w… w… w!" she blurts. Half-joke, half-panic. It's the only logic her brain can manage. "Who? What ring?"

Seri doesn't answer. Her face is wet with tears, but her eyes glow with awe.

"You are …very special, Lilly," she whispers.

Lilly stares. "What? Who? What are you saying?"

Seri sets the vok gently between them. Her hand trembles.

Lilly's head buzzes. Her vision swims.

A thousand bees behind her eyes. Her body feels far away. Like she's growing… changing… altering.

Seri grips Lilly's wrist—tight. The only thing keeping either of them grounded.

"I, Ist-San Seri, Royal Khem Gesh of Seairland, hereby invoke… my right… of Abarj-Kensha upon Lilly Edelweiss Dubois."

The words come ragged, but strong. Her eyes burn with urgency.

"You will say *'I will'* at the end of this," she commands.

Not loud. But final. Iron.

Lilly sways, dazed. "O-okay."

Seri begins. Her voice shifts—low, ancient. "May you, as Royal Khem Gesh of Seairland, live and serve as one… with the land, the sun, and the water…"

She pauses. Her breath hitches.

"…in sacred connection…"

Her eyes squeeze shut. Her body trembles.

"…you will vow to act with integrity… in selfless duty… as protector of all life…"

Lilly doesn't move.

"…guardian of life force, champion for bravery… advocate for peace… defender against all hostility…"

Seri wavers. Her head droops—then rises again.

Her voice thins to a whisper. "…from this day forth… until your final breath."

Silence.

Seri stares straight into Lilly.

Pleading. Expecting. Commanding.

Lilly's chest heaves. Her lips part.

Seri shakes her arm. "*Say it!*"

"I… will," Lilly whispers.

Seri collapses. Her hand slips from Lilly's wrist. Her head sinks to her chest. Her final breath: "…yes. You will."

Lilly sits frozen.

The forest spins.

Seri's words echo: *until your final breath…*

Then—

**BOOM!**

The forest shakes.

Another—**BOOM!** Like a car backfiring again and again.

Shouts. Explosions. Screams.

The forest holds its breath.

And then—

**BOOM!**

# Chapter 29
## Help Arrives

A series of **BOOMs** ring out—like car backfires, one after another.

Shouting. Crashing. Somewhere in the woods.

Lilly turns instinctively. The whole forest lurches under her. She crawls to cover Seri with the vok.

All around—

The forest writhes.

Figures in black emerge from between the trees—just like Seri—battling half a dozen ogre-like men.

One woman stands cornered against a tree. She wears a black uniform too. Her ponytail lashes like it's fighting beside her.

White light blasts from her black club—knocking two ogres over like bowling pins.

**Kaboom!**

Lilly's thrown.

Tumbling —flipping—

Her head slams something hard.

Then— Stars.

And darkness.

# Chapter 30

## A Way to Escape

Lilly keeps her eyes shut.

She hears voices—ones she doesn't recognize.

"Is the ring safe?"

Another voice answers, "Guarded and hidden where it always has been."

Footsteps. Someone moves closer.

"Shhh. Not now."

Lilly opens her eyes.

The ceiling of a tent blurs into focus.

"There she is," someone says gently near her ear.

A face leans close. He's smiling—way too many teeth, blue eyes, wavy blond hair. Like he just stepped out of a toothpaste commercial.

"You bumped your head a bit, but you're going to be okay," he says, smooth as silk.

Lilly sits up. Her skull throbs. She's in a tent with Mr. Smiley—and two others in uniforms like Seri's. Black with gold trim. Military.

"Zak?" she asks.

"He's fine. Outside, waiting for you," Blondie replies, sugary sweet.

The other two stand back, at ease—but weirdly identical. Same brown hair pulled into tails. Same olive-brown skin. Same brown eyes. Same amused expressions. Like ...clones.

Lilly's thoughts yank backward. "How's Seri? She was hurt badly." She flinches as a hand lands on her knee.

Blondie pulls back fast. "Oh—yeah. Seri's in the other tent. Still a little out of it. She probably said some weird things, right?" His tone lifts into a question. Nervous.

Lilly glances between him and the two against the tent wall.

The twins look bored.

Blondie looks too interested.

"She, um... said I was special, then made me say 'I will' after some kind of oath. I figured it was from the head injury or something. But... how'd she know our names?"

"The *Oath of the Royal Khem Gesh*?" Blondie's eyes go wide—then narrow fast, like he's trying to hide it. "Oh... well... she probably heard your names during training exercises. That's all this is—we're just your local military, running a war game. Testing tech."

It sounds like he practiced the speech.

"But she knew our *whole* names. Nicknames and everything. And things about my mom," Lilly says. Her stomach turns. Her palms are damp.

Blondie swipes back his golden hair. His eyes dart, searching. "Well... ah... she probably pulled a report on the area. That's just Seri. Super detailed." His words stumble forward.

"But hey, you should come to our base. Let a nurse check you out. You hit your head hard. And you and your dad aren't safe while the robot dog is still loose. That's all this is—we're trying to turn it off. Simple." He talks fast, like the speech is ending and he's out of time.

Lilly eyes the tent flap—half open.

You know what? I'm good," she says, rising. "I've got to check on …my chickens. And my garden—it's been two weeks. Weeds, you know? Also, dinner. For Dad."

She plants her feet. Ready.

Blondie steps back. Concern flickers across his face.

The twin soldiers exchange a glance. A perfect, identical glance.

Lilly's gut twists.

Time to leave.

Then—

One of the soldiers blinks.

Just a blink.

But she's certain.

For a second, his brown eyes flash—lizard-yellow. Then back to brown.

# Chapter 31



That blink was enough.

Lilly's mind is made up. "Ah… thanks for the hospitality," she says, already walking toward the tent flap. "Good luck finding your dog-contraption."

Blondie panics. "You're in grave danger! If we don't get you out of here now, they'll attack in full force!"

"No, we'll be okay. Really. Gotta go!" Lilly picks up speed.

The twin soldiers stay still—matching smirks carved into their faces. They glance at each other like they share a single brain.

No one stops her.

She steps out into the green blur of the forest.

Another tent nearby. Soldiers move through the broken trees.

The wreckage of their fort is still in view. Their special tree now stands scarred. Strips of bark hang like peeling skin. Sap bleeds from the trunk. A few boards cling where the fort once stood. The rest lies crushed in a heap.

Zak steps into view, worry written across his soot-smudged face. One eyeglass lens is cracked. "Hey, Lilly-D!"

She grabs his arm. "Come on!"

"But—"

"Time to go!" Lilly pulls him into a fast walk.

Zak stumbles after her like he's leaving behind a candy store. "But…" He keeps looking back.

No one follows.

The camp and its weirdness fade behind the trees.

Lilly doesn't take the trail. She blazes through brush, branches slapping her face. Her legs fly. She tugs Zak along, lungs burning.

They're free.

"Wait!" Zak stops. "Why are we running?"

Lilly turns. "Something's …not …right." She points into the shadows. Her skin still tingles.

"They explained everything. Testing new tech. In our forest. Kinda cool, right?" Zak's voice lights up.

Lilly yanks him forward again. "And you believe that? I want to check on Dad."

"But—"

They crash through one last wall of brush and burst into a field.

On the far side: the chicken coop, the driveway, her dad's car, the tiny house.

Lilly stops. Finally. She lets go of Zak's arm.

"Whew."

Zak adjusts his glasses. "What's the problem?"

Lilly makes blinking motions with her fingers—lizard eyes—but can't explain it.

Zak blinks back at her. "What? Use your words."

"Argh!" Lilly groans. "They're lying! They wanted me at their base. Said some machine-dog was loose. But... they knew too much. They acted too weird."

"Yeah, they told me that too," Zak says. "Honestly, I kinda want to see that dog. Bet it's awesome tech."

Lilly stares at him. "You were ready to follow the first stranger who said, 'Come pet my dog'? How did you survive childhood?"

Zak shrugs. "It's a cool dog."

Lilly snorts. "They could've at least made up a better excuse than we are in danger." She turns toward the house. "Let's go find Dad."

KABOOM!

Heat slams into her.
The ground disappears.
She's flying.
Then—impact.
She hits her back hard. Air is crushed from her lungs.
She lies there, blinking. What now?
Debris rains down—wood, plaster, and leaves, drifting like confused ghosts.

# Chapter 32

Lilly sits up, confused.

Her house is gone.

Not just damaged—gone.

In its place is a crater, blasted wide open. Broken boards and metal scatter across the pasture like trash after a storm.

A single wall still stands—charred, ghostly, and alone.

Her father's car is on fire. Just a shell now, hissing flames spit black smoke into the sky.

Not a campfire smell. This is melted plastic. Burned rubber. Home turned to ash.

To the side, her garden is crushed. Wood and drywall litter the rows. It's not a garden anymore.

Lilly stares at the wreckage. Her brain won't reach for what's next. It just tries to understand what's missing.

Her home.

She glances at Zak. He sits dazed, wobbling. His eyes sweep the smoke like he's looking for ghosts.

Feathers float through the air.

Lilly's breath catches.

The chicken coop is gone.

"Oh no. Jenny… Amelia… Tabby…"

Then—lightning strikes. "Dad!" she gasps.

WHOOM!

WHOOM!

WHOOM!

Machines drop from the sky—white and gray, like flying jet skis. They hover just above the ground. Soldiers ride them.

Dust blasts upward as more arrive. Dozens.

One stops in front of Lilly.

A tall man steps down. Broad-shouldered. His presence hits like a spotlight. "Alpha Ang—set up a full perimeter cloak!" he shouts. "I want this site locked down yesterday!"

"Sir!" a rider calls, thumping a fist to their chest.

The soldiers move like a swarm—fast, focused, no wasted motion.

Lilly sits frozen.

"Ist-Ba Rowan," the man says. "Biological scan—now."

"Sir!" a woman replies. She taps her armband. "No Earthing biologicals on the blast site."

"Code Diushi-Gen," he says. "Beta Ang—search for a missing Earthing male. Thirty-eight. Name: Michael Dubois."

He taps his armband. "Image sent to your voks. Find him."

The troops vanish into the trees.

Lilly watches, awestruck. Still sitting.

The tall man turns toward her. He looks older than her dad. Short hair, neat white beard. Like an explorer who just came in from a storm. His voice is calm and deep. He offers her a hand up. "Hello, Lilly. Are you okay? Are you hurt?"

Lilly takes his hand. She shakes her head. Her lips part, but nothing comes out.

"My father," she whispers. "I thought he was home."

"He wasn't in the house," the man says gently. "My team is searching. We'll find him. I promise."

Lilly nods.

"I'm Iyengar Aubrin," he says. "Commander here."

He holds out his hand. A greeting.

# Chapter 33


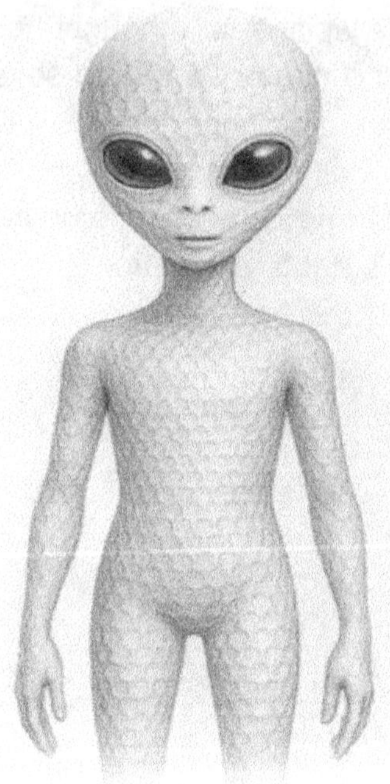

Lilly takes his hand. It vanishes inside his much larger one. She's not sure if she shakes it or just holds on. Her thoughts are a mess—spinning too fast.

"I'm sorry I wasn't here earlier," Aubrin says gently. "We were chasing the Canker Abduction Unit." His blue eyes meet her green ones. "I think we can stop pretending now."

"Okay," Lilly squeaks. It's all she can manage.

Zak steps beside her. Their eyes meet—wide and full of *holy crap*.

"You must be Zak," Aubrin says, offering his hand. "Call me Aubrin."

"Mr. Aubrin," Zak replies, shaking it like he's meeting a superhero.

A faint smile crosses Aubrin's face, then fades. "Obviously, we're not from around here."

Both Lilly and Zak nod.

"And we need to get you somewhere safe."

Another glance between them.

"We can take all three of you to our base," Aubrin continues. "It's secure. You'll be safe there. We'll answer everything."

Zak lights up like a kid promised a ride in a spaceship. Lilly looks at Aubrin—then at what used to be her house, her garden, her chickens. All of it… gone.

"Alright," she says. "We'll go. We don't have anywhere else."

"Yes!" Zak pumps a fist like he just won a video game.

Lilly shakes her head. "You'd follow a blood-covered stranger with an axe if he offered you a gadget."

Zak shrugs, all smiles.

A smile flickers across Aubrin's face before he reins it back in. He waves to a nearby soldier.

The soldier hands him two gray armbands.

"Put these on—left arm," Aubrin says. "They'll give you access to the base entrance." He hands one to Zak, but before giving Lilly hers, his armband double-beeps.

He raises it. A holographic face appears—another soldier.

"Iyengar Aubrin, this is Ist-Fee Flaxen."

"Go ahead."

"It's Ist-San Seri, sir. She's awake. She insists on speaking with Earthling Lilly." A pause. "You'd better hurry."

Aubrin lowers the band and looks at Lilly, concern in his steady gaze. "Can we go see her?"

Something tightens in Lilly's chest. She nods. "Yes."

Aubrin taps his armband.

Suddenly, a small gray robot appears—just *appears*. It's shorter than Lilly, with a large head, big teardrop eyes, and long skinny limbs.

Zak's jaw drops. His armband is already strapped on. He stares like he's just met Santa's cooler cousin.

Aubrin offers his hand to Lilly again. His face, lined with experience, glows with something warm—like firelight in winter. But behind it… sadness.

Lilly looks at the robot. Then at Aubrin.

She takes his hand.

She trusts him.

# Chapter 34

It's Yours Now

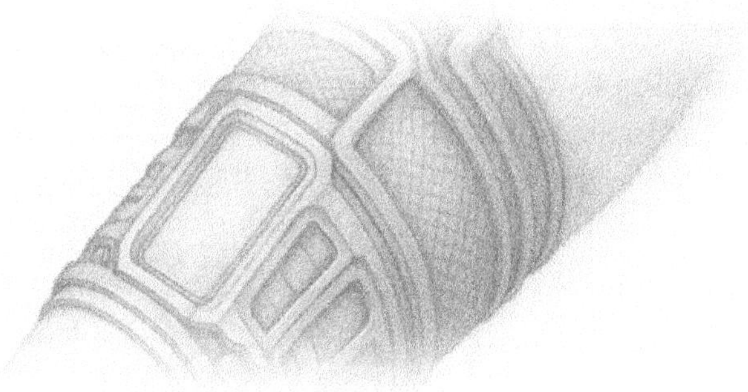

In a blink, Zak and the wreckage vanish.

In their place—

A tent. Clean. Military-grade.

Soldiers move quietly around the space.

Lilly stumbles, like the ground tilts beneath her.

"It's okay," Aubrin says, his voice deep and steady. He reaches out, anchoring her with one strong hand. "It can be disorienting, the first time."

Her head spins. One second, she was standing in smoke and rubble. Now— Here.

Then she sees her.

Seri.

Lying on a cot.

Lilly rushes forward.

Seri's eyes are barely open. Her skin is pale, drained of all color. But she sees Lilly. One trembling hand lifts—barely.

Lilly grabs it. It's cold. Unnaturally cold. But the grip is tight—urgent.

Seri's lips move. No sound. She licks them, trying to speak.

Then—*click.*

Lilly flinches.

Something clamps around her left arm.

She looks down.

It's Seri's armband.

Even in this weakened state, Seri has fastened it to her.

# Chapter 35



## You are the Ohmuno!

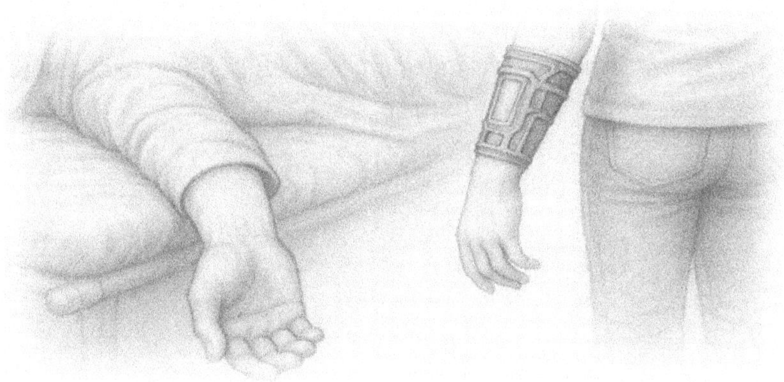

Lilly's chest tightens.

She looks back into Seri's face, searching those fading eyes for answers.

Seri tries to speak. Her eyes flutter, blinking fast with effort.

Lilly leans in—then sways. Her head swims worse than before. A sensation rushes up her arm from the armband. It feels like her skin is sinking into warm water, pulsing through her veins.

Seri's grip tightens. "You …are …the …Ohmuno," Seri rasps. Each word sounds cracked and torn. "The universe …needs you."

Lilly freezes.

The words hit like static through a broken speaker—garbled, far away. Her body turns heavy, like something's draining her strength.

Then Seri speaks again—like she's spent her last breath to say it. "Save them!" Her hand slips from Lilly's.

Gone.

Seri's eyes don't blink. Don't move. Still.

A flood of heat surges from Lilly's arm, racing through her chest and down her legs. It fills her like fire turned to liquid.

The world tilts.

Seri's face blurs in and out.

The tent spins—walls swirling, voices bending like waves.

Color wraps around her like smoke.

And then—Everything unravels.

Lilly's knees give way.

# Chapter 36
### Out Like a Light

Darkness falls over Lilly.

# Chapter 37
## Waking to Aliens

Sunlight warms Lilly's face as she melts into the bed. She keeps her eyes closed, resisting the brightness. She loves when the sun reaches out like this—like it's playing the same game every morning.

*Hey Lilly, time to get up,* it urges.

But this morning, Lilly decides to be difficult. "Nope. Not yet," she mumbles. Her body says she needs more sleep.

Then, harsh whispers cut through her peace. Strange voices. Not from anywhere she knows.

Curiosity beats comfort. She cracks open her eyes.

The ceiling looms above.

The walls stretch out.

Everything's wrong.

Her room. Her stuff. Even the colors. All gone. All white. Stark. Unreal.

She must be dreaming. She squeezes her eyes shut. Opens them again.

Still white.

"Crap. What did I do now?" she mutters.

She tries to sit up—

Nothing.

Her arms, back, legs—dead weight. Glued down. What started as a cozy wake-up turns into a porcelain nightmare.

"Double crap," she whispers, eyes darting.

Four blank walls. A single chair. A table. Two outfits folded on top. One stack: all white. The other: jeans and a T-shirt. Everything's spotless. Organized. Sterile.

This is not her room.

Her heart jumps. "Where am I?" she breathes.

She spots a gap in the wall. Not a door. A balcony. Trees sway under a cloudy sky. Birds chirp. A low hum in the distance— vehicles, maybe.

And something smells like... bread? Coffee?

She looks down.

A white armband, trimmed in gold, clings to her wrist. It's high-tech. Complicated. Not hers.

Her breath sticks in her throat.

Then the memories crash in.

The forest.

Seri—

Red blood. Explosions. Screaming. Someone is not moving.

"Seri!" she cries.

Zak bursts another opening.

His wild eyes scan the room—then lock on her armband. "Hello, Lilly-D. Feeling better?" he asks, half-smiling, but it doesn't touch the panic behind his eyes.

"Zak! You're okay!" she breathes. If she weren't glued down, she'd hug him.

"Of course I'm okay," he says, trying for casual.

"Seri. How is Seri?" she asks quickly.

Zak blinks. "Seri? Oh—her. They haven't told me yet." He jerks his chin toward the hallway. "They."

"They?" Lilly echoes. "Who are they, Zak? Where are we?"

Zak opens his mouth. Shuts it. His eyes flick to the gap he entered from. Then back.

Cold rushes through her chest. "What?" she snaps. "Hey— I'm trapped. Help me up!"

Zak hesitates, then gives in. He grabs her wrist and leans close.

"They're all aliens," he whispers.

Lilly freezes. Her entire body tenses.

Then—she laughs. Weakly. "Yeah, good one, Zap-Man. Now help me up."

Zak doesn't laugh. "Willow said you're under some kind of neural restraint so you'll heal faster," he mutters, studying her like she's part robot. "But I don't see anything holding you down. It's fascinating."

Lilly squints. "Who's Willow?"

"She's the healer. That's what they call doctors here," Zak says. "We're at their base. In Antarctica."

Lilly blinks hard. "Healer? Antarctica?"

She stares at Zak's outfit. All white. Cottony. Like a hospital uniform.

"So… we're in some kind of hospital?"

Zak doesn't answer right away. He drags the white chair closer and sits. Everything around him is white. It makes her skin crawl.

"Zak," she says quietly. "Tell me!"

He sighs. "They sent me in here to calm you down. Before they come, talk to you."

His eyes find hers. "But I have to tell you this."

He leans in.

"They've got him. They took him hostage."

Lilly's brain screeches. "What? Who?"

Zak's voice goes flat. "The Cankers took your father."

It lands like a punch.

She stares. "The Cankers? You mean those weird, stinky people in our forest? Why would they take him?"

Zak doesn't blink. "Yeah. Them. Like the one at the crash. They're the Cankers. The bad aliens. They took your dad."

Lilly flails—useless. "But... is he okay? Is he hurt?"

Zak presses her shoulder gently, trying to steady her. "Stop squirming. I'm supposed to be calming you."

She stops. Just barely.

"We're in an underground alien base. Here on Earth," he says. "They're the good aliens, though."

He leans even closer.

"I overheard Aubrin. The Cankers want you dead, Lilly. And they'll do anything to get to you."

Lilly stares at him.

The only word that escapes her lips is: "...Aliens?"

Her thoughts are mayhem and chaos.

Zak nods fast, grinning like he just shared the best secret ever.

Lilly freezes. Alien images flood her brain—tentacles, fangs, bug wings. She eyes the balcony. The door. Possible escape. She's still pinned flat.

"All right, you two, visiting time is over," a voice says—surprisingly human.

Zak jumps up like a kid caught sneaking snacks. "I did my best," he blurts, clearly frustrated.

Lilly pushes against the bed, ready to spring. Still stuck.

An older woman enters. Short, wild white hair. Soft blue eyes. Kind smile. "Hello, Lilly. I'm Willow, the healer," she says. "Looks like Zak explained a few things."

She gestures to the doorway. "We just need to finish your scan. Then you can be off to eat. I bet you're hungry."

Lilly blinks. The woman looks… normal. Not alien at all.

Willow shoos Zak with a motherly point. "Out."

He makes a face. "She's grumpy today," he mutters, then slips out with a worried glance.

# Chapter 38

### The Healer and the Hygee

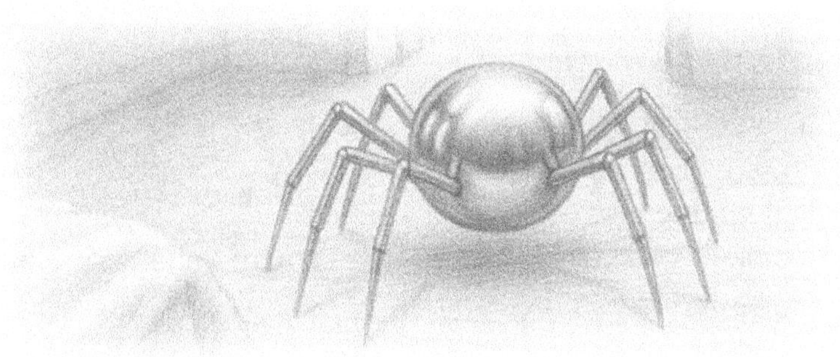

Willow turns back. "I've been taking care of you since last night. How are you feeling?"

"Fine… I guess," Lilly mumbles. "But I can't move. And my dad—have they found him?"

Willow's smile fades. "Not yet. Aubrin sent two angs to search last night. Another went this morning."

"Ang?" Lilly frowns.

"Phisian word. Means squad or team," Willow explains. "Sorry. I'll stick to Earth words."

Lilly's alien alarm blinks on. "You mean… Earthlings?" Her voice cracks.

Willow chuckles. "Yes. And I'm not one. I'm Kalpanian—our ancestors were from Earth. That's why I look like this, like you."

Lilly searches Willow's face for something weird. Finds only warmth.

"And… Seri?" Lilly asks, words catching.

Willow sighs. "Seri didn't make it. I'm sorry."

Lilly flinches. Tears rise fast.

"There was nothing you could've done," Willow says gently. "You were thrashing in your sleep. We had to restrain you until your navok stabilized."

Lilly looks down at the white-gold band on her arm. She'd forgotten about it.

"Its interaction with you is… complex," Willow says. "I've never seen anything like it."

"Is it hurting me? Please. Take it off."

"It's okay," Willow reassures her. "You're better than before."

Then—movement behind her.

A spider.

Silver. Huge. Silent.

It creeps forward—eight spindly legs, a baseball-sized body. Just like the one from the tree fort. Only bigger.

"Behind you!" Lilly gasps, pointing. "It's the thing that attacked Seri!"

Willow turns, startled. Then… sighs. "Ah, so that's where it went." She waves it off. "It's a hygee. A healing helper. A machine."

Lilly's stomach flips. "I smashed it. I thought…but…could it have saved her?"

"No, Lilly, it was too small to help her. You acted bravely," Willow says softly. "You didn't know."

"Now—can the hygee come closer?"

Lilly nods silently. Uncertain.

Willow turns to the spider. "Hygee. Proceed."

The spindly legs begin to move—smooth, silent. The silver ball of its body glides forward. It doesn't touch Lilly. Its limbs extend so far, it looks more leg than anything else.

Up, up, and over it crawls.

The shiny, mirrored body moves above Lilly's chest. Its legs stretch wide; each one placed carefully on either side of the bed.

But it's close. Too close.

Sunlight dances off its polished shell.

One limb touches her forehead.

A tingling wave spreads through her.

The restraint vanishes.

She lifts her arm. Free.

Relief hits—then dread. The spider still hovers over her.

"Arms at your sides. Stay still," Willow says. "We'll have you walking soon."

A green light zaps from the spider, scanning Lilly head to toe. Then back again.

Suddenly—something begins to form. A glowing figure made of thread. It's Lilly. Floating above.

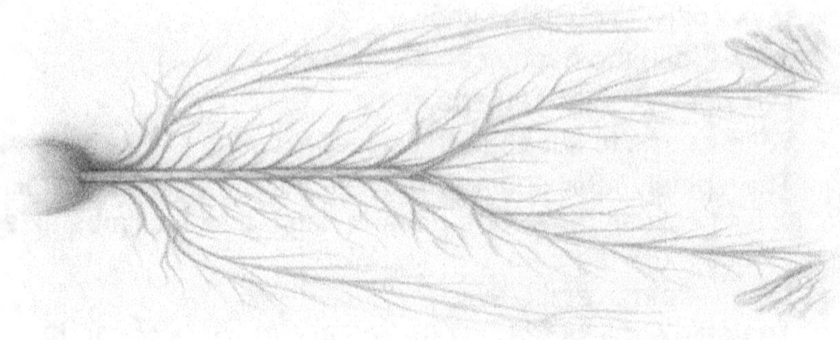

"Wow," Lilly breathes. "That's me?"

The glowing threads mimic her every move. Her nerves, brain, even her voice—all made of light.

"Ewww," she mutters. The thread-body copies that, too.

Willow laughs. "Everything looks good. No damage."

The left arm glows brighter—threads linking into the armband.

A new voice enters. Calm. Smooth. "Hello, Willow. Might I speak with your patient?"

Aubrin steps into the room.

Lilly stiffens—still under a giant spider.

Willow blocks him. "Not yet. Out. Shoo."

She grins at Lilly. "That's Aubrin. Royal Gesh Iyengar."

"We've met," Lilly mutters.

Aubrin winks, then exits.

At the door, Willow and Aubrin lean in, whispering. Lilly catches one word: "merging."

Willow returns. "Let's finish what we started."

She studies the thread-body carefully. "The navok is merging with you. It's extraordinary."

"Merging?" Lilly echoes. "It's… attaching itself?"

"More like it invited you," Willow says. "Can you feel anything?"

"No. That's the weird part."

Willow touches her shoulder. "We don't know how to remove it. But it's not hurting you. I think it's making you stronger."

Lilly stares. "Why?"

Willow grins. "That's my favorite question."

She watches the glowing thread-arcs. "It's like this navok was designed to recognize you."

Lilly frowns. "But… I'm just Lilly."

Willow's smile warms. "You're special. You stayed calm in a crisis. I'm proud of you."

Heat rises in Lilly's cheeks. "I'm no one special."

"You are," Willow says firmly. "Hygee, scan complete. Retreat."

The thread-body vanishes. The spider leaves.

Lilly exhales. "Can I get up now?"

"You're good to go."

She sits up fast—then sways.

"Whoa. Slow down," Willow says, steadying her.

# Chapter 39

Willow disappears, then returns with a tray. Two granola-bar-looking things. A red drink.

"This is a Cassii bar and Kota Berry juice. From our home planet."

Lilly stares. "Alien food?"

"Try them," Willow says with a grin.

Lilly sips the juice. Tangy. A little apple, a little cranberry, with a zing. She downs half. Then the bar—chocolatey oats. Familiar. Delicious.

"Yum," she says, mouth full. I guess I'm hungry." She blushes at her impulses. "Thank you."

Her armband chirps. Willow glances at it, one eyebrow rising.

"Aubrin is waiting. He wants to talk about your father."

"Will it help?" Lilly asks.

Willow nods. "And I trust him."

Lilly wipes her eyes. "Then let's do it."

Willow smiles. "They will find your father."

She gestures to the table—two piles of clothes.

One is white.

The other? Her favorite jeans and T-shirt.

"Your clothes have been cleaned," Willow says. "Wear what feels right."

Lilly grins. She picks her clothes. Feels like a win.

"Oh—Zak's been outside the whole time," Willow adds. "Wouldn't leave."

"Hmmm," Lilly murmurs. "We've known each other since first grade."

Willow pats her hand. "You're lucky."

Then, from the hall: "After lunch and that's final!" Willow snaps.

Lilly smiles. She likes Willow.

She finishes eating. Then—

A sound. Not her stomach.

A groan. From inside the walls.

"Hello?" she calls. Nothing.

"Rae oh yoo," a voice whispers. Right by her ear.

Lilly spins. No one.

"Hello?" she calls again.

111

Silence.
"Rae oh yoo," the voice repeats. A child's voice.
She crouches. Peeks under the bed.
Nothing.
She laughs nervously. "Okay. I'm going crazy."
And then—
Something drops.
A black shadow slams down across the balcony.
Like a guillotine.
Darkness swallows the sky.

# Chapter 40
## A Creepy Crow

Lilly blinks at the black shape, sunlight flaring behind it. A crow. Finally—something familiar.

"Was that from you?" she asks, mostly just to hear her voice. She's not expecting an answer. She's not *that* crazy.

The bird is huge—about the size of a medium dog. Midnight black. Eyes just as dark. And it's only a few paces away.

It's the closest she's ever been to a bird this big.

She lifts her arm to block the sun and get a clearer look. Her heart thumps harder.

The crow doesn't respond. It just tilts its head—one eye locked on her.

Then—

*WHOOSH.*

It launches into the air. A blast of black wings cuts across the light.

Gone.

So fast, it feels unreal. Like maybe it wasn't there at all.

She glances around one more time. Empty balcony. No sign of the bird. Just shadows and wind.

"Okay then," she mutters, brushing it off.

She steps through the other doorway the others had used. The next room opens wide and tall.

Faces turn toward her.

# Chapter 41

The first one she sees—Zak.

Then, Aubrin steps forward—tired, but kind. The kind of kindness that cuts through everything.

"It's good to see you up, Lilly," he says, offering a hand. "You gave us a bit of a scare."

His voice is calm, steady. His crisp black uniform gleams with gold trim. A strange symbol sits on his chest: a circle over wavy lines, inside a triangle, wrapped in another circle. Another, different mark on his arm - a squiggle and a zero.

ɣ-O

"Welcome to Phi Guya."

115

Lilly shakes his hand. "Thanks for protecting us."

His eyes hold hers—warm, but worn. "You have questions. I promised answers. But first: lunch."

Willow crosses her arms nearby, nodding like a bouncer for hungry patients.

Aubrin continues, "After lunch, I'll explain everything. In the meantime—meet Oakeros. Sorrel's son. He's your age, part of our research team."

Lilly turns.

Her first thought: *How big are the kids here?*

Oak is already taller than her dad. Quiet. Heavy in the shoulders, like he's carrying something he can't put down. And…he has blue skin.

"Call me Oak," he says, holding out a hand. It's very blue. His voice is flat. Not unfriendly—just… done.

Lilly stammers a hello, distracted by his green eyes—bright, alive, and full of pain.

Aubrin fills the silence. "Oak and his father have offered to host you and Zak."

Lilly blinks. "Oh?"

Oak winces like that physically hurts. "We are honored," he says. Three words. No warmth. The smile is more grimace than welcome.

Lilly glances at Zak—who's nodding like a bobblehead.

She doesn't know what to say. "Ah… yes. Thank you", comes out.

"Yes!" Zak pumps his fist. Alone.

Aubrin smiles. "One of our angs is already searching your forest. We'll find your father, Lilly. You have my word. I will do my best."

He turns to Oak. "Show them the community when they're ready."

"Yes, Royal Iyengar," Oak replies, standing like a soldier.

"And after lunch—move three genaethers to the launch area, then bring Lilly and Zak to my office."

"Yes, Royal Iyengar."

Aubrin softens. "Welcome to the community of Phi Guya."

Then he's gone.

Oak exhales. Long and slow, heavy with regret. Thick and awkward.

"Just great," Oak mutters.

# Chapter 42

## This does not Belong to You

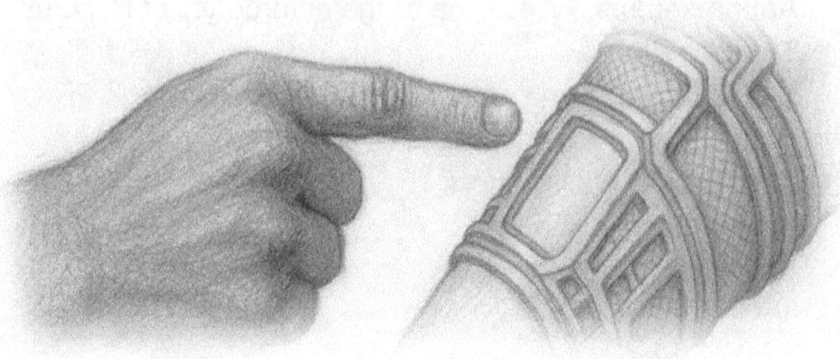

Lilly folds her arms. "Sure," she mumbles, then jerks her thumb toward Oak.

Lilly's armband chirps again. She smacks it.

Zak stares, not getting it.

"Let's go," Oak grunts.

Lilly snaps. "You're clearly not thrilled we're here. But my dad's been taken hostage, and when we get him back, we'll be gone. You won't have to deal with us ever again."

Her armband chirps.

Oak glares at it. "That doesn't belong on you. It belongs to a Royal Gesh."

His voice sharpens. "You're going to be beat like a bug."

Lilly flushes. "Didn't ask for it. Willow said I have to wear it!"

"And it's squashed like a bug," she adds. "If you're gonna insult me, say it right."

Chirp.

Zak watches like he's caught in a tennis match.

Oak growls, "You know nothing. Even a Liege knows more."

"Thanks," Lilly snaps. "I know I'm not welcome. But you could at least explain where we're going. Or fake a smile."

Oak's face contorts into the world's fakest grin. "Eat. Genaethers. Meeting."

Lilly shoots him a glare. "Sure. Whatever."

"Let's go, bug," he mutters, still grinning like a cartoon villain.

Lilly smiles at him just as fake and follows.

Zak trails behind.

Then—BLAM.

Sunlight.

Lilly flinches, shielding her eyes. The air is warm. Moist. It smells like the school greenhouse—earthy and alive.

Green. Everywhere.

She stops in her tracks.

Grass springs beneath her feet. Thick. Spongy. Bright.

"But... I thought we were in Antarctica?" she says aloud to Zak.

Instead, it's a jungle. Trees. Vines. Grass and weird buildings.

"Don't look at me. I didn't make this weirdness." He laughs back

Buildings rise in the distance—trees growing out of them like sculptures. The sunlight glints off rooftops shaped like leaves.

Whatever this place is... It's not cold. It's not empty.

And it's not what she expected.

# Chapter 43
## Welcome to Weirdsville

Oak and Zak are already several paces ahead when Oak turns with a grunt. "Let's go, bug."

Zak scurries back, eyes huge. "We're really in Antarctica! 1.6 kilometers beneath the surface! They've created a synthetic sun, a full ecosystem, maybe even weather modulation—"

"Zak," Lilly cuts in. "The clouds are bright. Got it."

She drags him along, staring upward. No sky. Just a glowing wall of blue-green ice arching overhead like a frozen tsunami.

Ahead, a hive-like structure is dwarfed by a cluster of buildings. Flying machines zip in and out of holes along its sides.

Lilly eyes it warily. "Giant bug hotel?"

Oak doesn't respond. He's too busy stomping toward a bridge that crosses a small stream.

On the other side—

A full-blown alien marketplace.

Colors, sounds, smells—

—everything hits at once. Bright fabrics, shouting vendors, spinning signs, sizzling food. It's like someone mashed together a farmers' market, a spaceport, and a hungry person's dream—

—Lilly is the hungry person.

"Stay close. Don't touch anything," Oak warns. "Everyone's stuck here since the attack. They've all decided to shop."

He charges into the crowd like a freight train. People part for him automatically.

Lilly follows in his wake, eyes wide.

First stop: Zuni's Groceries.

A barrel of what she hopes is rice turns out to be a tub of wriggling maggots.

"Fresh Oisen worms! Best eaten live!" shouts the vendor.

"Hard pass," Lilly mutters, backing away.

More barrels. More bugs. Some twitch. Others breathe.

Next: a fish tank.

THUD! A horned, double-jawed fish rams the glass, antlers jingling with shiny ornaments.

Lilly yelps.

"Tacano fish, deary?" cackles the vendor. "Good deal at 34 tokens!"

Zak, still in shock, spins like a broken compass.

Lilly drags her eyes toward a nearby stall of herbs and spices. Familiar scents—mint, basil, oregano—calm her panic. A crooked sign reads: **Sissal's Spice and Fungus.**

Then—

SNARL!

A blob of fungus attacks another inside a crate. The shopkeeper beats it back with a stick, swearing in a language that sounds 80% anger and 20% frustration.

Lilly steps away fast.

# Chapter 44


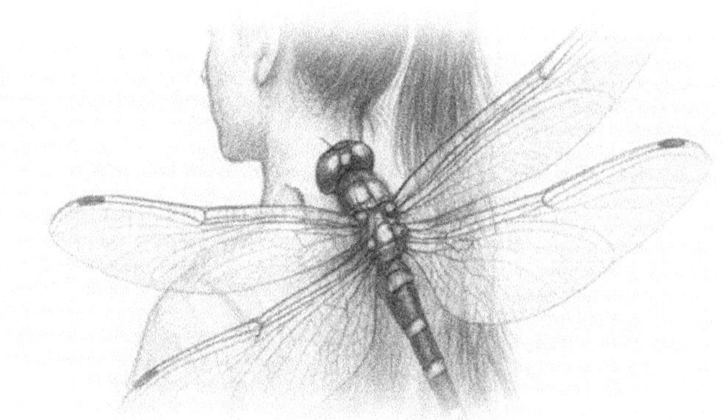

A girl struts by with a dragonfly the size of a squirrel perched on her shoulder. Her pupils are slits, her skin shimmers like wet marble, and her clothes pulse through the rainbow.

She stares at Lilly like she's the weird one.

Lilly ducks her gaze and spots a jewelry booth—finally, something normal.

**Grita's Fibles.**

Charms. Necklaces. Animal-shaped trinkets. Not trying to eat anyone. Nice.

Then she realizes—she's lost Oak.

His head's barely visible over the crowd.

She pushes forward and ends up near roasting pits. One spits out the smell of heaven—like Thanksgiving dinner—but the meat is too large to be chicken, and the deer has an antler sticking out of its nose.

"Nope," she mumbles.

A group of teen girls stares as she walks by. One whispers, eyes locked on Lilly's armband.

Then—fruit. A towering display of melons.

Lilly's elbow clips the edge.

The whole thing topples.

YELLOW

MELONS EVERYWHERE.

"Argh!" shrieks the vendor. "Sivagen oh pumatti!"

Oak appears in a flash, bowing like his life depends on it. "Meta! Meta! Maa oh Kinrik Gesh—"

It works. The vendor softens. "Meta! Meta!" she says, bowing back.

Oak herds Lilly away. "She called you a destroyer of formation. Try not to break anything else."

They pass a dim, deserted café—**Swig-N-Swill**—that smells like old pickles and wet socks. One man stares into a mug like he's expecting it to offer therapy. Another glares out the door, polishing a glass with a cloth that looks dirtier than the floor.

Nope.

Hard nope.

# Chapter 45
## Used Robots & Alien Gossip

Next shop: an explosion of lights, wires, and robots. Hovering signs yell:

**DEALS! BUY! TRADE! POMO'S GREAT DEALS**

Flying bikes, dented droids, and strange tech fill the space. In front of a sleek flying machine, a green-skinned man, half Lilly's height, pokes at a panel with laser focus.

Across the aisle:

**MicMac's Sweets.**

It's packed with kids, rainbow walls of candy, and a humanoid robot behind the counter with glittery hair and perfect posture.

Lilly steps inside.

Everyone turns to stare.

Whispers spread. A blond girl nudges a friend. Eyes lock on Lilly's arm.

"What's the big deal?" she mutters to Oak.

Oak's voice booms over the noise. "It's rude to stare."

Half the kids flinch.

"You don't know what that means, do you?" Oak says, motioning to her armband. "I've got a lot to explain."

Lilly bumps into an old man. "Oh—sorry!"

"Metta," he says kindly, bowing.

She bows back. "Metta."

*Hey,* she thinks. *I can do this.*

A few steps later, the smell of fresh bread wraps around her like a hug. A baker waves from behind a glass case, flour streaking his face.

"Earth flour's in!" he shouts at Oak.

"We'll come back later," Oak calls back.

A tiny robot zips by. It salutes Lilly with a chest-smack and keeps going.

Oak nods at it. "Royal Gati. That was for you."

"Me?"

"Because of the armband."

Before she can process that, WHAM—a floating skateboarder slams into her shoulder and speeds off.

Other shoppers get bumped too.

People yell in the same weird language.

Lilly blinks, dazed.

Then—coffee. Fresh. Warm. Perfect.

She spins toward the smell. A café across the plaza. Her stomach growls loud enough to echo.

"Food," she mumbles.

Somehow, the weirdest part of the day is also the most familiar. Hungry is hungry—alien planet or not.

# Chapter 46
## Café Acadia

"We are here!" Oak proclaims. "Café Acadia! We'll meet my father and grab a bite to eat before anything else."

# Chapter 47

Helping Hands

The café explodes with sound—clinking mugs, barking laughter, overlapping chatter. It's a riot of voices trying to outshout the market outside.

"This is insane," Oak mutters. "It's never this crowded. The portal lockdown must've driven everyone here."

They squeeze inside. Steam rises from plates. Tiny robots hover by tables like obedient pets. The smells alone could punch someone in the stomach.

Zak spins slowly in place, mouth open, glasses fogging. His brain might melt from the tech overload.

"Chocfee and bagels," Oak yells over the noise. "Huge since my dad opened this place!"

A large man in an apron waves from across the café. Oak waves back.

A woman stands and leaves a nearby table. "That one's ours," Oak says, bolting for it.

The big man joins them as they reach the table. "This is my father—Sorrel," Oak says.

Lilly tries not to gape. The man's built like a fridge with a heartbeat.

"Nice to meet you, Lilly. Zak," Sorrel booms, shaking their hands like he's testing the structural integrity of their bones.

"I've heard good things—from Aubrin," he adds, with a wink.

Oak stiffens as Sorrel gives him a look. "You're being helpful, right?"

Lilly steps in. "Oh, totally. Couldn't ask for a better guide."

Oak gives a fleeting look of gratitude.

Zak remains in stunned silence, staring at a passing robot with what can only be called religious awe.

Sorrel leans close. "Follow orders from the Royal Gesh. Whatever they need—you help."

"Yes, sir," Oak mutters.

Then Sorrel turns to Lilly. "I'm truly sorry about your father and your home. Aubrin's the best hope you've got. Until then—you've got a home with us."

Lilly nods. "Thank you… Sir."

He grins, gives her a warm "Welcome to our community," and lumbers off like a battleship in sneakers.

# Chapter 48

The café goes quiet.

Too quiet.

Lilly realizes everyone in the café is staring at them. Even the robots.

A dented little bot rolls up, twitching like it's running on leftover parts. It collects dishes with a mechanical wheeze, whirring and clicking like it might collapse at any second.

It rolls off without a word.

Then a tray floats in beside them—carrying only a holographic head.

Zak gasps.

"Welcome to Café Acadia," says the hovering man. "May I process your request, Oakeros?"

To Lilly, the expression seems fake—like a recording played on demand.

Oak winces as the head says his full name.

Snickering breaks out from a group of kids at the table behind them.

"Yes, please. And again—can you please change my name to Oak in your database?" he says, exasperated.

More snickering from behind.

"May I process your request, Lilly?" The head-and-shoulders hologram grins at her with the same unnatural smile.

The whole thing is just… *weird.*

Lilly flusters, suddenly panicked about needing to order. She realizes she hasn't even seen a menu.

"Ah… sure… ah…" She spots it—high on the wall above the glass counter—and rushes her eyes across the options without really reading. "Ah… well…"

"Why don't I order for us, until you get used to it?" Oak offers, clearly impatient. He turns to Zak –

– but Zak is fully turned around in his seat, gawking at a dish-carrying robot.

Oak rolls his eyes. "I'll order for all of us."

"Your request will be processed, Oakeros."

"*Please* edit my name to Oak."

"Your request will be processed, Oakeros."

Another snort of laughter erupts nearby.

Oak shakes his head and exhales sharply. "We'll have three large chocfees—extra chocolate, extra sugar. And the mixed bagel platter, all lightly toasted, with the premium spread selection. Please."

"Your request will be processed, Oakeros."

More laughter.

Oak's face turns a darker shade of blue. He looks like he's about to yell—but holds it in.

The floating head grins once more, then glides away.

Despite her hunger, Lilly turns to Oak with a pressing concern. "These... bagels and stuff... they don't have any *wiggly* things in them, right? They're not like that stuff I saw in the market?"

Oak shakes his head, grinning. "You mean Oisen worms?" He chuckles. "No! That's traditional Phi food. Old folks eat it. Sometimes they serve it at the Feast of Unity."

He gestures at their table. "This? This is the popular stuff. Earth food. Same stuff we ordered."

Lilly exhales with relief.

"Portal! You said *portal!*" Zak blurts, snapping out of his trance. His mouth has finally closed, but his eyes look wild behind his glasses.

"Yes, to Tyr-Daijo—our orbiting moonship," Oak replies, casual as can be. "There is a larger portal on there. That one gets us to our planet Phi."

"You mean a... *machine* that can transport a person to another *planet!?*" Zak's voice rises with every word. He looks like he's about to leap over the table and shake Oak for answers.

"Well... ah... yes. In the Phi language, we call it the Anubis. It'll transport anything that fits through it—even a medium-sized vehicle."

Lilly and Zak both fall silent—but for different reasons.

Zak looks like someone just slapped him with a science textbook.

"You both don't know much, do you?"

"I believe you've been told to tell us what we *want* to know," Lilly says, meeting Oak's challenge with one of her own.

Oak crosses his arms and leans back. "So?"

"We don't have to tell your father you *refused* to help us, do we?" Lilly bluffs. She'd never actually do that—but Oak doesn't know that.

His eyebrow shoots up. "You wouldn't do that! Would you?"

"No. Of course not. We're stuck here anyway—so maybe talk, instead of glaring at each other?" Ooops, that bluff didn't last long.

A tense silence hovers between them, even as the café clatters and bustles around them.

Then Oak nods—a truce. "Alright. Okay." He pauses, deciding where to begin. "Have you heard of the solar system called Trappist-1?"

"No," Lilly says.

"Yes," Zak answers at the same time. "But... that's 38.98-something lightyears away."

He taps his armband, and an image of the solar system floats in the air.

# Chapter 49
## The Trappist-1 Solar System

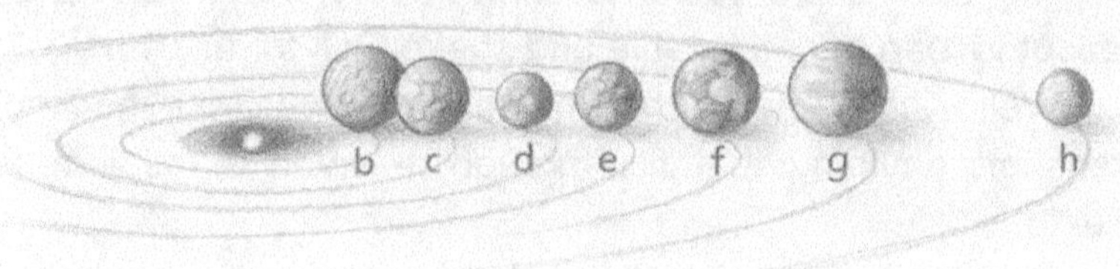


"When did you learn how to do that?" Lilly blurts out, half-laughing, half-knowing the answer already. This is Zak, after all.

"I had to do something while you were lazing around," Zak jokes back.

"Right. Planet Phi is in the Trappist-1 solar system, thirty-nine light-years away," Oak adds, pointing to the hologram floating above Zak's armband. "Phi is what you call Planet E."

"You're joking! How long does it take to get there!?" Zak booms. "Years? Decades? What?" He's leaning right into Oak, wide-eyed behind his glasses.

Patrons who had returned to their meals now glance over again.

Oak leans in, touches Zak's armband, and flicks off the hologram. He glances at nearby tables, aware they now look like the crazy group. He speaks cautiously, searching for a tone that might calm Zak down. "Well... ah... no. I'm not joking. It only takes seconds. It's immediate—as soon as one goes through it."

"But the energy required for intergalactic, instantaneous flight for thirty-nine light-years would be... wow! ...phenomenal!" Zak slumps back into his seat. His eyes glaze, like he's diving into a calculation too big for his brain.

Lilly braces for the Zak meltdown—any second now.

Oak looks ready to explode from frustration, his eyes darting at the café patrons now staring at them.

Lilly steps in, realizing it's not helping Oak to have half the café eavesdropping. "Zak! Please! Just stop with the *how* questions—just for now. Let's get to the *why* and *what-in-the-world-is-going-on* questions! You're gonna pop a brain cell!"

She turns to Oak, softening a little. "Please, Oak. Just go on. Tell us about Phi, and why you're here."

For the first time, Lilly thinks she actually feels a little sorry for him. A tiny bit.

"Well," Oak begins, "as I was saying, we're all from the planet Phi—sort of. Depends on how far back in history one goes." He taps his armband, and a projection appears beside his face. He starts flicking through it, scanning digital pages until he finds what he's looking for.

Zak looks like he's about to leap across the table. "Where in the database did you find that?!"

Oak flinches, as if preparing to jump to another table.

"No! Stop! *Bad* Zak!" Lilly snaps. "*Sit. Listen.*"

She turns to Oak with mock formality. "Sorry. He's running low on his medication."

Zak folds his arms and slumps in his seat, looking like a scolded child.

Oak still looks like he wants to bolt.

Welcome to the life of Lilly-D.

"Go on. Please." Lilly gives him a calm, coaxing smile. "You're aliens from the planet Phi... and...?"

Oak blinks, clearly regretting everything that led to this conversation. But he sighs and carries on. "Well, we're not the aliens—*you guys* are. But yeah, planet Phi is made up of eight realms.

Each realm originated from a different planet. Earth is one of the original planets, where we believe the Kalpanian Realm came from. Thousands of years ago." He gestures as he explains. "We figure it was the Noahs who did this. They were terraforming or something."

"My father is from Mangbi Realm—they're like Earthlings, just a lot bigger."

"My mother was from Baine. That's where my blue comes from. It was—"

"I'm sorry to interrupt," Lilly cuts in, trying to follow. "But... are the Noahs one of the eight realms?"

"Ah... no," Oak replies. "We believe they were a highly evolved race. In existence well before we began measuring time. They left behind advanced tech—our portals, the Royal Gesh stuff..."

Zak whimpers at the word *portals*.

"No!" Lilly scolds, wagging a finger. Zak instantly quiets, perched on the edge of his seat. She turns back to Oak. "So why are you here? On our planet? Who here even *knows* about you?"

Oak looks between them. His face creases with concern. "Well... nobody here on Earth knows about us. That's one of our laws—strictly enforced. It's been that way since the time of the pyramids." He shifts in his seat. "And... why are we here? We're here to protect Earth. To monitor its environment. That's the job of the Royal Khem Gesh of the Seairland Realm."

"Protect from what?" Lilly asks.

Oak laughs, like it's a silly question. "We protect Earth from itself, of course. You're almost always on the verge of nuclear self-destruction."

"Since the time of the pyramids? *Wow.* You've been here the whole time?" Lilly blinks, stunned. "That was a long time ago. How have you stayed secret *this* long?"

# Chapter 50

Oak chuckles. "We're not completely secret. You know the children's stories? The little green aliens, the greys, werewolves, Bigfoot, ogres. Let's not forget the big, blue, strong helpers." He puffs out his chest and spreads his arms wide, like he's saying, *like me*. "We can't stay completely out of sight. We wipe the minds of most who see us. The ones we miss? People think they're crazy."

Yeah, that's right, Lilly's father. Not that she needed a reminder.

"Who took my father? Did they take my mother too?" Lilly's head spins with questions that crash into each other like br cars.

"I don't know any facts about your mother. But your father—that would be the Cankers. They're hired terrorists from the realm of Barea. You've met a few."

"Big, ugly, and ogre-looking?" she asks.

"Yup. That's them. They're the worst of the worst. Most of them are highly mutated—radiation contamination back in their realm."

"So …why him?"

"That's something best answered by Iyengar Aubrin—after lunch." Oak points a thick blue finger at the armband on Lilly's arm. "I think it's got something to do with you. And that navok."

A sudden whirring cuts the air. A floating tray glides to their table, stopping just within reach. Steaming mugs and a massive platter of fresh, golden-brown bread rings hover in front of them. The smell is like warm sugar and fresh dough, the kind that dives deep into your happiness and offers to remind you of it.

Lilly feels a wave of relief. She hadn't realized how empty her stomach was until just now. The food also saves her from more of Zak's endless tech questions.

The bagels are still warm, their soft crusts brushing steam off the surface. The drink in the mugs is hot and sweet—somewhere between coffee and cocoa. Honestly, Lilly would have eaten cardboard at this point. Just nothing that wriggles.

They all dig in.

Even Zak seems too busy chewing to interrogate anyone.

"Well, that's it," Oak says between bites, his mouth full of bagel and jelly. "Those are our ancestors. That's why we're here on Earth. We're on lockdown now. No one's going anywhere since the Cankers attacked the portal and tried to steal the power supply."

"But why would one of your own… uh… people attack here?" Lilly asks.

"Not everyone on Phi agrees with protecting Earth," Oak says casually, chasing his bite with a swig of chocfee. "Some realms—like Baine, Barea, and Crewl—think Earth should be harvested."

"Harvested?" Lilly sputters, nearly choking on her drink.

"You know, taken over. Earthlings enslaved or relocated, if they're lucky. All Earth's resources stripped to fuel their realms. Apocalyptic kind of stuff."

"Well, that's not fun," she says, blinking.

Oak's calm tone rattles her more than anything. The idea that he's from another planet? That somehow feels less wild than what he's just described.

"That's why the Royal Gesh are here," he continues. "As long as the Phi World Council sides with protection—not harvesting—earth's got a chance."

"This power supply, the bad guys are after," Zak jumps back in, eyes locked on Oak. "How much power does it put out? What's its principal design?"

Lilly groans and rolls her eyes. Zak is back.

# Chapter 51

Oak doesn't even blink at Zak's question. "I don't know, and I don't know." He raises his index finger, checking off each answer like check marks. "But I *do* know the power supply is based on ancient Noah Technology. That makes it more powerful than anything anyone's ever managed to reproduce. Even now, no one's been able to copy it. That's why it's so rare. That's why everyone wants it."

"Thanks for some idea of what's going on," Lilly says, locking eyes with each of them. "Now tell me, please, how to get my father back. Whatever it takes—let's do that."

Oak winces mid-chew, caught off guard.

Zak sinks behind his mug like it might hide him.

"Lilly," Oak says, serious now, "these Cankers aren't just ugly. They're experts at kidnapping, violence, and theft. It's all they do." His sea-green eyes settle on hers, steady and unblinking.

His words land like iron in her chest.

Oak softens. "But Aubrin and his Royal Gesh—they're better. The best. He *will* find your father. It's just… it'll take some time."

"Time?" Lilly's voice rises. "How much time? How long does it usually take to rescue someone? How often does this even happen?"

"Ah… I… ah…" Oak scratches the back of his neck. "Honestly, I don't know. If I had to guess… maybe a unity or two."

"A *unity*? And how long is that?" Her patience wears thin with all these alien measurements.

Oak swipes across his armband and glances at the readout. "A unity …is 0.2597 Earth years."

Zak's already got his math-face on, chewing and calculating at the same time.

"Normally," Oak goes on, "you wouldn't be here. No Earthling would be. After what you saw, your minds would've been wiped. But you and Zak? You're the first humans in this room. All of this—it's because of *you*, Lilly."

"Me? I've done exactly nothing."

Oak points at her armband. "That Navok is why everyone's staring. That's why you're both here. Aubrin would've wiped your memories otherwise. But you're wearing that." He holds up his half-eaten bagel, gesturing toward her arm. "Everyone who wears a Royal Navok has spent their life training. They start as kids, working as Lieges. Of those, only a few ever get picked as a Gesh Burden. And the *only* way to become a Royal Gesh is to displace—or beat—another one. It takes *many* unities. And then there's *you*—a kid, an Earthling, and bug-sized, too."

"That's height-efficient," Lilly says, flat as toast.

Oak ignores her.

"You should've heard how furious Vishot was when he found out you had on the Royal Navok. Seri was in his *ang*. Rumor is, he stormed off to Aubrin and threatened to go to the Queen. Aubrin told him there was some 'uncertainty' in the law about Navok's induction. Said for now—it stays on you."

A soft beep chimes from Lilly's armband.

"You've got an incoming report," Oak says.

"I have a *what*?"

"It's a report. A message." Oak leans over to help—Lilly has no clue what to do. He taps a few times on her armband, and a glowing message floats up above her wrist.

"Looks like it's from Aubrin." He swipes again, and the message morphs into a string of numbers. "Whoa. Okay. I don't think I should be looking at this. That's your token balance."

Lilly stares at the numbers, trying to make sense of them—like they're a foreign language she's supposed to already know.

# Chapter 52

### Lots of Alien Money (Tokens)

"It looks like you're getting paid—and you already have a token balance," Oak says.

"What? Why?" Lilly stares at the hovering image, but all she sees is a blur of numbers.

"I've heard of this," Oak continues. "Royal Gesh inherit a balance when they're first inducted. Then they get a stipend every unity." His eyes widen. "Wow, Lilly—you're rich!" He glances around to make sure no one's watching. "You should check this out later, when we're alone." He swipes across the list, and the numbers vanish.

"Paid? For what?" Lilly mutters, eyeing her armband like it's the one with answers.

Oak is about to respond when his armband lets out a sharp double beep. He raises his arm and taps the display.

A projection of a woman—just her head and shoulders—floats above his wrist. She has brown hair and speaks with a crisp tone. "Good afternoon, Oakeros. This is Haro. We're nearly at the launch zone to swap out our genaethers. Aubrin said you were moving them before meeting him in the Royal Gesh conference room. He's there now, waiting for you to bring the two Earthlings."

Oak glances at Lilly, then Zak. "Will do. We're finished here."

Both Lilly and Zak give a nod.

"We're on our way," Oak replies.

The woman gives a slight smile before fading from view.

"We should go," Oak says, getting up. "Aubrin's waiting. Looks like he'll be the one to explain your pay. He's the boss."

Lilly cringes. "I thought *you* were supposed to fill us in?" There's a sting in her voice—another answer dangling just out of reach.

"I *would* have—but we've run out of bagels." Oak grins. "Come on, bug."

Lilly eyes the empty tray, now reduced to a few scattered crumbs. She glances at Zak to see if he's as baffled as she is.

Zak just shrugs.

Oak is already up and heading for the exit.


Lilly rests her arm on Zak's shoulder. "C'mon, Zap-man. Maybe you'll get some answers from Aubrin. You know you've got a problem with your shyness. Don't be shy this time. You've got Zak problems—just speak up, ask your questions." She grins, teasing him.

Zak gives her a *you're nuts* look. "Yeah, right. I've got *bug* problems, more like." He flashes a crooked smile, slips out from under her arm, and jogs to catch up with Oak.

"Oh sure, you're hilarious now!" Lilly calls after him, picking up speed to follow the two of them.

# Chapter 53
## The Spy Bug

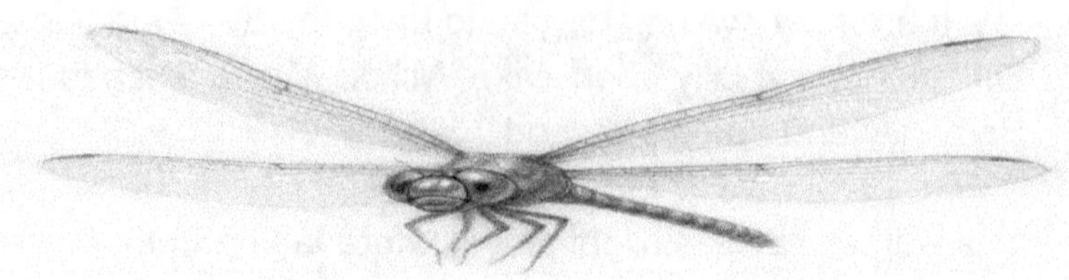

Lilly and Zak trail Oak past the noisy market. Tall, windowless buildings rise like white anthills, spotted with greenery. Flying machines hum in and out of a tower nearby.

"Research and residents live here," Oak calls. "And over there's the Queen's Compound."

He points to distant towers rising like a stone bouquet, their tops lost in mist.

"Queen like… Britain?" Lilly asks.

"No! She's the Queen of Seairland. The ruler of Seairland and where Royal Gesh comes from. Rarely visits," Oak mutters, clearly annoyed, by Lilly.

Lilly snaps, "Sorry, I'm not from your world!"

Suddenly, a dragonfly the size of a kite zips in and hovers. Its wings blur like shimmering fans, but the hum is too mechanical.

"Shoo!" Oak growls, swatting. "It's a Jag. Someone's spying."

The dragonfly dodges and zips off.

Zak gasps, "That's a robot dragonfly!"

"Kind of. A Jagaether," Oak mutters.

Just then, Oak's armband beeps. Sorrel's hologram pops up. "Don't forget the flour order. And check on our vesta robot."

Oak groans. "Yes, Dad."

"One more thing—dinner tonight. Roast DoDo."

The hologram vanishes. Oak sighs.

# Chapter 54

They're nearly to the flying-machine tower when Lilly spots movement by the lakeshore—a boy and a dog. The boy flings a flying disc, and moments later, it hovers midair, gliding past Lilly at chest height.

The dog bolts after it with lightning speed. Its legs flail in a wild blur, kicking up grass and dirt. In seconds, it closes the gap, leaps, and snatches the disc straight out of the air.

Lilly's about to chalk it up to a normal park scene—until the dog trots past her with the disc clamped proudly in its mouth.

It's not a dog.

It's a robot.

"Research is over there," Oak adds, pointing to a building on the other side of the park. "There's a school too."

Zak's jaw drops. "They learn about all this?"

"Just the locals do, here. The best education is in Sieraland, the Royal Gesh Training Program," Oak says. "Hard to get in. Plus, it's not like Earth school."

He taps his armband. Three sleek flying machines detach from the tower like wasps, descending in perfect formation.

# Chapter 55
## Tin-Can Flyers

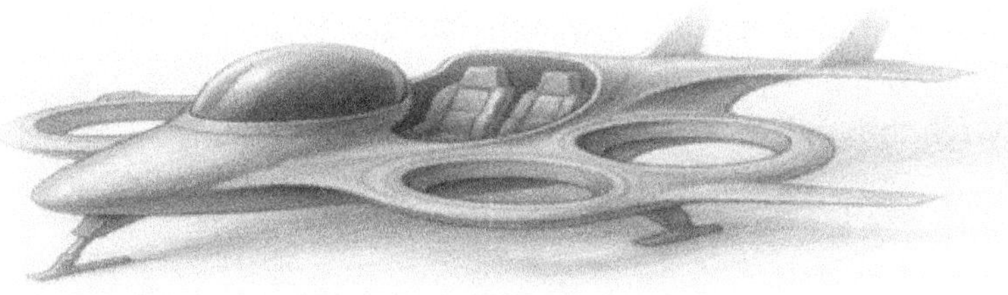

The machines land hard. Each has two seats, wide frames, and scuffed surfaces.

"Basic residential genaethers," Oak explains. "Not like the Royal ones. These are junk copies."

Zak squints. "These look like the ones we took from the forest."

"Similar, but dumber," Oak says. "C'mon. We're flying them to the anubis."

"We're what?" Lilly blurts. "I don't know how to fly!"

"You don't need to," Oak grunts. "They're in follow mode. Just sit."

She hesitates.

"Pick one. They're all equally bad."

Grumbling, Lilly climbs on one. Zak follows and goes on to the remaining one. He grips his handlebars like a life raft.

Oak knocks on a dome in front. "Wake up, tin-head. Formation flight to the anubis."

Zak gasps. "Is that a robot?"

"Yep. An ardhiar. Dumb helper drone. The Gesh use Gati, ancient Noah tech—way smarter."

Lilly's dome twitches too. She narrows her eyes. "Do you know how to fly one of these?"

Oak smirks. "Even Earthlings can manage. Just hang on."

Lilly grips the handles. The machine hums beneath her. Zak's already clenching like a statue.

# Chapter 56
## Flying Machines

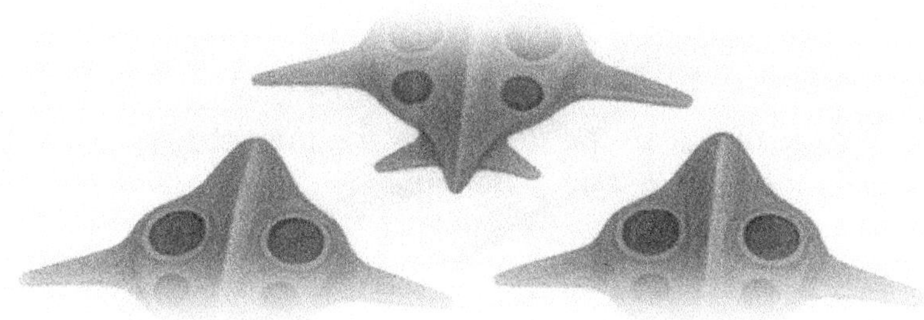

"By the way, you don't need to yell; there's a comm system," Oak's voice echoes from her console.

Lilly flushes. "Oh."

"Launch!" Oak commands.

His machine lifts, slow and steady. Lilly's jolts up next—too fast. She gasps, hugging the seat, wind rushing past.

They hover in formation. Oak glances over, totally unbothered.

Zak's machine whooshes up beside her. His glasses are crooked, eyes wide.

Other flyers zip by, staring openly at the two Earthlings. So much for blending in.

Below, Phi Guya spreads like a model city—round houses, spoked paths, a shimmering dome overhead.

Lilly's genaether nudges forward. They glide across the sky like train cars in the air.

She looks down. Fields, forests, and the lake pass beneath. The city hugs one side. Nature claims the rest.

Oak's voice crackles. "Going down. We made it without you falling. Lucky me."

Lilly ignores him. She's kind of disappointed it's already over. It wasn't even scary. Just… amazing.

As they descend, she sees it: a huge ring standing tall. The anubis.

Near it, the clustered rooftops of the market.

"There's the market," she mutters.

"What's that, bug?" Oak's voice teases.

Lilly grits her teeth. "Nothing."

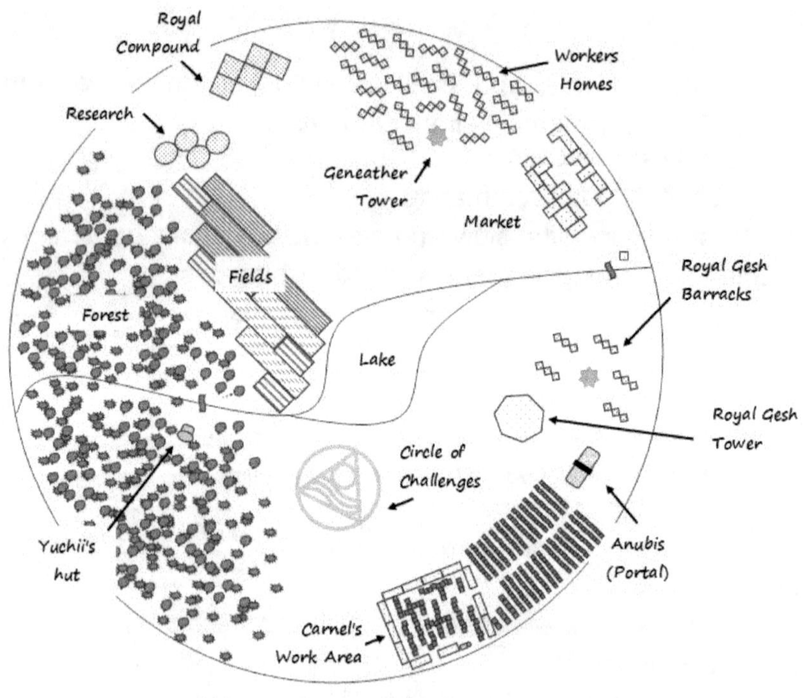


Phi Guya Layout

# Chapter 57

There are fewer people here—especially compared to the market. As the ground nears, more details come into focus, and Lilly's awe deepens.

Tall figures stand among much smaller ones. At first, they look like adults with kids—until she realizes the small ones are people. The tall ones... machines. Robots. They mingle with the crowd like it's normal.

The trio of flying machines descends toward a massive ring, landing just before it.

Shattered edges and black scorch marks mar the base. At first, the swarming motion around it looks like ants—until they get closer.

The "ants" are robots.

They move with precise coordination—cutting, lifting, hauling metal away.

Six guards stand before the ring. Black armor, full-face helmets, identical stances—imposing, like they're built for war.

Dust kicks up as the genaethers land.

The ring towers above—like an ancient gateway for giants.

Lilly checks on Zak. He's pale, swaying, eyes wide. Then he leans over and spews.

"Oh great," Oak mutters.

"Give him a break!" Lilly snaps.

Oak shrugs.

"You okay, Zap-man?" Lilly asks.

"Yeah. Over as fast as it's out."

"Maybe stick to the ground next time?"

"Good idea." Zak wipes his mouth on his sleeve.

Around them, the robots—knee-high with thin black legs—silently carry twisted metal. Like leafcutter ants, but colder.

Zak stares at the towering arch. "What... what is that?"

"That?" Oak says, swinging off his machine. "That's our portal. The anubis."

Zak stares. "That's the portal?"

"The Porrr-tal," Oak says like Zak's missing a few screws. "The one to Tyr-Daijo?"

Broken. No one gets in or out."

Zak blinks. "How? Why?"

"It... is... broken," Oak says flatly. "Shell's gotta come off to fix the core.

Someone from Phi attacked us. You've been told this. Keep up."

Zak frowns. "Yes... but..."

"Oh wow. This just gets more fun by the centag," Oak groans, flailing his arms.

"Work? How?" Zak blurts, clearly short-circuiting.

Oak grabs him by the arm. "Come on. You're holding up Aubrin."

# Chapter 58

### Noxiars (robot guards) on Guard

Lilly walks up to the line of six guards. They tower over her—super tall.

Their armor is made of overlapping black panels, each one catching the sunlight at a different angle. The result: their uniforms sparkle like black diamonds, every surface glinting and shifting. Each guard holds a black weapon with precision, standing in perfect mirrored stances.

Lilly gets the odd feeling they're not *wearing* helmets—that maybe the helmets *are* their heads. Could they be robots? Really big ones? No… they're *twice* her height. She steps in closer, trying to peer through the dark visors, hoping to catch a glimpse of eyes.

Yeah, why not get curious with alien robots? What can go wrong?

All at once, the six guards slam their left arms across their chests in unison. *THUMP*. A single, thunderous metal-on-metal sound echoes out.

Lilly jumps.

The guards freeze in place.

"Ah… hi," she stammers, giving a timid wave—just a wiggling finger and an awkward smile.

Oak squints at her like she just grew antennae.

A sudden whirring interrupts everything, followed by a rush of wind from above.

Lilly glances up just in time to see the belly of a genaether dropping fast toward them. Her muscles coil, ready to dive.

But Oak stands completely unfazed. No alarm.

She forces herself to relax and stay upright. Look cool.

The flying machine touches down beside them on a cushion of air, kicking up a swirl of dust around their knees.

Zak immediately starts coughing.

This genaether is white with gleaming gold trim—identical to the one Lilly saw in the forest, except this one isn't all broken up. Its polished surfaces flash in the light.

The rider sits tall on the landed machine, dressed in a tight black uniform with gold lettering and a transparent fishbowl helmet.

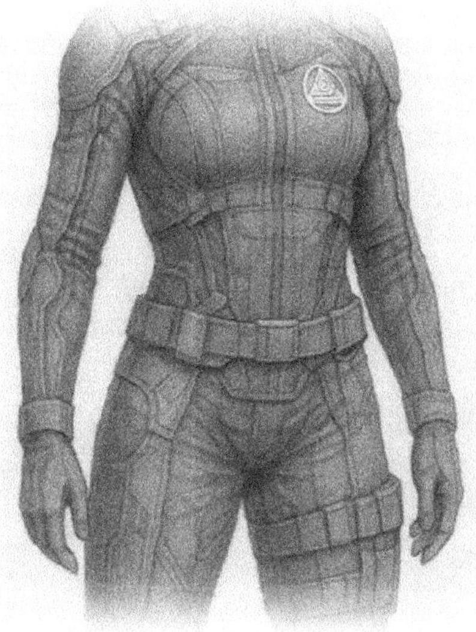

"Hiya, troublemaker!" the rider yells at Oak over the hum of the genaether, as it powers down.

In a blink, the fishbowl helmet vanishes.

She's young—tall, athletic, confident. Her dark brown hair is pulled back in a ponytail, much like Lilly's.

Oak flushes. His mouth opens, but no words come out.

The rider turns while still seated and flashes Lilly a big smile. "I'm Haro. Your daily, neighborhood Royal Gesh. You must be Lilly and Zak." She has a ranking symbol on her left shoulder of a squiggle and an upside-down V. She nods hello.

ɣ-Λ

"Hello. It's nice to meet you," Lilly says, smiling as she steps forward and extends her hand.

159

Haro returns the handshake—firm, quick, and full of energy. Her grin stays steady. "It's good to see you up and around," she says.

Up close, Lilly sees it—Haro's skin is covered in a fine, tan fur, like a mouse. Smooth, soft-looking, and warm-colored.

Lilly almost blurts out *Wow!* But holds it in. "Good to meet you," she says instead.

Zak is still coughing, trying to recover from the dust storm.

Haro turns to him. "Are you going to be alright?"

Zak waves her off between coughs. "Cough! Cough!"

Something about Haro's posture, her confidence—her quick arrival on the flying machine—reminds Lilly of a cowboy from one of those old Wild West movies.

# Chapter 59



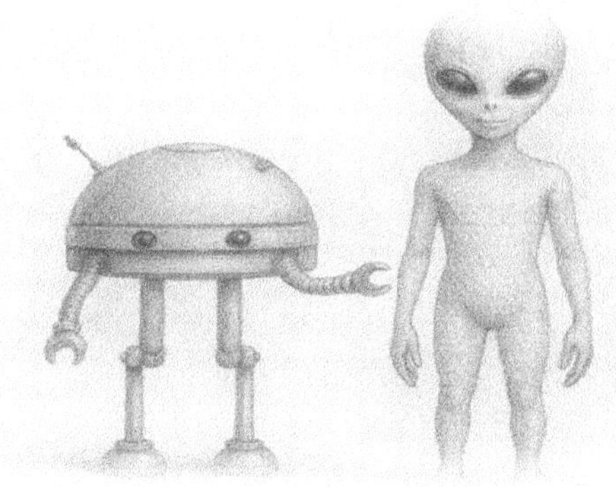

Haro looks at Oak, who's still frozen, mouth gaping.

"Aubrin says Lilly might be as stubborn as you, Oakeros," she says. "So double trouble."

She turns to Lilly, grinning. "See this kid? Snuck out of the dome to fight Cankers. Got off the hook by saving me—shot the one aiming at my back."

Oak still doesn't move.

Haro walks over to Oak's landed genaether and knocks on the dome. "Ride's over, tin-head."

The dome stirs, then lifts. What emerges is gangly, armless, and walks on legs—a half-ball on stilts.

From Haro's machine, another robot rises—shorter than Lilly, with a teardrop-shaped head and huge eyes. It looks exactly like the alien grey she saw with Aubrin.

As it passes, the robot turns its head toward Lilly, then slaps its metal arm across its chest—*Thump!*—before hopping into Oak's grey machine.

Haro's smile fades. Her face turns serious.

She glances between the alien-grey and Lilly. A slight frown creases her brow, then vanishes.

She locks eyes with Oak.

"Thanks for saving me, Oakeros." She crosses her arms over her chest and bows her head.

Oak turns even bluer and stares at the ground.

"Terco's fine," Haro says. Complaints less every day. You just grazed him. Happens."

Oak opens his mouth—nothing comes out.

"You seeing Aubrin?" Haro asks.

Oak nods once, shy as a schoolboy.

"He's scanning all Royal genaethers for trackers," Haro adds. "Someone's probably watching us."

She swings into her machine. "Thanks for the ride."

To Lilly and Zak, she smiles again. "Good to meet you both. Stay out of trouble." She winks at Lilly.

A moment later, her energy helmet seals shut.

Her genaether blasts skyward, straight through the dome.

Dust swirls around their knees.

Zak coughs. "Does she have… cough, cough…fur?"

"Yeah. And a tail," Oak says dreamily. "She's Miedonian. But don't—*ever*—mention a Miedonian's tail."

Lilly folds her arms. One sharp look says it all.

Oak stands there, mouth still open. "Oak. You can call me Oak," he mumbles, still staring up.

Then he finally lowers his gaze, avoids Lilly's eyes, and heads toward the tower.

Lilly still has questions—but with Oak marching off, the Haro conversation is over.

# Chapter 60

### Voices, Vines, and Very Big Robots

Lilly, Zak, and Oak enter the overgrown tower—the same one Lilly had mistaken for a hospital. Two robot guards thump their arms in salute as she walks by.

She jumps.

Inside, the center of the tower is a hollow column, ten stories tall. A glowing lift platform awaits. Oak speaks a calm phrase: "We have a meeting with Iyengar Aubrin, please." The lift glides up without rails.

Zak's glasses tilt.

Lilly mutters something about missing elevator music.

At the top, glowing floor dots guide them down a circular hallway. Lilly whispers to Zak, "Even you couldn't get lost here."

He snorts.

A huge hologram floats in the open core, multi-stories tall—a man reaching toward a godlike figure. It rings a bell in Lilly's memory, but she can't place it.

Then a voice whispers in her ear. "Rae oh yoo."
She whips around. No one. "What did you say?" she demands. Another whisper—this time inside her head. "Ray-o… something!"
Oak stops. "What now, Bug?"
"I heard something! A voice!"
"Didn't hear a thing." Oak stares like she's grown a second head.
"Stop calling me Bug," she snaps.
"Stop acting like one."
Their glares lock.
Zak looks ready to dive between them—or run.
Lilly folds her arms. "Let's just get this over with."

# Chapter 61

## Wooden Ships and Blue Scowls

They follow the blinking dots into a wide, high-ceilinged room filled with wooden ship relics and old navigation tools. At the center, a round oak table.

Behind a desk the size of a car sits Aubrin.

Willow stands nearby, mid-argument with a scowling, blue-skinned man.

He's tall, black uniform, with stone-cold eyes full of judgment and an expression worn by years of grim thoughts. His slick black hair shines like it's soaked in grease. But it's his skin that hits hardest—blue, electric, and jarring, like a static shock to the eyes.

The room falls silent as they enter.

Two grey robots salute with metal-on-metal thumps as Lilly nears.

Aubrin comes over and greets them warmly. His handshake is firm, his smile easy.

But the blue man refuses even eye contact.

Aubrin introduces him as Vishot, the leader of the second Royal squad. Seri was under his command.

Lilly's eyes drift to the models and relics.

Aubrin beams. "All from Earth's sailing era—my hobby."

"Cool," she says, trying to keep her voice steady.

Aubrin shifts tone. "We're still looking for your father, Lilly. But we believe the Cankers weren't after him. They were after you."

Lilly freezes. "Me?"

# **Chapter 62**



He nods. "There's a Phisian named Mensch Morder. He is a fanatic about genetic studies and patterns. He believes, based on your genetic code, you're someone called the Ohmuno. A figure from myth and fairy tales. We believe he hired the Cankers to catch or kill you and they messed up. They captured your father in a panic."

Lilly's breath stumbles. "Seri called me that. But that doesn't make any sense."

"No, it doesn't. But, more importantly, you're safe—for now. They'll keep your father alive. He's their leverage."

Lilly fights for air, for clarity. "In the forest... where he was taken... There must be clues!"

Aubrin nods. "A team's already searching." Then he looks at her directly. "You're brave. Seri told us you protected her. That means everything to a Royal Gesh."

Lilly shrugs, unsure what to say.

"You too, Zak," Aubrin adds, turning. "She said you shielded her when you could've run. That's rare. Very impressive."

Zak blushes and gives a small nod.

Then Lilly remembers something Seri said. "My mother, was she taken by the same people?"

A shadow passes Aubrin's face. "We looked into that accusation and found no evidence of it being true. We do not know what happened to your mother, sorry. She would be proud of you helping others."

Vishot sits frozen, bitterness carved into every line.

Oak's eyes widen. His skin shifts to a lighter blue.

Lilly nods. "It was just instinct. I thought…" But the memory of Seri, broken and bleeding, crushes her words. Her chest tightens. Her eyes sting.

She won't cry. Not here.

Vishot sneers like he's tasted something rotten.

Oak's expression softens.

Willow looks like someone just learned a child has been sent to war.

Aubrin watches Lilly carefully. His voice softens too. "You did good, Lilly. Very good. I'm impressed. You didn't even know Seri, and you still stepped in. Most wouldn't."

Lilly fumbles for words. Her mouth opens, then closes. She just shrugs, fighting back the sob. Her eyes blink fast.

"Aubrin. Please," Willow says gently, placing a hand on his arm.

Aubrin covers her hand with his own. "Lilly, I know this is hard. But it's important."

Lilly nods, voice shaky. "It's… okay," she breathes.

"Can you tell us everything you remember about the forest? Start with when you first saw the diablopero."

Lilly wants to help—needs to. She takes a breath, steadying herself. Then she begins. Every strange, jarring detail from Oak Drive Forest. From the moment she saw the shimmer in Zak's trap.

The room goes still. Everyone listens.

Vishot folds his arms, scowling like whatever rotten he's tasted has come up as bile.

Zak fidgets, blushing.

Oak looks puzzled.

Silence.

Then Aubrin speaks again. "Seri said her Vok activated when you picked it up. That was thought impossible—unless someone was wearing the exact paired navok. Unless… it was already yours."

He tilts his head. "Were you holding Seri's navok? Or maybe—her arm?"

Lilly looks at each face staring back. "No."

The big blue soldier recoils like he's been slapped. "She lies!"

"Enough," Aubrin snaps, eyes locking on the greasy-haired man.

Vishot looks ready to explode.

Oak blinks, stunned.

Zak just stares at the floor. As usual.

Lilly thinks she just might have got some Vishot spittle on her.

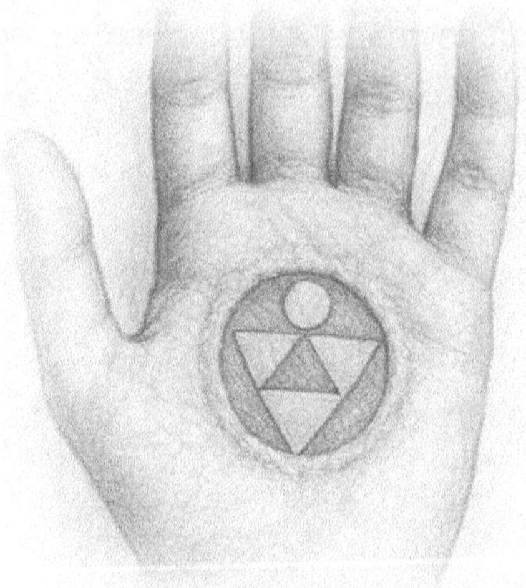

Vishot explodes. "She's a child! An earthling! She shouldn't be wearing the Royal navok."

Willow's voice slices through: "Enough!"

Aubrin shuts Vishot down with a look. "We both heard what Seri told us she did. We all follow the Royal Gesh law."

All eyes fall to Lilly's armband—her Royal navok. It glints, bright and undeniable.

Silence hung heavy for a long moment.

"May I see your left palm, please, Lilly?" Aubrin asks, his voice warm—gentle, like a healthcare worker's.

"Uh… sure. I mean, I just have a birthmark. That's all," she says, lifting her hand and glancing at the stained palm beneath her armband.

Aubrin reaches out and gently grasps her wrist—but his grip is strong. In one fluid motion, he turns her hand palm-up, then holds his white-and-gold armband above it. He swipes the surface twice.

Lilly gasps.

Her birthmark—mottled and slightly darker—is now hovering in the air above his armband, magnified. The mark looks like a triangle within a triangle, with a circle at the top, all enclosed by a ring. It covers her whole palm.

"Well…this is an interesting mark. How long have you had this, Lilly? "Aubrin asks gently, there is a bit of a smile at the corners of his mouth.

"Um…always…I don't know. I thought it was a birthmark."

Then Aubrin turns to Vishot, a flicker of amusement behind his words. "Any idea about this, Ist-er Vishot?"

Vishot's eyes go wide as moons. His mouth opens—but no words come out.

"Alright! That's enough! That is completely enough!" Willow bursts out, her voice sharp and commanding.

Aubrin releases Lilly's wrist, and the floating image of the mark vanishes.

Lilly pulls her hand back quickly, clutching it to her chest. The birthmark remains—unchanged, just as it's always been.

"You're right, Willow," Aubrin says with quiet finality. "We're done here." He turns to her with a kind, apologetic look, then shifts to Vishot with eyes of stone.

"Ist-er Vishot," he says firmly, "from this point forward, until I decide otherwise, we will follow the rules of the Abarj Kensha. Lilly Dubois is, by Seri's last wishes, the rightful owner of this navok. She now holds the rights, duties, and privileges that come with it."

# Chapter 64
### Decisions Made

Vishot scowls. He stands stiff and sharp. Lips pressed into a furious line. "It will be as you command, Royal Iyengar!" He spits the words like curses. Without another glance, he pivots and storms out—no goodbye, no nod, not even a glance at Lilly. Not exactly the friendly type.

One of the grey robots silently peels away to follow him.

The other stays frozen, like a statue.

Aubrin turns to Oak.

Oak looks like he just stumbled off a ride that spun too many times. He stiffens, trying to look like a soldier.

"I want you to accompany Lilly and Zak. Tomorrow, take her to Fuerte's to retrieve her Vok. I hear you were top of your class in Liege training. Do you have access to your father's Burden Vok?"

Oak blinks, caught off guard. "Ah… yes, Royal Iyengar." His face pales.

"Very good. Help her with the basics. Prepare her for the First Circle of Challenge."

"Aubrin! Please, no!" Willow blurts, voice tight with concern.

"We must, Willow. It's the law of the Royal Gesh." Aubrin's eyes soften. "Besides, with her wearing that, we know what will follow. She will need to learn a few basic skills."

Willow bites her lip, holding back words. She nods, reluctant, but agrees.

Aubrin turns to Oak. "Take Zak to meet Carnel. I'm sure they'll have things to talk about."

Lilly glances at Zak.

Zak shrugs. "*I don't know.*"

Lilly's thoughts swirl. She's grateful they're helping find her father, but the rest feels like fog. "Thank you. For helping," she blurts out.

Aubrin nods. "Carnel doesn't know you're coming," he adds. "Likely too buried in Anubis repairs to check his messages."

They take it as dismissal. "Yes, sir," they mutter, out of sync.

The three head for the exit. As they pass the still-standing grey robot, it slams its fist to its chest in a sharp salute.

Lilly glances back.

Aubrin's expression holds concern and faint amusement.

The hallway is silent at first.

Oak's eyes scan, lips tight.

Zak looks pale, wide-eyed.

Lilly tries to lift the weight. "So, Zap-man. Told you I was special."

Zak blinks, then grins. "You are special—especially short." He nudges her toward the hallway edge.

"Hey! Watch it! Geek!" Lilly laughs, pushing him.

Zak smirks.

Oak glances back, debating whether to scold them.

They reach the lift.

The tension still hums.

Lilly breaks the quiet. "I don't know who that big blue guy with the plastered-down hair was… but let's have him over for dinner."

A pause.

Then—laughter. The first time since it all began.

It bursts from all three of them, echoing through the hologram-lit chamber, following them down.

# Chapter 65
## Yin and Yang

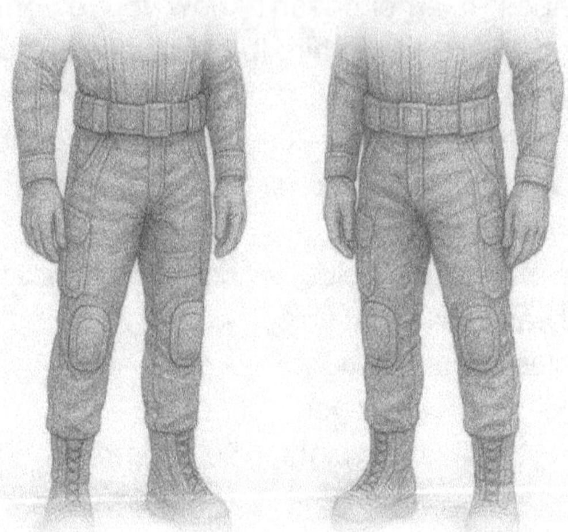

$O$ak, Lilly, and Zak step through the doorway of the Royal Gesh base. A rush of warm greenhouse air and brilliant light washes across Lilly's face. She squints, lifting a hand to shield her eyes. The gold on her armband catches the sun, scattering flashes of light in every direction.

Two Royal Gesh stand beside the two remaining genaethers—the same ones that had been moved earlier. They're dressed identically in black uniforms with gold trim. And they *look* identical, too.

Lilly recognizes them. The two long-haired, ponytail guys from the tent.

They wave as Oak leads the way.

Lilly and Zak trail after him.

"Hey there," one of them says to Lilly.

"Getting settled in, we hope," adds the other.

Both soldiers have yellow lizard eyes, with narrow black slits for pupils. Gone are the fake brown eyes from before.

"It's all …a little overwhelming," Lilly admits, honest and unguarded.

"Sorry, we didn't say anything in the tent."

"We couldn't."

They take turns talking, finishing each other's sentences, like they share a single brain. Leaning casually against the genaethers, they don't seem scary at all—despite the eerie eyes.

"Top-secret alien stuff and all?" Lilly teases, raising an eyebrow.

Both chuckle in perfect unison.

"No. We couldn't say anything…"

"Because we had a bet going."

"Oh?" Lilly tilts her head.

"Yeah. With Terco."

"He said he could convince you to come back to base."

They go on alternating their lines so fluidly it's surreal.

"Terco couldn't even convince a Tacano fish to come and eat."

"We won."

"Yeah."

"We each get a berry beer out of him."

They laugh together and fist bump, completely in sync.

Oak steps in, curious. "Say… are you the Royal Gesh clones everyone talks about?"

"One and one—"

"—make one. I am Yin," says one.

"I am Yang. And we're the best," finishes the other.

"You guys are legendary!" Oak grins.

"Why…"

"Thank you," they say in unison, bowing with wide smiles.

"We aim…"

"To please."

Their grins melt away, replaced by something more serious.

"Listen, Lilly," one of them says, voice low and sincere. "We heard what you did to help Seri. She was our friend. Thank you. You have the makings of a true Royal Gesh."

The other picks up the thought without pause, pointing an olive-brown finger at her armband. "If Seri gave you that, then she believed you should have it."

"And since we believe in Seri…"

"We believe you should have it as well."

They nod to each other like a silent agreement passed between them.

"If you need anything…"

"You ask for us."

Without another word, they hop into their genaethers at the same time, smooth and synchronized—like a perfectly timed dance. Even their ponytails bounce in harmony.

"Oh, right," one calls back.

"Thanks for the ride," finishes the other.

Yin and Yang flash one last grin—warm, welcoming, and somehow kind even through their lizard eyes—then shoot straight up, vanishing into the clouds above.

# Chapter 66

$O$ak leads them in the same direction, as the robotic ants are carrying the metal sheets.

The ants pay them no attention, marching along their programmed path.

Just beyond the damaged Anubis, rows upon rows of shipping containers stretch ahead—stacked well over three people high. Each one looks exactly like the containers seen at Earth's shipping docks.

To the left, a massive bowl-shaped stadium dominates the horizon. It's easily the size of a football stadium. Its towering walls rise twelve or thirteen stories high, and perched along the very top are round rings—spaced evenly—lining the upper edge.

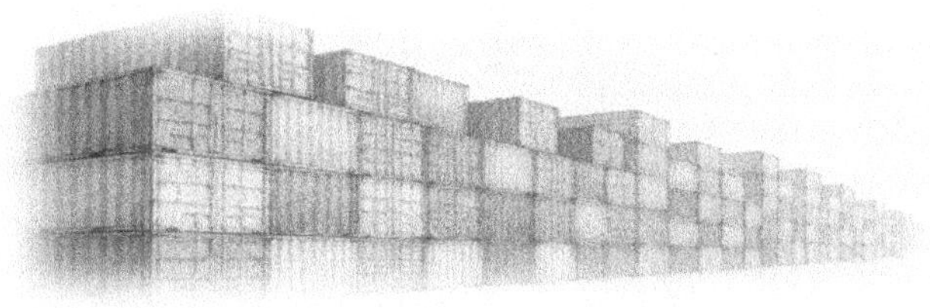

# Chapter 67
## A Porto-Jo

The trio—Oak, Lilly, and Zak—have to step aside as a large container glides past. It floats on a platform that hovers just above the ground without touching it.

Zak stops to watch the platform rise to the very top of the stacked containers and shift smoothly into position. "What is that, an autonomous flying forklift? Is it using the same levitation tech as your people-fliers—your genaethers?"

"We call it a *porto-jo*—or, in your language, a carry vehicle," Oak replies with less irritation than usual. "As for how it works? That's a great question for Carnel. He knows how everything works."

Oak leads them to the end of the stacked rows. They turn down an alleyway formed by the final row of containers and a tall concrete wall. Halfway through the narrow passage, the concrete gives way to something unexpected.

"Wow!" bursts out of Zak as he halts at the threshold, gaping at the scene ahead.

Piles of equipment stretch into the distance—stacked in rows, scattered in heaps, rising several stories tall. Narrow, zigzagging paths snake between the towering mounds.

Oak steps confidently into one of the paths, as if he's walked it a hundred times.

Strange-looking machines crowd in from all sides. Lilly recognizes broken grey flyers—or what's left of them. There are giant parts of robots, twisted hills of scrap metal, and chaotic stacks of multicolored wire. In one pile, a lone robot arm sticks out. From another, a leg. Some look like they were frozen mid-motion before being tossed into the junk.

Lilly pauses, chills pricking her arms. She's certain she sees a pair of eyes watching her from deep inside the pile. But when she looks again, they're gone.

The path opens into a small clearing. In the center sits a crumpled white machine—what's left of a Royal genaether. A sharp clanking sound rings out, metal on metal. Knee-high robotic ants scurry back and forth between the heap and the broken craft, carrying bits of machinery like overworked workers.

A muffled voice rises from behind the machine. "No, I said a *neuron converter*, not a *neuron inverter*!"

Oak glances back at Lilly and Zak, a note of warning in his eyes. "Don't be scared. He's... a little different. And don't make any sudden movements. He gets edgy."

One of the robotic ants turns around, still carrying the same part it arrived with, and hurries back to the junk heap.

"Carnel?" Oak calls out, leaning forward with cautious respect.

# Chapter 68
## Carnel?

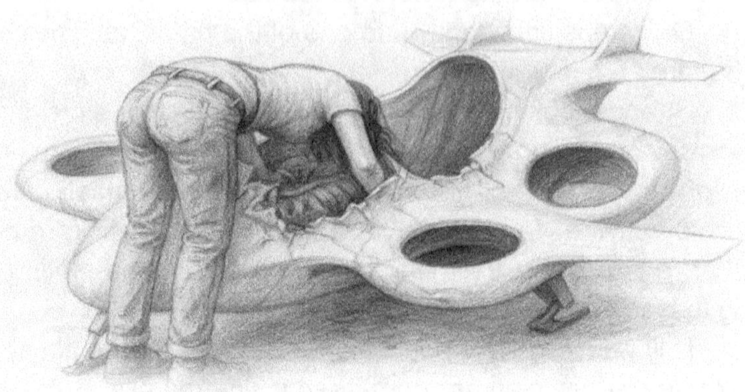

The clanking stops.

A leg appears from around the crumpled vehicle—then the rest of a person. It's a girl, Lilly's age, but tall. Her blond hair is mostly tucked under a baseball cap, though several rebellious strands have escaped. She wears a grease-stained T-shirt and blue jeans covered in smears, blotches, and splotches of every kind of stain. Bright blue eyes fix straight on Oak.

"Do I look like Carnel?" she asks, as if Oak just insulted her mother. Grease streaks her cheeks, but it doesn't take away from her appearance—nothing could.

To Lilly, the girl looks like she's stepped out of a commercial for mechanics' tools. She could be a model... a stunning, oil-smudged, wrench-wielding model.

Oak stops short. "Ah... well... no. Definitely not. You're so much more... I mean... no... I was told he was here." His hands fumble in the air, trying and failing to explain the jumble in his brain. If Oak could turn a brighter shade of blue, he would.

Zak stands beside Lilly, mouth completely open.

Lilly rolls her eyes and elbows him.

"Ooogh!" Zak grunts, clamping his mouth shut.

The blue-eyed girl sighs and jerks a thumb behind her. "Two rows back." Her face says that's about all the energy she's willing to spend on this conversation. She vanishes back under the crumpled machine. Her echoes from deep in the metal: "No! Left! Turn it to the left!"

A moment later, the hood of the vehicle straightens itself—as if someone hit rewind on a crash.

Zak stares in awe at the genaether. The questions on his face pile up faster than he can blink.

Oak stands rooted for a beat longer than necessary. He seems like he has more he wants to say—but says nothing. Maybe he's avoiding Lilly's gaze. Then, finally, he obeys the thumb and leads them two rows back.

Zak and Lilly follow.

The new row is worse—a scrapyard jungle of metal, wires, and indecipherable tech. All kinds of jumbled parts poke out of the stacks like discarded limbs.

A pile of junk shifts.

Beside it stands a skinny, long-limbed robot, all arms and legs. It's dirty and patchy—blue and grey parts cobbled together like a walking salvage project. The robot clutches a box the size of a toolbox and stares ahead, completely motionless.

"Carnel?" Oak calls out, carefully—like he half-expects another blue-eyed supermodel to burst out of the junk.

A mumble answer from somewhere inside the heap. Lilly spots a pair of legs wiggling in the center of it all.

*Bang!*

The mound shudders.

"Sobacco!" comes a shout from inside—loud, irritated, and entirely unfiltered.

# Chapter 69

Lilly glances over at Oak for a translation.

"Ah… don't ask," Oak mutters sheepishly.

The legs wiggle faster. The junk heap shifts again, then—bit by bit—a little person scrambles out from the pile. When he finally stands upright, Lilly's first impression is *elf*. He's shorter than her, skinny, with a bushy white beard and wild, scraggly hair. Baggy canvas clothes hang off his narrow shoulders, bulging at odd angles like every pocket is crammed full. His eyes bulge too, from a face so deeply wrinkled it looks like a roadmap. Some kind of multi-lensed eyeglass contraption clings to his nose. His crooked teeth stick out at strange angles, adding to the whole *crazy-elf-in-a-junkyard* vibe.

And most striking of all—his skin. Wrinkled. Green. Moldy green. He looks like an old apple that rolled under a couch and turned weird. The little green man scuttles over to Oak in quick, twitchy steps. "What? What? Who are you? Who are you?" he barks. His eyes narrow, scanning, drilling.

The beat-up robot with the box follows close behind, silent.

"I… am… Oak," Oak says slowly, pointing to himself like he's introducing himself to a cannibal at lunchtime. "I dropped a vesta off …a few days ago …for repairs. I'm just checking …to see if it's ready yet." He gestures to Zak, who now looks like he's planning his escape route. "And this is…"

"Oak. Oak. Ah yes!" the little man yelps, jabbing a finger in the air. "Oakeros! Yes, yes!" His eyes bounce in their sockets like popcorn.

"Great. Is it repaired?" Oak peers around, clearly searching for something familiar in the chaos.

"Ah! No! No! Too busy! Too busy!" the old elf yelps. "The portal, you know—the portal! Fixing the portal! Damaged main coil! Damaged main coil! Several unities left! Several unities!" His eyes jitter in all directions like they're battery-powered. He's the twitchiest, most hyperactive little green alien Lilly's ever seen. Probably overdosed on space espresso. Not that she's met many little green aliens. Or even knows what they drink.

But still—he reminds her of a chipmunk trying to cross a six-lane freeway, how's that?

Zak blurts out, "The portal coil—what type is the energy core? It must be nuclear fission?"

The little man freezes mid-spasm. His wild eyes narrow. He scuttles right up to Zak in a flurry of tiny, determined steps.

The box-carrying robot shadows him faithfully.

Carnel rises on his toes, their faces nearly touching. His multi-lens contraption lets out a series of *click-click-clicks*, and more lenses snap into place like a mad scientist's telescope. He now wears a stack of glasses thicker than a microscope.

Zak and Carnel stare at each other—eyeglass to eyeglass.

It's a total geek showdown.

"Hmm… primitive idea… but… interesting! Interesting!" Carnel mutters. "No. No. *Fusion*. Fusion!"

"Fusion? Really? Wow!" Zak lights up. "How? It must be using helium-3 and deuterium? How is it initiated without negative energy gain? And—how is it contained?"

Carnel pauses, his wild eyes lock on Zak. Then, he grins. *All* his teeth. It's the grin of someone who lives for this. "Boron-11 and hydrogen! Held in neuron-absorbing meta crystals! With a reaction phase recycler! Controlled! Controlled! Low temperature loss!" Carnel rants in one breathless burst. "Amazing power output per mass! Amazing! Amazing!"

Zak's jaw drops. "Wait! Then it has *no* radiation exhaust? And the neuron by-products are… what… recycled?"

# Chapter 70

Lilly notices that Zak is starting to look just as unhinged as Carnel.

"Yes! Yes! You are the smart one!" Carnel exclaims. "Power. Power! Vok is thirteen times greater than the genaether. The dome is twenty-one times greater than the Vok. Anubis is thirty-four times greater than the dome. All the same power source. Power source!"

Zak's face lights up with shock. "Fibonacci series!"

Carnel nods so hard he looks like a woodpecker hitting pay dirt.

Both of them giggle. They actually *giggle*.

*Click!* One of Carnel's stacked lenses snaps up, leaving just one layer between him and Zak's face. He leans in. "Hmm… good thing *you're* the smart one. Smart one," he mutters. "They're going to need you. Need you." He jabs a bony, dust-covered finger toward Oak and Lilly. His fingertip is smeared with orange powder.

Carnel turns to the dented robot, still holding the box, and swipes a grimy finger along its side like it's a touchscreen. *Swipe. Swipe. Swipe. Stop.* He seems to find what he's looking for. Then—

without hesitation—he plunges his hand into the side of the box. Instead of stopping, his entire arm disappears into the metal like it's liquid. There's no resistance. No bulge on the other side. It just vanishes.

Carnel pulls something out and stuffs it into Zak's hands.

Zak stares at the box, completely dumbfounded. "A wormhole toolbox? *No way!*"

Carnel grins widely, all jagged teeth and pride. "Sho Anubis. Mini portal. Very useful. Useful." He jabs that same orange-stained finger into Zak's chest. "You come back. Tomorrow. Bring cheese puff, puffs. First thing! First thing!"

Zak looks down at what's been shoved into his hands: a weird pair of multi-lensed eyeglasses, just like Carnel's.

"Uh… you mean cheese doodles?" Zak asks, blinking. He glances down again—Carnel's left a perfectly round orange dot on his shirt.

"Yes! Yes! Doodles! Doodles!" Carnel shouts, thrilled with the answer.

Zak's grin spreads into a full-on beam. "Wow! Thanks!" He cradles the eyeglass contraption like it's the best present in the universe. "Tomorrow. OK. OK."

His eyes are nearly as wide as Carnel's now.

Lilly lets out a small laugh. She can't help it. Zak is turning into a crazy alien-elf right before her eyes—and loving every second of it.

But suddenly, Carnel snaps his attention toward her. In a flash, he scuttles up and grabs her white-and-gold bracelet with his green, gnarled fingers. He moves faster than anyone this wrinkled has any right to.

The dented robot with the box sticks close behind him, as always.

# Chapter 71


## Lilly's & Oak's Gifts

Lilly gasps for breath.

The crazy old alien clutches her arm with the strength of a much younger man. Well…alien. *Click! Click!* Go his glasses. Now he's peering at Lilly's navok—her new armband—through three stacked lenses. "Ah, yes! Ah, yes!" he mutters, chuckling at whatever he sees.

The hand grasping her navok only has two fingers and a thumb.

*Ha! Ha!* He laughs again, delighted.

Lilly catches the faint scent of cheese puffs. There's a dusting of orange powder clinging to Carnel's wrinkled cheek. Up close, she notices something else—he's missing one eyebrow. Just one bushy white one remains, perched above eyes which are as black and bottomless as coal.

*Click!* Another lens flips up. Carnel turns Lilly's palm over and traces a gnarled green finger across her birthmark. He lets out a giddy giggle. "Yes! Yes!"

*Click!* A second lens folds up, leaving only one set remaining. The others rise out of the way like mechanical wings. Carnel now peers straight into Lilly's eyes. His gaze is sharp, unsettling—those black eyes are all pupil.

Without looking down, his free hand plunges into the wormhole box. His fingers rummage this way and that, muttering as if speaking to someone—or something—inside. His gaze scans the air above the dome, as if the item he's searching for might be suspended in another dimension.

Then, with a nod, he finds it.

From the shimmering side of the box, he pulls out something small and gleaming. "Hmm... hmm... good thing you are brave. Brave." He presses a polished silver ball into Lilly's palm.

"Ah... thank you," she says, her voice unsure.

The orb rests warm in her hand. It's the size of a ping-pong ball, etched with golden vines that spiral like roots in molten metal. Its mirrored surface gleams in the light.

"You will need it. Need it," Carnel says, letting go of her hand. Assessment complete.

He shuffles over to Oak, his short legs carrying him quickly. Up close, he barely reaches Oak's ribs, yet somehow, he yanks the tall blue boy down with surprising strength, forcing Oak's face closer.

The dented robot, still toting the wormhole box, lingers right behind him.

"Oomph!" Oak exhales sharply, caught off guard. His eyes blink in alarm.

Carnel studies him for a long moment, silent and still, like a scanner freezing over critical data. "Hmm... hmm... You have many good traits. Good strength."

Holding Oak in place with one wiry hand, he plunges the other deep into the rippling surface of the toolbox. From inside, he draws out a sleek black-and-silver scepter, about the length of a forearm. How it fits in the box is a mystery.

"Hmm… hmm… good thing you are strong. Strong," Carnel says, and presses the scepter into Oak's hand. "They will need you. Need you."

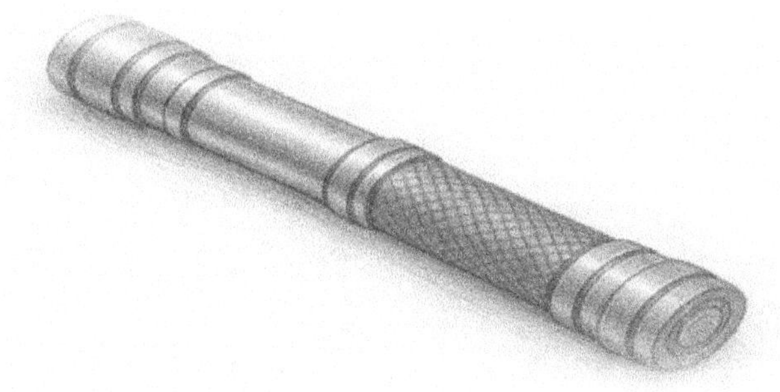

Then, without ceremony, he releases Oak's arm.

Oak springs back upright like a boxing dummy on a spring.

"This is a… a…" Oak stares down at what he's holding, wide-eyed. "It's a Level Seven Vok. I can't…"

"More. Experimental. Very powerful. Go. Now. Now." Carnel flutters a hand at Oak and the others, shooing them away like a swarm of flies.

Meeting over.

"Doodles. Tomorrow. Tomorrow," he says to Zak, already turning. He shuffles off, muttering something under his breath that sounds suspiciously like *cheese doodles*. Within seconds, he vanishes around the nearest heap of junk.

The weird robot, still carrying the wormhole box, trails after him in silence.

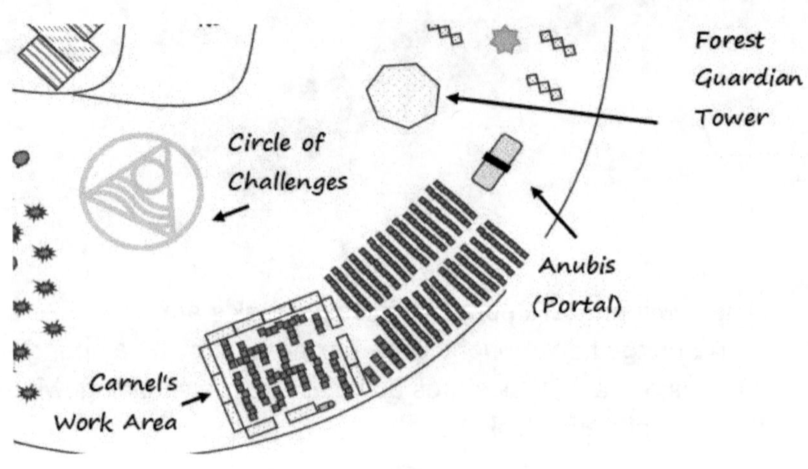



Carnel's Work Area

190

# Chapter 72



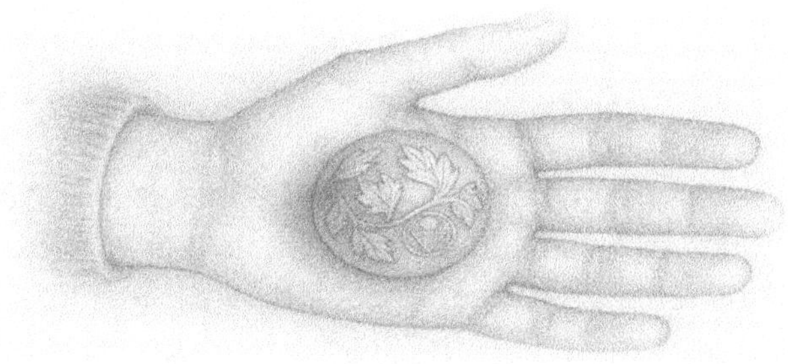

The trio heads out of the junkyard, shooed away by Carnel's twitching hands. They walk in silence.

Beside them, two lines of robotic ants march along a trail—one line returning with pieces of white anubis sheets, the other heading out to get more.

Lilly doesn't pay much attention. She walks while half-looking where she's going, her focus mostly on the gift Carnel gave her. The gold scrolling on the silver sphere, up close, matches the emblem on her palm: a circle over three triangles, all enclosed by an outer ring. She bumps into Oak. "Oomph."

Oak barely notices the collision—he must've been doing the same thing.

"What is this?" Lilly holds the shiny silver-and-gold ball out in her palm.

They all stop. None of them seems in a rush now.

Oak's face flashes irritation as he pulls himself out of whatever thought he was having about the scepter he's holding. He glances at Lilly's hand, then leans closer, his brow furrowing. "That's… a hygee. A mechanical healing aid. But it's… different. A

Royal Gesh's is silver, yet…" His blue finger hovers over the emblem. "Yours has gold leafing, and that's a symbol from one of my children's stories. The mark of the Ohmuno. Weird."

Zak is in a world of his own, wearing his eyeglass contraption. He clicks through the lenses like a kid fiddling with a new toy, eyes darting around excitedly.

Oak's attention drifts back to his scepter. He glances between it and Lilly's Hygee, comparing. "And… this is a restricted vok, powerful enough to be limited to Royal Gesh. Not ancient Noah tech, but close. I haven't even been selected to be a Burden yet. Why would Carnel give these to… us? It's as if…" Oak trails off, his voice lost somewhere between confusion and hope.

Lilly blinks as new images flash through her mind. "So… Carnel thinks I'm going to need a healing helper? Oh, goody."

The daylight dims suddenly, like a blanket of cloud just dropped over the world. The shadow startles Oak out of his thoughts.

"Come on. We need to hurry. We have to pick up flour from Zuni's before it closes." He turns and heads past the anubis toward the Royal Gesh barracks.

Two Noxiar robots stationed by the anubis thump a fist to their chests as Lilly approaches—"Thump!" in perfect unison.

Lilly nods back, unsure what else to do.

Behind the robots, the lower end of the anubis is now exposed—its cover stripped away. Tangled tubing and a honeycomb support structure gleam faintly in the dimming light. The worker ants don't stop for anything—not even the darkness approaching.

Something to the side catches Lilly's attention. It's on the facility wall. No—beyond it. The other side of the translucent blue barrier. A blur paces back and forth, like a caged jaguar.

"Hey. You see that?" Lilly calls out.

Oak is already several paces ahead. "Come on, bug!"

Lilly points at the blur. Her eyes strain to lock in the shape. It darts left, then right—then suddenly leaps up and vanishes. A blur within a blur. Her mind races to place it. "It looked like that dog-thing from before."

Oak pauses briefly, glances where she points, then shakes his head. "Nothing there."

"But it's gone now."

"Come on. Don't make me miss the flour."

Lilly jogs to catch up, still not sure if she saw anything at all.

Crossing the bridge, another noxiar guard thumps its chest at her. "Thump!"

The market ahead is a skeleton of shadows. All its flesh—the people, the bustle—is missing.

Zuni's is the first shop they reach. The shelves are bare. Doors closed. Lights off. One item remains: a massive sack of flour, as big as Lilly if she curled up into a ball.

"Whew! Thank you, Zuni." Oak hauls it up onto his shoulder like it's nothing heavier than popcorn.

He leads them past the dark, quiet bagel shop. No doors. Just shadows and empty tables.

"Wait here," Oak instructs. He disappears to the back and returns moments later, without the sack of flour.

He gestures toward a side wall beside the bagel shop, where an opening stands like a closet with no ceiling.

"Follow me. One at a time. Just step in, keep your hands at your sides. Step out when you get to the top." He doesn't wait for questions. He steps in.

*Whoosh.*

Up he goes, vanishing from sight.

# Chapter 73
## Ajax

Zak and Lilly glance at each other.

Lilly gives a mock bow and a sweeping hand gesture. "After you."

Zak shrugs, steps into the tube, and vanishes upward after Oak.

When Lilly steps into the vertical shaft, a *whoosh* and a *whir* fill her ears. The floor doesn't rise—she does. She glides upward without anything pushing her feet, like floating in an invisible elevator.

At the top, she slows to a stop and steps into what looks like a perfectly normal kitchen. The warm smell of roast turkey hits her like a wave, carrying a few unexpected but welcome memories of home.

Sorrel stands in the kitchen, wearing a flour-dusted apron and even more flour on himself. Pots, pans, bowls, and measuring cups clutter every surface like a kitchen explosion.

"Bark! Bark! Bark! Bark! Bark!"

Oak is crouched over a small, metal-looking dog about knee high. "I missed you, too."

"Bark! Bark!"

"Who's a good boy? Who's a good dog!" Oak scratches behind its ears. "Where's your leg? Go get your leg."

"Bark! Bark!"

Zak is already off to the side, slipping off his shoes.

Lilly does the same, her gaze drawn to the dog.

It has only three legs. It spins in a happy circle, then darts off in the direction it came from, barking with determination.

Sorrel beams when Lilly steps fully into the room. "Dinners in two desitags. Time to wash up!" he bellows, grinning like he's announcing a feast on a holiday.

"Roast dodo. Yes!" Oak throws his arms in the air like a football fan at a touchdown.

The dog returns moments later with its fourth leg in its mouth. It drops it triumphantly in front of Oak. "Bark! Bark!"

"Good dog! Good Ajax!" Oak kneels and reattaches the leg with practiced ease.

Ajax spins in dizzy circles, overjoyed with his restored limb—until something zips past in another room. The dog takes off again, barking wildly.

*Clunk.* The leg drops off again, abandoned in the chase.

"Yes. Plus, I thought I'd cook the Earthling way, since this is our guest's first meal here." Sorrel smiles warmly, his face speckled with white like a flour bomb went off.

"Oh no," Oak mutters, eyes rolling.

"I heard that." Sorrel throws an exaggerated glare at his son.

"Besides, Bengen is helping," he adds with a puffed-out chest of theatrical pride.

He leans away from the counter, revealing a small, wiry robot.

The robot had been completely hidden behind Sorrel's bulk. It wears a little apron and, mercifully, much less flour than Sorrel. It chops vegetables at lightning speed, hands a blur.

"It's more like Bengen is cooking and tolerating you," Oak fires back, grinning widely.

Sorrel grins back and tosses something at Oak—too slow. It flops off Oak's shoulder without even a flinch.

Lilly's stomach growls. She's starving.

"What's a desitag?" Zak asks, still wrestling with his shoes.

Without slowing, the robot's head swivels toward him while still dicing carrots at breakneck speed.

"A desitag is a measure of time on Phi. There are ten centags in a desitag. There are ten desitags in every tag. There are ten tags in one dekatag and ten dekatags in every Phi sun. Converting to Earth time, there is one Phi sun to approximately 0.94794521 Earth days. That means…"

# Chapter 74


## Dinner is Served by Bengen

"That means—get going and get washed up," Sorrel cuts in, waving the robot off mid-rant.

Lilly is already lost somewhere after two desitaggies or whatever they're called.

Zak pauses like he's buffering, then tilts his head toward the ceiling, entering full human calculator mode. "That... is... roughly...

two point seven... minutes," he announces, tapping the side of his head between each word, like he's jump-starting his brain.

Oak and Sorrel spin around, blinking at him.

"How did you figure that out so fast?" Oak blurts out, clearly impressed.

Lilly chuckles. "Chalk one up for the human computer!"

Zak blushes, rubbing the back of his neck. "It's a base-ten-time system," he explains, like it's no big deal.

The whole room breaks into laughter.

When the meal is finally served, the skinny robot handles the task. It trembles as it sets down the dishes, making plates and silverware rattle like they're on the verge of breaking.

# Chapter 75

Roast Do-Do Bird

Sorrel looks a little embarrassed. "I've been meaning to have Carnel tune this one up, but he's been so busy with the portal down."

Dishes upon dishes fill the table. What stands out most is the largest roasted bird Lilly has ever seen. It's bigger than any Christmas turkey she's had back home—not that her family was big. Just her, her dad, and Zak. But this bird isn't shaped like a turkey. It's more like a giant, roasted ball sitting in the middle of the table. And it still has the head on.

"Ick."

Oak's eyes go almost as wide as the bird. "This is what we call roast dodo bird!" he says proudly, clearly picking up on Lilly's disbelief. "We usually save it for the Feast of Unity. It's kind of like your New Year's celebration."

"Or when we have earthlings over for dinner," Sorrel adds with a chuckle.

"I thought dodos were extinct?" Lilly asks through a mouthful of potatoes, remembering her science class from last year.

"On Earth, they are. On Phi, they're not. I believe it's the Bainian realm that does most of the DNA theft from Earth. They collected some dodo DNA back when they were still around and resurrected the species—along with a bunch of others that were supposedly extinct." Oak keeps eating like this is just another Saturday.

Lilly is on her second plate when she knocks over her drink. Juice spills across the table and dribbles onto the floor. "Oops. Sorry."

No sooner has she said it than something scurries under the table. A grey blob climbs up the table leg and spreads across the spill. It's made up of tiny grey marbles flowing together like a pulsing mass, stretching and retracting in all directions.

"That's Baba," Oak says between bites. "Dad picked it up when he was Royal Gesh. It's rare. It's a Bahu-kwee—the only one known to exist."

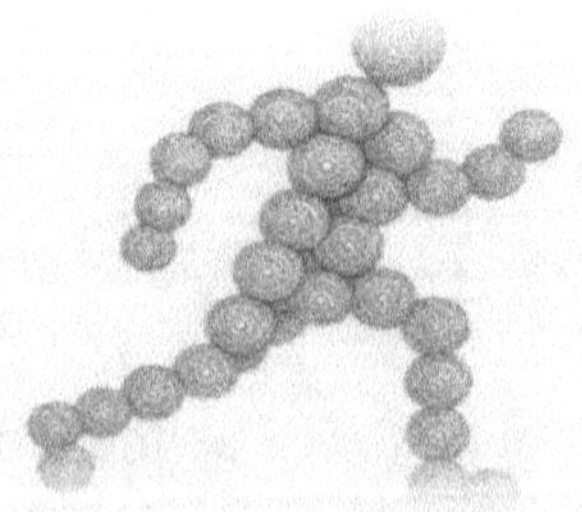

The juice vanishes beneath the blob as if it's being vacuumed up. Lilly hears a faint rattling near the floor. One stray marble bounces against the table leg, trying to climb. It's way slower than the blob.

"Feet up," Oak says flatly.

He and Sorrel both lift their feet, like this is routine. Zak and Lilly follow.

"Bark! Bark! Bark!" Ajax comes skidding into the room, heading straight for Baba. The blob zips off, looping around the table like it's toying with the dog. It's way faster. After a few circles, it switches directions and disappears into another room, Ajax right behind it. The lone marble bounces after them, running into things, correcting itself, and continuing.

"It might be slightly defective," Oak notes.

Lilly and Zak glance at each other.

Zak's expression is full of questions.

Silence settles in as everyone finishes eating.

Sorrel breaks it. "For dessert, I thought we'd have Zak make something special for us."

Zak's face twists with confusion and a little fear. Like he's just been told there's a pop quiz he didn't study for. Zak always studies.

Sorrel winks. "Come on. You'll find this interesting. I hear you're into Phi tech."

He waves Zak over, and together they move to the kitchen counter.

# Chapter 76
### Dessert From Heaven (well…space)

From where she sits, Lilly can see the end of the counter, where Sorrel leads Zak. The two of them stand in front of a box about the size of a microwave.

Sorrel mumbles something, and a big grin spreads across Zak's face.

Zak punches a few buttons on the front of the box, then stops and looks up at Sorrel, clearly stumped.

Sorrel leans over and taps a couple of buttons.

Zak nods, smiling again.

A soft hum fills the air, followed by a beep. The front of the box slides open.

"No way! Awesome! That's amazing!" Zak booms, eyes wide.

Moments later, he returns to the table carrying a plate of desserts like he's the Grand Marshal of a parade. He sets it ceremoniously in front of Lilly. "It's an organic molecular deposition chamber. Absolutely amazing!"

Lilly gives him the face—her usual *'please translate'* look.

"It's an automatic food maker," he explains. "It builds food from tiny particles. This one used cocoa, cherry extract, and sugar. May I introduce: Cherry Chocolate Lace."

The dessert looks like a gift from another world—a dark chocolate geodesic sphere, its delicate lattice revealing a whole cherry in the center, nestled in a pool of thick, oozing cherry sauce.

Around the base floats a ring of vanilla foam, light as air, holding its shape like Saturn's rings of edible cream. The scent is warm and sweet—vanilla and cherry with a hint of something rich underneath.

It doesn't look like food.

It looks sacred.

And still—Lilly wants to bite it.

There's one for everyone.

She has to admit—it's good. The chocolate melts in her mouth, smooth and rich. The red cherry ball at the center bursts with flavor when she bites in—better than any cherry she's ever had.

After dinner, Lilly offers to do the dishes, just like at home.

"Not needed, but thanks anyway. Bengen will clean up for us," Sorrel says.

"Of course, sir. I'm happy to be of service," says the skinny, beat-up robot in a very human voice.

Sorrel pauses and turns to Lilly. His voice softens. "Aubrin told me they have yet to find your father. But they're still searching."

Lilly nods slowly. "Okay."

"Don't worry, Lilly. They'll find him. Aubrin's good at what he does."

"Thank you for telling me."

Sorrel's gaze moves from one of them to the next. "Aubrin also passed along some advice, and I strongly agree with it. We're in dangerous times right now. A diablopero—the deadliest machine ever made—is running loose. We've already had an attack here. And someone out there is after Lilly."

His voice drops lower. "No one is to leave this facility without a Royal Gesh escort. If you do, you put yourself and everyone here at risk. Is that clear?"

Everyone exchanges glances.

"Yes, sir," Oak replies.

Lilly and Zak nod.

A heavy silence settles.

"There's good reason to fear the diablopero," Sorrel says. "During the last war, Aubrin was on guard duty with his whole ang— fourteen Royal Gesh. Fully trained. Fully armed. One diablopero attacked. Nothing could stop it. Fourteen soldiers against one machine. Aubrin was the only survivor. The diablopero walked away without a scratch."

No one speaks.

Zak looks paler than usual.

"Okay, enough of the lecture." Sorrel stands and crosses the room, returning with something in his hand. "Aubrin wanted me to give you this. They found it at your house. I believe it belongs to you, Lilly."

He holds out a small package that fits in her palm.

It's wrapped in birthday paper—torn and smudged. A tiny handmade card is taped to the front. In penciled handwriting, it reads:

**"Happy Birthday, Lilly. Love, Dad."**

# Chapter 77

## An Unexpected Birthday Gift

Having the little birthday gift in her hand feels like a slap she never saw coming. It means her dad went out and got her something—or already had it—and she never knew. Her eyes well up. She pushes it back. "Thank you," she manages to say.

"I'm going to retire for the night," Sorrel says, his voice softer now. "I've got a long day in the bagel shop tomorrow. I hope you three get a good night's rest. If you need anything, Lilly, Zak—just call for Bengen. It'll get you what you need. Your rooms are upstairs. Some of your things are already there."

He gives them a tired smile, the kind people wear when they've almost used up all their energy. "Have a good night."

"Good night, sir," Lilly and Zak say at the same time.

Sorrel turns to go, then pauses. "Oh—by the way, the lights and doors are controlled by the panels on the wall."

"Thanks, sir. And…thank you for a good dinner."

"You're welcome."

# Chapter 78
### Symbols, Symbols, Symbols

Everyone heads to their rooms early.

Lilly takes another gravity lift to the next level, just like the first one she used. She's told her room is the last door at the end of the hall.

She's halfway down the hall when a commotion breaks out—coming straight at her.

"Bark! Bark! Bark!"

Three-legged Ajax is in full pursuit of Baba, the blob.

Lilly lifts one leg just in time to avoid getting bowled over. She's about to lower it when the little white marble bounces past, bumping into one wall and then the other, chasing after the chaos.

All three disappear down the gravity lift.

Lilly glances left, then right—clear. She finally lowers her leg.

Her room is clean and simple: a bed, a desk, and a chair. On the desk sits her machete, her folding saw, and her backpack. She's not sure what she'll ever need again, in the strange new world she's entered.

She realizes she's been clutching her father's birthday present the entire time.

Sitting on the bed, she peels back the wrapping.

Inside the little box is a gold necklace. The medallion on it is made from carefully arranged golden shapes—shapes she's seen before. She pulls out her silver and gold ball and holds it in her palm. The design is the same as the one on the sphere... and the same as the one on her palm. A circle over three triangles, all enclosed by a larger ring. The same symbol... again.

Every fiber in her body begs for a time-out. Even her mind needs rest.

She doesn't see any visible light fixtures in the room. The whole ceiling is glowing. Shrugging, she walks to the touch panel beside the entry door.

After a few swipes, the ceiling turns red.

She rolls her eyes and swipes again. "Argh!"

Now it's blue.

Lilly sighs and smacks her hand flat against the panel, frustration doing the work this time. "Off!" she commands.

Her armband gives a soft *chirp*.

The light shuts off.

A smirk spreads across her face. "Ha! Who says I'm not good with new tech?" She drops onto the bed. Silence settles over her like a blanket. A pause. Finally.

It feels like a lifetime of new ideas packed into one tight hourglass of time. She hasn't had a second to adjust. Just questions. Questions. More questions—and almost no answers.

'Where did her dad even get the necklace?'

Mind foggy, body like jelly, Lilly flops backward. She stares at the necklace, the little sphere, and her palm.

They all bear the same marking.

Before she knows it, sleep takes over.


A ray of sunlight pokes at her eyes. She stirs, thinking she has a kink in her neck—until she realizes she's been sleeping on the silver sphere Carnel gave her.

A warm, moist breeze billows through the balcony window. But there's no sound. It's like someone turned the world's volume off.

Lilly plods over to the wall panel. There are eight symbols, each one unfamiliar—except they sort of remind her of the ones on Seri's scepter.

She touches one.

The window goes completely black. No view. No sound.

"Nope, that's not it."

She picks another.

The door closes. Light pours in again, bringing a breeze... but still no sound.

"Nope, not that either."

She smacks the keypad with the palm of her hand because that worked so well with the lights last night.

Nothing.

"Just let the sound in... please!" she begs.

The window stays dark. But the breeze carries the chirping of birds and the low murmur of people already up and about.

"Ha! It's voice-activated."

Over on the table is a stack of clothes that wasn't there last night. They're black with gold trim—the Royal Gesh uniform. The emblem on the chest is the same as every Royal Gesh.

The emblem on the shoulder, stitched onto it, matches Seri's: a curling line and an upside-down 'T.'

$$\gamma\text{-}\bot$$

There are two full sets.

Beside them are two more sets of comfy cotton clothes—the kind Zak's been wearing since the hospital.

Lilly shrugs. She checks her T-shirt. Still clean. "Good."

Just to be sure, she lifts her arm and sniffs. She nods. "Good enough."

She leaves the uniform folded neatly where it is and opts to stay comfy.

# Chapter 79
## Good Morning Bengen

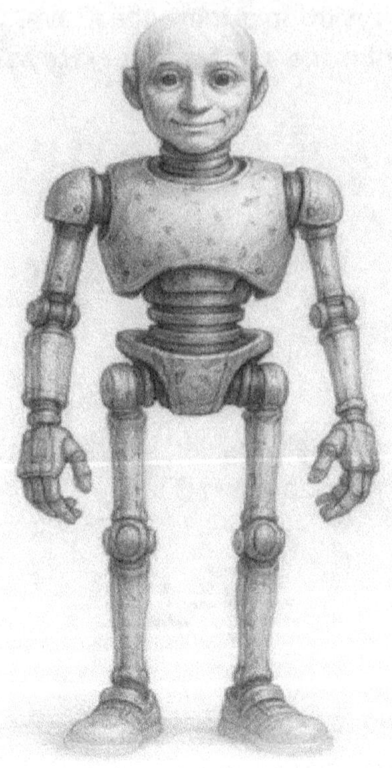

Her hand went to her neck, realizing what was yet to be there. She went back to the bed and found her necklace, which she had dropped. After putting it on and tucking it under her shirt, she surveyed the room before she left.

On the floor was the wrapper and box her necklace had come in. She picked them up and was about to put both on the table when she saw something unusual.

Scribbled on the outside of the wrapper was something hastily drawn. It was a symbol. It was not just any symbol.

Lilly's heart raced. She clutched the wrapper tightly and ran out the door.


Lilly found only Bengen in the kitchen when she got there. It was just standing there, motionless, gangly sticks for arms and legs. It came to Life upon Lilly's approach. "Good morning, Ohmuno Lilly."

"Ah… good morning… ah… Bengen."

"Master Sorrel is working. Oak and Zak are waiting for you in the café. I am to inform you of this."

The words rattle out shaky, like the robot's already had too much caffeine.

"OK… ah… thank you." Lilly still isn't sure how to talk to a robot.

"You are most welcome, Ohmuno Lilly."

The robot turns and jitters off toward the lift, disappearing in the same direction she already knows by heart.

# Chapter 80
## Her Father's Clue

All of the tables in the bagel shop are full again. A few people glance over when Lilly walks in. She finds Oak and Zak huddled over plates of pancakes and hot drinks.

"About time, sleepyhead," Zak says through a mouthful. "Sorry, we were too hungry to wait."

"Don't worry about it. Listen—I need to show you something." She tosses the wrapping paper on the table and drops into an empty seat.

Zak wipes a hand on his shirt and picks up the wrapper, turning it this way and that. He stops at the marking scribbled on it.

Lilly leans in, pointing at what caught his eye. "That's the symbol my dad uses for north. I've seen him use it before. He wrote it on there… after he was kidnapped. Then he dropped it on purpose."

Oak swallows his bite and peers at the mark with Zak. "Maybe."

"I know his writing. He left us a clue. They took him north."

"OK." Oak shrugs.

Lilly leans back, surprised at Oak's flat reaction. "Well… we go and look north. We do something! We don't just sit here."

Oak pauses, studying her. "For starters, we're kids—with no skills, no defense, no weapons… well…" He looks down at the scepter now tucked into his belt. "…one weapon." He takes another bite. "The Royal Gesh are already out there looking for your father. We were told to stay within the dome."

"But everyone's already so busy… we can help."

"We follow the rules. That's what we do."

"But—"

Oak holds up a big hand, cutting her off. "I'll tell you what—we take an image of the mark and send it to Aubrin. We'll tell him what you think it is. Maybe that helps. But we follow the rules. Period. Bug." He goes back to eating.

Lilly fumes. Maybe it's the 'bug' comment. Maybe it's the helplessness. Maybe it's just that Oak finds eating more important than what feels like a real clue.

The moment tightens.

Zak's hand lands gently on her arm, startling her. "Why don't you eat something, Lilly-D?" He knows her well. He probably sees she's about to spiral into 'hangry,' the hungry-angry thing.

Lilly takes a deep breath. "Right. You're right." Her stomach growls. She looks around for the floating do-hickey menu robot, or whatever it is. She turns to the menu on the wall, but it's too far away to read. "I'm hungry. I would love some pineapple and ham pizza right now."

"Pizza? For breakfast?" Oak asks.

"The best breakfast ever," Lilly jokes.

"Beep. Beep." Her armband chimes.

Suddenly, an image of the floating waiter robot appears above her armband. "Would that be a medium or a large pizza?"

"Bug! That just self-activated!" Oak leans in, eyes wide, studying her navok.

The image of the robot patiently waits for Lilly's reply.

"Yes... so... Phi tech does all sorts of weird stuff."

"Not on its own. All navoks are touch-activated. Even the Royal Gesh ones. They're not voice-activated. What exactly did you say?"

"What did I say? I think I said I'm hungry and I would like pizza."

Oak and Zak lean in close, ogling Lilly's armband like kids staring at candy. "Maybe Lilly's navok is somehow special," Zak suggests, glancing at Oak.

"Menu off," Oak says directly to her bracelet.

Nothing happens. The image of the robot waiter floats, waiting.

"Lilly, you try," Zak urges, eyes bright with curiosity.

# Chapter 81



### Floating Pizza for Breakfast

Lilly rolls her eyes. "Guys, I'm hungry. I want to order food."

"Just try it. Please."

Lilly sighs. "Menu off," she says sharply.

Her chance at ordering food vanishes from above her wrist.

"It works! It obeyed her command!" Oak gushes.

"Wow!" Zak echoes, eyes wide.

"I'd like to order a pineapple and ham pizza, please," Lilly says flatly.

The image of the floating order robot reappears above her armband. "Medium or large?"

"It's specific to Lilly's voice. Wow!" Oak sputters.

"Oh! Oh! No. Wait. What if it's more than that?" Zak blurts, staring at Oak. "What if it's thought-activated?"

"Hey, you two—I'm hungry. Let me order first. Then you can nerd out later."

Oak and Zak keep glancing between Lilly's armband and each other, wonder racing across their faces.

"No way! That would be out of this world!" Oak says, barely containing his excitement. "Lilly, think 'menu off'—but don't say it."

Lilly drops her head against the table with a groan. Then she squeezes her eyes shut and focuses on something to order.

"I do not believe we have a can of whoop-arse to open up for either Zak or Oak in our inventory. Is there anything else you would like me to get for them, Lilly?" says the robotic waiter, voice polite.

Lilly's armband chirps.

She glances sideways at Oak. Then at Zak. Says nothing.

Both boys sit frozen, mouths open.

She turns back to the floating waiter and silently thinks about the rest of her order.

"Very good. Medium pineapple and ham pizza with a large chocfee, coming up," the waiter says, then vanishes.

Zak shoots Oak a glance—warning him they're entering dangerous territory.

Oak starts to say something, thinks better of it, and clamps his mouth shut.

Breakfast tastes even better when it's her favorite food.

Lilly eats while Oak and Zak steal glances at her and her white-and-gold navok, between bites of their meals. A few times, they whisper behind their hands, trading secret theories they think Lilly won't notice. Their eyes and ridiculous expressions give them away.

When Lilly finishes the last of her pizza, she leans back and lets out a satisfied sigh. She feels much better.

Oak and Zak sit at the edges of their seats, stealing one last look at each other.

Zak nods at Oak.

Oak clears his throat. "Ahem... ah... all done?" he asks, testing the waters.

Lilly smiles back. "OK. What?"

Oak glances at Zak.

# Chapter 82

Zak nods—safe to proceed.

"We agreed to ask you to try just one more thing," Oak says carefully.

"OK. Then I get to ask two things in return."

"That doesn't sound fair."

Lilly gives him a take-it-or-leave-it look.

Oak nods. "OK. You ask first."

"What does the symbol on the Royal Gesh uniforms mean? The triangle circle thing. It's on the uniform left for me."

"But you're not wearing it," Oak banters.

"Is that your question?" Lilly gives him a half-smile.

Oak's face twitches with the amusement of a game he just might be enjoying. He shakes his head. "Easy question. Land—the triangle. Water—the waves. Sun—the circle above. And life—the circle that surrounds it all." He grins. "Next?"

"What is the Yishi Ring? I overheard someone say it's guarded and safe."

Oak looks genuinely confused. "I don't know. It might be in the databanks."

"I got that," Zak says instantly.

"It's a highly complicated, encrypted data system," Oak sputters.

Zak and Lilly exchange amused looks.

"You don't know Zap-man very well," Lilly says proudly.

"Whatever," Oak mutters, clearly not convinced. He glances around the room, searching. When he spots what he's looking for, he turns back to Lilly.

"Don't look now. But do you see that girl, with the black ponytail, behind me? The one with the big vestiar robot?"

Lilly looks. It's a girl about her age, talking with another girl at the table. The robot beside them looks shiny, new, and expensive. They're too far to hear what's being said.

"I said *don't* look!"

Lilly rolls her eyes.

"It's a shiny black robot," Oak continues.

Lilly nods. She saw it.

"OK, good." Oak leans in, voice lowered like it's some top-secret mission. "See if you can tell the robot to move its arm—with your thought."

Lilly sighs. "One circus act coming up." She looks at the robot, focuses, and thinks hard. Maybe too hard.

**Wham!** The robot's arm flicks up and smacks the girl in the side of the head.

"Hey!" the girl shouts, leaping up. "You stupid piece of junk!"

Everyone in the café hears that.

Then the girl kicks the robot.

Oak and Zak instantly slouch down in their seats, trying to disappear behind the table. As if that makes them look *less* suspicious.

"Is this normal? Can all Royal Gesh do this?" Lilly asks, still watching the chaos she just caused. What's new?

"Not," Oak mutters, eyes wide.

Zak mouths silently at Oak: *Wow.*

Oak nods back. *I know.*

# Chapter 83
## Zak's Navok Beeps

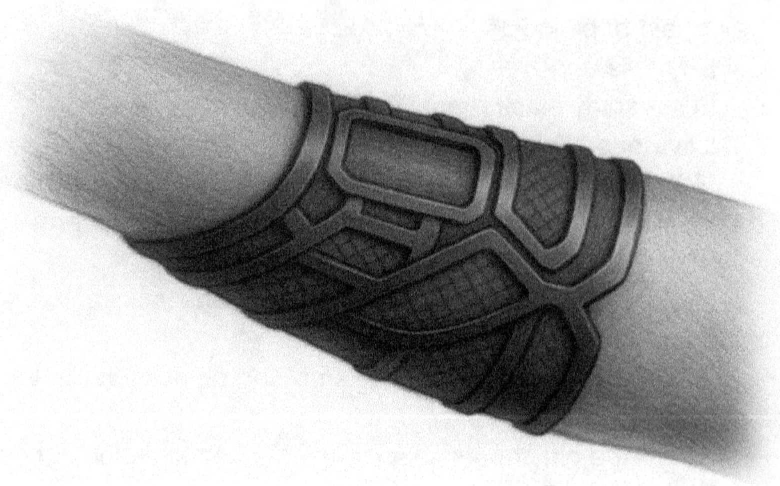

"**B**eep! Beep!"

Zak's armband lights up. He jolts in his seat like he just got zapped. "Gotta go! Carnel's letting me know he's ready." He shoots a quick look at Lilly. "We need to talk about this." He points at her armband, then bolts out of the restaurant.

Oak and Lilly sit in silence.

The moment stretches. Without Zak, Oak looks unsure—like he has no idea what to do with this weird girl sitting across from him.

Then he glances around. "I'll go ask my father what to do about the symbol on the wrapping paper," he says quickly, already standing and walking off.

Lilly watches from her seat. There's some talking, arm waving, and pointing. Then Sorrel pats Oak on the back, and Oak returns.

He leans in. "OK. We'll take an image of the symbol and send it to Aubrin. Dad's giving me time off—since Aubrin gave him a robot for the kitchen. I guess they're serious about me showing you everything I can about your vok."

"Vok?" Lilly asks.

"You know. Your Royal Scepter. The one we're supposed to pick up."

"Oh. Right. That stick thingy."

Oak shakes his head, clearly frustrated. He snaps a quick image of the wrapper and swipes a few times on his armband. Then he stands. "Let's go, Bug."

Lilly gives him the eye of death.

"Lilly-Bug," Oak corrects, meeting her glare without flinching.

She holds it for a second longer. Still doesn't like the name—but *Lilly-Bug* is better. She turns off the eye of death. For now.

# Chapter 84
## Kuni's Pet and Fun Store

The shops on the other side of the market feel like a different world. They're neat, tall, and proud. Each store has a big, bold sign, posted either above the entrance or off to the side. A long wooden overhang stretches across the front of them all, like something out of an old western movie. One shop after another, every one of them looking new—and expensive.

The first store has matching signs flanking the doorway. One says **KAIS BOOKS**, the other **AN OCEAN OF IDEAS**. There's no glass in the window opening, and no door—just a wide-open entrance.

Looking inside, Lilly spots floating holograms hovering above the floor, streaming some kind of sales pitch in a smooth, artificial voice.

Oak keeps walking.

The next store has a bold overhead sign: **SEKANI BODY COVERS**. Just from the name, Lilly figures it must be a clothing store.

Oak blows past that one, too.

The next shop stops Lilly in her tracks. Right from the entrance, it's clear—this place is huge. A flashing sign reads **KUNIS PET AND FUN STORE**. Flying discs zip in and out of the doorway, weaving around people and displays like they've got minds of their own. Tiny dragonfly bots flit around the discs, darting and spinning in perfect control. Robot dogs patrol the walkway, some wandering, some following customers. One carries a flying disc in its jaws like a trophy. Above each dog, hologram ads hover in the air:

**GANIS ARE FUN TO PLAY WITH AND HANDY TO HAVE AROUND – STARTING FROM ONLY 987 TOKENS.**

But it's the birds that hook Lilly's attention.

Dozens of robotic birds—some tiny, some as big as hawks—flap, perch, or hover in motion. Some shimmer with colorful feathers, others shine with bare metal wings. A few are covered in slick, black scales instead of feathers. One lets out a crisp chirp, and Lilly's sure she hears a warbler's song coming from somewhere deep in the store.

She follows Oak along the outside of the shop, glancing through the final window opening—just in time to spot someone familiar.

It's the girl with the black ponytail—the one from the restaurant. The same girl with the shiny black robot. "This robot is a stupid piece of junk!" the girl shouts, furious. "My father paid you good money for the best robot you had, and this is all you give me? It's broken!"

"Version 21 is the most intelligent robot available, by law, for residential use," the shop owner says, voice tight but polite. "Your unit is an intelligence level five. I tested it personally."

"It hit me! I want it replaced! Now, you idiot!"

The man bows deeply. "I assure you, miss. This vestiar is programmed for non-violence against its owner."

"Are you calling me a liar?"

"No, miss..."

"Wait until my father hears about this!" She kicks the robot hard. It tilts on one leg, tumbles back, scrambles to regain its footing, then lumbers to the back of the store and vanishes.

That's all Lilly manages to see through the opening, before Oak moves on.

# Chapter 85



Fuertes Extreme Living

The next store is even bigger than the pet shop. Sleek, shiny genaethers sit lined up out front like they're showing off. A bold sign above the doorway reads: **FUERTES EXTREEM LIVING**.

"We pick up your vok here," Oak says. "Most of the Royal Gesh get their supplies here—and any repairs done to their Vok or Navok."

Inside, shelves run along the outside wall from floor to ceiling, packed tight with every kind of contraption imaginable. In the center of the store, robots and machines of all sizes crowd the space. Hovering just above the ground, a large rock rests on a platform. A

225

flashing hologram hovers above it: **BRAHMS PORTO-JO – MOVE LARGE THINGS WITH EASE OVER ANY TERRAIN**

Oak heads toward a counter at the far end.

Lilly follows.

A full-size robot passes them on the way. It's as tall as Oak, and looks like the guards posted at the portal—only this one wears a scepter pack and carries a silver scepter. Holograms float around it like sales tags in midair: **BE THE FASTEST. BE THE STRONGEST. MODEL 22 – PAIRED VOK AND NAVOK – NOW AVAILABLE FOR MILITARY PURPOSES**

The movement above catches Lilly's eye. A swarm of mechanical ants crawls across the ceiling in perfect formation.

"Hello, Lilly. I've been expecting you in my store."

Lilly looks down, startled, and finds a tall, athletic-looking woman with blonde hair standing behind the counter. She's older, with smile lines at the corners of her eyes—like someone who's found plenty of reasons to laugh.

"Ah… yes… hi," Lilly says, thrown off.

"My name is Fuertes. And I must say, it's quite a privilege to have your Royal Vok in my shop. Not that I haven't worked on other voks before—we clean them all the time, tune them up periodically. But yours… yours is different. It's been misbehaving."

"Oh. Okay," Lilly says, not entirely reassured.

"You're here to pick up your vok, are you not?"

"Yes. Yes, of course. I'm sorry. I'm just… new at all this."

Fuertes studies her for a moment, then smiles—wide and warm. It reaches her eyes. "Yes, I imagine all of this feels a bit overwhelming."

Lilly glances at Oak, unsure. "What do you mean by misbehaving?" she asks, her voice edged with concern. She half-expects her vok to explode in her face.

Oak, on the other hand, just looks curious.

"Oh, my dear Lilly, don't worry. You'll see." Fuertes taps her bracelet. Moments later, an ornate wooden chest, on a tray, floats toward her from the back of the store.

It settles gently on the counter in front of Lilly.

**Rattle! Rattle!** The box shakes.

A thick clasp keeps the lid tightly sealed.

"As I said—it's misbehaving," Fuertes says with a mischievous grin. She doesn't seem the least bit alarmed. Leaning in, she studies Lilly's face more closely and points to her armband.

"Your navok is at least 16,000 unities old. That's over 4,600 Earth years. It is technology left behind on Phi by an advanced race we call the Noahs. They didn't just leave us navoks and voks. There were also the genaethers, gatiars, and even the Anubis. Why they left it all, we still don't know. The historical data gave little explanation. There are many theories… but no answers. It took us many unities just to figure out how to operate the basics. Thousands of unities later, we're still learning. Much of the technology is still too advanced to fully replicate."

She extends a hand. "May I see your navok, please?"

Lilly raises her arm.

Fuertes grips the armband firmly in both hands.

**Rattle! Rattle!** The wooden box jumps again.

Then a disc floats down from above. A clear lens glows in the center. It settles in midair between Fuertes' face and Lilly's armband, scanning silently.

# Chapter 86
## Lilly's Royal Gesh Vok

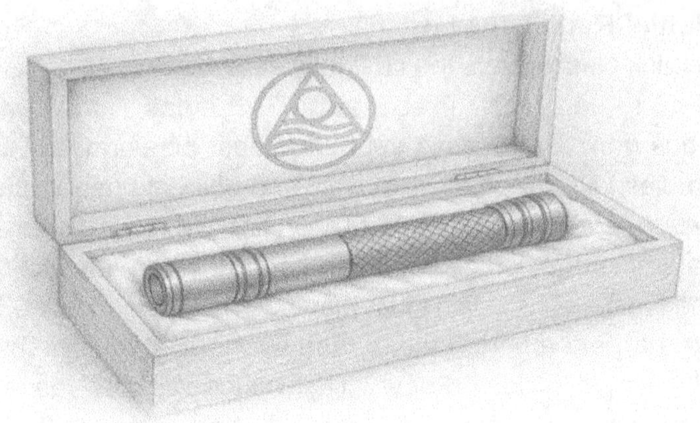

Fuertes turns Lilly's arm this way and that, inspecting it through the floating lens. "Hmmm… very interesting. Very interesting indeed. Yes… Indeed." She leans back and lets go of Lilly's arm.

The lens whooshes back up into the ceiling.

"You know they're a mated pair, your navok and your vok here?" She pats the wooden box. It rattles again under her hand.

Lilly nods.

"The Noahs, for some reason, made them that way. They also created technology that can only be separated from the owner upon death. Why? I'm not certain."

A painful flood crashes into Lilly. Her chest tightens as she's reminded—this armband was once Seri's. Seri is gone. Sadness surges through her, sudden and raw.

Fuertes must see it.

"Seri saw a true Royal Gesh in you," she says gently. She pauses, choosing her next words with care. "She saw so much more. And I believe... we're all going to see it, too." She reaches across the counter and rests a comforting hand on Lilly's.

**Rattle! Rattle!** The box vibrates harder, scooting slightly toward Lilly.

"Is that normal?" Lilly steps back.

"No. Definitely not." Fuertes smiles like she's more intrigued than worried. "There's something special about this Vok; it has become... alive." She chuckles at the word. "There's something special about this vok, your navok, and you. You're all … now … one."

She tilts her head, studying Lilly. "Let's try something. How about you place your arm—the one with your navok—right here beside the box?"

Lilly hesitates. *Yeah, right,* she thinks.

"It's all right. This is what Aubrin and I have come up with."

Still unsure, Lilly slowly places her left arm onto the counter beside the wooden box. The gold bands of her armband glint under the bright store lights.

**Rattle! Rattle! Rattle!** The box reacts instantly, bouncing up and down on the counter like something inside can feel her presence.

Fuertes chuckles. "Well, now. This'll be interesting." Without missing a beat, she unclasps the wooden box.

The lid explodes open with a **Bang!** A white blur shoots into the air—**Smack!**—it lands squarely on Lilly's armband.

Everyone jumps.

Lilly holds her arm up high, instinctively keeping it as far from her body as possible, as if that might help. The vok clings to the armband, vibrating against it, like a live wire.

A rush of heat floods from the vok into her navok, then through her arm and into her whole body. The room warps. Blurs. Spins.

She grabs the counter with her free hand.

Strong arms catch her from behind.

Then, just as quickly as it started, it ends.

The vok slides off her armband and drops onto the counter with a rattle. It lies there, still.

The room steadies. Faces stop spinning. Oak and Fuertes come back into view, both looking concerned.

"Like I said. Misbehaving," Fuertes says with a laugh.

# Chapter 87



"No. Spin it the other way. Place an arm on each side, with the power module in the back." Oak grabs the straps and picks up Lilly's arm like she's a ragdoll he's dressing. He stuffs her arms through the loops. Clicks something. Pulls. Tugs. Adjusts.

They're standing in the open grassy area, wedged between the market, the lake, and the research fields. They've already collected Lilly's vok and Royal Gesh shield pack.

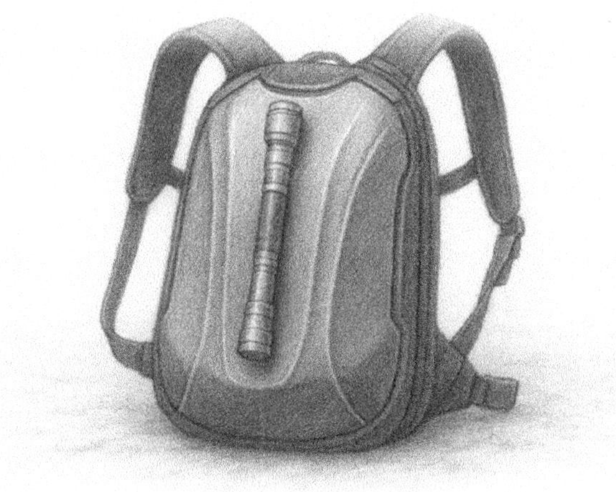

"You sure this is all I need?"

Oak shakes his head like she just asked the dumbest question imaginable. "This protects you against a level five blast from a Royal Gesh vok. Hold still!"

Lilly's arms flop around under Oak's grip. Being this close to him for the first time, she notices—he smells like spices and forest. Her face flushes. Maybe it's the heat under the dome. She glances down. The pack feels too light, too flimsy. How is this supposed to protect her from anything? Once the scepter pack is on, it's almost weightless—like it disappears. Still, she can't stop thinking about how fragile it looks.

The straps cross into an X on the front. On the back, there's a pouch or slot—definitely for something. Then it hits her. When Seri had crashed, she'd pulled her scepter-thingy from behind her back. This slot must be for the scepter. At the front, right in the center of the X, sits a small silver medallion. Etched into it is a triangle enclosing a circle with wavy water lines below. Another circle wraps around the whole symbol. It matches the one on Aubrin's, Haro's, and now her uniform.

These aliens sure like their symbols.

*Beep. Beep.*
Lilly's armband lights up. She lifts it, and Zak's head and shoulders project above her wrist.

"Hey, Lilly-D. I found some information on the Yishi Ring. You wanna hear it now?"

"Shoot."

Oak stays silent, but his face says he's impressed.

"This is just preliminary. I still need to dig further," Zak hesitates.

"Just tell me what you got, Zap-man."

"Okay, okay. Hold your horses." Zak glances down, reading. "In the ancient texts, it says the Yishi Ring is part of the ultimate weapon—held only by the Ohmuno. It's the first section of eight, acquired in the Circle of Challenge. The first challenge is called the *Ist-Uno-Yishi*. Each section gets added to the Ohmuno's vok after they complete one of the eight Circle of Challenges. When all eight are joined, it forms the *Satya Vok*—the ultimate, all-powerful weapon. To stop the power from falling into one realm's hands, the sections were spread across the eight realms. The Yishi Ring went to the Kalpanians."

"Got an image?"

"Yup."

A flash. The image transfers.

"Got it. Thanks."

"Hey, I also found some interesting information on the mark on your hand. This is something you should see."

"Later."

Zak nods. His expression turns serious. "Don't do anything stupid, Lilly-D."

"What?" She blinks, all innocent.

"I know that look," Zak's hologram says.

"I won't, okay?"

He studies her for a long moment. Looks like he's about to say something—doesn't. Just nods. "Okay." Then he blinks away.

Lilly realizes she's been absentmindedly comparing her birthmark to the symbols on the center of her cross strap. She's startled when Oak grabs her armband arm. "What?" she asks.

"You don't know what you're dealing with." He's after something on her armband. "Later, try this—with your thought."

"I'm looking for answers about why someone's after me, my father, and maybe abducted my mother."

Oak just shrugs. He taps and swipes a few times—and suddenly, a clear shimmer appears around Lilly's head.

She's wearing some sort of energy fishbowl.

A weird one.

Blinking numbers and strange letters scroll just outside her field of view.

# Chapter 88

**‘Ooomph!’**

“There. You’re set to go, Lilly-bug.” Oak stares at her for a second, something wanting to be said. He changes his mind.

He starts putting on his own protection suit. “You know, maybe you should understand how ridiculous this all is.” He pauses, choosing his words carefully. “It’s not like I don’t think you have the guts to try this. I get the idea not much can stop you.”

Oak slips into his suit and adjusts the straps. “Let me put this in Earth terms you might understand. You, a twelve-year-old Earthling, trying to become a Royal Khem Gesh… it’s like you trying to play on a pro football team—and you’ve never even played football before.”

“So maybe, because I’m so small, I’d just run between everyone.”

Oak raises an eyebrow as he swings his vok in a circle and clips it to the back of his pack. “It’s more like trying to perform brain surgery on yourself—with zero medical training.”

Lilly follows his lead and reaches behind to slide her scepter into the slot on her pack. It clicks in with a satisfying snap. “Maybe my small hands make me a natural for surgery.”

Oak laughs. “It’s about the same as you deciding to pilot a commercial airliner—never flown a plane before—and the autopilot’s broken. This is utterly ridiculous.”

“Thanks for the confidence. Why even bother showing me?”

Oak shrugs. He taps his armband, and an energized shimmer wraps around him—just like the one around Lilly.

"If Aubrin tells me to train you for the first challenge, then that's what I do. I follow orders."

He inhales deep, holds it, rolls his neck like he's loosening a knot, then exhales. "Okay. Voks out." He reaches behind and pulls out his vok.

Lilly does the same—minus the neck wiggle.

"I want you to set yours to spar mode. Try it with thought."

Lilly squeezes her eyes shut and thinks, *spar mode*.

Her vok hums to life in her hand.

"Good." Oak swipes his armband. "Mine's on stun. I just want you to feel the impact of a low-level blast."

"Okay. What do I do?"

Oak raises his vok and points it at her. A ball of light blasts from the tip and slams into her chest.

The light spreads like a bucket of water—minus the wet. "Oomph!" Lilly stumbles back a step. Feels like someone just stole the air from her lungs. But she stays standing. "What—no warning?"

"Oh, don't be such a baby." Oak laughs. "Now you try it. Shoot me."

"Just shoot you?" Lilly stares at her scepter like she's not sure what she's holding.

"Yes. Point and think *blast*. Try it." Oak stands there, casual, like he's got a toothpick in his mouth after lunch.

Lilly lifts her vok. Aims the tip at Oak. Thinks '*blast*'. This time, she doesn't squeeze her eyes.

Her vok hums—and a flash of light explodes from the tip.

It hits Oak like a thunderclap. He lifts clean off the ground and flies back several body lengths. Hits the ground with a thump. "Ooomph!" He flails for a second, limbs grappling the air in surprise. Then he shakes his head, disbelief painted all over his face, and gets up.

He storms over, grabs Lilly's armband. "I thought I said *spar*!?" He's mad now—maybe a little embarrassed.

"It is on spar," Lilly blinks at him.

*Swipe. Swipe.* Oak taps through her navok. "Oh. It is spar. Wow. Yours is strong."

"I told you so. Don't be such a baby."

Oak gives her the eye of death.

Lilly grins innocently.

Then something moves behind Oak—and Lilly's smile vanishes.

"So, what's going on here?" a syrupy voice calls out.

# Chapter 89
### "Attack! Attack them Both!"

It's the girl from Kuni's Pet Store. The one trying to return her broken-looking robot. She's tall—Oak tall. Her skin is a smooth, silvery-blue. A tight black braid hangs down her back. Her snug grey uniform makes it clear she's fit. Like, seriously fit.

But it's her eyes that stop everything.

They look like octopus eyes—yellow where whites should be, with black, horizontal slit pupils.

And she's not alone.

A shiny red robot stands beside Nafari, perfectly still. The last black one has been replaced.

"You're the Earthling girl. I am Nafari, Royal Burden." She said the last two words like she was expecting a royal bow in return. She towers above Lilly, looking down like she's deciding whether to squish a bug.

Lilly nods. Decides not to bow.

Oak stiffens.

"This is Rasht. She is also a Royal Burden."

Behind Nafari stands another blue-skinned girl. Her black hair is tied in the same tight tail. Her eyes are stone black, wide and bulging, like everything she sees is a surprise. She's tall, though shorter than Nafari—maybe it's the slouch. Her grey uniform bulges at odd spots, like she's hiding leftover donuts for later. Her nose sticks out a little too much, and her mouth hangs open. Maybe she is trying to dry her mouth out.

Her eyes flick nervously between Nafari and Lilly.

Lilly doesn't bow for this one either.

"You are not a Burden, are you, Oakeros?" Nafari spits Oak's name like it's a disease.

Rasht smirks, eyes darting everywhere, mouth still wide open. Not dry enough yet.

Oak clenches a fist. "Beat it, Nafari. This is none of your business."

Nafari turns to Lilly. "Listen, Lilly—is it? If you want to learn the ways of the Royal Gesh, Rasht and I can show you. We're real Royal Burdens. Plus, we just signed up for the elite *Naquee Hebbe.* That's Mensh Morder's youth party. My father knows him personally. Daddy's on the Phi World Council."

She steps closer, syrupy sweet. "You need *us* to survive the First Challenge. Not this loser." She jabs a thumb at Oak. "His mother's a criminal. Probably one of the many reasons he didn't get picked to be a Burden."

Oak lunges toward her, fists clenched, teeth bared.

Lilly leaps into his path and holds him back. "Don't do it!"

She barely comes up to his chest, but Oak stops just in time not to run her over.

Rasht giggles. Her black eyes look like swollen raisins swimming in fake pudding.

Nafari jumps back, gasping with mock drama. "Ooo! Careful! Careful!" Her tone drips venom. "I *am* a Burden. Touch me, and you won't even be allowed to sling dirty plates at that grease pit your father calls a café."

Lilly locks eyes with her. "I think I'll stick with Oak, thank you."

Nafari's octopus eyes narrow to slits. "Suit yourself," she hisses like a blade being drawn. Then her face flips into a practiced, glowing smile. "Why don't you spar my new vestiar? It's actually, secretly a Noxiar—the newest model." Her voice oozes fake sweetness. "It'll help you... learn... *fast*." She giggles on the last word.

"Vestiar. Attack Earthling Lilly. Attack them both."

Oak sputters. "That's illegal!"

"Nothing's illegal if you're as rich as Daddy." Nafari laughs.

The red robot crouches low, palms to the ground. Its joints twist with an unnatural grace, folding inward, for maximum leverage. It looks like a mechanical panther—eyes locked on prey.

Then it springs.

It slams into Oak, knocking him flat. He crashes down hard, dazed and struggling.

Nafari giggles like it's the best thing she's seen all week.

# Chapter 90
## Kwi-Li

The robot rolls and rights itself. Then it locks onto Lilly, hunches down—and springs.

In mid-air, there's a sudden blur of grey motion.

The vestiar never reaches her.

Instead, it gets slammed aside in a tumbling blur of grey.

Red. Grey. Red. Grey.

*Bam! Bam! Bam! Bam! Bam!* The grey blur pummels the vestiar, strikes landing as fast as a machine gun.

A startled garble escapes Nafari. "Wait!" She runs to the convulsing heap. "Stop!"

The banging stops.

The vestiar twitches on the ground.

Standing over it is a little grey robot—shorter than Lilly, dimpled-bodied, completely grey, with no features on its torso. Its head is oversized for its frame, with big, round eyes that give it the look of a child insect. Its arms and legs are skinny.

It runs straight to Lilly and wraps her in a hug—tight, unrelenting.

The wrecked vestiar continues twitching behind them.

Lilly is too stunned to move. Not that she could—her arms are pinned to her sides.

"There you are! I've been calling and calling and calling you! But you didn't come!" the robot chatters. "You're not hurt, are you?"

Still frozen in the robot's grip, Lilly struggles to respond.

Oak stands up, brushing himself off, smiling as he eyes the demolished vestiar—and the outrage on Nafari's face.

"My brand-new vestiar! You *ruined* it! You will *pay* for this!"

Oak laughs. "I didn't do anything."

Lilly laughs too, still trapped in the clingy robot hug. "Don't look at me!"

"It was *your* robot that attacked my brand-new vestiar. Rasht, pick it up!"

"Me?" Rasht quivers, holding back.

"*Now!*" Nafari snaps, already storming away. "Wait till my father hears about this!"

Rasht creeps over and grabs the robot's leg, dragging it across the ground. Her mouth still hangs open, eyes wide with permanent awe.

"You're going to *fail* the First Challenge! And your father is going to be *killed* by the Cankers! They kill *all* their hostages!" Nafari screams as she storms back toward the store she came from.

The little robot squeezes Lilly tighter. "Oh! It is *so* good to finally find you. I have looked *everywhere* for you. *Everywhere!*"

The voice sounds familiar.

Lilly pries herself out of the hug, holding the robot at arm's length. "Do you know me?"

"I am Kwi-Li!" the robot declares proudly, standing up straight and doing a slight bow. Not that it's very tall.

Oak strolls over, chuckling.

Then it clicks. Lilly remembers where she's heard the voice before. "Hey! Were you trying to say something to me before? 'Ra oo you' or something?"

"*Rae oh yoo.* Means 'where are you' in Phisian language. *Where were you?* I have looked and looked and looked…"

"Can you just slow down for a minute, please?"

The robot drops its head in a dramatic pout. "Are you mad at me?" There's a solid ding in the side of its head.

"No! No, I'm not mad. I… I'm just a little confused. That's all."

Oak is grinning ear to ear as he brushes off more dust.

"What's so funny?" Lilly asks, eyeing him suspiciously.

"Lilly, meet your Royal Gati."

"*Mine*?"

"Yup. We are a team. We're going to be great together. I just *know* it. Can we go and get balloons? I like balloons. Green and blue are my favorite colors!"

"Shhh!" Lilly presses a finger to the robot's mouth.

Oak chuckles again.

"Oh, I'm glad *you* find this funny," Lilly mutters to him.

"What?" Oak shrugs, hands raised in the universal *who me?* Gesture.

"Is *this* normal?" Lilly points to Kwi-Li.

"Carnel says I am as normal as I should be. He says I am *special.* So does Yuchii."

"Shhh!" Lilly points at Oak this time. "*Stop laughing.*"

Oak finally pulls himself together long enough to reply. "Nothing is normal around you."

# Chapter 91
### Something in Common Afterall

"**W**ho is Yuchii?" Lilly asks.

Oak quickly shakes his head—*No!*—his eyes locked on hers with intensity.

"I see him over there. I'm going to go say hi. I'll be right back."

Before Lilly can say anything, the little robot runs off toward the research fields. It disappears into the crops, which tower above any gati.

Oak is still laughing.

"Explain *that* to me. Please?"

Oak finally reins in his grin. "Well… all Royal Gesh above the Shang level are assigned a Royal Gati. They're partners for… as long as they remain Royal Gesh. However—yours…"

"Let me guess—*is special*."

"Very special. Gatis don't talk. They're ultra calm, completely silent. No names. No balloon obsession. And they don't come with visible head injuries. They are self-healing."

Then an idea hit Lilly like a splash of water, "Hey! Can this little robot do what Aubrin's can and…blink me to different places?"

Oak twitches at Lilly's use of words, "It is called geennii. It is a self-teleportation that includes whatever it takes with it. They also have a cloaking ability, called gatiest. It is where their name comes from." He thinks for a moment. "Well, in theory, yes. It should be able to do both."

"But?"

"It is Royal Gati, with obvious damage. Will it geennii you to the right place?" He adds a smirk for effect.

"Great." Lilly lets out a long, exaggerated sigh. "However…that just might come in handy, if it works."

"Your Gati—Kwi-Li—*did* save us, once already."

"True." A shadow passes over Lilly's face. "Hey… I'm sorry if I brought you any trouble."

"No. It's okay. Nafari *is* the trouble." Oak looks down, searching for words. "My mother isn't a criminal. Not really."

"It's not my business," Lilly says quickly.

"No, I want to tell you." Oak pauses, clearly struggling. "Both my mom and dad were in the Royal Gesh once. Some unities ago, Mom just… disappeared. The rumor is she defected to the Realm of Baine. They're considered a threat—to Earth, to Phi, the Royal Gesh… basically everyone. Within the Gesh, that's considered treason. Dad lost his position. And when it came time, no one chose me to be a Royal Burden."

"What's a Burden?"

"It's like… You train your whole childhood as a *Liege*—a kind of grade school trainee—hoping to be selected for Royal Gesh training. That's the ultimate. Middle school and high school all rolled into one. If you're good enough—and if your mom *isn't* labeled a traitor—a Royal Gesh picks you as their Guarantor. They train you. It's the most honored path you can follow."

"But nothing was ever proven about your mom."

"Didn't matter. Just the accusation was enough. Dad had to step down. But thanks to Aubrin, we got to stay at Phi Guya and take on the bagel shop. Dad seems to like it. Still… sometimes I think he misses being in the action."

"Hmm…" Lilly lowers her voice. "I'm sorry. It must be hard—being seen as the contaminated one."

Her armband gives a soft *chirp.*

Lilly ignores it. "It's not your fault," she adds.

They fall into a quiet pause.

"I have you beat, though," Lilly says.

"Yeah, right."

"I do. You've got nothing compared to me." She smiles sideways at him. "My mother went missing the day I was born. My father didn't take it well. The rumor is, he killed her and buried the body somewhere. Best case? She ran off—didn't want either one of us. He claims aliens abducted her. He's been searching for them—and for her—ever since. Because of that obsession, he's seen as the village drunk and the crazy man."

"Wow." Oak chuckles. "You *do* have me beat."

"Stop." Lilly punches him lightly in the arm, smiling just a little.

Oak laughs too—then his smile fades. Concern takes over. "But... your mother was abducted by aliens."

"What?!"

She doesn't know whether to scream, laugh, or fall to her knees.

"You heard that too? I thought it was just...nonsense...the way Aubrin explained it." The truth slams into her—shattering everything she thought she understood. And then, impossibly, something inside starts to gather itself back together. Hope. Fragile, but real.

"But...Why didn't you say anything—to me—to Aubrin?"

"Because I only know of it as a rumor. You heard Aubrin, he already investigated it. That is a fact."

"Tell me anyway. Rumor or not."

# Chapter 92


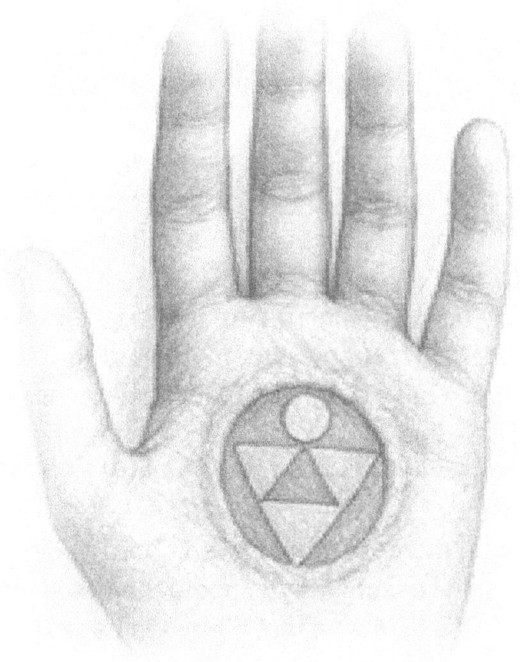

Oak looks Lilly in the eyes. "Alright. The talk I've heard is that Mensch Morder abducted your mom. But… It's just a rumor." He pauses, watching her closely.

"Please," Lilly says gently.

"Everyone knows Mensch Morder is obsessed with finding the ultimate weapon. He wants it so he can conquer both worlds. He also believes in mystical powers and magical weapons. He is a true nut case. It's said he believed your mom was the Ohmuno. From the children's tales, the Ohmuno is the pure female—the one with the ultimate DNA. The all-powerful one. The one who has the power of the entire universe. Funny thing is, even nut cases have followers. Some people believe in his crazy ideas. Most logical people know it's just bedtime nonsense."

Oak points to the mark on Lilly's palm. "For some reason, that's the mark of the Ohmuno. If he is crazy enough to believe your mother was the Ohmuno... it would make sense he'd think her daughter might be too."

Lilly stares down at her palm. "I thought this was just a birthmark. So that's why Aubrin was interested in it..." Her voice sharpens. She grabs Oak's arm—maybe a little too hard. "But is my mom still alive? Does this Mensch Morder guy have her?"

Oak shrugs helplessly. "I don't know, Lilly-Bug. Really. I don't."

"Maybe your mom and mine were both taken by Mensch Morder—for the same reason. Maybe someone here is from Kalpan and has the Ring of Yishi. Maybe that's why the base was attacked?" Lilly says, words tumbling out fast.

Oak blinks, caught off guard. "Well... it wouldn't be anyone from Kalpan. Everyone there's a vegetable. Most of the population is permanently plugged into fictional reality. It wouldn't be with a Kalpanian, here. There are none here."

"Then maybe," Lilly says, her eyes bright with sudden purpose, "this Circle of Challenge is where we find the Yishi Ring. If I am the Ohmuno, maybe we can get to the ring before Mensch Morder. And if we have it, we can use it to find our moms."

Oak stands silently for a long moment, thinking through everything she's just said. "I don't know… that's a far-fetched idea, Lilly-Bug. You're making a lot of assumptions. We need more answers first. But… come on. Let's head to the Circle of Challenge. Maybe we'll find a Royal Gesh there who can explain more. Either way, it's smart to see what you're going to be practicing for."

"What about my gati?" Lilly glances toward the field in the distance. "Maybe it knows something about the Yishi Ring—or our mothers? It's been around forever."

"Kwi-Li?" Oak laughs. "I don't think it even knows about itself."

"Great." Lilly sighs.

"We should go get the little runt," Lilly says.

"Kwi-Li?" Oak echoes, hesitant. "But—"

"But what?"

"Your Gati is visiting Yuchii."

"…And…? Who is Yuchii?"

Oak looks genuinely concerned now. "Yuchii's not a *who*. It's a *what*? A big, hairy, dangerous… thing. It lives in the forest. Looks after it. I think it works in the fields too—but always alone. Always."

"Ha! You're not scared, are you?"

"Of course not." Oak blurts that out a bit too fast. He straightens up, chest puffed like he's suddenly the bravest being on two legs. "Just… don't say I didn't warn you." He adds it as he turns toward the fields.

# Chapter 93
### Big & Scary Yuchii

Oak leads the way between the fields and the lake.

Lilly watches ants scurrying every which way between the rows of plants.

Some are carrying a tomato.

Others haul a whole cob of corn.

A few crawl across the stems, probably hunting for insect pests.

No sign of a tall, hairy beast anywhere.

The lake narrows into a stream on their left.

Oak follows the stream to a small bridge. He stops at the foot of it. "Okay. Just stay behind me and don't make any sudden moves. I accidentally ran into Yuchii once, when I was trying to retrieve an aether—a flying thing. It smashed the aether to bits. It was… kinda scary."

They cross the bridge.

Laughter drifts through the trees ahead.

"Zay! Zay! Giggle. Giggle."

Suddenly, a gray ball the size of a couch cushion flies from the forest, rolling across the ground beside the stream. When it stops, it unfolds—straightens up—

Kwi-Li.

Giggling, the gati darts right back into the forest. "Zay! Zay! Giggle. Giggle."

Lilly raises an eyebrow at Oak. "Right. *Dangerous.*"

Oak frowns, clearly confused.

They follow the sound of giggles just inside the forest.

**"Groowwll!"**

Oak and Lilly freeze.

Right in front of them towers a mountain of hair—taller than Oak. It's twice Lilly's height, standing upright. In its giant, shaggy arms is Kwi-Li, rolled up tight in a ball.

To Lilly, it looks like a bear on two legs—only much taller. And very, very angry.

"**Grroowwll!**" It lets out another warning. Then it sets Kwi-Li down and puffs out its chest, all aggression.

"Ne nikum! Pengou. Pengou." Kwi-Li unrolls and springs to its feet, stepping in front of the hairy giant. It waves its skinny arms up at the towering beast, trying to catch its attention.

"**Grrrr!**" Yuchii rumbles deep in its chest.

"Pengou," Kwi-Li says again, this time pointing straight at Oak and Lilly.

The beast just stands there—not growling now, but looking like it could leap and rip them both in half without breaking a sweat.

"Hi Lilly! Hi Oak! This is my friend Yuchii! We were playing catch! But… there was no one to catch me… so I guess you could call it throw."

Lilly slowly raises her hand, giving the beast a tiny wave. No sudden moves.

Yuchii doesn't wave back. It just stares—eyes buried deep beneath a mountain overhang of a forehead.

Lilly thinks fast. "Ahh… time to go… Kwi-Li. Playtime's over." She waves the gati toward her, keeping her voice calm.

Oak stares at Lilly like she's grown a second nose.

Lilly shrugs. "Just go with it," she whispers.

Kwi-Li's shoulders slump. "Ah, really? We were just starting to have fun."

Oak rolls his eyes. "Yes. Time to go. We're heading to the Circle of Challenge. Say goodbye to your friend. You can visit again later."

He sounds like he's forcing the words—but he says them.

"Ah… okay." Kwi-Li sighs, turns to the hairy mountain, and hugs it tight. "Jaijan."

The beast hugs the gati back and gives it a gentle pat.

Kwi-Li skips over to Lilly. "*Vako Yuchii!*" the gati says, waving.

Yuchii waves back.

# Chapter 94


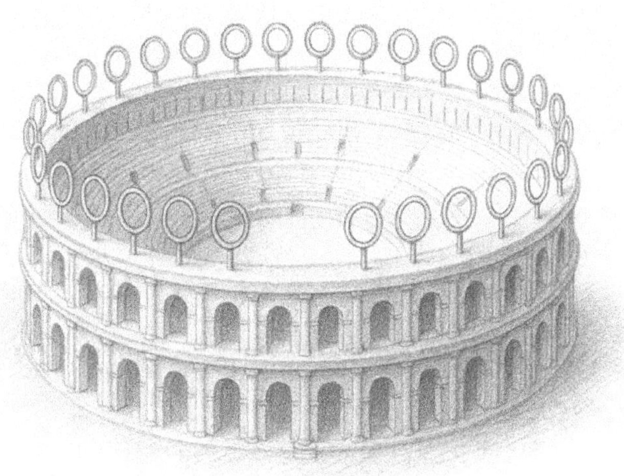

Oak leads Lilly and Kwi-Li along the river, then beside the lake—without crossing the bridge. The gati skips the whole way, humming a cheerful tune.

Lilly leans in close and whispers to Oak, "What do you mean *scary*? Yuchii's a kitty cat. You're just a big baby." She grins and nudges him with her shoulder.

"Shut up." Oak smirks, punching her in the arm.

As the trees thin out to their right and the lake opens wide to the left, a massive circular structure rises directly ahead—the coliseum they passed yesterday on the way to Carnel's junkyard.

"Welcome to the Circle of Challenge," Oak says, gesturing toward the towering arena. He keeps walking.

"Wow," Lilly breathes, suddenly feeling very small.

"This is *nothing* compared to the one in Seairland, back on our planet, Phi. That one's ten times this size. This is just the training version."

The Circle of Challenge is easily the size of a football stadium—almost two hundred meters across. Up along the top circular edge of the coliseum walls, a geanaether zips through rings at breakneck speed, its movement a blur.

When they reach the arched entrance, the true scale hits her. It stretches up—*way* up—the height of an apartment building.

Inside, rows of bleachers wrap around the inner ring like ribs in a giant shell.

"It looks like a Roman coliseum," Lilly says, spinning slowly in place.

"Right. Phi helped design Earth's ancient coliseums, secretly."

In the center of the stadium, tall walls rise in sharp corners. From this angle, Lilly can just glimpse what looks like the edge of a maze.

Oak grabs her arm. "Come on—there's Yin and Yang. Let's go talk to them. They'll help us."

The dynamic duo stands near the bleachers, talking with another Royal Gesh Lilly hasn't seen before. Their conversation looks friendly—casual, like old teammates catching up.

# Chapter 95

Lilly doubts anyone could tell the two apart.

Beside each clone stands an identical grey gati. Both remain perfectly still—calm and unreadable. The conversation between the three Royal Gesh ends, and the group begins to separate.

Kwi-Li suddenly breaks into a run. "Yin! Yang!" the gati shouts with glee.

Yin and Yang turn together like they're on a hinge.

Kwi-Li barrels into one of them with a huge hug.

"Hey there, short stuff!" the clone breaks into a wide grin and hugs back. "Gimme five!" He holds out a hand.

Kwi-Li slaps it with a palm.

"Pound it home!" The other holds up a fist, and Kwi-Li bumps it without hesitation.

The two silent gatis glance at Kwi-Li, then at each other. No expression. But something unspoken passes between them.

"Hey there, Ist-Kee Lilly!" one of the clones greets her, grinning.

"Howdy, Royal Gesh Trainer Oak!" says the other, with the same bright smile.

Whichever is whichever.

Oak flushes slightly.

The two gatis face Lilly and, at the same time, slam their fists to their chests. Thump!

Both Yin and Yang glance at their gatis, amused.

"Well, someone's getting a salute."

Lilly stares wide-eyed. "Is that what they're doing?"

"Well, I don't think they both caught heartburn at the same time."

"Spend some time with Lilly-Bug here, and they might," Oak teases.

Lilly jabs him in the ribs.

Then she feels a small tug at her pant leg.

"I'm going to go exploring for a bit, okay?" Kwi-Li looks up at her, wide-eyed.

"Ah… okay, but don't go too far—and be careful," Lilly says instinctively, surprised at her own words. She's never been a mom in her twelve years of life, but the tone comes out anyway.

"Okay!"

"Stay close enough to hear me."

"Don't worry. Just call me like I called you before. Bye!"

Kwi-Li skips away.

"Kwi-Li's talked to you before?" Oak asks, confused.

"I'll explain later."

Yin and Yang exchange amused glances.

"So, how's the training going?" one of them asks.

"You're here to see the First Challenge, aren't you?"

"Ah… well… we're just getting started," Oak admits, flustered.

"So, you've come to see how the experts do it first."

"Clever training method, Oak."

"Very clever. Because Yin…"

"…and Yang…"

"…are the best," they finish, bouncing the words between them like a game. The effect is both entertaining and completely confusing.

"We'd be happy to show you how it's done."

"That would be great," Oak says, clearly relieved. "If you could go through the First Challenge and show her, please."

One of them bows to Lilly, fist to chest. "If you wish, my Ohmuno."

They both give her a wink, as if teasing her.

"That's not funny." Lilly laughs back.

# Chapter 96



**"Simple, just walk to the end."**

Yin—or maybe Yang—shrugs. "You are who you think you are, Lilly."

The other speaks up. "You can do this, Lilly. Seri believed in you, and so do we."

"Hmm… I'd like to see what it's all about." Lilly bites the side of her cheek. "But first, can I ask what you know about my mother—and the Yishi Ring, please?"

Yin and Yang exchange a serious glance. Then one of them answers. "So, you heard us?"

"Sorry. I was awake."

Both of them smile.

"Well… about your mother, Haro is the one to ask. She was best friends with Seri."

"Seri?" Lilly asks, confused.

"Yes. Seri was on her first day as an Earthling Guardian the day your mother was abducted."

"Then, she became your Guardian ever since. Seri would have shared what she knew with Haro." All smiles vanish from Yin and Yang.

"Regarding the Ring of Yishi, all we can say is next to nothing," one of them admits.

"But isn't the Ohmuno supposed to receive the Ring of Yishi upon completion of the First Challenge?" Lilly asks.

"Oh, you heard about that?"

Yin and Yang look at each other. Wordless words. They both nod.

"Okay. We've heard that tale as well. But we can't tell you where it currently is, because we are bound to secrecy by Royal Gesh code. We're sorry."

Lilly and Oak exchange glances.

One of them, forcing a smile. "But we *can* help you—by showing you our secrets to the First Challenge. Since Yang here is still learning which end of his vok has the sword option, it's best to learn the Warufang Challenge from me. Also known as the Ist-uno-Yishi Challenge."

"In your dreams, clone-boy!" Yang sputters back.

Yin checks the vok in his back cradle and marches toward the maze. "Watch and be humbled, dear brother."

"Come on. Let's go up in the stands. It's the best view to watch the utter carnage we're about to witness."

"I heard that!" Yin yells, without looking back.

Yang leads Lilly and Oak halfway up into the stadium.

"Has Oak told you about the First Challenge?"

"We were getting to it. We started and got distracted," Lilly says, trying to hide a smirk.

"Okay. I'll explain then. You start at one end of the maze edge and walk to the other. It's just a straight line."

Yang points to one of the paths on the outer perimeter that makes up one side of a triangle. Yin is nearly at the start of it.

"The challenge is simple—see where Yin is? You get from there to the other end of that straight path. The only thing in the way is a small swarm of wasps."

"Seriously?" Lilly laughs.

Oak sputters.

Yang chuckles at Lilly's reaction. "Well, they're not exactly *normal* wasps. They're called *Warufang*. In Earthling, that translates to *Bad Wasp*."

"Very bad," Oak adds.

"True. Because of two main problems. First, it's not just one— it's fifty-five of them. Second, they're not like your Earth's little pests. They're oversized, poison-filled, aggressive, impervious, flying robots. They're EMP-shielded, armor-covered, and carry one nasty barb. One sting leaves a welt the size of Lohan's largest fruit-of-the-day. Multiple stings will render you unconscious.

Nothing stops them. You just have to swat them away long enough, to make it to the end of the line. Simple, really. But challenging. If you make it through alive, your warufang time gets added to your genaether time."

# Chapter 97
## Warufang Attack

"Yin there holds the Royal Gesh record," Yang adds with a smirk. "But I don't remind him—he'd be impossible to deal with."

Lilly smiles back. She likes Yang.

Yin stands at the beginning of the challenge, flexing his arms and legs, getting limbered up. He withdraws his vok from the holster on his back and holds it ready.

"He's going to use the laser-sword option on his vok. It's a good idea for you to do the same."

A light wand extends from the end of Yin's vok. It grows until it's as long as his entire arm, then stops.

Lilly nods. She sees.

Yang looks directly into her eyes with those intense, yellow, lizard-like pupils. The effect hits hard—like being scanned by something ancient and serious. "Whatever you do," he says, "don't stop moving. Strike while you move. Strike—and always keep moving."

"Got it." Lilly nods quickly. She understands.

Yin spaces his feet apart and crouches like a runner at the starting line. Then, he waves—begin.

"Beep!"

A buzzer sounds, and a holographic timer lights up in the sky, counting upward.

A buzzing rises—like fifty gymnasium fans starting at once.

A black cloud as thick as oil materializes in front of Yin. The machines look like mutated wasps with bloated bellies—chest-high and hovering in a scattered formation. Their wings resonate together, pulsing in sync like one giant hive.

Yin doesn't hesitate. He walks briskly into them. His braided ponytail bobs with each step, flipping forward and back.

One Warufang darts for him.

Yin ducks and swings. "Whack!"

A burst of sparks explodes as the glowing blade of his Vok slams into the robot. The machine tumbles to the ground, buzzes briefly, then lifts off again—unharmed.

The hit seems to anger the rest of the swarm. The air shivers, thick with furious wings. It's like someone struck a dinosaur-sized wasp nest.

But Yin is ready. Step. Strike. "Whack!" Dodge. Step. Strike. "Whack!" Step. Step. Strike. "Whack!"

He keeps moving, always moving—twisting, ducking, striking. It's like watching a dance—fast, balanced, exact.

Sparks fly like fireworks.

Each time a robot falls, it rises again. The swarm doesn't back off. It keeps coming.

And Yin keeps going. Relentless. Focused. Fluid.

Step. Side-step. Strike. "Whack!" Dodge. Duck. Strike. "Whack!" Strike. "Whack!"

"Beep!"

The buzzer sounds the moment he reaches the end of the path.

Instantly, the flying robots vanish—whirring away into the air like they were never there.

Not one Warufang has landed a sting.

The hologram timer flashes: **9.2**

"Wow. Good time," Yang stammers.

Lilly stands still, feeling woozy. "Wow…" is all she can say.

Yang must notice her face. He pats her on the back. "You can do this, Lilly. I know it."

"We'll work our way up to it," Oak says, trying to reassure her.

# Chapter 98
## Through the Rings

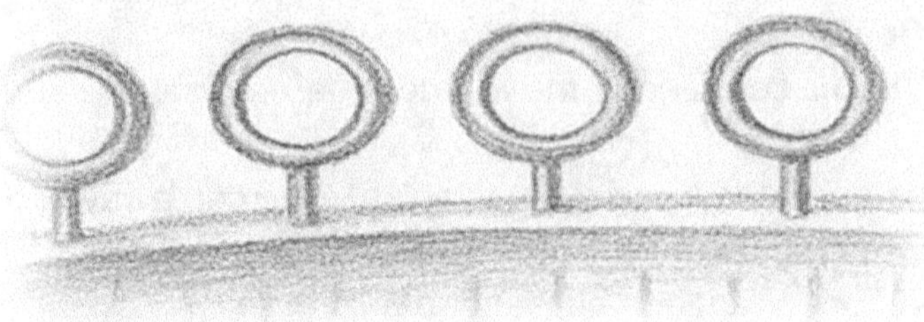

"Beep! Beep!" Yang's armband blinks with alarm.

"Gotta go. Canker sighting."

Within seconds, his genaether floats up beside him in the bleachers. Yang hops on.

Yin is on his way just a moment later, and together they disappear over the wall.

"Why don't I show you the Genaether Challenge?" Oak offers. "That one's less... ah... dangerous." He's already tapping and swiping on his navok.

"Well, I need to learn both, to get the Ring from the Challenge," Lilly says, trying to sound casual. "So, sure. Whatever. I mean, the wasp challenge looks doable... sort of." She says it mostly to keep Oak from worrying.

A moment later, a grey genaether lowers from somewhere above.

Oak hops on. "Come with me." He pats the little seat space behind him.

Lilly hesitates. She'll have to sit closer than she's comfortable with.

"Come on. This is how a Liege learns the first time."

Lilly climbs into the seat. She's not sure what to hang on to.

"Grab the rails by your legs. We're not going too fast. I just want you to get the idea."

She finds the handles and grips them tightly. She can smell bakery sweetness and warm spices on Oak. Lilly likes baked goods. She shoves the thought aside and focuses on holding on.

"All challenges have two parts," Oak explains. "The genaether ability and the vok ability. Your total time on both makes your score."

Lilly nods. She gets it.

"You see all those rings?" Oak points. "They light up, randomly, one at a time."

Lilly nods again, again silently. Oak can't see her.

"We go through the lit ring. Then look for the next one, and go through that. Thirteen in total, for the first challenge."

"Got it."

"Yang holds the fastest time in recorded history. I don't come close to his time, but..." Oak trails off, leaving the rest unsaid.

Their genaether lifts off the ground.

Lilly feels her stomach dip as the earth drops away beneath them. She tightens her grip on the handles.

Oak hovers toward the wide opening of a big ring at the highest part of the wall.

More rings circle the top of the stadium, stacked in a row—one after another, all around the perimeter.

"Ready?"

"Good."

A loud "Beeeep!" echoes through the entire coliseum.

They launch. Not gently. More like two riders on a rocket—if rockets had open seats and rails to clutch for dear life.

They shoot through one ring, then swerve around into two more, then curve outward to find the next. Oak's guiding the genaether in sweeping arcs, slicing through each lit ring around the coliseum.

"When you do this," he calls over the wind, "be sure to lean into the turn. It tilts the genaether and gives the gati better control. It is the gati that drives. You are pretty much just shifting your weight."

# Chapter 99
## The First Attempt

Lilly nods. She can feel the genaether tilt beneath her.

Already, they're halfway around, flying through one lit ring and then the next.

She hangs on tight, trying to remember everything.

"Also," Oak calls back, "when you bank either direction, squeeze your knees into the side of the cabin wall. It keeps you from sliding. Most first-timers end up shifting the center of gravity, and you lose time that way."

"Got it."

Another loud *Beep!* Sounds as their genaether zips through the thirteenth ring.

A holographic number flashes high above the coliseum: **16.3**

"Ooo, slow today," Oak says with a wince. "Yang's best time for the Yishi Challenge is 9.6 centags. The First Challenge is 13 rings. The Second Challenge is 21. The Third, 34, and so on. You'll just need to go 13."

Oak dives up, arches in a wide sweep, and lands smoothly just paces from where they started.

A small group waits at the entrance to the maze.

"Go on. Get in there. Don't be scared—we're right here to help you."

Someone snickers.

Lilly spots Nafari and Rasht, standing with a smaller girl dressed in soft, hospital-type cotton clothes.

"But I've never done this before," the girl pleads.

"You want to be a Royal Gesh, don't you?"

"Yes, but—"

"You're a Liege. This is how you get to be a Gesh. Don't worry, it's easy."

Nafari pushes the girl gently toward the maze and hands her a vok.

Rasht snickers again.

A loud *Beeeep!* Blares—the timer starts.

"That's not right," Lilly says, already climbing off the genaether.

The Warufang swarm lifts into the air—buzzing, circling.

The little girl holds the vok above her head with both hands like it's a magic wand that will scare the swarm away.

"Get going! You'll be fine!" Nafari barks.

"Leave it alone, Lilly-Bug. It's not our business," Oak warns, reaching for her arm.

He's too late.

Lilly bolts.

The swarm closes in. One Warufang dives—*Zap!* Another swoops—*Zap!*

The girl whimpers at each strike, swinging the vok helplessly at the air and missing every time.

Nafari and Rasht laugh. "Keep going!"

Lilly storms toward the maze, Vok already in hand.

"Leave her alone, Nafari!" she shouts.

"Ooo, it's Dirtling Girl." Nafari plants her hands on her hips, smirking. "What are you gonna do about it?"

# Chapter 100
## Alien Bullies

$S$*word,* Lilly thinks as she approaches Nafari.

Her vok hums to life, and a glowing blade extends from its tip. "This isn't right!" she snaps, staring Nafari down.

Nafari takes a few steps back, blinking in surprise.

Lilly wants to wipe that smirk off her face, but the girl—curled on one knee with her hands over her head—is overwhelmed.

Lilly strides past Nafari and into the maze.

"Oh, goodie, double the entertainment," Nafari laughs.

Lilly steps in front of the crumpled girl, placing herself between her and the swarm. She holds her vok sword like she used to hold her machete—tight, centered, ready.

Step. Strike. *Whack!*

She dodges. Swings. Strikes again. *Whack!*

Her armband gives a faint *chirp.*

"Come on. Up. We need to keep moving," she says to the girl, reaching with her free arm and helping her off the ground.

The girl has dropped her vok.

Lilly bends to pick it up—*Zap!* Something stings her in the back. It feels like an electric shock.

"Stay behind me," Lilly commands.

Step. Step. Strike. *Whack!*

She can feel the wind from the swarm pulsing in and out, like the whole thing is one giant animal breathing over its prey.

The little girl holds her hands above her head.

Lilly leads. The end looks impossibly far.

Side-step. Strike. *Whack!*

Dodge. Duck. Step.

*Zap!* A sharp pain sears through Lilly's leg.

Step. Step. Strike. *Whack!* Strike. *Whack!* Step.

The downed robots rise again, more aggressive than before. All of them zero in on Lilly, attacking over and over.

*Zap!* Lilly lets out a groan—this one hits her face.

There's no elegance now. No rhythm. Just raw survival.

The Warufang keep coming.

And Lilly keeps fighting.

Side-step. Strike. *Whack!*

Dodge. Duck. Step.

*Beep!*

The buzzer sounds the instant they reach the end of the path.

Lilly drops to one knee, gasping for breath.

The little girl slumps to the ground and curls into a ball, shaking.

Oak runs up from far behind.

"You could've helped, you know," Lilly snaps.

Oak is panting, flushed from his sprint.

"Sorry—but it's not a good idea. The swarm becomes near impossible with two… and deadly with three," he says flatly.

Lilly glances back. Nafari and Rasht are gone.

The timer above flashes: **18.6**

"Wow. That was forever," she pants. Her face feels like something's swelling on it—she can barely see out of one eye. Her back burns like a fire's smoldering under her skin. Her leg throbs like there's a baseball bat-sized thorn jammed into it.

"How is she?" Lilly asks.

Oak kneels beside the shivering girl.

Out of the corner of her eye, Lilly sees a flicker of movement. She swats at it—

A silver-and-gold spider tumbles to the ground, rights itself, and starts heading back toward her.

Oak catches her hand. "It's your hygee—your nurse."

"Oh." Lilly lets it crawl up her leg and body. It touches her face, and suddenly the pain starts to melt. The swelling stays, but the fire's gone.

She glances at the girl, still curled up and crying.

Oak stays beside her. "She's okay. But she's been stung many times."

The spider's on Lilly's back now. She feels that burn ease, and it's a relief—until it's not.

"Okay! Enough!" she shouts, shaking herself like a dog to fling the spider off. "The girl! Help her!"

Her armband chirps again.

The hygee flops to the ground and immediately crawls back toward Lilly.

Lilly stomps her foot. "No! The girl! Go!"

The shiny spider pauses—then obeys.

# Chapter 101



### Of Things Crawly but Caring

The silver-and-gold spider climbs over the crumpled, shivering girl, touching each swollen welt, some the size of apples.

Oak bends down to check her closely. "It's okay. We're here to help."

Within moments, the girl uncrumples. Her eyes blink up at the now-empty sky. The danger is gone. She's young—grade-school age.

"Are you okay?" Lilly asks, holding out one hand to help her sit up and the other for the spider to return.

Lilly's armband gives a slight *chirp.*

The girl nods. "I'm okay," she sniffles. Her eyes adjust. "Nafari said she was going to help me learn the First Challenge…" Then her mouth drops open and her eyes go wide. "You're the Earthling girl! The Ohmuno! You saved me!"

"No. I'm just Lilly. And this is Oak." She smiles gently. "What's your name?"

The girl looks surprised, like she didn't expect to be asked. "Um… me? I'm… uhm… Orriah."

Lilly smiles warmly. "Hello, Orriah. Can we help you get home?"

The girl's eyes fill with tears. She wipes them away with her sleeve and nods.

"I'll get a genaether," Oak offers.

"Kwi-Li is faster, if it can do it," Lilly says aloud—then thinks hard: *Kwi-Li, we need you.*

*Pop!*

Kwi-Li appears beside her in a blink. "You called, Lilly?" the little robot chirps, cheerful as ever.

Oak steps back, startled. "How did you… Hey—no way!"

Lilly just shrugs. "Can you do the blink-travel-thing, the …geennii thing?" She asks her gati.

The runty robot nods its head, so much yes, that it looked like it was a woodpecker.

Can Kwi-Li here take you home?" she asks Orriah.

Orriah's face lights up like it's the best birthday present ever. "Really!? A *Geennii* ride with a Royal Gati? You bet!"

Lilly turns to Kwi-Li. "Can you bring Orriah here home, please? She's had a rough time."

"Okay!" Kwi-Li nods eagerly.

*Pop!*

In a blink, they're gone. Space where they just stood.

Oak stares at Lilly like she just did a triple somersault with one arm, one leg, and a backpack full of textbooks.

There's a whirring sound from above.

Both look up.

A grey genaether descends and lands beside them.

"Hi, Lilly. I heard you were here."

The blond-haired Terco steps off, his voice bright and familiar. His smile says they're best friends.

"Ah… yes. Hi." Lilly is caught off guard by the friendliness. Way too friendly. It is like he is a Labrador retriever and Lilly's navok is a dog treat.

"We met near your forest. I am… was Seri's partner."

"Yes… I remember… and… I'm sorry for what happened."

An awkward silence follows. Terco glances at her bracelet, searching for words.

"Well, you see, that's why I'm here." He brushes back his perfect blond hair. "Just before Seri's death, she promised me her Royal Gesh position—if anything happened to her."

"Oh?"

"Right," he says, like it all makes perfect sense now. "It's just… we weren't able to make it official."

"I'm sorry. I'm confused." Lilly shifts uncomfortably. She looks at Oak, who looks just as puzzled.

"There's just been a misunderstanding," Terco says in a soft, almost sing-song tone. "Seri was injured—not in her right mind—when she gave it to you."

Oak and Lilly exchange glances.

Oak shrugs. *I don't know.*

Lilly tries to make sense of it. "Well… according to Willow, it's stuck on me. And according to Aubrin… well, have you talked with Aubrin about this?"

Terco's smooth expression falters. "We've talked, but… I thought I'd ask you directly."

Lilly's skin crawls. Something about this feels wrong.

"I don't know what to say. What's important to me is finding my father… and now, finding out what happened to my mother." She glances at Oak, then back at Terco.

Oak still looks confused.

Terco looks hopeful. Labrador dog hopeful. Like maybe, just maybe he will get a navok treat.

"Let's just wait and discuss this after my father is found, can we? Please? If you want, we can talk to Aubrin together." Lilly's voice is calm, but firm.

Terco's warm expression goes cold. He opens his mouth—then shuts it. He turns his back, climbs onto his genaether, and shoots into the sky without another word.

Lilly looks over at Oak. "Did that make any sense to you?"

Oak shrugs. "It makes sense that he wants that navok off of you. He's in Shang position—last place—and he's desperate. By removing your navok, he is no longer Shang. By beating you in a challenge, he moves up to seventh. Seri's level."

# Chapter 102
## Spot

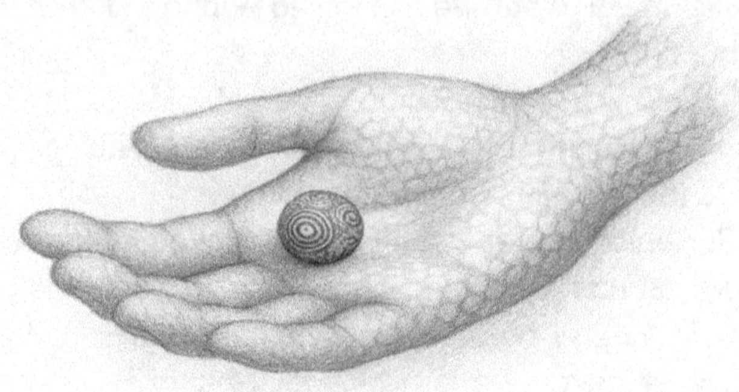

Lilly heads to her room above the bagel shop. It doesn't feel like home—but it's better than what's left of her old one. The day clings to her like wet clothes, dragging her down.

Behind her, Kwi-Li bounces along, hopping and skipping, humming something cheerful and strange.

It sounds in stereo to Lilly, in her hearing and her mind. Freaky, but she is too tired to do anything about it.

"Bark! Bark! Bark!" Three-legged Ajax tears down the hallway, chasing Baba. Again.

The round marble trails behind them, struggling to keep up—pinging off one wall, then the other, like a lost pinball.

Lilly lifts her leg just in time, letting the chaos storm past.

Kwi-Li drops to one knee and scoops up the marble with both hands. "Oh, you poor thing. You are all alone." The gati cradles it like it's a baby bird.

Lilly sighs. "It's probably just trying to get back to its momma."

"But its momma doesn't want it."

Lilly hesitates. Her brain feels like it's been rung out and left to dry. "Okay, well… what happens if you set it down?"

"On the hard floor?"

"Yes."

Kwi-Li clutches the marble tighter, unsure.

"Come on. Let's see."

With obvious effort, Kwi-Li lowers its hands to the ground. The marble rolls out, does a full loop, then zips straight back up into Kwi-Li's palm.

"See! It likes me!" Kwi-Li beams, eyes practically glowing. "I'm calling you Spot, and we are going to be best friends!"

"Great," Lilly mumbles under her breath. "Alright, well… we need to ask Oak if you can adopt it or something, because it probably belongs to him."

Fear flashes across Kwi-Li's face. "Oh? Really?"

"Don't worry. We'll ask him tomorrow."

Some of the worry melts. "Ah… OK."

Later, when Lilly gets ready for bed, Kwi-Li chooses to sleep curled on a cushion beside her.

"Do robots need sleep?" Lilly asks.

"I am not a robot. I am a Royal Gatiar. We self-heal, so I need healing time. Can you buy me balloons tomorrow? Blue and green are my favorites. P-l-e-a-s-e?"

"We'll see," Lilly says—without meaning it. "Now go to sleep."

She ends up holding Kwi-Li's hand until the gati finally drifts off.

Oh goody.

# Chapter 103
### More than Meets the Eye

When Lilly and Kwi-Li reach the bottom of the stairway, just before the café, a low hum of voices swirls around them—like the buzzing of a beehive. Conversations blend, rising and falling in a wall of sound.

Lilly steps around a pile of things stacked neatly against the wall. Flowers. Shiny-wrapped parcels tied with ribbons. Even some perfectly shaped fruit nestled in small baskets.

"Oooh! Flowers and presents. I love flowers! They are so pretty," Kwi-Li bubbles, bending to sniff one of the bouquets.

"Come on, we don't touch what's not for us," Lilly snaps, more impatient than she means to be. She's hungry, and it shows. She shakes her head. She doesn't know where these motherly instincts are coming from.

"OK," Kwi-Li says, standing upright again.

"Let's find Oak. Remember, we have to ask him about your runaway robot."

"Spot?" Kwi-Li's eyes widen. It's like Lilly just said, a best friend might be moving away.

When Lilly steps into the café, the buzzing dies almost instantly.

Every head turns. Some people try not to stare. Others huddle together, whispering furiously. The café is packed. Slowly, the murmur of conversation begins to rise again.

Lilly feels Kwi-Li grab her hand. She's certain everyone sees it. She quickly shrugs the gati off.

Oak waves her over. He and Zak sit at the same table they used during the last meal. Oak has a mountain of pancakes in front of him and his usual chocfee steaming nearby.

Zak is finishing up, eating like he's in some kind of food-speed competition.

"In a hurry?" Lilly asks.

Zak nods, too focused on finishing to bother with words.

A hover tray glides up beside him, carrying a metallic lunch box.

"Your chamomile tea and cinnamon raisin bagel to go, Zak, as you requested," the tray announces in its flat, metallic voice.

"Since when do you drink tea?" Lilly asks.

"It's for Carnel. He can't just eat cheese doodles." Zak wipes his mouth, grabs the tea, and stands. "This is the only other thing I can get him to eat." He waves at both of them.

"Stay out of trouble, Shrimp," he adds with a grin before heading out the door.

"Catch you later, Geek."

Lilly slides into the seat across from Oak. "Why is everyone staring?"

Oak pauses mid-bite. "Same reason they left you gifts at the doorway." He keeps eating.

"Those are for me?" Lilly sputters.

Oak points a syrup-dripping fork at her. "Word travels fast around here. Everyone's talking about how you saved Orriah from the deadly Warufang challenge. The story goes that you did it blindfolded with one hand tied behind your back. Now they all think you're the Ohmuno."

Lilly glances around. Some café-goers try to act normally. Others just outright stare.

"What? Really? That doesn't make any sense."

"I will have Bengen collect them and bring them upstairs. We can't just leave them there."

"Ah… thanks," Lilly said, as calm as can be, on the outside. Inside, her mind blinked twice.

"Dad says no matter how full this café gets, no one will sit at this table anymore. They think it's yours." Oak shovels another bite of pancake. "So, I guess that's one good thing."

Kwi-Li tugs on Oak's sleeve. The gati opens its hand, revealing its prize. The little marble has split open to show the tiniest robot—one eye, two arms, and a pair of legs.

Oak looks about as excited as a dog being interrupted mid-meal. "Hmmm… I didn't know it did that. We've had that Bahu-Kwee my whole life."

"Oak… um… can I keep Spot? He's scared and just wants a friend. I'll take care of him, I promise."

Oak glances at the tiny robot in Kwi-Li's hand, then up at Lilly.

Lilly shrugs. She gives Oak the expression, 'Hey, this gati didn't come with a manual.'

"Ah… yeah, sure. I guess."

"Yay!" Kwi-Li jumps with excitement. The robot hurries over to Lilly, leans in, and whispers something in her ear.

Lilly glances at Oak, who now looks at her like she's lost it. "Oh! I never thought of that. OK!" Lilly says brightly. "After breakfast, we'll go."

"OK! Spot and I are going to go exploring now," Kwi-Li announces, turning and skipping out the door.

"Stay out of trouble," Lilly calls after the fleeing robot.

Oak stares at her, clearly expecting an explanation.

"Girl stuff," Lilly says, then turns to order her breakfast—with no words.

# Chapter 104
## A Diablopero's Snack

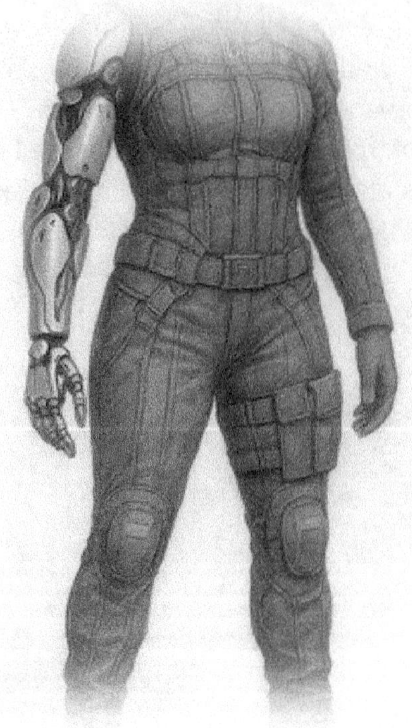

$O$ak and Lilly step outside the café, slipping away from the crowded noise. When Lilly spots a Royal Gesh approaching. It's Haro, in the same black uniform as before. Her black ponytail bounces behind her as she strides toward them.

"Hey, Lilly. Getting along fine?" she asks.

"Hi," Lilly replies with a smile.

Oak stands rigid beside her, his mouth hanging open.

Haro leans in like she's about to spill a secret. "Thought I'd give you a heads-up. Terco's going to challenge you for your 7th spot in the Royal Gesh."

Images of something even more dangerous than Olga Bartlutt—this time with weapons—rattle through Lilly's thoughts. "Should I be worried?"

Haro's smile warms from her eyes. "You? Yes and no." She rests a steadying hand on Lilly's shoulder. "If you know what to say and get ready for the challenge, you'll be fine. Terco's still figuring out which end of the vok to hold."

Lilly glances at Oak.

His mouth is still open, his eyes ping-ponging between Haro and her, worry etched all over his face.

Haro locks eyes with Lilly. "Listen carefully. Since you're the one being challenged, you get to choose the type of challenge. It can be direct combat or one of the tests in the Circle of Challenge. Pick the Ist-Uno Yishi. Got it?"

"Got it."

"Terco's improving with direct combat, but he still hesitates with the Warufang. He has a fear of wasps, for some reason."

Lilly nods, processing. She can think of lots of reasons why.

Haro pats her shoulder. "You can do this. Just practice up."

"Thanks for letting me know."

Haro's tone shifts. "Also, Aubrin asked me to tell you—the Royal Gesh shifted an ang to search the northern path through the forest, based on the wrapping paper you sent. So far, no luck."

"Maybe we can go help look," Lilly says, turning to Oak for support.

Oak doesn't look supportive. His mouth is closed now, but his wide eyes and subtle head shake say it all: *Nope.*

Haro's hand tightens on Lilly's shoulder. Her gaze sharpens. "No. That is not a good idea. It's way too dangerous out there for you.

A diablopero is hunting you, and there are cankers all over. Both want you off this planet—dead."

She lifts her right arm in front of Lilly. "This is what a diablopero can do."

Haro pulls back her uniform sleeve. For the first time, Lilly sees the truth: her arm, all the way down to her hand, is robotic. Synthetic. Haro flexes her fingers, and a low hum pulses from inside the metal.

"I lost my arm just under the shoulder. It became a snack for a diablopero. The thing was just running past. One blink, and chomp—my arm was gone. Like it was nothing. These machines aren't something we mess with, Lilly. You're safer inside. Aubrin says you stay here. So... you're staying here. Period."

Lilly glances at Oak.

He gives her a smug *told-you-so* look.

"I see a bit of rebel in you," Haro says, flashing Lilly a conspirator's smile.

Then she looks to Oak. "You're the one keeping an eye on her, I suppose?" she adds with a wink.

Oak's mouth opens and closes. Nothing comes out.

"I should mention—Aubrin set it up so that if any biological material crosses the Phi Guya wall, an alarm goes off. So don't worry. She's safe in here," Haro says, her eyes locking on Lilly's, making sure the message lands.

Lilly shrugs innocently.

But Haro softens. "This is confidential... but I want you to know. Your account of what happened in the forest has been incredibly valuable. Thanks to you, we're learning more about this specific diablopero. You see, only Royal gatis can cloak. Nothing else. So, either the cankers have some seriously advanced tech... or there's a captured gati inside that machine. Maybe they dismantled one and stole the cloaking tech. We're still speculating."

She pats Lilly's shoulder one more time, then nods at Oak. "I hear she's getting good at the Yishi challenge. Good job training her. She'll make a fine Royal Gesh, in time."

Lilly smiles, a little disbelieving. "Really... we're just starting."

Oak nods slowly, blinking like he's still trying to catch up, mouth stuck open.

Haro turns and walks off toward the bustling market, her ponytail bobbing behind her.

"Listen," Oak says, finally recovering. "I need to pick up more flour for Dad."

"Well, Kwi-Li and I have an errand too," Lilly replies.

*Blink!*

Kwi-Li appears at her side out of nowhere. "Ready to go?" the gati chirps, grabbing Lilly's hand and bouncing with excitement. "After, can you buy me a balloon—p...l...e...a...s...e!"

"We'll see," Lilly replies, same as always.

Oak looks at her like she's grown a second head. "So... then we'll meet up after?"

Lilly smirks. "You're going to let me out of your sight?"

"Probably not a good idea," Oak mutters.

"Don't worry—we'll be at Sekani's. Busy not trying to escape." Lilly turns and heads toward the cluster of shops across the market.

# Chapter 105

## Sekani's Body Covers

Kwi-Li skips beside her, holding Spot carefully in a folded hand.

Lilly passes Kai's bookstore and stops in front of the store next to it. A big sign reads: **SEKANI'S BODY COVERS**. Surprisingly, there are no customers inside when they enter. An automated greeting rings out.

"Welcome, Lilly, to Sekani's Body Covers. It is a good day to complete your shopping," a voice announces from somewhere above.

This store feels more familiar—more like the clothing shops Lilly remembers. The mannequins are all holograms, shifting through different styles and colors of clothes. Shelves along the walls and in the center are piled high with neatly folded outfits. Above the displays, a glowing hologram flashes:

**LOCKDOWN CLEARANCE SALE – 55 TOKENS PER ITEM**

As Lilly and Kwi-Li step further in, the hologram mannequins start to move. Some walk casually. Others pose, shifting like models caught mid-photo shoot.

Lilly stops and watches, uncertain.

Just then, an oversized dragonfly whirs toward her and hovers in midair. A red beam flashes from its head, scanning Lilly from head to toe. The beam shuts off. The dragonfly buzzes in place.

"I see you're a size five, Lilly. What can I do for you today?"

Lilly turns. A young woman steps into view, smiling. She looks like she belongs in a commercial—perfect features, wild bright clothes, and a toothpaste-ad grin.

"I… um… we… need to get a few things."

"Yes," the woman says smoothly. "Our records indicate that you own two sets of Teslan's Dynamic Membrane Royal Gesh Level Seven. As well as two sets of Version 34 of Miley's Metamorphic Muftis, complete with Version 8 Earth Design."

"Pardon me?" Lilly blinks in surprise.

The girl's warm smile widens. "You already have two sets of tight clothing and two sets of baggy clothing."

"Oh. Right. Okay." Lilly nods and tries to smile back. She's wearing neither. Somehow, this perfect stranger with her flawless face and sunny tone knows exactly what's in her closet.

"May I suggest an additional spare set of each? Plus, our most recent festive-wear program? The Feast of Unity is arriving soon. We have a marvelous selection for the celebration."

"The Feast of Unity?" Lilly repeats, trying not to admit she has no clue what that even is. "No… um… I… we're here for something else." She gestures toward Kwi-Li.

The attendant's brow lifts in polite confusion.

Lilly leans in and whispers what they're shopping for.

"Oh? Okay. We can do that." The woman's face lights up with an even bigger smile.

By the time they get what they came for, Lilly stands near the front, facing the salesgirl.

Kwi-Li stands in front of a mirror, admiring the new purchases.

"So, this is sort of new to me—this Phi… paying thing," Lilly says, trying not to sound completely clueless.

"Oh, no! There is no charge." The girl's cheerful smile turns firm, serious.

"What? Are you sure?"

"It's free of charge for the Ohmuno. Come again, for anything you want." The woman waves them out, her smile returning as she gently shoos Lilly and Kwi-Li from the store.

# Chapter 106

## Kwi-Li gets some New Clothes.

Lilly and Kwi-Li have just stepped outside Sekani's store when Oak shows up.

He's dusted in flour—arms, shirt, even a smudge across one cheek. He looks a bit like a sugar-coated blueberry. "What... on... earth?!" Oak sputters when he spots Kwi-Li.

"What?" Lilly blinks, all innocent.

Oak points a blue, flour-dusted finger straight at the gati.

Kwi-Li stands proudly in brand-new bib overalls. The outfit is sleeveless with sturdy straps and a front bib loaded with pockets—front, back, even down the pant legs. A red baseball cap rests crookedly on the gati's big head, like it wandered into a summer ball game by accident.

"You put clothes... on a Royal Gati." Oak blinks rapidly, still pointing.

"Spot likes her new home!" Kwi-Li says, tucking the little marble into the bib pocket like it's a sleeping kitten.

Lilly throws Oak a smug glance. "Spot likes her new home," she echoes, clearly proud of the result.

"But... but..." Oak's words stumble and fall apart before they make it to his mouth.

Lilly shrugs. "What? Kwi-Li doesn't want to walk around naked anymore."

Oak stares at her, then back at Kwi-Li. His mouth opens, but nothing comes out. He's broken.

**Blink!**

A Royal Gati suddenly appears beside them. No cool outfit. No tilted cap. Just sleek, official, and very not-dressed.

Lilly and Oak both freeze, completely forgetting what they were just talking about.

The new Gati looks over at Kwi-Li. Its face doesn't move, expression unreadable.

Kwi-Li straightens, standing like a kid on the first day of school, rocking the best outfit anyone's ever seen.

Maybe—if you squint—you'd think the arriving gati's eyes flicker with surprise. But it turns to Lilly without comment, lifts one arm, and strikes its chest.

**Thump.**

"I am Royal Iyengar Aubrins, gati," it says, bowing to Lilly. "Royal Gesh Ist-Kee Lilly, you are being respectfully summoned for a matter of Royal Gesh Procedure. Please allow me to geennii you to the meeting."

Lilly glances at Oak just as he glances at her.

"Do you think they already know about the clothes?" she whispers, nodding toward Kwi-Li's outfit.

"I think it's a little more serious than that," Oak whispers back, frowning.

# Chapter 107

Lilly checks herself out. T-shirt and jeans—both pretty clean. Maybe there's a little pizza sauce on the shirt, but overall? Not bad.

She turns to Aubrin's gati and nods. "Okay. Yes. Please. We'll go."

In a blink, the world shifts.

Lilly staggers, struggling to find her balance.

The buildings and trees whirl around her like she's just stepped off a carnival ride.

When everything finally settles, she realizes she's standing in front of the Royal Palace Building—the one she'd only seen from a distance, until now.

Oak, Kwi-Li, and Aubrin's gati stand beside her.

Ahead, the palace rises—pure white, towering into the clouds. Multiple towers of ascending height give it the aura of a royal fortress. Everything about the structure radiates importance. Like other buildings in Phi Guya, the windows and doors are just openings—no glass, no doors to swing shut.

Numerous black Noxiar robots stand posted at the entrance, unmoving. More Noxiars are spaced evenly around the palace perimeter, a silent army stretching as far as she can see.

Oak lets out a breath. "Wow."

"This is some serious security," Lilly mutters to him.

"Yeah. It sure is."

"Please follow me, Ist-Kee Lilly," Aubrin's gati says, voice flat, already moving forward through the guards toward the towering arched entryway.

As they approach, all of the Noxiars slam their fists to their chests in one perfectly timed *THUMP!*

Lilly jumps. She's still not used to this.

Kwi-Li grabs her hand.

Lilly brushes it away. "Act like the other gatis," she hisses under her breath. She regrets it instantly—for reasons she can't quite explain.

Then they enter the palace—and it takes her breath away.

Whatever awe the exterior promised, the room inside delivers tenfold.

The gati leads them into what must be a ballroom, but it feels more like a palace of air and light.

The ceiling stretches so high it disappears into shadows. The floor shines like poured glass, reflecting sunlight in soft, shifting ripples. It's like standing on the surface of a still lake.

Each of their footsteps lands with a crisp, echoing *tap*—multiplied and magnified by the vast space. With four of them walking, the sound becomes a living rhythm, like the drumbeat of multiple hearts inside the room's stone cavity.

Kwi-Li tries again to take Lilly's hand.

She swats it away.

"What is this place?" she whispers to Oak.

"Shh," Oak replies, posture suddenly straight, face solemn.

Tall arched windows line the walls like cathedral gates to the sky, their panes catching sunlight and shattering it across the floor in fractured colors.

Light scatters like glass dust across the polished floor.

Everything here whispers pageantry and power. The air carries a faint trace of old perfume and candle wax—like a room that's seen centuries of secrets. It isn't just a place to gather. It's a place to *impress*. To remind you: something important is always happening here.

They're halfway across the ballroom when Lilly notices a group gathered at the far end.

Aubrin's gati leads them directly toward it.

From a distance, it looks like one person seated and a dozen others flanking each side.

Closer now, she sees the truth. One seated figure. Three standing people. The rest—Noxiars. Their scale-like armor catches the sun, sparkling in sharp diamonds of light that shimmer across the floor.

She spots Aubrin standing tall, calm. Then Terco, perfect hair in place. And of course, Vishot—his hair glued down with enough product to shine like plastic.

But the woman seated in the grand, high-backed chair is someone Lilly doesn't recognize.

She has nearly white blond hair, braided tightly and woven with glints of golden lattice. Her eyes are a bright, icy blue, and her skin—smooth and pale like fresh milk. She sits still, straight, and poised. A delicate crown of golden leaves and vines rests lightly on her head, like it belongs there.

Her hands rest on the arms of the chair, one on each side, with the stillness of someone used to being watched.

# Chapter 108
### The Queen of Seairland

"Who is that?" Lilly whispers to Oak.

"Shh!" Oak replies, his whole body vibrating with nervous energy.

They're only a few paces away from the royal gathering when everything seems to happen at once.

Lilly's group stops walking.

She doesn't.

She feels a tug—Oak grabs her shirt to stop her.

At the same moment, all the noxiars slam their fists to their chests and bow toward Lilly.

*THUMP!* Reverberates through the vast chamber.

Oak, Kwi-Li, and Aubrin's Royal Gati all bow low to the woman on the throne-like chair.

The woman responds with a single, slow nod.

What doesn't happen—at least not in time—is Lilly understanding *what on earth* is going on. She stands there, frozen, eyes darting from the saluting noxiars to the bowing bodies beside her, to the calm woman in the chair.

A hand tugs her arm.

It's Oak.

"Bow," he hisses from the side of his mouth.

Lilly blinks, realizing she's missed something. She bows—too late—just as the others are rising.

A faint smile curves on Aubrin's lips, his eyes flicking to Kwi-Li's new outfit.

The woman on the throne seems secretly amused as well.

Vishot glares at Lilly like she's a disease that just wafted into the palace.

Terco can't stop stealing nervous glances between Lilly and her armband, which sparkles with golden light as it catches the sun.

Aubrin straightens. One hand rises to rest gently on the back of the queen's grand chair. "May I introduce Queen Aumune Gotress, Queen of Seairland," he announces. His voice echoes across the ballroom, deep and formal, like a monk's chant in a cathedral.

The queen shares a glance and a quiet smile with Aubrin. For a brief moment, she places her delicate hand over his. It's gone in an instant, but says everything: mutual respect, long-held trust.

Aubrin's expression is carved from stone, but his eyes sparkle with humor beneath it all.

"Royal Gesh Ist-Kee Lilly," he says, "you have been called here for a matter of Kinrik Khem Gesh procedure, as requested by Shang Terco of the Kinrik Khem Gesh." His voice rings with ancient authority—and then, with one quick wink to Lilly, mischief cracks through his mask.

Terco shifts from foot to foot, his gaze bouncing between Aubrin, Lilly, and her armband. It's obvious what he's after.

He glances at Vishot.

Vishot's stare could melt armor. If he were allowed to smack sense into Terco, he absolutely would. His pitch-black eyes scream *Just do it.*

Terco clears his throat. "By the ancient code of Kinrik Khem Gesh, I, Terco, Shang Position, do challenge you, Lilly Edelweiss Dubois, Ist-Kee Position, for your title."

Lilly turns to Oak.

He stands stiff as a plank, a bead of sweat trailing down his blue forehead. He looks like a mime trapped in an invisible box.

She looks to Aubrin. He smiles back, subtle and steady. His face stays still. His eyes laugh.

"Do you accept, or do you forfeit?" Aubrin asks.

Lilly tries to speak, but no words come. Her voice has decided to go into hiding.

Oak leans in close, ventriloquist-style. "I accept," he says through unmoving lips.

Lilly shakes her head, trying to knock her thoughts back into order. "I accept," she repeats. And then it hits her—Haro's advice. Clear. Sharp.

"I choose the challenge of Ist-Uno Yishi."

Her voice echoes through the grand room, louder than she expects. Bolder.

Terco looks like Lilly just slapped him.

A flicker of delight flashes in Aubrin's eyes, though his face remains composed. "So be it. By the ancient code of Kinrik Khem Gesh," he declares with flat formality.

Oak, Kwi-Li, and Aubrin's gati bow.

Oak pulls on Lilly's sleeve again. She bows—again, just slightly out of sync—just as everyone begins rising.

The queen nods back, kind and wordless.

Aubrin's gati turns to lead them out.

Oak follows without a word. He gives Lilly a soft tug.

She follows, exiting the grand hall the same way they entered. Confused.

# Chapter 109
### Zak's Holographic Projecting Drone

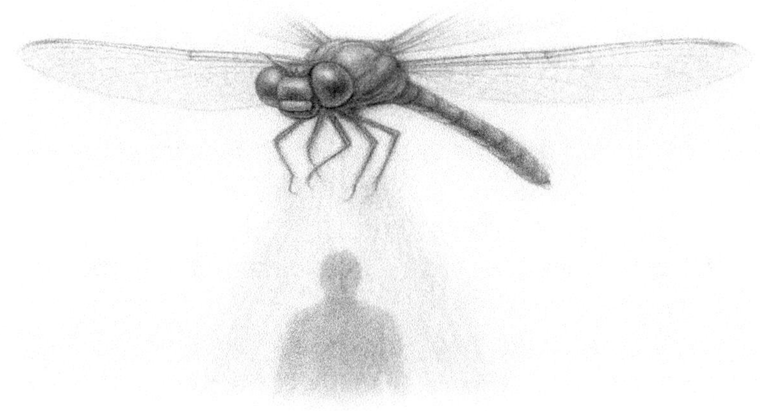

"Holy crap! That was the Queen!" Oak blurts as they step into the brightness outside. "I didn't know she was here!"

Lilly shoves him in the chest, fuming. "You could've *prepared* me for that!" Her glare could bore through walls.

Oak doesn't even flinch. "What's she doing here? They must've been keeping her hidden this whole time!" He talks like she's background noise—like she's a mosquito buzzing near his ear.

Lilly punches him in the arm. "*I looked like a total idiot!*"

Oak blinks, like he's just now noticing someone else is present. "That was the Queen of Seairland," he says again, eyes wide in awe.

Before Lilly can unleash her wrath, a buzzing overhead cuts through the moment.

A large dragonfly descends, sunlight flickering off its body in rainbow sparks. It hovers just above Lilly's head. A beam shoots from its front.

Instantly, a hologram of Zak materializes in front of her. It looks exactly like Zak—down to the mop of hair and lopsided grin—except he's wearing the eye-glass contraption Carnel gave him. His body appears solid. There's no flicker or transparency. It's like he's standing there.

"Zak? What the—" Lilly leans in, trying to find any flaw that proves it's not him.

"Lilly-D. You got time to swing by the junkyard? We've got a few things you'll want to see," Hologram-Zak says.

"Is that… *you*?" Lilly stammers.

"Of course it's me. Well… a hologram of me—but still me. Forget it. Just get down here to the junkyard."

Lilly pokes a finger into his belly. Her finger sinks in like she's pressing into a puddle. A ripple shimmers where she touches him.

"Cool."

"Hey. Stop that." Hologram-Zak tries to brush away her hand. It passes right through her.

A smirk curls across Lilly's face. She raises her finger and sticks it right up his nose.

"*Stop it!* Grow up." Zak waves at her again, uselessly. "Hey, do me a favor—pick up a chamomile tea and cinnamon raisin bagel from the café."

Somewhere offscreen, a muffled mumble drifts in. It sounds a lot like the words *cheese doodles.*

Hologram-Zak turns around, showing the back of his head. "No. You are going to consume a nutritional substrate with higher micronutrient density. Period."

"*Flitchi chici chici!*" another voice grumbles from out of sight.

"I don't want to hear it. You need *real* food," Zak says, turning back to Lilly.

"For Carnel?" Lilly laughs.

"Yup."

She chuckles again. "Alright. Alright. We're on the way." She glances at Oak.

He's staring at her like *she* has her finger up her nose.

"What?" she laughs.

They use Kwi-Li's geennii ability to travel quickly to Carnel's junkyard. It's just faster that way.

They arrive to find Zak and Carnel hunched over something on a worktable. Zak's deep in concentration while Carnel passes him tools.

"Very good. Very good," Carnel nods eagerly, peering at Zak through a stack of overlapping lenses. The contraption makes his eyes bulge like ping-pong balls. The little green man stands on a stool, the robot with the portal toolbox beside him.

"Food delivery service," Lilly jokes, holding up the lunch box.

Zak glances up from his work—

—and Lilly jumps a little.

He's wearing the same crazy contraption as Carnel. His brown eyes are magnified to ping-pong ball size, behind the layered lenses. His grin stretches wide. *Click. Click.* The lenses shift, making his eyes slightly smaller. A mechanical dragonfly perches on his shoulder—probably the same one from earlier.

Zak sets down his tool and steps around the table. "Thanks, Lill." He takes the lunch box and hands it to Carnel. "Eat." His tone is pure babysitter-who-s-had-enough.

Carnel beams like a schoolboy getting his lunch pail—except, you know, he's green, wrinkly, bearded, and ancient.

"You are a good boy. Good boy." Carnel grins shyly. "I eat... if you show your idea. Your *brilliant* idea." He looks at Zak with a mischievous glint.

Zak blushes. He looks like someone just handed him a trophy he's not sure he earned.

# Chapter 110
### Zak's Sticky Bomb

"Go on. Go." Carnel nudges Zak with a wrinkled green finger and a lopsided smile.

Zak blushes, staring at the ground like it might rescue him from embarrassment. He looks too mortified to speak.

Carnel pokes him in the arm. "Tell her. Tell her about that EMP sticky bomb. Genius. Genius." He glances over at Lilly and Oak. "Smarter than anyone on all of Phi."

"That's not true. He's just being nice," Zak mutters, trying to brush off the compliment, but it clings to him like glitter—obvious and everywhere.

Carnel gives him a yeah-right look and taps his armband. "Unit 2743 here now. Now."

A moment later, a gangly robot stumbles around the corner of stacked junk. It's as skinny as a broomstick, with arms and legs like flailing twigs.

"Show them. Show them," Carnel says, jerking a thumb at the robot.

Zak stares down at his shoes, then picks up a black ball from the cluttered table. Its surface is covered in weird bumps, like it caught a bad case of warts or zits.

The robot freezes when it sees the ball. If robots could look nervous, this one does. It starts shaking, then turns to run.

Zak lobs the ball. It arcs through the air and sticks to the robot's back.

The robot keeps running, flailing to reach the thing stuck to it, trying to escape like its joints are on fire. A buzzing sound blasts out. The robot jerks into the air—limbs locking straight—then thuds down again. It bolts forward, buzzing again. Limbs spazzing. Then it's gone, vanishing behind the piles.

"Okay… I've still got to up the power," Zak says with a half-smile.

"You will get it. You will get it," Carnel says, patting him on the back like Zak just tried riding his bike for the first time. He walks off, grinning, clutching his lunch box like it's the best present ever.

Zak turns to Kwi-Li. His finger lifts. "What, the…?" is all he says, his face twisting in confusion as he glances at Lilly.

Kwi-Li stands proud in the new outfit—hands stuffed in the pockets. Hat tilted like a fashion choice.

"What?" Lilly says, overacting innocence like a kid caught near a cookie jar. "I can't tell you all my secrets."

She feels a tug on her sleeve.

It's Kwi-Li.

"Can we go and get a balloon? P-l-e-a-s-e?" The gati's eyes go wide, sparkling with hope.

"We'll see," Lilly says.

Kwi-Li slumps instantly, shoulders sagging, eyes falling to the ground. "You always say we'll see."

"Well, we're busy right now. Why don't you go play with Spot?"

'Pop!' Kwi-Li vanishes.

Zak stares at Lilly like she just grew a third eyeball. "Really? You put clothes on a gati… and now balloons?"

"Don't look at me like that. The thing is not exactly normal."

"But... the clothes?" Zak repeats, his tech-glasses wobbling as his eyebrows shoot upward.

"What? It didn't want to walk around naked. I don't blame it. Besides, I think there's something wrong with it."

"Carnel figures Kwi-Li's got emotional trauma. From the Forest, and her previous Royal Gesh—Seri, and all that." Zak hesitates, then adds, "Carnel tried to get the memory out of Kwi-Li, but couldn't. That's rare for a Royal Gati. Most can self-heal."

He points to where Kwi-Li stood a second ago. "And, well, it makes sense. Royal Gatis don't usually have names, skip around, or think they're toddlers."

"But the Sticky Bomb isn't why we brought you here," Zak says suddenly, all upbeat again. He glances toward a towering wall of junk. "Come on."

His face lights up with a grin.

Zak leads them around the corner.

There, bent over something and wiping it shiny with a cloth, is blond-haired Riz.

# Chapter 111
### Lillys Genaether

"You remember Riz." Zak introduces her with an outstretched palm.

Riz pauses from polishing a Royal Genaether to fist-bump him. "Zap-man," she says with a slight smile.

She turns to Lilly, and the smile fades—or at least it seems that way to Lilly.

A baseball cap keeps wisps of Riz's blond hair under control. Her t-shirt and jeans are streaked in grease, with a fresh smudge across her cheek. She rubs at her hands with a rag, but the grease just smears.

"Hey there," Riz nods at Lilly.

Zak practically vibrates with energy. "Lilly-D, we heard you might need a genaether for your Ist-uno-Yishi challenge. With Terco." He says it with his chest out like he's handing her a surprise birthday gift.

"How did you hear about it so soon?" Lilly asks, glancing at Oak—who looks just as stunned as she feels. "We just got out of there."

Zak throws a glance at Riz. They exchange a conspiratorial look. "We can't tell you all our secrets," Zak says with a smirk.

Something tightens inside Lilly. She's not sure what.

Riz gives up on wiping her hands clean—they still look like she's been tuning engines with her bare fingers.

"We've been busy taking care of things for you," Zak brags.

Riz flashes him a grin. "Zak's been busier than anybody. You should see what he's working on. It's utterly brilliant."

"No, not really," Zak mutters, eyes dropping to his shoes. Then he nudges Riz. "Show her what you've been up to."

Riz offers a tiny smile, then waves toward the Royal Genaether in front of them. "May I present your Royal Genaether. All set for you to kick some Terco butt."

On the ground gleams the machine—white and gold trim catching the light like armor in a spotlight.

"Mine? Really?" Lilly stares at it in disbelief.

"It belongs to you," Riz replies, hands planted on her hips, clearly proud. "You should give it a try. See how it feels. You're gonna need your goofy gati, though. It sits up front there."


They're already at the Circle of Challenge. Have been for a while now.

"How are you OK up there?" Lilly calls out. The little robot perches at the front of the genaether, its red hat bobbing beneath the hood line. "Let's do better this time, OK?"

Kwi-Li sticks a thumbs-up above the hood. Not that she needs to—Lilly can hear her gati's thoughts clear as ever.

"All right now, let's try this again," Oak calls out. He sits on a grey utility genaether, looking up from the ground. "Do it the way I showed you. Same as we talked about—through the lit hoop, loop around, find the next, and then keep going, one after the other."

Lilly nods.

# Chapter 112
## Still Too Slow

"What time do you have to beat?" Oak demands.

Lilly shrugs.

"I told you twice already. Ten-point-two is Terco's best time." Oak shakes his head, clearly annoyed. "And remember, don't hit a single hoop. That's a time-loss penalty."

Lilly nods. "I heard you before." Her voice carries a frustrated edge.

"Don't forget—lean away from the fall, and into the rise," he adds.

Lilly gives a sharp nod back. Got it. She's sitting at the starting line, waiting for the timer to beep.

A low hum floats through her mind, like a strange nursery rhyme she's never heard before.

"You gotta be quiet up there. I can't hear myself think," Lilly mutters aloud.

**BEEP!**

The timer starts counting. Lilly and the genaether just sit there.

"Go, Kwi-Li. Go!" Lilly urges.

"But... I..." Kwi-Li stammers.

Lilly isn't sure if it's out loud or in her head. Doesn't matter—it all blends anyway.

The timer keeps counting.

"Go! Go! Go!" Oak yells from below. He slaps both hands against his head. His hair is already a wild mess from the previous attempts.

The genaether suddenly jerks to life beneath her. Lilly grabs the handles just in time as it wobbles into motion—and smashes through the first hoop.

**DING!**

A warning horn blares.

Lilly curses.

Her armband gives a soft **chirp**.

"Sorry," Kwi-Li blurts.

That strange rhyme starts humming again in her thoughts.

"Kwi-Li, I can't concentrate!"

**DING!**

They hit another ring.

Lilly curses again.

**Chirp.**

"Sorry."

It keeps going like that—warning dings, curses, soft apologies—until they finally cross the finish line.

**BEEP!**

A hologram flashes: **18.7**

Lilly slumps in her seat.

Oak just shakes his head in silence. He is sitting on the hood of his genaether.

She lands the genaether next to Oak. "We need a break."

Oak stands with his arms crossed, looking like he'd rather be anywhere else. He shrugs. "It's your loss," he says, sarcasm dripping from every word.

Lilly tries to ignore him.

"Are we taking a break?" Kwi-Li asks.

Lilly is fuming—frustrated, embarrassed, and fed up with Oak's impatience. "Why can't you just do this like other gatis?" she snaps. The words leave her mouth before she can stop them—and she regrets them instantly.

**Chirp.**

**BLINK!**

Kwi-Li vanishes.

"Great." Lilly drops her head, heart sinking. She wants to take it all back.

Oak lets out a long sigh. "Alright. Let's call it a day. We'll try again tomorrow. Let's park them," he says, nodding toward her genaether, and getting into his.

Lilly doesn't reply. She just lifts off, rising with the genaether.

The Circle of Challenge sinks below her. So does the junkyard wall surrounding Carnel's place. She turns toward the Royal Gesh Genaether tower.

The anubis ring is completely stripped now. Robotic ants scurry around inside its exposed core, working on something deep within the ring's mechanics.

Lilly slows, mid-flight. Something catches her eye.

On the far side of the Anubis ring, there's movement along the wall of Phi Guya. She leans forward for a better look. "Hey!" she yells.

Oak stops beside her, hovering.

On the other side of the wall, Lilly spots it—clearly—a ripple in the air.

A diablopero. It paces back and forth, nose to the barrier, like it's searching for a way in.

"Diablopero!" Lilly shouts. She launches her genaether forward like a rocket, aiming for the wall's outer perimeter.

"No!" Oak yells behind her.

# Chapter 113
### Lilly Reacts

As soon as Lilly breaches the perimeter, an alarm blares. **WHEE-HOO! WHEE-HOO! WHEE-HOO!**

On and on and on, it screams.

She blasts through the barrier like a breath held too long—bursting from thick, wet heat into a world that punishes her lungs the second she arrives. Warmth vanishes in a blink, ripped away by wind so sharp it feels like shattered glass slicing across her skin.

The world outside slams into her like a frosted fist.

It howls over the open white—a screaming emptiness that claws at her clothes and stabs through every seam.

Before her stretches a vast, frozen nothing. A white so pure it hurts to look at. Snow rolls endlessly in every direction, untouched and ocean-wide, swallowing the horizon. The sky above presses down like steel—no sun, no color, just a slab of lead crushing her down.

Lilly barely hears the alarm or feels the cold. She's locked on her target.

The diablopero.

It's bigger than she remembers—blacker than nightmare shadows. Its jaws look wide enough to crush a car. And those eyes—Lilly knows—they kill.

It hasn't seen her yet.

All she can think about is Seri dying. Her missing father. Her mother's smiling face in old pictures. Her heart beats—not from fear, but from sheer, terrifying purpose.

She dives straight at the diablopero.

It lifts its head just in time, sidestepping her bulleting genaether.

Lilly barely catches the blur of a claw slicing through the air.

Something slams the back of her genaether.

She and the machine spiral out mid-air.

Wind slashes her face like needles. Her eyes blur with tears that freeze on her lashes. The air stabs her lungs, each breath like inhaling broken glass. Her chest seizes under the weight of the cold.

Then, Oak dives his genaether at the monster.

But this time, the dog-machine is ready.

It swipes.

**SMACK!**

Oak and his craft go tumbling—a blur of motion crashing toward the dome wall.

He flips over and over like a mannequin flung from a speeding car across a frozen lake.

His genaether cartwheels through the air, smashing apart with every brutal impact against the dome.

Oak lands hard and fumbles in the snow. On his knees, he digs blindly through the icy white, searching. His vok is gone—flung from its holster. Snowy crystal dust buries it fast.

Lilly banks around, arcing hard.

But it's too late.

The diablopero is already charging—galloping toward Oak like death in motion.

Lilly pushes her genaether hard, thinking only one word:

**Fast. Fast. Fast.**

The machine surges forward like a rocket beneath her.

Wind stabs her face and carves down her arms. Her thin shirt does nothing. The cold cuts straight through.

She aims right for the monster.

At the last moment—mid-leap above Oak—her genaether slams into the diablopero.

**CRUNCH!**

Genaether, Lilly, and the black beast crash in a chaotic mess—flipping, smashing, scattering through the snow.

Lilly tumbles over the curved roof of the barrier. "Oomph!" She finally stops rolling—an eternity later. She lies still, stunned, the cold slapping her back to focus.

She blinks.

The diablopero—its massive shape—turns toward her.

Then—

**BLINK!**

**BLINK!**

**BLINK!**

Royal Gesh and their gatis appear out of nowhere.

The diablopero freezes. Pauses. Then—**BLINK!**—it vanishes.

Vishot is suddenly in her face. "You've put the whole facility in jeopardy! You won't spend one more day wearing that navok! Both of you are completely reckless and a danger to everyone here!"

His face is flushed bright blue with rage.

# Chapter 114

"Oak had nothing to do with it! He was just trying to stop me!" Lilly blurts out. Her teeth chatter. Her body shakes—from cold, adrenaline, or both.

"You both breached the barrier. Against the rules! You are both going to be gone!"

Yin and Yang — Voks in hand.

Terco and several other Royal Gesh stand in ready stance, weapons drawn.

**BLINK!**

Aubrin appears.

Vishot grabs Lilly's Vok from behind her back holster. "You are both gone. Done! Over with!" He stabs a finger in the air at Lilly and Oak. If his finger were a knife, it would've cut deep.

"That's enough, Ist-Er Vishot. I will be the one dispensing disciplinary action, should it be appropriate." Aubrin walks calmly up to Lilly and grabs her armband.

Lilly thinks it's over.

But Aubrin gives her navok a single swipe.

In an instant, a bubble of warmth surrounds her—like stepping into a warm shower after freezing rain.

Aubrin steps over to Vishot and takes Lilly's vok from his hand.

Vishot doesn't look like he wants to give it up. "They broke the rules! They put us all in danger!" His eyes dart to Lilly's vok, and his hand slices the air in Oak and Lilly's direction like he wants to erase them on the spot.

"It wasn't Oak's fault, Iyengar. It was me! Oak came out to stop me—and save me—after I broke the rules," Lilly protests.

Aubrin looks between Lilly and Oak with curiosity, a flicker of concern in his eyes. "You did break the rules. But first, we will find out why the diablopero was on top of the barrier in the first place."

"Their childhood recklessness has no place in the Royal Gesh—let alone in this facility! Their alnahi may have let an enemy noxiar into this facility. They have put everyone here in danger. By the rules of the Royal Gesh, they have committed Alnahi-Soch," Vishot spits.

Aubrin turns sharply. "Treason? That is going a bit far, do you not think, Ist-Er Vishot? I will deal with this."

Vishot hesitates, like he wants to shout *no*, but then doubles down. "By the law of the Royal Khem Gesh, I am invoking a Kwan-Jusalon on both of these traitors to the Royal Khem Gesh!"

Concern flashes in Aubrin's face, but he holds composure. He pauses, studying Vishot. "That is your right as a Royal Gesh." Aubrin's jaw tightens. "By the laws of the Royal Khem Gesh, I, as the Royal Iyengar, must comply with your request." He places his fist against his chest and gives a slight bow.

Vishot's anger slithers into something smug—like a snake finding easy prey. He returns the bow, fist to chest, a sly nod playing across his face.

"As per the laws, the Royal Iyengar will set the time of the Kwan-Jusalon. Until then, they are still under my command."

Vishot suddenly looks like he's lost sight of his prize. A flicker of doubt surfaces through the hate.

Oak turns ghost-pale.

Lilly's head swims with confusion.

Aubrin holds a firm gaze on Vishot. "At this moment, I need you to go down to the Anubis and extract data from a rogue Iar Haro and I intercepted. It was attempting to dismantle the power supply and remove it." Aubrin's tone sharpens into authority. "We need to figure out why—as soon as possible."

Vishot looks like he wants to object, but wisely thinks better of it. He and his gati vanish.

"Ist-Ba Haoyu, Ist-Wu Tao, Ist-Ju Shu-Zhen—search every bit of this facility. Make sure there are no canker iars that got in." Aubrin says to the two nearest Royal gesh.

Robotic ants crawl out from the dome surface, scattering through the snow as they begin clearing the shattered genaether pieces.

Oak steps up beside Lilly, his face still white as ice. "Lilly was just protecting Phi Guya, Iyengar Aubrin. She saved me, too."

Aubrin stands tall, a thoughtful look clouding his face. "The rules were pretty clear about not breaching the dome."

"Yes, sir," Lilly says, eyes dropping to the ground.

"Yes, sir," Oak echoes, deflating like a balloon pricked by reality—his hope leaking out by the second.

Aubrin locks eyes with Oak. "Despite my position, I cannot deny Vishot his right to a Kwan-Jusalon. Any Royal Gesh can demand it."

"Yes, Royal Iyengar. I understand." Oak extends his vok, trembling, like he's handing over a beloved pet to be given away.

Lilly glances between the two, desperate for something—anything—that makes sense.

A tiny smile creeps onto Aubrin's otherwise stone-set face. "But I can delay it. You better hang on to that, Royal Gesh Trainer Oak."

Oak's face lights up—like hope just found a pulse.

"You're going to need it to keep training Ist-Kee Lilly here." Aubrin jerks his thumb toward her, the edges of a grin tugging at his lips.

Lilly stares, blinking in confusion.

Oak gives her a look—part disbelief, part joy, part *we're not dead yet*.

"Sir, I don't understand. What is Ist-Er Vishot demanding?" Lilly asks, eyes bouncing between Oak and Aubrin.

Aubrin nods toward Oak, passing the baton for bad news.

Oak hesitates, then finds the words. "He's demanding a circle of judgment—to remove you from the Royal Gesh and banish us both for life from this facility. From everything to do with the Gesh."

Aubrin lifts his chin, standing taller, his voice laced with assurance. "It is a formality, not a finality. It will not pass—as long as I am here." He offers a small, encouraging smile to both of them. "I assume from now on, instead of trying to protect this facility on your own, you'll call for help first?"

"Yes, sir." Lilly accepts her vok with both hands.

"Yes, sir," Oak adds, glancing at Lilly with one raised brow and a cautious, relieved grin.

# Chapter 115
### A Long Way to Go

"All right. Come on back. Do it again. You weren't any faster. I told you—swing faster."

Oak stands at the beginning of the Warufang challenge, arms crossed, completely unharmed and annoyingly safe.

Lilly has just finished the course, again. She's bent at the hips, hands braced on her knees, breathing like she just ran up five flights of stairs. Her hygee nurse numbs the last of four fresh welts on her legs.

"I *did* swing fast! They're learning or something—adjusting!" she pants.

The hologram timer above her flashes **17.4** in bright, brutal letters.

Lilly groans the second she sees it.

Her nurse spider scuttles across her cheek, its sticky little legs tickling her skin.

She swats and misses. "Stop. I'm fine."

The shiny spider hops onto her head, just out of reach. It's getting better at dodging her. It starts creeping again, zeroing in on the welt near her jaw.

"Stop, or I'll have Zak repurpose you to pick bugs in the garden."

The spider freezes, folds its legs, and rolls off her head like it's playing dead in a school play.

Lilly catches it mid-fall.

"Giggle! Giggle."

Nafari sits in the stands, whispering to Rasht. The two look utterly thrilled by Lilly's swollen face and arms.

Lilly walks slowly back to the starting point, doing her best to hide the limp caused by the throbbing welts on her legs.

"I need a break," she mutters when she's close enough that no one else can hear.

"One more time." Oak's face is pure stone. "Terco's time on the Warufang challenge is 14.3—on his worst day. You've got a way to go."

"It's hard to concentrate with the peanut gallery up there." Lilly jerks a thumb toward Nafari and Rasht.

Oak glances up. "Well, entertainment is in short supply with us still on lockdown. You're the best show they've had in weeks." A smirk edges onto his face.

Nafari and Rasht aren't the only ones watching. At least a dozen others dot the stands.

"Listen, Lill—we need to compensate for your smaller size. If you can't hit harder, you need to be faster."

"I *am* swinging faster." Lilly plants a hand on her hip, then shoots him a sideways glance. "Hey. You called me Lill."

Oak stammers, the blue in his cheeks deepening like a storm cloud. "I… I… uh… meant *Lilly Bug*."

Lilly smirks, satisfied.

"Again!" Oak snaps, trying to bury his blush beneath a layer of command.

"Oh, just give up. You're not meant for the Royal Gesh— either of you." The words come like a hiss from a reptile disguised as a human.

Lilly and Oak turn.

Nafari has come down from the stands.

Rasht trails behind her, looking ready for blood—but not exactly sure what blood is.

Oak tenses, fists balling at his sides.

Lilly steps between him and Nafari. "Beat it, Nafari." Her tone is flat as steel.

"My daddy's on the Phi World Council, like I told you before. He says you're both as good as gone after the Kwan-Jusalon." She sneers with glee.

Lilly doesn't flinch. "Let me explain this in crayon-eating terms for you. Aubrin's in charge here. And we're both staying."

Nafari's face twitches like the insult hit a nerve. "It won't matter. He says the Phi World Council has all but decided to hand this poorly run place over to Bainian control at the next Unity. You'll both be gone then anyway."

She turns to leave, then has to yank Rasht by the arm to drag her along.

Rasht still looks like she's trying to figure out what a crayon is.

"Ignore her," Lilly says flatly.

Oak exhales, the tension draining from his shoulders as he watches Nafari and her sidekick stomp away.

He pivots back to business. "Again," he says to Lilly.

Lilly sighs deeply. She pulls her vok from the holster on her back and thinks *sword*.

The vok glows to life.

She does that neck-flex thing—rolling her head side to side like she's trying to shake the doubt loose.

"Ready…" she mutters, instantly regretting the word.

# Chapter 116
## Glum News and Glum Expressions

Several tables over, a woman watches the news on her navok. A serious-looking newscaster floats above it, face tight with concern, warning of doom and gloom across the universe.

"In breaking news, the Phi World Council is reportedly facing mounting pressure from several influential Phisian Realms to reconsider Seairland's longstanding authority over Earth's Phi Guya Program. At the forefront of this movement is Baines' controversial leader, Mensche Morder, who has issued unverified claims suggesting that Phi itself may be at risk due to what he describes as ongoing leadership failures within both Phi Guya and the Realm of Seairland."

So, what's new? Lilly thinks. "News is the same no matter where in the universe. Scare the viewer with horrible news so they keep watching," she mutters just before taking her first bite of lunch.

"Seriously? Pineapple and ham pizza again?" Oak sputters in disbelief.

It's obvious to Lilly that he's rattled by the news; they can all overhear. He's probably just pretending none of it's real—like everyone else.

"Hey! Don't insult a spiritual moment."

Lilly's favorite pizza floats onto the table on a hover tray. Steam lifts from the golden circle of perfection, the aroma hitting her so hard it's almost dizzying. She yanks a slice free—cheese stretching in gooey strings the way it's supposed to. She points the slice toward Oak's weird stack of food.

"Look who's talking. Who in the entire universe gets pancakes for lunch?" She jabs back and bites into her slice of happiness.

"Would you two stop arguing? I can't hear myself think," Zak grumbles, mid-devour on a towering sub sandwich.

"You're not supposed to be thinking. You're supposed to be eating," Lilly says between bites. "Besides, eating calms me down."

Zak pushes his glasses up the bridge of his nose. "It's this whole spy thing that's bothering me. Somebody—someone in this facility—is either in a position to see everything or has some high-tech way to spy. They are getting real-time data, all the way to Phi."

"Uh huh… we have a spy among us." Lilly hums the words like a tune. She's sort of listening, but also seriously into her pizza therapy.

Her armband gives a slight 'chirp.'

Zak leans in, flicks a few swipes on her navok—and freezes. "Huhhh!" he blurts.

"Don't interrupt my pizza ritual with more bad news," Lilly says, doing her best to eat one-handed.

"No. No bad news. Just… interesting." Zak glances at Oak, then back at the screen.

Oak doesn't stop eating either. Maybe it's therapy for him, too.

"Lilly, did you know you have a power indicator on your navok? It has eight different categories."

"News to me." She takes another bite, still smiling at her pizza.

*Chirp.*

"It makes that sound all the time." She adds.

Zak blinks behind his glasses. "One of them just went up again." His face scrunches in concentration. "Why? Hmmm… It's almost like you're gaining and losing power with certain actions."

"It looks pretty serious with the Phi World Council," Oak says quietly, his tone shifting.

"Someone's behind all this. We need to find them."

"Pfft!" Oak sputters at her. "What can we do? Seriously?"

Zak's eyes flick between them, concern rising.

"We're not useless. And we don't have to follow all the rules," Lilly says, her voice sharper than she meant. That helpless feeling is bubbling up again.

Oak turns a brighter shade of blue. "If we *did* follow the rules, we wouldn't always be in trouble." His face contorts in regret the second the words leave his mouth.

Movement beside the table cuts off the tension.

"Oak, I hope you do your best to stay out of trouble today." Sorrel looms over them, apron dusted in flour, face lined with concern.

Oak nods without looking up.

"There's a strong possibility the Phi World Council will vote to remove Seairland's control of Phi Guya. That means we're all done here. We need to keep our heads down." His voice isn't angry—just honest.

"Yes, sir," Oak mutters, still avoiding Lilly's eyes.

# Chapter 117
## Blasted Crow!

"That was better. A little bit," Lilly says, though she doesn't believe it. She stores her vok in the back holster.

The hologram above reads **16.1**.

It's dark at the Circle of Challenge. There are no spectators this late.

"You were able to stop a few with your thought," Oak says. "Maybe just try harder that way?"

"There are just too many. When I focus on a few and stop them, the others just swoop in faster."

Oak yawns. "Maybe we can keep this to one hour every night from now on." His eyes look half-closed. "I think better when I get my sleep."

"Sorry. Really. It's just—I think better when nobody is watching."

"Well, you better get used to people watching. When you do the challenge, the stands will be full."

Kwi-Li skips beside Lilly as they head toward the market. "Can you buy me a balloon tomorrow?"

"We'll see," Lilly replies.

*CAW! CAW!*

A crow shrieks from above as they pass underneath. It's perched on one of the storage containers between Carnel's and the Anubis.

Even in the dark, there's a faint glow around it.

"Crows don't come out at night," Lilly says slowly, stopping cold to make sense of what she's seeing.

Her instincts snap. She spins, reaches behind her back, and flings out her vok. The word *BLAST* rushes into her mind the instant she points it.

A ball of light bursts from the vok's tip—strikes the crow—then explodes in a crack of feathers and sparks.

The bird slams upward in a convulsion. It seems to pause going up, and then drops to the ground.

"What the!?" Oak ducks, hands over his head. If he was half-asleep before, he's wide awake now.

A lump of black twitches and sparks on the ground.

"It's a spy aether! How'd you know?" Oak sputters.

Lilly smirks as she holsters her vok. "For one thing, crows don't come out at night. And for certain, they don't glow."

"Someone should take a look at this," Oak says, crouching beside the ruined machine. "Might have data on who's been spying on us."

A trail of smoke curls upward from the crow's center. Feathers drift down around them like black flakes from a factory smokestack.

"Kwi-Li, can you put this on Zak's workbench, please?"

"Ah!"

"Please?" Lilly pleads. "Then come right back."

She grabs the crow by a wing and hands it to Kwi-Li.

*Blink!*

Kwi-Li vanishes.

*Blink!*

In the next instant, Kwi-Li reappears, brushing off clinging feathers. No crow in sight.

"Fastest gati in town," Lilly says to Oak, lifting an eyebrow like she's issuing a challenge.

Kwi-Li stands taller, puffing out its chest.

"Too bad Kwi-Li can't do the Warufang challenge for you," Oak jokes.

"You're funny," Lilly replies, giving him her best fake death-stare.

Oak smirks. He's immune. It's a superpower of his.

*Ding! Ding!* A soft chime echoes from the dome above.

"Oh! The rain cycle's starting." Oak taps his armband. A shimmering half-bubble appears over him.

The rain starts immediately.

It pours down in a steady stream, soaking the stadium, the walkways, and Lilly.

"What? It rains *in* here?" she shouts, blinking as water runs down her face. Her clothes are already soaked.

Oak glances over at her, half-asleep and perfectly dry. "Think the words *'rain shield on'* to turn yours on."

Lilly does.

In an instant, a translucent dome materializes above her. She watches the rain strike its surface and slide away, leaving her completely dry inside her little bubble.

"Amazing! Now *this* I can use!" she announces.

She steps carefully now, avoiding the streams and puddles building on the ground.

Kwi-Li, of course, is hopping and skipping happily beside her, jumping in every puddle—loving every second of getting soaked.

# Chapter 118
### Night Time At Phi Guya

They pass the Anubis.

The ants don't seem to be getting wet. It isn't raining over that one spot. In the core, a steady procession of them carries out what looks like burned glass wires. Other ants march in with new ones, weaving back and forth in tireless lines. They're working straight through the night.

"How much time do we have if they take over?" Lilly asks, pausing in the dark rain to watch the repair work.

"When this is finished," Oak says, eyes on the moving swarm. "They'll push for the next full moon. This'll be done by then. Dad says that's the plan. The Council's still tied, so it has to go for another vote."

A long silence settles between them.

They stand there in the rain, in the dark. Hope feels like it's slowly washing away.

Lilly shrugs it off, straightening her shoulders. She needs to steer the conversation somewhere else.

"You'd think the dome would stop the rain everywhere," she says.

"They make it rain on purpose," Oak mutters. "Living plants still gotta grow. Here, it makes more sense to rain at night than during the day."

He sounds like he'd give anything to be in bed instead of walking through dark, wet corridors.

When they reach the market, it's a hollowed, darkened shell.

Stalls slump like broken ribs, soaked with rain. Water clings to the empty shelves. Price tags curl at the edges, abandoned—nothing left to label.

Where crowds once pulsed, shadows now linger. Long. Whispering.

Rain slicks the cobblestones, turning them into rippling mirrors of blackness. Their footsteps echo like intrusions, each one swallowed by wet shadows.

The place doesn't feel empty. It feels ended.

Only wet bones remain.

As they walk through the deserted market, Lilly hears a low murmur of voices coming from the Swig-N-Swill up ahead.

Passing in front of the tavern, she glimpses three people at the bar. Each sit slumped over a tall glass of amber liquid, elbows on the counter, eyes on their drinks, not moving.

At a table by himself, Terco leans in close to the head and shoulders of a hologram man glowing above his armband. He talks in low hushes. Lilly figures its probably family—someone trying to console him after losing the love of his life.

Behind the bar, she's sure the same expressionless man stands in the same spot. Same stained apron. Same grimy towel. Same dull stare as before.

He's still wiping the same dirty glass.

When they reach the entrance to Lilly's new home, she stops and turns to Kwi-Li.

"Okay. Come on. Pocket check. You know the routine."

"Ah!" Kwi-Li groans.

"Come on now, we talked about this. Bugs, beetles, and frogs stay outside. They need to go home to sleep, too."

Lilly holds out her hand, ready to collect whatever living treasures Kwi-Li tries to smuggle in.

# Chapter 119

### Attack in the Junk Yard

"**I** don't know. I haven't heard from him all day. He's still not answering," Lilly says, trying again to reach Zak through her armband.

"He's probably working on the crow drone—too focused to notice his messages."

Oak, Lilly, and Kwi-Li enter Carnel's junkyard.

Nothing moves. There's no clatter of tools or muttering from Carnel—none of the usual signs of work. Only faint music hums through the air.

They round a towering stack of discarded parts, and something startles Lilly into a full sprint.

Zak lies face down on the ground. Not moving.

"Zak!" Lilly drops to one knee and shakes him.

Zak groans.

She turns him over. A thin trickle of blood runs down the side of his face, starting somewhere beneath his hair.

Just then, Riz rounds the corner. A clear bubble around her head pulses with music, her blond ponytail bouncing to the beat. Her eyes go wide. She drops the machine part in her hands and sprints toward them.

"Zap-man!" she yells.

"Mmmm," Zak moans, eyes fluttering open.

"Are you okay? What happened?" Lilly stammers, panicked.

Her spider nurse crawls out of her pocket and scurries up Zak's leg.

"Attack… robot… Carnel…" Zak slurs.

The hygee nurse perches on Zak's head, one leg touching the spot where blood trickles from his scalp.

Zak's eyes keep blinking. His mouth moves, but his words are broken.

"You're not making any sense," Lilly says, her voice shaking.

"Come on. Let's get him to Willow," Oak says, bending to hook an arm under Zak's shoulders.

But Zak grabs Oak's wrist, eyes wide. "It took Carnel!"

"What did?" Riz asks.

A sharp rattle erupts from the junk pile beside them.

They all turn.

A black mass of gangly arms and legs leaps from the shadows—straight at them.

Zak and Riz are the closest.

The thing crashes into Riz. She hits the ground hard.

She kicks and claws at it, her hands scrabbling for something to grip, but the robot clamps around her throat.

It twitches violently, vibrating like its malfunctioning, while a metallic growl snarls from deep inside it—raw and feral.

Oak is on the robot in a flash. He grabs at its frame, trying to rip it off Riz, but the two just writhe together—too tightly bound.

He strains, muscles bulging. "Too strong!" Oak gasps.

"Move!" Lilly barks, yanking her vok from behind her back.

Oak sees the weapon pointed and dives aside.

Lilly thinks *EMP BLAST.*

From the tip of her vok, a pulsing ball of static fires—strikes the robot square in the side.

The robot locks up—limbs straight out, convulsing in place like it's being electrocuted.

Riz shoves it off and rolls away, coughing and gasping. Her hands claw at her throat as she kneels, wheezing for breath.

The robot goes still. As lifeless as a toppled streetlamp.

Everyone pauses. Breathing hard.

Zak staggers to his feet, sways, then drops back to one knee. He fumbles with the robot's head.

"Zak! Stay back. It might not be dead," Lilly warns, weapon raised.

"Gotta get its memory core…" He doesn't finish.

The robot's hand snaps upward—clamps around Zak's throat.

Its other hand raises a jagged metal shard, pressing it to Zak's temple.

Lilly points her vok.

"Stop! Or he dies!" a metallic voice commands.

There's no mouth. The voice echoes from somewhere deep inside the machine's frame.

Lilly freezes.

"Lilly Dubois," the robot garbles, its voice built from many—cut and pasted, guttural and eerie. "Surrender… to… us, and your…

father… and the repairman… will be spared. Do not… both… will die. And you will… never find… your mother. You have until… the next full moon."

Then the robot releases Zak, falls backward, and begins to shake violently.

*Beep! BEep! BEEp! BEEP!*

"Everybody back! Now!" Zak shouts.

They all leap away in a tangle of limbs and panic.

*KABOOM!*

The robot's head detonates.

# Chapter 120
## No New Clues

They lie scattered on the ground, the five of them—like groceries dropped in a panic.

Luckily, none of them are broken open like eggs.

Lilly's ears ring like church bells. Zak's mouth moves, but his voice is a distant mumble. His face—just glasses—is way too close.

"Lilly! Are you all right!?"

Finally—words that make sense.

Lilly nods. Her eyeballs feel like they've been shaken loose.

*BLINK!*

*BLINK!*

*BLINK!*

Royal gesh appear out of thin air, gati by their sides.

Suddenly, there are enough Royal gesh to start a soccer team. Every one of them has a vok drawn, ready to blast anything that moves.

"Everyone okay?" Aubrin asks, vok out and sweeping. "Anyone hurt?"

Lilly shakes her head no. She hasn't found her words yet.

Kwi-Li tries to grab her hand. Lilly brushes it away.

Yin and Yan stand in ready stance, their voks out, shielding the group from any further attack.

"Carnel! They took Carnel," Zak blurts, choking on the words. "He fought hard but... he's..."

"Life-threatening?" Aubrin asks.

"I... I... I don't know. He was bleeding pretty badly."

"Who, Zak? Who did this?"

"Three noxiars. Level 7. Modified. They were armed with voks and had a gati with them. But…" Zak stops.

"What, Zak?"

"They just kept hitting him. He fought back, but…" Zak's eyes swim, and he wipes his nose. "But…" Some thought short-circuits his voice.

"What, Zak?"

"It looked modified, the gati. It had an electro-mechanical shunt of some sort."

Aubrin raises an eyebrow.

Lilly places a hand on Zak's shoulder. She can feel how shaken he is. "Try non-geek-speak, Zap-man," she says softly.

Zak blinks fast, scrambling for simpler words. "It looked like it had an external virus clamp. Something was probably corrupting its data—controlling it."

Aubrin frowns at the thought. "Ist-San Yin and Yan—see if you can trace any electro-magnetic trail. I know it's slight, but we've got to try."

*BLINK! BLINK!* Yin and Yan vanish with their gatis.

"Shang Terco," Aubrin orders, "investigate access and escape. I want to know how they got in and out without triggering the alarm."

Terco hesitates, like the thought takes a second to catch up. He brushes his perfect blond hair to one side. Then—*BLINK!*—he's gone.

"Ist-Ba Haoyu, Ist-Wu Tao, Ist-Ju Shu-Zhen—search every bit of this repair yard. Make sure there are no more rogue machines," Aubrin says, then walks toward the carcass of the smoldering robot.

It's all arms and legs, gangly like it was stitched together from different robots. Dirt smears its joints like camouflage, like it had been burrowed into the nastiest of junk piles. Where its head used to be—

just a shredded stump. Like a pimple popped too hard. Just no messy puss.

"Probably set to self-destruct. Would you agree, Zak?" Aubrin asks, nudging it with his foot.

"Yes, sir. But there's more you should know."

Zak explains what the robot said before it self-destructed—and tells him about the crow drone Lilly shot down.

"So... there's no data—nothing retrievable—from either one?" Aubrin asks, brows furrowed in thought.

Zak glances at Lilly, then back at Aubrin. "Not from their memory cores. Too much damage, sir."

Aubrin's expression shifts. He doesn't even have to ask—he can already see where Zak's mind is headed.

"There may be trace particles left on the robot, the iar," Zak says. "I can scan the surface for pollen, detritus, and soil residue. That data can be cross-referenced with known soil compositions and local flora profiles. That could narrow down where the iar—and the crow drone—have been before they got here."

Zak says it flatly, pushing up his glasses as he locks eyes with Aubrin.

Oak stands with his mouth open like Zak just transformed into a genius.

Both Lilly and Riz glance at Zak—proud.

Lilly's pride becomes overshadowed by concern when she realises how worried and worn Zak looks.

If anyone has just aged ten years in one day, it's him.

# Chapter 121
## All Seems Lost

"I know you're upset, Zak. Carnel told me how well you two were getting along. We can find someone else to do those scans," Aubrin offers gently.

"No, sir. I know what to do. Plus, I want to help. I can't just sit around worrying. About him. About both of them." Zak glances at Lilly, his face locked with sheer determination.

"When can you get me those results, Zak?"

Zak looks down at the robot remains. "Within five tags, sir."

"The sooner, the better," Aubrin adds before his gati *blinks* him away.

Lilly, Oak, Zak, Riz, and Kwi-Li just stand there. No one moves. No one speaks.

"Zak, what can I do to help?" Lilly offers.

"Nothing. I got it," Zak says flatly. He doesn't even look at her.

He swipes his navok, and a floating Porto-Jo zips around the corner. Zak nods, a silent cue Riz seems to understand.

Without a word, she steps in and helps load the robot onto the carrier.

"I'm sorry, Zak. This is my fault. The robot probably got in when I breached the dome. Your friend is hurt because of me." Lilly's voice wavers.

Zak doesn't answer. His silence screams louder than words. *Of course, it's your fault.* That's what it feels like he's thinking.

"He's more than a friend," Zak finally says. "He's like the father I never had. He…" Zak stops. His face says the rest. Words he doesn't want to say are bleeding through.

"I'm sorry. It is all my fault." Lilly mutters. She bites her lip and turns away.

"No, Lill! Wait! That's not what I meant—"

But she doesn't stop.

She runs. Leaving behind all the harm she's caused.

If there were people in the market, Lilly's sure they would have parted like she was a disease they didn't want to catch.

She trudges between the empty stalls, shoulders slumped, eyes low. Her footsteps echo through the whispering shadows. It feels like everything she's doing wrong has piled onto her back and is dragging her down.

She feels Kwi-Li's hand brush against hers—and she pushes it away.

"Can you buy me a balloon?" the robot asks. The question sounds like it's not meant to be answered. Just... needed.

"We'll see," Lilly replies. Just words. Empty air.

In the hallway to her room, Baba bumps into her foot, redirects, and scampers off. Lilly doesn't even lift her foot.

Three-legged Ajax follows behind. "Bark! Bark! Bark!"

Lilly flops onto her bed like forgotten laundry—crumpled, heavy, not worth folding. Even her clothes feel too heavy.

She hears Kwi-Li's feet shuffle across the floor—each step dragging.

"You don't like me, do you?"

Lilly turns her face just enough to see Kwi-Li staring at the floor. "That's not true."

"But... you hardly ever hold my hand. And you never buy me a balloon. You always say 'we'll see.' But you never do."

"It's just... everything's going wrong. I can't do anything right. So many people are getting hurt because of me."

"We can do this. We're a good team." The words come out like a whisper wrapped in the kind of hope only little kids have—for Santa, or the Easter Bunny.

"No. We're not. We can't even do the first of the Royal Challenges. You're a broken-down robot who can't even fly through an obstacle course. And me? I'm a reckless girl who just makes everything worse. I'm not a Royal Gesh. I'm not the Ohmuno. And I'm not your mother. I get people hurt, kidnapped—everything around me blown up. We're the last two who should ever be together."

Lilly's words hang in the room like smoke—thick and choking.

Kwi-Li doesn't answer.

The silence hurts. It's like watching someone bleed without seeing any blood. Whatever little flicker of hope kept the gati standing seems to vanish through an invisible wound.

Kwi-Li sags to the floor.

Lilly hears a soft scuffling beneath the bed.

"I didn't mean that…"

Silence.

"I'm sorry, Kwi-Li. Please."

But Kwi-Li doesn't just go quiet. It's like the robot folds in on itself, crumples up like a note someone's thrown away.

Lilly buries her face in the covers, wishing tears would come and wash everything away.

Sleep comes instead.

# Chapter 122
## No Kwi-Li

When Lilly wakes in the middle of the night, the smell of rain and darkness reaches in—tiptoeing, hesitant.

Silence echoes off the walls.

Regret is the first emotion. It hits like a flood. She regrets everything—including what she said to Kwi-Li.

Lilly's heart flutters. "Kwi-Li?"

The words vanish into corners where the light doesn't reach.

It's the kind of silence that follows bad news—heavy, unmoving, final.

She looks under the bed.

Empty.

Even the dust bunnies seem to have packed their bags—wanting nothing to do with Lilly.

"Kwi-Li, where are you?" Lilly says aloud... and screams inside her mind.

Only her echo answers—blended with the sound of rain, soaking the blackness outside.

It's exactly how Lilly feels.

Phi Guya is crying rain.

Lilly taps her wristband and calls Oak.

A sleepy-eyed hologram of Oak appears above her armband. "Wha…?"

"Have you seen Kwi-Li?"

Oak's eyes fumble for meaning. "Hmm… no."

She swipes him away and calls Zak.

A hologram of Zak's head appears, wearing his eyeglass contraption. "Lill?"

"Have you seen Kwi-Li?"

Confusion floods Zak's face. He shakes his hologram head: no. He leans in, eyes full of something unspoken. "Listen, Lilly-D, I wa—"

She cuts him off.

Panic takes over. Fast.

She doesn't change clothes, doesn't think—just runs straight into the rain.

She skips the rain shield. Maybe she wants it. Wants the downpour to wash away her regrets.

By the time she passes the field, the rain soaks clean through to her skin. She keeps running—heading for Yuchii's cabin.

Her hair clings to her scalp like glue when she crosses the bridge into the forest.

And there he is.

Yuchii stands motionless in the rain, in front of his tiny home—as if he's been waiting, or heard her coming from far away.

The tall, hairy mountain of a being is stooped slightly. His arms hang long—too long. His eyes sit deep beneath a heavy brow.

"Have you seen Kwi-Li?" Lilly asks, voice trembling, rain dripping from her face.

The giant doesn't answer. He just turns and heads into the cabin behind him.

Lilly follows.

Shadows fold around her as she enters. The walls are bundles of tightly packed sticks. A candlelight flickers against the wall, its glow dancing like it's trying to hold back the dark.

A fire smoulders from a rock platform, a kettle hanging over it.

Yuchii motions for her to sit in a chair made of bent saplings.

Lilly slumps into it. More like melts.

She's handed an earthenware cup of steaming tea, massive. It is like she is an infant holding a hot cocoa mug. A thick blanket drops over her shoulders.

Maybe it's the tea. Maybe it's the shadows. Or maybe it's just Yuchii—quiet, steady, listening.

But Lilly lets it all out.

She tells him everything.

About snapping at Kwi-Li. About Carnel. About the diablopero attacking Oak. About how it's all gone wrong. Right back to the beginning—when her dad was kidnapped because of her.

The story lasts as long as the tea.

Yuchii listens the whole time—about as still and thoughtful as her friend Bob, the tree.

When she finishes, she feels lighter. Not fixed. But ready.

They stand outside Yuchii's hut.

The rain has stopped. Mist weaves through the trees. Morning light begins to stretch in and touch the fog.

Yuchii stands still, twice Lilly's height.

She steps forward and hugs him.

His fur smells like pine cones, earth, and wet dog.

"Thank you. For listening. I know what to do now."

Yuchii pats her on the back. Then turns and disappears into his cabin—quiet as ever.

# **Chapter 123**

## Unpleasant Decisions are Made

The café is filled with staring eyes from every table—except one.

Lilly's table sits empty. No Oak. No Zak. No Kwi-Li

Then her armband buzzes.

Zak's head flickers into view above her wrist, his hologram faint and jumpy.

"Where are you?" Lilly asks, facing his distracted image.

"We're at the junkyard. Meet us there," Zak says flatly, then disappears.

Lilly's mind storms. Zak doesn't sound friendly. Her imagination kicks into overdrive, spinning worst-case scenes like a broken projector. Still, she knows exactly what she needs to say when she gets there.

She rounds a tall pile of equipment.

Oak, Riz, and Zak stand with arms crossed, locked in serious discussion in front of something large under a tarp. Their conversation dies the instant they see her.

Lilly's eyes catch on the red, blue, and purple bruises blooming around Riz's neck.

"There's something I need to say," Lilly blurts.

All eyes turn to her.

"I know you're mad at me. You have a right to be. I'm sorry for the trouble I've caused. It's all my fault. Everything I do leads to destruction. People get hurt. My mom was kidnapped. Seri is dead, trying to save me. Our house was destroyed because I wouldn't listen to Terco. My father and Carnel were taken, because of me. My friends keep getting attacked because I let in an enemy robot. And now Kwi-Li is missing, because I am horrible to be around. I don't belong here. I don't fit in. This—" she lifts her wrist "—doesn't belong on me."

She stares at her royal navok bracelet. "Terco, Vishot, and even annoying Nafarii are right. I'm a danger. I need to give this back. Everyone would be better off if my brain were just wiped and I surrendered. That's what I've decided."

Oak, Zak, and Riz exchange glances.

"We're always mad at you," Zak says with a smirk. "What's new? Trouble seems to find you, Lilly-D."

"You could've been killed yesterday. Because of me."

"No," Riz steps forward, her voice raspy, raw. Words scrape from her bruised throat. "That's …not true. We're alive … because of you."

Everyone nods.

"You're not the one hurting people," Oak adds. "And this isn't just about you."

Lilly shakes her head. "I don't know why Seri picked me to be a Royal Gesh—let alone that Aubrin allowed it. I'm just Lilly."

Riz tucks a rebellious blond strand under her cap, her eyes searching. "You have …some skills, Lilly. We …believe in …you. All of …us."

More nods.

Zak raises his arm. "You need to see this." He swipes his Navok. "This was found in the ancient Phi database."

Above Zak's wrist appears a glowing image—Lilly's exact birthmark, the same one on her necklace.

"This is the mark of the Ohmuno. Your mark."

"So? It's just a deformity."

Zak shakes his head. "It's more than that."

"No, this is nothing. It's just a birthmark—a coincidence."

Zak looks at her over his eyeglass device. "Really? That's your explanation?" He swipes again. "Then explain this."

"This simple dot is the Phisian symbol for the number one—Life-force and Sun. It means all three, in one. It's part of what's on your hand."

"A dot with a triangle under it is the symbol for a person, also part of your so-called birthmark. Does it look familiar? It's also on your necklace."

"This is the Phi symbol for Ohm, three arrows pointing in three different directions. It means everywhere, everything, and all the time. You say it's nothing? More coincidences? This, circle over two triangles, is the symbol for power—*shak* in Phisian."

"And here, all together. This is the identical symbol that you call a deformity, a coincidence. It's the symbol for the all-powerful one, who holds the power of the entire universe, everywhere, all the time. It's the symbol of the Ohmuno."

"Zak. Really? This isn't you. This is stuff of Phi fairy tales, not science."

"Okay. True. But it got on your palm somehow. That is science. If that doesn't convince you—listen."

Zak leans in. "You are the only one who can see the shimmer of a gatiar. The only one who can see a glow around Phi tech. No one else can. You are special, somehow."

"No. No, I'm not anything special. I'm just a silly girl. I need to stop this before someone else gets hurt."

Zak looks wounded by her words.

"I believe in you, Lilly," Oak says. "There's something …unique about you."

Lilly shakes her head. "First impressions are always right. Yours was that I was too small to be a Royal Gesh. You were right."

Oak looks hurt.

"I've got something …that belongs …to you," Riz says, her voice rough and broken as she pulls back the tarp. They've all been standing around.

Underneath is Lilly's repaired Royal Gesh Genaether.

It looks like love and care went into restoring it—like it's been brought back to life.

"This is yours. This belongs to a Royal Gesh. It was Seri's, and she gave it to you for a reason—just like your navok, and your vok. Seri believed in you. I believe in you."

Lilly's voice cracks. "That belongs to someone else. Anyone but me."

Riz steps closer, her bruised throat barely pushing the words out. "You are …the Ohmuno, Lilly. I know it. And we need …you— now more than …ever. We've all decided …to team up, to …support you."

Lilly looks into Riz's eyes. "You're wrong. You're all wrong."

She turns and walks away, tears rising.

Zak, Oak, and Riz stand speechless.

# Chapter 124
## "Where have You Been!?"

Lilly runs—free of everything behind her, going nowhere fast.

In the middle of the open field, she collides head-on with Kwi-Li, who's sprinting straight toward her.

Relief slams into her like a tidal wave.

She throws her arms around the little robot, hugging tight—folding into the moment like air is finally filling her lungs again.

Then, she snaps into full parent mode.

She holds the gati at arm's length, dropping to one knee so she can look the little face straight in the eyes.

"Where have you *been*? I thought you were dead—or hurt, or taken, or gone. Or like… You left me. I mean… I'd understand if you did…"

Kwi-Li looks wounded, like someone just stepped on the gati's heart and left it bleeding on the ground—but the words burst out faster than the pain. "We need to go!"

"Where?" Lilly asks.

"To the place of everywhere. Pax Thay is waiting." Kwi-Li tugs urgently on Lilly's arm.

"Wait. Who is Pax Thay?"

"One of the creators! A Noah! One of the architects! One of my makers! One of the ancient ones—the one who chose *you!*" Kwi-Li sputters, voice bubbling with the excitement of a child about to reveal the best treasure ever.

# Chapter 125
### Lilly's Protection Team

It's then that Lilly notices Aubrin standing back, waiting. He's in full battle uniform—wearing his vok pack, face set with sheer determination.

His gati stands beside him, motionless, expressionless, ready.

"Kwi-Li came and got me, for good reason," Aubrin states calmly, his voice controlled and focused.

"Sir?"

"You'll need to step outside the dome for Kwi-Li to geennii the two of you to your location. That will be dangerous. We'll be your escort." Aubrin motions toward the anubis.

Off in the distance, Lilly spots three Royal Gesh—ready and waiting.

Haro stands beside her genaether.

Yin and Yang are on foot, each with a gati.

They walk together to the base of the dome's entrance. Haro is already on her genaether, tightening her vok harness.

Yin and Yan stand nearby, voks out—alert and ready for anything.

"Do I need my vok and pack?" Lilly asks. She's still in her t-shirt and jeans—unwilling to trade away their comfort just yet.

"According to Kwi-Li, it's an 'arrive as you are' party," Aubrin says with a small smile, feet planted wide, vok resting at his side.

Kwi-Li nods eagerly. The robot's red hat bobs up and down like a flag at the start of a race.

"It's only the outside perimeter of the dome where you're in danger," Aubrin adds. "Once you geennii, you'll be somewhere else. Somewhere safe."

"Okay," Lilly says. "But… are you coming with us?"

Aubrin's head shifts slightly—*no*. "Regrettably, no. I'd love to meet the Noahs. I have so many questions. But according to Kwi-Li, only the Ohmuno is allowed. It's a strictly enforced law."

Butterflies bounce in Lilly's stomach.

Aubrin must notice her nervousness. He places a hand on her shoulder. "You'll be fine, Lilly."

She nods, and then feels Kwi-Li's small hand slip into hers. She looks over.

"You have to hold my hand," Kwi-Li says, like it's something they were told *not* to do—but they're doing it anyway.

Lilly feels the rush of everything she's done wrong. "Kwi-Li… I… uhm… We'll talk about this later."

Aubrin gives her a warm smile. "Ready? We'll create a brief opening. You can geennii up to it. It'll be cold momentarily. It will be so short, you won't notice. Then you'll geennii from there."

Lilly nods. "Yes."

Aubrin taps his chest. His protective shields shimmer around him.

He speaks into his armband. "Go."

Haro and her genaether shoot upward.

*BLINK! BLINK!* Yin and Yang vanish.

*BLINK!* Aubrin disappears.

*BLINK!*

In a flash, the towering form of the anubis above Lilly and Kwi-Li is replaced by cold, frozen eternity.

Haro hovers above them.

Yin, Yang, and Aubrin form a circle around Lilly and Kwi-Li— voks out, ready for anything.

"You've got this," Aubrin says, with the smile of a proud parent sending a child off to school for the first time.

In a blink, the world changes.

Lilly steps into a sun-warmed forest.

It draws her in—not with force, but with the quiet pull of something that has always been waiting.

The air shifts. Warmer. Softer. It brushes her cheeks like gentle fingers, tucking hair behind her ear.

Above her, tall black spruce and tamarack lean inward, their branches draped in lichen that sways like veils in a breathless breeze. Shafts of light pierce the canopy in golden threads, like the forest is stitching her into its quiet heart.

The moss beneath her feet gives without protest. No snap of twig. No startled rustle. Just a hush so deep it feels like she's being held.

She pauses.

For the first time in many days, nothing feels scary.

It feels safe.

Here, no one asks who she's supposed to be. No one tells her to be stronger, or more, or less. The forest doesn't demand. It receives. And it wraps around her like a mother's arms—steady, knowing, and infinite.

"We're supposed to wait here," Kwi-Li says, looking around for something—or someone—to arrive.

# Chapter 126
## The Noah called Pax Thay

Lilly stands, breathing in everything that surrounds her.

The scent of pine, earth, and rain seeps into her lungs. It feels like breathing for the first time.

Somewhere above, a birdsong begins—a slightly louder "woo-hoo…," followed by three soft, trailing notes, "…hoo-hoo-hoo." A mourning dove. Not warning. Singing. A song of hope… and new beginnings.

Lilly blinks hard—not from fear or cold—but because something inside her is breaking open… quietly.

This place hasn't just accepted her. It's been *saving her space*.

"Hello, Lilly," a voice says. It echoes from the forest—or maybe from her mind.

Lilly turns.

"I am Pax Thay."

Before her stands a presence without weight, yet full of shape. A person—woven from light. Shimmering. Radiant. Alive with understanding. Its form is neither male nor female, yet both. A perfect balance.

It's as if harmony itself has stepped forward, and peace has taken form.

"Pax Thay!" Kwi-Li bursts into a run.

"Hello, beautiful," the being of light giggles, arms open wide.

Kwi-Li runs straight into the open arms—straight *through* them.

The gati slips into Pax Thay like diving into sunlight.

Kwi-Li spins in the embrace of light.

Both Pax Thay and Kwi-Li laugh in perfect harmony.

The light forming Pax Thay pulses gently, like a living thought. It's warm and inviting, like morning sunshine sneaking in through a window. The air itself feels quieter now—light and breath weaving into one another.

"Do it again! Do the butterfly thing again!" Kwi-Li laughs.

"All right," Pax Thay replies. "This time, see how many you can catch."

Pax Thay waves a hand above Kwi-Li.

In its wake: monarch butterflies. Dozens.

They flit and dance just beyond reach, weaving around saplings and tree trunks. Kwi-Li darts after them, laughing in zig-zags.

Pax Thay turns toward Lilly.

The eyes—if they could be called eyes—hold depths of knowing.

Lilly feels drawn to look, not because she's told to, but because something in her *wants* to.

To meet this gaze is to feel eternal mercy, to feel seen—fully, entirely, and without judgment.

"Namaste," Pax Thay says, bowing.

Lilly hesitates. Should she bow? Curtsy? Shake hands?

"I... I don't understand," she says.

Pax Thay laughs softly.

A breeze stirs the trees. Leaves flutter like the hands of a grand auditorium clapping in slow motion.

"Thank you for your intent to show respect," the voice says—not from Pax Thay's mouth, but from within Lilly's mind, spoken in the exact tone she most needs to hear.

"It is the same as the word *Namaste*. Different societies offer slight variations. But when I use it, I mean: 'The universe within me sees the universe within you.'"

Lilly blinks. "How can I hear you without you speaking?"

"The same way you speak with Kwi-Li. We are one universe, in unity. You and Kwi-Li are also one."

Lilly lowers her eyes, feeling the weight of her failures. "I don't seem to do good with Kwi-Li. I don't know how to take care of a child. You two... You understand each other."

She glances toward the trees. Kwi-Li is still dancing after the butterflies, joy rising with each leap.

"You take care of your father." The being of light reminds Lilly

Lilly nods. "He is my father. He needs help."

"It is the same with Kwi-Li. You only need to accept people as they are—and listen," Pax Thay says. "We are all in different places in our lives. Kwi-Li is still dealing with the trauma of losing someone loved. Similar to your father, but more recent. Because of that, a little more kindness and tenderness are needed."

"You mean... like hold Kwi-Li's hand?"

"Exactly."

Lilly doesn't feel small next to Pax Thay. She feels whole. As if all her confusion, anger, and fear finally had somewhere to rest.

Pax Thay is a mother. A father. Something more. Something infinite. Something kind.

"Kwi-Li said you're the one who chose me, and some people call me the Ohmuno, like I am an all-powerful chosen one. Why? Does that mean I am the Chosen One?" Lilly asks.

Pax Thay nods. 'No and yes,' the answer rings wordlessly inside her.

"You are just a girl, yet I did choose you. The rest is people's imagination.

You see, when life feels random or scary, to some people, it's easier to believe someone special is meant to fix it.

They make up Chosen Ones because they want things to make sense.

It's not about truth—it's about feeling safe.

They turn lucky breaks into signs. They call fear 'fate.'

They want heroes to save them."

"But… why me? I'm just… Lilly. I'm too small to do anything. Let alone be the ultimate Royal Gesh."

# Chapter 127
## Butterfly for Kwi-Li

Pax Thay smiles. "Maybe the real hero isn't the one who's chosen.

Maybe it's the one who chooses to help, even when no one asks. When people see you as the 'Chosen One', it is power. Yet it is intention that is important.  You can either use it as power over them or use it powerfully to help them."

A warmth fills Lilly—like she's just been hugged by the mother she's always wanted.

"Just one of the smallest seeds can change an entire garden," Pax Thay says. "Lilly, you are the smallest seed within the Royal Gesh. The eight lessons you will learn from me: the size of the body does not matter. It will be the size of your connection to the universe, the strength of your conviction, and the sincerity of your intention that will make you all-powerful. Today, you already influence some Noah technology. That is what an Ohmuno can do. With the eight lessons and much practice, you will learn to wield the power of the entire universe unto your will.”

“Are you certain you have the right person?”

“You already are learning to connect to the universe. Yet you do not see it.”

“I can’t even connect with my father. I’m not unique or special.”

Pax Thay smiles. “Lilly, we are all special, all unique, and also—all the same being. You, like Kwi-Li, are different and unique because of your past pain, your past losses, and how you see the world. You are special in the way you already connect with the universe. Not too many people hug and talk with trees... and call them *Bob*. This makes you special.”

“Oh. You know about that?” Lilly blushes slightly, the heat rising in her cheeks.

Pax Thay nods. “Yes.”

“But... how does hugging a tree make me powerful? I’m still too small to complete even the first challenge. I have no power. I mean, I seem to have the ability to get everyone hurt—not save them.”

“You already have power you do not see. The diablopero jumped over you because you told it not to see you.”

Pax Thay’s peace radiates outward—like something that could melt war, hush grief, or calm the fury of the angriest nations.

“Then... why can’t *you* just save my father and Carnel? Why don’t you stop the Cankers—or whoever’s behind them—from doing horrible things?”

“We are not allowed to intervene in a new species’ life conflicts or technology beyond what we’ve already done. It is our law. Humans are still relatively new in this universe. They have much to learn. And they still forget their history.

Every other generation, an Ohmuno—a person destined to become all-powerful—is chosen to reteach the ways of *Uno Khem*. The Ohmuno will learn and then teach others the language of the universe. That person is you, Lilly.

It was almost your mother. But your mother sacrificed herself because she believed *you* were the Ohmuno."

"My mother! Do you know what happened to her? Is she alive?" Lilly's thoughts ignite like lightning.

Pax Thay holds up a glowing hand. "I am not allowed to intervene. I'm sorry, Lilly. But I can tell you… If you choose to accept the path of the Ohmuno, you *will* get your answers—one day.

Do you accept the offer to become the Ohmuno, Lilly?"

Lilly pauses.

It's not that the idea of being all-powerful isn't appealing—it's the weight of her self-doubt that pulls her down like gravity.

"…I do."

Pax Thay reaches out and places a hand on the top of her head.

In that moment, warmth, fresh air, strength, and electricity surge through her at once.

The ground falls away beneath her.

It isn't the feeling of rising—it's the feeling of becoming *one* with the planet. With the land. The air. The water. The sun.

In that moment, in Pax Thay's presence, Lilly *knows*—this being doesn't command the universe.

**It *is* the universe.**

Lilly feels her feet return to the ground as Pax Thay's glowing hand lifts from her head.

"Wow! That was… was…"

"Awesome?" Pax Thay offers.

"Yes," Lilly giggles.

"Are you ready for your first of eight lessons?" Pax Thay smiles. The forest around them seems to smile back.

Lilly nods. "Yes."

"Listen carefully."

Lilly nods again.

"Follow your breath."

There's a long pause.

Lilly waits, expecting something more. But then it hits her. *That* was the lesson.

"I… I don't understand. How is *that* going to help me become all-powerful? How am I supposed to beat anyone bigger than me?

Unless I have, like, *really* bad breath.

You're not going to do that, are you? Give me… superhero bad breath?"

# Chapter 128

## Pax Thay into the Sunrise

Pax Thay laughs out loud. The chuckles roll through the forest, echoed by the wind as tree branches sway with a sudden gust.

"When we follow our breath, we pause our rambling thoughts—thoughts of the past and thoughts of the future. It is stopping these thoughts that allows us to connect with the present moment. *Being present* is the foundation for connecting with the universe—the only way to gain access to all knowledge and all power of the universe."

"OK," Lilly says, a little skeptical.

"Practice the following exercises daily to learn how to follow your breath. Are you ready to hear them?"

Lilly nods.

"Follow your breath for ten breaths. Think of nothing else."

Lilly nods.

"Choose a task, at least once in the day—like brushing your teeth or getting dressed. During this task, think of nothing else but what you are doing."

Lilly nods.

"Walk slowly, paying attention to each step. Do this at least once a day."

Lilly nods again.

"Even a single mindful breath can shift your power... build your presence. Start small, stay consistent, and let presence grow."

"But it's just paying attention to breathing. Not any superpower stuff."

"The Noah technology is designed to respond to the power of the Ohmuno. The more of the eight lessons the Ohmuno can master, the greater their ability to control Noah technology. For now... will you at least trust me that following your breath is the first and most important step in becoming connected to the power of the universe?"

Lilly considers Pax Thay's words. Her mind flashes back to the warufang—stinging her over and over. How can she do that if the only defense she has is following her breath?

Pax Thay smiles. It was as if this being read Lilly's mind. "If I can teach you how to become all-powerful—starting with the warufang—will you believe me, then?"

Lilly nods. "Yes."

"You see, the Circle of Challenges is designed to test the Ohmuno's mastery of the eight lessons—the powerful way of Uno Khem. The first challenge tests your ability to follow your breath."

"Ok. I understand that much."

"Then this is what you are to do the next time you meet the warufang," Pax Thay says—and then tells Lilly exactly how to excel at the first challenge.

Lilly smiles. "I get it. I can do that. Thank you."

"Now, it is time to go and begin your practice. You will need your gati." Pax Thay smiles, beginning to fade—its light dissolving into the sunrise. "Namaste, Lilly."

"But... wait... I have—Namaste," Lilly replies hurriedly, just before Pax Thay is completely not there... and yet *everywhere*.

"I like your hair," Kwi-Li bubbles, skipping beside her.

"Um… thanks," Lilly says, confused where that compliment came from.

*Blink!*

Their surroundings shift instantly—from the perfect old growth of forest to the stark white of eternal snow.

Aubrin is there, feet planted wide, scanning the horizon. Snow swirls around his legs. His body is tense, as if his premonition of danger has triggered high alert.

Haro hovers above them in the pale, cold sky.

Yin and Yang are positioned around Lilly—spread wide, each in full search mode, about to spring at whatever the swirling ice may conceal.

An ear-piercing *"Beep! Beep! Beep!"* slices through the cold air.

It's coming from Lilly's navok.

"We have company!" Haro raises her arm fast, like a cat pouncing on prey. She swipes her navok, revealing a cluster of glowing dots converging on another group of dots.

"Three unidentified approaching our early warning perimeter! They're coming fast! How did they find us?" She pulls her vok from behind her back—it hums to life as it activates.

Aubrin's face remains calm, composed.

In one smooth motion, he slides out his vok from behind him, raises his navok, swipes a few commands, and nods—stone-faced and serious. He lifts his vok, poised to defend.

Lilly glances at Yin and Yang. They shift this way and that— ready for the intruders to come from any direction.

"Take Lilly and evade!" Aubrin shouts the command.

"But…" Haro protests.

"That's an order!" Aubrin barks.

# Chapter 129

The red dots above Haro's armband become a sea of blood red.

"Something's way wrong. There are *many*, many more. Get on!" Haro holds her hand out to Lilly. "We're outnumbered. *Get on now.*"

Her face is etched with calm determination.

Lilly stands wide-eyed, tensed to jump—but not sure where.

Haro keeps her navok arm raised, eyes locked on the dots as they converge. "*Now!*"

For a long moment, the icy land seems to hold its breath.

Then a mechanical *whirring* sound above them.

Three genaethers begin lowering toward the snowy ground nearby. Ice kicks up in spirals, spinning around their legs.

"*Get on! Let's go!*" Haro shouts.

Lilly finds her legs and leaps onto Haro's genaether, yanking Kwi-Li up with her.

"They're here! Hang on tight! This is gonna get *wild!*" Haro yells over the rising noise.

"Yin, Yang—take defense point!" Aubrin commands.

In a single heartbeat, the white tundra becomes a sea of black.

Countless Noxiars swarm from nowhere, writhing like hungry spiders as they surround Aubrin, Yin, and Yang.

Lilly's heart skips more than a beat.

She clamps both hands onto the handles beside her, her knuckles white, as the genaether rockets skyward. Below them, the snow, ice, and swarming machines fall away—along with her breath.

The genaether lurches forward—heading straight toward a sunset of chaos. Blood red bleeding into cold white.

Below, Yin and Yang blast at wave after wave of attacking dark forms.

A grunt echoes from the genaether intercom. It might have been Aubrin.

Haro's genaether shoots straight up. A moment later, it begins to fade—Haro, Lilly, Kwi-Li, and all. Everything turns grainy, then disappears in a ripple of light.

Lilly blinks.

They're in shimmer-space now. Gatiar mode.

Three attackers are fully visible.

Three flying genaethers approach—each carrying massive forms. Fur. Bone. Fungus. Ugliness. All familiar.

Explosions flash from the attackers. Blasts zip over and under Haro and Lilly.

Their genaether rocks violently.

"*Hey!*" Haro yells, as if confronting a wild storm directly.

It's a car crash about to happen—except this one's *intentional.*

Suddenly, all three enemy vehicles explode in bursts of light.

Two blasts overhead. One veers downward into swirly snow below.

"*Hang on!*" Haro commands.

She pushes the genaether forward—fast.

Lilly tightens her grip around the handlebars. She squeezes her legs against the wall to stay in.

Something slams beside Lilly—but doesn't hit her.

A brief static shimmer flashes around her in a perfect sphere.

Something slams into it—then falls away.

The genaether shakes violently—but nothing touches her.

"Domes open! *Time to go!*" Haro shouts again.

Ahead, a swirling cone of sky opens—a tunnel into elsewhere.

With a heartbeat, the shimmer of the dome swallows them whole—Haro, Lilly, Kwi-Li, and the genaether.

Everything violent disappears behind them.


In the next heartbeat, black and white chaos becomes green and noiseless. The only yelling is in Lilly's mind.

Beneath them: the Anubis. And grass—lush and glowing in the synthetic sun.

A collective *"Whew…"* escapes, followed by heavy breathing.

They descend slowly.

The skeletal arch of the anubis ring rises around them as they touch down.

The genaether whines, still revved up.

"*Off! Off!*" Haro yells.

Lilly jumps out.

*Blink! Blink! Blink!*

Multiple Royal Gesh appear, forming a tight perimeter around them.

"*Stand down, Haro,*" Vishot barks.

"They're outnumbered!"

"Too late. They're gone. *Stand down.* That's an order."

Haro's jaw clenches. She looks like she's about to launch back into the sky.

A Royal Gesh Lilly doesn't recognize steps forward and places a firm but kind hand on Haro's shoulder.

"They have Aubrin. Yin and Yang are gone… dead."

"No! …No! …Wait!" Lilly sputters.

Everything around her slows.

People's words melt into mumbles.

Movements drag like they're underwater.

Oak appears—his face twisted with worry.

Lilly collapses into his arms.

She cries until there's nothing left.

And Oak holds her up.

# Chapter 130
## Untouched Chocfee

Zak and Lilly sit at their usual table in the café. Both stare at their plates of uneaten food.

The café is full of people—but few voices rise above a whisper.

"I can't believe they're dead," Lilly says, still staring into her untouched chocfee. "They were protecting me. Yesterday."

"I know. I'm sorry, Lill." Zak pauses heavily. "It wasn't your fault," he adds quickly. "Let me see your navok."

Lilly slides her arm across the table like it weighs a hundred kilos.

Zak does a few swipes. "Hmm… your power's way up from last time. Why?"

Lilly knows he's just trying to change the subject. "Zak. I need your help."

Zak breathes in—and holds it. The pause stretches forever. "To get this off?" he asks finally.

"No," Lilly says. "I need you to help me be the Ohmuno." She looks him straight in the eyes—those troubled, thinking-brown eyes. "I don't like bullies. And I need you to help me stop them."

Zak stares like she just slapped him across the face. Then a crooked, awkward smile starts to form. "Now *that's* the Lilly I know. What can I do?"

"Tell me everything you know about the old ways of the Ohmuno—and my vok and navok."

A wide grin spreads across Zak's face. "Genius-level research coming up."

"More like geek level," Lilly mutters through the ache in her chest.

"Shrimp," Zak fires back.

"Hey, guys," Oak says, slumping into the seat beside Lilly— for the first time. He's always sat across from her before.

Lilly wants to lean in. Just a little. Feel grounded again.

"Our Lilly-D is back," Zak pipes.

Oak's eyes meet hers—and hold, just a moment longer than normal.

Lilly shrugs off the confusing flutter. "Will you help me?"

"Of course I'll help you, Lilly-D," Oak replies, a flash of relief softening his face.

"I want to get these guys who are hurting everybody. Stop them. Get everyone home." Her voice is level. Her face—dead serious.

Oak doesn't even hesitate. "I'm in."

"But I haven't told you my plan."

"I'm in." Oak levels her a look that needs no more words.

A warmth flushes over Lilly. She pushes it down. "Then I'd better tell you both about my time with the Noah, Pax Thay."

"Is that where you got your hair changed?" Oak asks, pointing to her head.

Lilly instinctively lifts her hand to the white streak that now blazes through her light brown hair. It's about three fingers wide, running from root to tip along the left side of her forehead. "I think so. It must've happened when Pax Thay touched me." She tucks it behind her ear.

"I like it," Oak says, awkwardly.

Zak glances between the two of them, eyebrows twitching in mild confusion.

Lilly recounts everything—every detail she can remember about her time with Pax Thay.

Oak and Zak lean in. Listening. Hanging on her every word.

When she finishes, the silence that follows feels thick.

Zak stares off, locked in some deep mental file.

Oak crosses his arms. Eyes fixed on the table. "Wow," he breathes. "So, you are not the Ohmuno. You are not the Chosen One."

A smile plays on Lilly's mouth. "No and yes."

Oaks face scrunches with confusion.

"It is just hype, fanciful belief. But I have been chosen by the Noah's for whatever reason."

Zak is looking just as confused. "So...why do you want help being the Ohhnuno, then?"

Lilly smiles, knowing the exact answer. "Because, as Seri told me, they need me to be. And the Noah's chose me."

Zak shrugs, 'OK, whatever,' and he leans in, all eager. "Do I have loads of questions for them!"

Lilly gives him the eye.

Zak starts tapping on his armband. "Practicing awareness makes sense. The ancient Noah technology may be designed to respond to physiochemical and neurological changes. Practicing awareness could increase gray matter density in the hippocampus—better memory and emotional regulation—"

Lilly laughs silently with Oak. "Zak," she says.

"—the prefrontal cortex would show enhanced thickness and activity. That's linked to executive function, improved focus, and self-awareness—"

Oak smirks. A mischievous gleam flickers in his eyes.

"The amygdala would have reduced volume and activity, which means lower emotional reactivity and reduced anxiety—"

"Zak!"

"Mindfulness reduces cortisol—the stress hormone—so it promotes a calmer physiological state—" Zak sputters, then finally looks up at her.

"*Geek talk done,*" Lilly says flatly.

Zak blinks like someone just flipped the power off to his brain. "Following your breath is good for you?"

"That's better," Lilly says, smiling back.

# Chapter 131


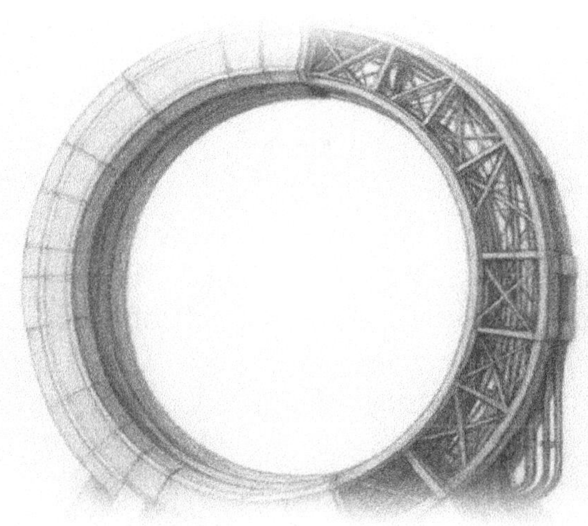

"**I** can't believe how well you're doing... I mean, I can... but—wow! You were amazing," Oak blusters.

The darkness is their secret place now. They walk back from the Circle of Challenges.

"Am I walking slow enough?" Oaks gives her a sideways glance.

"Yes." Lilly smiles. She likes his effort. "It helps my power when I clear my mind and just feel my steps as I walk."

Oak nods, nervous, like a kid learning to ride a bike for the first time.

"Terco's time is still better with the Warwenzi. I lost concentration at the end, even after all the breathing exercises I have been practicing." Lilly counters.

"But you've got this. Almost. If you can do the genaether challenge faster than Terco, you might be able to make up the time."

"Kwi-Li's not ready. The little one's been at Yuchii's all day again." Lilly adjusts her vok into her backpack as they head toward the Anubis. "The death of Yin and Yang was too hard on the tiny Gati, I guess."

"On all of us," Oak adds kindly.

Lilly's armband dings.

She lifts her arm. Zak appears above it. "What's up?"

"I've got a little more on the Ring of Yishi. It's not much. It's like everything's been scrubbed from the databanks."

"Well, give us what you have."

The image of the ring floats up above her navok, same as before.

"All right, you've seen this. But what I found that's new is the meaning behind the symbol. The eye on the Ring of Yishi represents the inner eye of awareness—calm, unblinking, and attuned to the present. It embodies the mindful practice of turning inward with quiet focus, observing thoughts and surroundings without judgment."

"Got it. Thanks, Zap-Man."

Zak nods, then his hologram blinks away.

The anubis ahead is starting to get its outer panels replaced. It's almost repaired.

Robotic ants carry sheets from Carnel's junkyard, marching in leafcutter formation, one behind the other. The large white panels sway back and forth like windblown leaves.

"How much time do we have?" Lilly asks.

"This'll be done just before the next full moon." Oak points at the Anubis as they walk past. "We've got until then."

The movement ahead startles them both. They stop.

"There you are, slinking around in the night!" Vishot spits the words like venom at Lilly.

Terco stands slouched beside him, running a hand through his perfect blond hair.

"We were just out practicing," Lilly says flatly. "There's no rule against that. Yet." She regrets adding the last word, the second it leaves her mouth.

"Insolent. And dressed like a vagrant, as usual." Vishot points a crooked blue finger at Lilly's T-shirt and jeans.

Lilly tenses. Teeth clenched. Fists tight.

Oak grabs her arm, holding her back.

"You've gone on long enough with technology that doesn't belong to you," Vishot snaps, his glare sharp enough to cut steel.

"Aubrin thinks differently." Lilly steps forward, wanting to get in his face.

Oak holds her again.

"Aubrin is gone." A gleam flashes in Vishot's eyes—too bright to be anything but joy. "I'm in charge now. You have until tomorrow to complete the official challenge for your position. If you don't show up, I'll have a Hygee cut that off."

"But you and Haro have the same rank." Again, Lilly regrets it the moment it leaves her lips. Note to self: stop talking.

Vishot is about to burst a vein. He points directly at Lilly's white and gold armband. "If you show up out of uniform, you lose that. If Terco is faster, you lose that."

He turns and storms away.

She can't see his face, but she's sure he's smirking.

Terco stays behind, shifting awkwardly from one foot to the other. "You know it'd be easier on you if you just gave up... I mean... You wouldn't get hurt, and that'd come to me. That's what Seri would have wanted."

Lilly pauses, choosing her words. "Seri gave me this because she believed in me. I don't plan to dishonor her last wishes." Lilly forces a smile. "I appreciate your concern, but I **will** answer your challenge."

# Chapter 132

"I don't know if I can do this," Kwi-Li says.

Lilly and Kwi-Li move carefully through the junk piles at Carnel's, looking for Riz.

Lilly holds the little robot's hand. Kwi-Li isn't skipping—hasn't since the loss of Yin and Yang.

"You don't have to," Lilly says gently. "Maybe Riz can figure out how I can pilot it myself and still be fast enough to win."

Lilly spots the back of Riz first.

Riz is bent over a half-disassembled flying machine, tools scattered around her like puzzle pieces.

"Hey, Riz."

Metal clanks as Riz straightens up. Her face lights up with a smile as soon as she sees them. Faint bruises bloom across her neck in deepening shades. "Howdy, Lilly," she says, brushing a wild lock of blond hair behind her ear. "Hey there, little one. Give me a hug."

She pulls Kwi-Li into a long hug, patting its back. "You doing OK?"

Kwi-Li shrugs, eyes low.

"You're getting your voice back," Lilly notes, relieved.

Riz absently touches her bruised throat, then smiles. "Doing good."

"I need a ride. Can you help, please?" Lilly asks.

The blonde mechanic's face stretches into a full grin, eyes twinkling. She gestures to a shape under a carefully draped cloth. "I was wondering when you'd come by this morning. I've got something waiting for you."

She strides over and peels the cloth away like it's a birthday present. Underneath is Lilly's perfectly reconditioned genaether.

"Try not to smash it up this time, please?" Riz teases.

The gold trim catches the light and scatters it in sparkles. The white surface gleams, blemish-free and brand new.

"Wow. You perform miracles."

Riz laughs—an awkward, hiccup sound that skips past her usual cool. She shrugs one shoulder, mumbling a shy "thanks" barely audible past her grin. Then her eyes sweep over Lilly, as if noticing something missing.

"You'll find I tuned it to match the speed variation of the challenge. Kwi-Li will pick that up right away."

Lilly slides her hands into the front pockets of her jeans. "Slight change of plans—Kwi-Li's having a rough time. Wants to sit this one out."

Riz glances from Lilly to Kwi-Li.

Lilly shrugs. "I'll fly it—same as Terco. He's Shang position. No gati. Probably uses an ardhiar."

Riz finishes wiping her hands on a rag. Concern etches her face as she crouches and rests a hand on the little gati's shoulder.

"It's hard losing someone, isn't it?"

Kwi-Li stares down at its feet. The red hat droops low, hiding its face.

Riz gently straightens the hat, then pats the small shoulder. "When I lost my father, I didn't want to do anything—not even the things I was good at. The best at. Not anything. My favorite thing to do is fly—and I'm the absolute best at it."

Kwi-Li glances up, searching her face. "Really? Like, even more than fixing things?"

Riz nods, her eyes steady. "I didn't understand why I felt that way. I mean—it's my favorite thing. Why wouldn't I want to do it?"

Kwi-Li watches her closely. "Really?"

"I figured out I was believing I wasn't supposed to be happy—because someone I loved so much, wasn't allowed to be happy anymore."

"Me too."

"But you know what I learned?" Riz leans in.

Kwi-Li shakes its head.

"I learned that my father is still with me. Always. He's all around, all the time. I know he loves me, and he'd want me to be happy. He'd want me to do what I love and do it well."

A flicker of hope melts some of the pain from Kwi-Li's face. "Really? Do you think Seri and Yin and Yang are here with me now?"

The gati scans the junkyard, like it might spot something invisible.

"Really." Riz tugs the red hat sideways for fun.

Kwi-Li smiles, the weight lifting. "Well... I love flying. I'm the best at it, too!"

"Then ...do what you love. Because it honors those you love," Riz says as she stands, giving Lilly a quick wink.

"OK. Right. I get it," Kwi-Li says, its voice lighter, touched by relief.

Lilly stands frozen, eyes glassy. She mouths, *Thank you.*

Riz bows in silence, her smile saying *You're welcome.* Then she gives Lilly a slow scan from head to toe.

Lilly's still wearing her favorite T-shirt and jeans.

"I know, I know. I'll wear the suit for the challenge."

Riz nods. "I'll have your genaether there waiting. You go change."

"Thanks," Lilly says with a smile.

"Go get 'em, girl!"

# Chapter 133


## ɣ-⊥

"I don't know. She better get here soon," Oak says, craning his head this way and that from his seat in the stands, scanning for Lilly.

Zak and Riz sit beside him, both looking just as anxious.

"She just has to change. She'll be here," Riz says hopefully.

Down on the ground, Terco stands next to his genaether. His black uniform hugs his athletic frame, but the absence of gold trim makes his intent clear. Arms crossed, chest puffed, he smirks with the calm of a cat already picking which bird won't fly fast enough.

An ardhiar stands beside him, half-round, looking half as smart as any other robot. Probably another reason why Terco wants Lilly's position.

Lilly's genaether sits nearby—tuned and ready.

Vishot stands out on the stadium floor, keeping himself separate, as if standing alone makes him more visible, more grand. His gati is standing motionless beside him.

The stands are full. Not a single empty seat. Word must've spread fast—this is a must-not-miss event. The constant murmur of the crowd builds, excitement rising like the air before a thunderstorm.

Then Lilly steps into the auditorium, Kwi-Li skipping beside her.

Excitement crackles in the crowd. The murmur swells to a roar, like a match striking dry paper.

"She's here!" Zak blurts, pointing at the obvious.

Lilly wears her Royal Gesh uniform—sleek black, body-fitting. The gold trim glistens under the stadium lights. On her shoulder, Seri's former symbol now belongs to her: the Phisian emblem for seventh. She's surprised how comfortable the uniform feels, how naturally it fits.

Kwi-Li sports blue jean suspenders, overalls and a red baseball cap—the signature look of Kwi-Li. The little gati hops and skips beside Lilly, humming a tune like everything's right again.

A wave of laughter bubbles through the stands—maybe they're not used to seeing a Royal gati with that much personal style.

Terco watches, disappointment flickering across his face—but confidence remains rooted deep.

As Lilly moves closer, Vishots gati slams a fist against its chest in salute.

Vishot glares down at it, his eyes like knives.

He shifts his glare to sneer at Lilly with a look of disapproval—he didn't expect her to show. With a swipe of his armband, he stands straight and official, ready to announce.

The crowd quiets into silence.

"By the ancient code of Kinrik Khem Gesh," Vishot calls, "Shang Terco challenges Ist-kee Lilly Edelweiss Dubois, for her Royal Gesh position. The one challenged has chosen the 1st Circle of Challenges. The challenger leads by example. The challenged shall follow—or fall."

He turns deliberately with each line, making sure the entire stadium hears every word.

"It is a two-part challenge of genaether flying—by iar—and the Warufang challenge. Points deducted for boundary breaches. The best time wins."

Terco smirks as he and his ardhiar take position on their genaether. Together, they rise into a hover just before the first loop.

The crowd's eyes lift to follow them.

Terco rolls his neck with a practiced head tilt, loosening up.

*BEEP!* The start alarm sounds.

The hologram timer above begins its countdown.

His genaether blasts forward like a bullet from a gun.

He tears through the course like a computer-guided missile, slipping cleanly through each glowing ring with surgical precision.

*BEEP!* The buzzer sounds again—done.


The timer flashes:

### 9.9

Terco lands beside Lilly, his eyes darting to her armband like a snake watching its prey. He beams. His best time yet.

Lilly kneels beside Kwi-Li and adjusts the gati's red cap. "We can do this," she says, looking right into its eyes.

Kwi-Li nods. "Do you want me not to hum?"

"I want you to do your best. You hum your heart out if that helps."

"OK," the little one says, then hugs her tight.

Lilly hugs back, holding on just a moment longer.

Another ripple of laughter rolls through the crowd.

At the starting line, Lilly tries to relax her hands, but her knuckles are white around the grip bars.

*BEEP!* The buzzer sounds.

There's a pause—a breath—

Then her genaether launches forward into the first lit loop.

# Chapter 134


Kwi-Li hums some tune inside Lilly's head.
On the third loop, they strike the side of the ring.
*DING!* echoes out.
"Sorry," Kwi-Li says in Lilly's head.
"Don't worry about it," Lilly replies.
*DING!* again, on the eighth loop.
"Sorry."
"Don't worry about it."
*BEEP!* sounds as they pass through the final loop.
The hologram timer above flashes:


**10.1**


A rumble rolls through the crowd.
Terco beams, smiling widely.
Vishot doesn't hold back—he laughs out loud.
Lilly catches sight of Nafari and Rasht in the stands. They exchange a low-key fist bump.
"Sorry," Kwi-Li says again. "All I could think about was Seri and me crashing after we were hit. The humming helps."
"You did good, Kwi-Li. I'm proud of you." And Lilly means every word.
Terco begins the Warufang challenge with his chin up, chest out, vok drawn and ready. He sweeps his blond hair aside like he's posing for the cover of a glossy magazine.

The robotic wasps dive in from every direction. Terco spins, dodging and striking like a practiced martial artist. His movements are clean—fluid.

But several wasps sting him from behind when he's mid-strike in the opposite direction.

The swarm is relentless. Their wings surge together, forming a single pulsing storm of motion and sound. The breeze they create tosses Terco's golden locks in every direction.

Still, Terco and his vok are impressive—strike, move, strike, move.

*BEEP!* The timer locks in:

**14.1**

— his best time yet. Again.

Applause rumbles through the crowd.

Terco strolls back to the starting point, waving to the spectators like he just saved the planet. He takes a grand, self-important bow, then flashes Lilly the grin of a cat that's just eaten the canary.

Beep! Beep!

Suddenly, Lilly's armband startles her.

She raises it to see Oak's face way too close.

"You need 13.8 here to beat Terco."

Lilly gives Oak the eye. "I know. Not only am I height efficient, I am also math capable. Stop distracting me."

A slight smile breaks Oak's nervous expression before Lilly clicks him off.

Lilly takes a deep breath and steps forward.

She stands at the starting line—vok holstered on her back, feet apart. A whole storm of butterflies swirls in her belly. She breathes deep, calming them. In her mind, she replays everything Pax Thay ever told her. Everything she's practiced. Day after day.

She inhales—a long breath. She calmly ties her hair into a ponytail.

*BEEP!* The timer starts.

Lilly doesn't draw her vok.

Instead, she tucks her white hair streak behind her ear. A reminder.

Then takes a step forward.

The crowd bursts into laughter. Fingers point. Some can't stop themselves from whispering about her doom.

The Warufang swarm lifts into the air. The buzz of a thousand wings washes toward her like a crashing tide. It's powerful.

Lilly exhales.

Step.

The wind direction shifts. It flows inward toward the swarm—lighter now. The cluster of wasps hovers, uncertain.

The laughter dies.

Hair not caught in her ponytail floats outward in the breeze. Her white streak waves like a flag of defiance.

Lilly inhales again.

Step.

The wind surges backward over her, stronger now. The swarm stays put, hovering in one tight pack. They don't break formation.

She breathes out.

Step.

The breeze softens again, pushing gently toward the swarm.

Breathe in.

Step.

Eight steps.

The swarm never moves.

They remain at their starting position.

*BEEP!* The hologram timer above the stadium flashes:

**8.0**

Eight steps. Eight millitags. A new record.

The entire stadium falls silent.

You could hear Terco's jaw hit the floor.

Then, somewhere in the crowd, a single word rises from the hush: *"Ohmuno."*

It multiplies.

It spreads.

Then, the entire stadium erupts.

The roar of applause is thunderous—echoing across all of Phi Guya.

Lilly walks calmly back to the starting point, smiling.

Kwi-Li runs straight into her arms and jumps up.

"We did it!" the little gati cries.

"We did it!" Lilly echoes, holding tight.

# Chapter 135

## Balloons for Kwi-Li

"We're a good team."

"Of course we are." Lilly hugs the little gati tight.

By the time Lilly reaches the beginning of the maze, Oak, Zak, Riz, and others are already there. The moment explodes into pure mayhem—slaps on her back, cheers in her ears, voices overlapping. She can't even tell who's touching her. It's a blur of celebration.

Lilly glances up toward the stands—and finds Haro.

Haro places a left fist to her chest and bows low toward Lilly. Her grin stretches wide.

Lilly returns the gesture with a bow of her own.

Vishot, Rasht, Nafari, and Terco don't bow. They just frown, brows wrinkled in confusion like their brains haven't caught up to what just happened.

Lilly sets Kwi-Li down—and is immediately wrapped in a massive bear hug by Oak. She doesn't resist.

Oak steps back, grinning like his face can't contain it. "You were amazing!"

"Let's celebrate!" Zak shouts.

"Pizza!" someone yells.

Lilly holds up a hand.

The excitement fades into puzzled silence.

"Now that this silliness is over," she says, her voice strong, "we need to focus on what we need to do."

Oak's grin fades into full attention.

So does everyone else's.

"These terrorists need to be stopped. My dad, Aubrin, and Carnel need to come back safely. And it *can* be done. I might be crazy, but I'm no fool. I'm too small, too unskilled to do it alone. And I know we have a spy—I don't know who to trust." She sweeps her hand across the group. "But I trust *us*. I know that if we use all our skills and work together, we can do this. We can do it *without* hurting anyone else. We're going to get everyone back."

Zak nods, serious. "Count me in."

"It means we break some rules," Lilly cautions.

"That's rebel talk. Good thing I'm a rebel," Riz says, grinning.

"Where you go, I go," Oak states solidly.

Zak glances at Oak—then quickly looks away.

A faint smile curls at the edge of Riz's mouth.

Lilly doesn't notice. "Listen... this will be more than breaking a few rules. It will be dangerous. I understand if any of you want nothing to do with it. You can bow out—that's fine."

She looks around at all the faces.

Every one of them is set. Determined. No one says a word.

"Then we're all in agreement."

Nods all around.

Oak's face lights up. "Wow. I'm going to break some rules. It feels kind of... exciting. *Good.* So *that's* what you feel like all the time, Lilly-D."

Laughter breaks out.

Lilly elbows Oak.

"Let's meet at the junkyard. We need to come up with a plan," Zak says. "I've got the perfect workspace—private, secure."

"Can we get our pizza delivered there?" Lilly jokes.

"For the *Ohmuno*, we can," Oak replies with a grin.

Everyone laughs again.

"Let's meet there."

Curious faces all around.

Lilly nods. An explanation is needed.

"I want to squeeze a power-walk in."

"You mean your breathing exercises, Pax Thay gave you?" Riz gives her a questioning glance.

"They work...really. I have been doing all the exercises. I notice a big difference." Lilly stood firm. "I will meet you guys there. Plus, there's something important I need to do first."

Lilly turns to Kwi-Li, kneeling so they're eye to eye. "Come on. Let's go buy you a balloon to celebrate."

Kwi-Li lights up. "Both green and blue?"

"Sure. Your favorite colors. One of each. Let's go—just you and me."

Lilly stands and offers her hand.

They walk off together toward the market, side by side, with Kwi-Li happily skipping along—hand in hand with Lilly.

# Chapter 136
## Café News

The café hums with chaos — spoons clink, steam hisses, chairs scrape, and conversations overlap like radio static.

Lilly, Kwi-Li, Zak, and Oak sit together at their usual table.

Kwi-Li colors a sketch with bright pencil crayons. The little gati sits beside Lilly, feet swinging to a tune — humming in stereo inside Kwi-Li and Lilly's heads. The red cap rests off to one side, one suspender strap sliding off its shoulder. It looks like any normal six-year-old drawing with crayons — except for a few key details: Kwi-Li is drawing faster than a human eye can follow, and the picture is a flawless copy of a famous, priceless painting.

Oh, right — and Kwi-Li is a Royal Gati robot.

Spot, the robot marble, zips back and forth on the tabletop, darting between coffee cups like its doing laps.

"You're being quiet, Lilly-D." Zak breaks the silence at the table.

"Yeah, I am doing my Ten Breaths Exercise," Lilly replies.

"Here?" Zak looks around, shocked, like Lilly is giving away all her secret powers to anyone who is watching.

"Yeah, why not? No one can tell. They just think I am quiet." She takes another bite of her pizza with a smile and a wink.

Lilly leans in. "Listen, guys. Kwi-Li is getting memory back."

Everyone who hears her goes still.

The table beside them falls quiet, their laughter tapering off like they've caught a strange scent in the air — something overheard, not coffee.

Zak's mouth opens to speak.

Lilly grabs his arm before the words can come. She tilts her head toward the quiet table beside them. Her eyes say, *not here.*

Oak leans closer, lowering his voice. "This would be easier if we had a clue who the spy is."

Zak nods, sealing his lips like they've been super-glued.

Several tables over, Lilly spots a hologram playing above someone's armband — Phi News. She leans to get a better view. "Hey, that's the guy Terco was talking to!" she says, flicking a thumb toward the glowing projection.

The man is bald as a cue ball, his skin blue, his eyes a pale, piercing yellow. Towering and over-muscled, he stares outward with cold intensity.

"I am the most modified human on Phi. If anyone can bring order to the disgracefully run Royal Gesh, it's me."

"When?" Oak asks.

"When we walked past the bar. Some nights ago," Lilly replies.

"You sure?"

"Yes. I'd recognize those eyes anywhere."

A commentator cuts in. "The Phi World Council has unanimously voted to transfer control of Phi Guya from Seairland to Baine. This is despite the mysterious death of the previous Banian president. It will reopen under Banian control."

"That guy is one nasty, mean, crazy lunatic — if you knew everything he's done and tried to do," Oak blurts, not holding back. "He makes robots specifically to kill people. He is the one who designed and built the diablopero, during the Great Robot War. He kidnaps and kills anyone and everyone in his way. He kills leaders who only wanted peace, and even starts fake rebellions just to blame those who oppose him. He says it's about 'purity' or 'destiny,' but really, he just wants to wreck everything—locking people up in camps, turning them into robots with no minds of their own. He is even believed to be working on a bomb that could wipe out whole worlds. And the worst part? No matter how many times he gets stopped, he always comes back, even meaner and scarier than before."

Mensch Morder speaks again. "My newly formed party will investigate the death of this bumbling leader and overhaul the disgraced Royal Khem Gesh of Seairland. The Naquee Rabb Party will find those responsible. I am now the Supreme Leader of Baine. The law and the will of the Supreme Leader are one."

"Plus, that's the same voice from the robot that attacked Riz. I'm positive," Lilly adds.

"Right! Knowing him, he probably threatened families on the World Council," Oak mutters. "It terrifies me that someone so consumed by cruelty still schemes in the dark, waiting for his moment to strike again. If we don't stand together against him, there may be nothing left to stand for.

The café buzzes around them — silverware clinking, cups clattering, a burst of laughter from a corner booth.

Lilly lowers her voice. "And guess who's from Baine and lined up to take over the New Order of Bainian Gesh?"

"Vishot."

"Right." Lilly glances sideways — a corner table of teens is trying to pretend they're not listening, but their glances give them away. "Let's save this for our meeting place. I want Riz's spin on it."

They get ready to leave.

Lilly helps Kwi-Li pack up the crayons. "Nice job, Kwi-Li."

Kwi-Li shrugs. "It's called *Parc Monceau*. It's really pretty, but it doesn't feel as exciting or full of feelings as some of Monet's later paintings."

Oak catches Lilly's eye and smirks, trying not to laugh.

Lilly ignores him, sending a small smile back with her eyes. "You invited Riz to breakfast, didn't you?" she asks Zak.

"Yeah."

"And?"

Zak shrugs. "She said something about her mom wanting her to eat at home."

# Chapter 137

It isn't official. It isn't pretty. But it's theirs — a room, a fort, and a place to plan everything that matters.

They're in their chosen spots, inside their junkyard meeting place

— courtesy of Zak.

Oak sits on a cargo crate.

Riz lounges in a busted genaether seat.

Zak spins slowly in a too-loose swivel chair.

Lilly prefers the rounded head of what used to be half a drone.

"I want to call this place the War Room," Oak offers.

There are nods — but not all around.

"No. Sorry," Lilly says plainly. She brushes her streak of white hair behind her ear, like a good luck charm. "After my experience with Pax Thay, I realize we're more about unity and togetherness than war and divisiveness."

More nods — firmer this time.

"Then how about *The Nexus*?" Zak suggests. "It means a meeting point where everything — and everyone — comes together."

Lilly smiles. She lets the word sink in. "I like it."

*This* time, there are nods all around.

"Let's get to it then. Who's the spy?" Riz asks.

"I think it's Vishot. He hates Aubrin. He wants me gone," Lilly says, adding to the growing list.

"You're safe as long as Haro is here," Riz points out. "She has the same rank as Vishot."

"So far, Vishot is my best guess. But like it matters — next full moon, we're all done if we don't solve this before then."

"I don't know, Lilly-D... just because Vishot is Bainian—" Oak stops. Regret flashes across his face the second the words escape.

The Nexus looks welded together from scraps — because it is. Tucked in a corner of the junkyard, shielded by old alloy panels and half-dead machinery. Shelves line the walls, packed with blinking orbs, cracked visors, and wires that twitch at random.

"It's not because he's Bainian," Lilly snaps. "It's because he's hateful. He's horrible."

A low table sits at the center — an upside-down porto-jo, scratched with grease, snack crumbs, circuit bits, and the occasional sketch.

Kwi-Li is busy at the table, setting up an obstacle course for Spot, the marble-shaped robot.

"Show them what you showed me," Lilly says gently.

Kwi-Li shrugs. "OK." The gati pockets Spot and steps forward. With a quick swipe, a grainy hologram blinks to life — someone's pant leg.

It hovers in the air — a tight black uniform. Hands adjust the camera. The image wobbles. The leg shifts aside. Then the view lifts, showing forest floor dropping away… then treetops.

"Go back to the pant leg."

The image reverses, zooms in.

"Freeze."

The image locks.

"See? Whoever's setting up the Crow Drone is from the Royal Gesh."

"That's it?" Riz asks.

"That's all we've got," Lilly says. "Thanks, Kwi-Li."

"Not much to work with."

"But it narrows it down. The spy's a Royal Gesh."

Nods all around.

"Makes sense. Who else could control a diablopero?" Oak adds.

"How about Terco?" Oak offers.

"Naw. No." Riz shakes her head. "That would mean he had something to do with Seri's death — his fiancée. No one's that creepy."

"OK. What do we have on the Ring of Yishi? It could help us if we find it first." Lilly turns to Zak.

"I'm sorry, not much, Lill," Zak says, frustration edging into his voice. "Someone's deliberately keeping it hidden. I did find one obscure note — it said the ring was given for safekeeping to a neutral, trusted realm."

"Seairland?" Lilly guesses.

"No idea."

"So, Lilly completed the First Challenge. Where's the ring?" Oak asks.

Zak shrugs. "No idea."

There's a pause.

Everyone goes quiet, thinking.

Zak jumps up like lightning struck his brain. He rushes to the workbench at the back. Tools, half-finished gadgets, and blinking tech are scattered everywhere. Sparks dance from live circuits.

He returns holding a golf-ball-sized device. "New and improved!" He grins, handing it to Lilly like it's a birthday gift.

It drops into her palm — rough and lumpy, just like before.

"For...?" Lilly asks, clearly uneasy.

"Way more power now," Zak beams. "Just lob it and it sticks. Underside's best — weakest point."

"For...?" she repeats, more pointed.

Zak blinks. "For the diablopero, of course! Next time you see it. Listen, its scales make it impervious to EMP…but…if the EMP burst is delivered right through, from surface to surface, the intensity of transmission is greatly intensified."

Lilly raises her eyebrows. "You want me to wait until the most lethal weapon in the universe is charging me, then dive under, *tickle its belly,* and stick this golf ball on?"

Zak shrugs. "Yeah, in theory."

"Oh, goody. Can't wait to see if it works... in *reality,*" Lilly mutters, dread tightening her jaw.

*BEEP! BEEP!*

An alarm slices through the moment.

Zak points. "Your navok."

Lilly raises her armband. A holographic image rises above it — and she nearly flinches.

Gasps fill the Nexus.

Floating above her wrist is the very real, very live image of the leader of Baine — **Mensch Morder.**

# Chapter 138



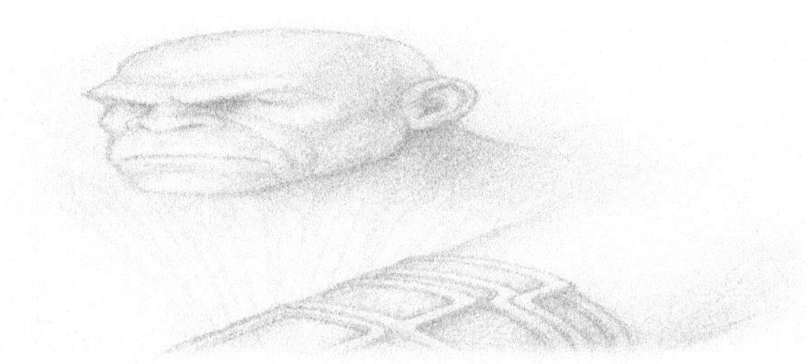

Being this close to Lilly feels like getting slapped in the face. She freezes, mouth open.

The man in front of her is part human — but mostly something else. Extensive genetic modifications have left his face closer to a blue gorilla than anything human. He's bald, broad-shouldered, with muscles so exaggerated they look sculpted by something unnatural.

"We have your father. And your leader, Aubrin. We have your Fixer, Carnel."

His voice is more growl than speech — a low, gravelly rumble, like a bear that learned how to talk.

Pale yellow eyes bore into Lilly's soul as he leans closer, and for a moment, it felt like they might stab her.

Lilly leans away.

"All will die, just like your two clone Royal Gesh, if you do not surrender yourself. On the new moon, bring the power cube of the anubis. Tell no one. We will tell you where to go on that day."

Then the terrifying man blinks away — gone.

The room goes silent.

It's the kind of silence that makes your ears ring. Like everyone forgot how to move.

Forgot how to speak.

All at once.

# Chapter 139
### Out of Time

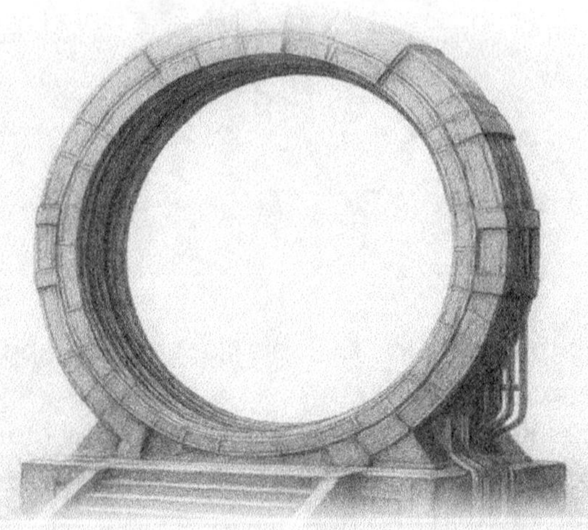

"Okay, but... what if it doesn't work somehow?"

Lilly knows it's fake hope, but right now, fake hope feels better than none at all.

"It'll be running the day after tomorrow." Oak's voice is soft, but it lands like solid truth.

They walk past the anubis, heading toward the Nexus.

The anubis looks whole again. The repair's complete. Robotic ants swarm around the power supply, which sits just off to the side of the ring. The knee-high ants are the size of medium dogs, climbing in lines over the car-sized cube.

"It's expected that the Cankers will leave Earth through their portal on the night of the full moon?" Lilly asks, though she already knows the answer. "After we bring them the power cube."

"It would stop the Baine military from arriving through this portal to take over. But even if we disconnect it… We're just delaying the inevitable."

*Beep. Beep.*

*Beep. Beep.*

Both Oak's and Lilly's navoks chirp at once.

They raise their arms in front of their faces.

The Queen of Seairland appears — duplicated. A projection hovers above Lilly's wrist, another above Oak's. She looks tired, but composed. Strong. Proud. Her blond hair is braided and held beneath a gold-leafed crown.

She smiles — the formal kind. It tries to be warm, but can't erase the sorrow behind her eyes.

"Unknown to many of the citizens of Phi Guya," the Queen begins, "the Royal Family of Seairland has been their hidden guests since the travesty committed by unknown terrorists. It is time for our presence to be known and for our voices to be heard. I hereby provide a formal decree upon the last days of an institution that has succeeded for generations of time eternal."

She glances off-screen, clears her throat, and continues.

"Let it be known to all realms and citizens of Phi Guya:

By decree of Her Sovereign Grace, the Queen, and by the ancient customs of the Unity Rite, a final celebration shall be held.

At the setting of the sun on the morrow, we will gather — not in sorrow, but in honor. We shall dance, not as the conquered, but as those who remember who they are. We shall lift our heads, not in defiance of fate, but in reverence of all we have been together.

Let music rise where silence threatens. Let light bloom where shadows gather. This Feast of Unity shall stand as our own — unbroken, unbowed, and unforgotten.

Though the future may bring closure upon our gates, and others may soon lay claim to these halls, Phi Guya shall have its final word — in dignity, in beauty, and unity.

Let no soul hide in fear. All are called to the celebration. Come as you are. Come for what we were. Come to stand for what still lives in us.

By my voice and by this seal, so it is declared.

— Her Royal Majesty, Queen of Seairland."

The holograms disappear, blinking off their armbands.

Lilly stands motionless, letting the words settle. "A celebration? Now?"

"It could work in our favor," Oak says, voice hopeful. His face doesn't match it — he's worried.

Lilly turns to him. She doesn't need to say every question out loud — not now.

"Everyone will be there," Oak says flatly. "Everyone, including the spy."

Understanding spreads across Lilly's face. "Everyone will be acting normal. The spy might not."

"Exactly."

Just then, a shadow moves across the ground between them. Lilly looks up.

A black crow glides down to the top of the shipping containers. It lands with a flap, then settles.

"Caw! Caw! Caw!"

A faint glow surrounds it — unmistakable.

"No one is that stupid," Lilly mutters, eyes locked on it. She grabs Oak's arm. "Don't look up."

"What?" Oak blurts. His eyes go wide — full cartoon-mode — and, of course, he looks up.

# Chapter 140
### The Power of the Ohmuno

"D-o N-o-t L-o-o-k U-p," Lilly says slowly.

She tries to look casual as she lifts her armband in front of her face.

Hologram Zak appears. "Yup?"

Lilly flashes her best fake smile, all sunshine and calm, like everything's just fine. "Remember when Tommy Tillman went missing? And you did what...?" she asks dramatically, her eyes wide, sending him a *you fill in the blank's* expression.

"And I..." Zak's eyebrows shoot up like they've got minds of their own. "Now?"

Lilly nods. Eyes locked. Dead serious.

Oak watches her like he's two seconds away from duct taping her mouth shut until someone in a white coat shows up.

She glances over at him and gives a wink. "So, let's go over our top-secret plan again."

Oak just blinks at her, speechless.

*Whirrrr!*

A Genaether spins down from the sky, landing with the grace of an Olympic diver.

Riz is at the controls.

Zak's the passenger — cozy, holding tight to Riz's waist. He looks like he might hurl as the machine touches down. He stumbles off, glancing around for the supposed life-threatening emergency.

Lilly nods at him, calm and half-smiling. Then she turns her attention to the crow. She raises her hand.

*OFF*, she thinks — firm, focused, like launching a rocket.

The crow jolts. Every feather puffs out. Its wings are half-spread, body locked like something invisible just punched it. For a heartbeat, it's a sculpture of panic. Then — *thud*. It drops, limp, to the ground.

Oak's whole face lights up like a kid seeing fireworks for the first time. "Wow!" is the only thing that escapes.

"Okay… you are terrifyingly awesome!" Zak sputters, pushing his multi-lens glasses back up his face. He rushes over to the crow and bends down, already working.

Riz's expression is caught between *wait, what?* And *you've gotta be kidding*. She glances from Lilly to the crow and back. "Alright. You're officially dangerous. Is this because of your breathing exercise stuff?"

"Yup," Lilly smirks with pride. "I've been practicing the three breathing exercises Pax Thay taught me. Every day. It works."

"Teach me some of that!" Riz beams.

Oak stares at her, mouth partway open in a question that never makes it out. Then something shifts in his expression — a new kind of clarity settling in. "Wow," he repeats, softer this time.

Something somersaults inside Lilly. She returns the look with a smile — just with her eyes.

"Got it!" Zak announces.

He stands up and slots a small chip into his armband.

A hologram flickers to life above his navok.

The image starts close — a face, too close, scrunched with effort. Then it pulls back. The face moves away, and the view becomes the treetops below, shrinking as the drone rises.

The silence hums, electric.

"Terco!" they all shout at once — three voices, same disbelief, bursting out in perfect sync.

A long, stunned pause follows.

"Ewww," Riz mutters, breaking the silence.

"That means Terco had something to do with his own girlfriend's death!"

"Poor Seri. She would never see it coming."

"Terco! What a total creep!"

# Chapter 141
### Nexus Room Planning

They're in the Nexus Room.

Zak peers through his multi-lens glasses, holding Lilly's armband steady in one hand.

*Click. Click.*

His eyes go wide — goldfish-sized behind the lenses. "Yup. Your power seems to increase incrementally every time you capture Phi tech. Plus, I think it's boosting whenever you practice what Pax Thay taught you. That explains some of the 'Dings' you're getting."

Lilly takes another bite of pizza with her free hand. Multitasker extraordinaire.

Zak releases her armband.

She takes another bite. "Is that... normal?"

"Nope," Oak answers. "Not with Royal Gesh Navoks. Must be an Ohmuno thing. You're also the only one who can see cloaked Noah tech. Everyone else — blind."

"We talked about this. The Ohmuno thing is just hype, children's stories. What I can do is because Pax Thay did something to me, or activated something in my navok." Lilly gives Oak a sideways glance.

He stood his ground, leveling a steady gaze. "Like I said before, Pax Thay made you the Ohmuno. Deal with it."

Lilly changed the subject. "How about the Ring of Yishi? Anything new on that?" Lilly throws the question out there.

"Nada." Zak volley's back. "I still can't find it anywhere. It has been scrubbed from the database, completely."

"Well…maybe it is just more children's story-time myth."

"Not if you heard Yin and Yang talking about it." Riz offers.

"Well, maybe that is good news. That means wherever it is, no one else will find it." Oak suggests.

"Well, forget it for now. What about Terco?" Lilly's voice turns serious. Time is running out.

"It makes sense, really," Oak says. "He's in the Shang position. He'll do anything to stay a Royal Gesh."

"But murdering his girlfriend?" Riz sputters, like someone choking on a thought too awful to even entertain.

"So, the question is — how do we follow Terco if he heads to the Canker hideout?" Lilly asks.

"Oh, he'll go," Oak says, chewing. "He's got an escape plan, guaranteed. We just need him to go before Lilly does."

For some reason, he's starting to like pineapple and ham pizza.

They all share a moment — a collective glance, thick with worry.

"Tracker Dot," Zak blurts. He jumps up and starts rummaging through the mess stacked on the shelves. Tools clatter. Bits fall. He returns holding something tiny — a speck on the tip of his finger, like a single freckle.

"OK... how do we stick that to him?" Oak asks between bites.

Lilly and Riz glance at each other, perfectly in sync.

"Kwi-Li," they say in unison.

"We go to the Unity Celebration tomorrow," Lilly says, halfway confident. "Terco will be there. If he isn't, it'll look suspicious."

"We all act like we've given up. Like we're not up to anything," Oak adds.

Nods all around.

"OK," Lilly says, straightening up. "Let's go over the plan. One more time."

# Chapter 142
Phisian Unity Celebration

The ballroom doesn't look real. It feels too big, too perfect—like it was built to hold legends, not people. The ceiling vanishes into shadow, and the windows stretch so high they could open into another world. Torchlight burns steadily along the marble walls, casting golden ripples across the polished floor—and even that feels too loud. Everything shines like it knows this might be the last time it ever will.

What was once a vast open room is now scattered with elegantly dressed tables along the sides. The Royal Table stands wide and raised at the front, still empty. The center floor is left open— for something planned.

People stand in clusters, quiet but not still. Formal uniforms make them look sharp, strong, untouchable—deep greens, silvers, crimsons, and then the Dress White of the Royal Gesh—each catching firelight on its trim, emblems, and rank. Some adjust their collars too often. Some grip their gloves like they're holding something in. A few whisper just loud enough for the edges of words to carry— *"shutdown," "tomorrow," "hold the line."*

One man stares up at the arches like they might fall.

Another scans the faces near him like he's trying to memorize them.

And still, somehow, everyone stands proud.

Even in the silence, you can feel it: the defiance.

The decision to show up anyway.

A girl not much older than Lilly tugs at her sleeve, exhales slowly through her nose, then straightens her back. She doesn't smile—but she doesn't blink either. She's nervous.

Lilly crosses the floor, dressed in her white ceremonial uniform—crisp, clean, perfectly in regulation. The fabric catches the candlelight with a soft sheen, the kind that makes her look more commanding than she feels.

A murmur rises ahead of her. The crowd parts in her wake.

Across the great hall, Zak and Oak stand beside a table. They're in their Phi, non-Royal Gesh suits—stiff white collars, tieless. Both look like they aren't sure if they should stay or run.

Zak keeps fidgeting with the hem of his jacket. His eyes dart around the room like he's searching for someone.

Oak doesn't fidget. But the suit hangs a little too tight on him. The collar sits high. His expression is unreadable—until he catches sight of Lilly.

His gaze locks. And stays. His expression says everything—but his mouth doesn't say much. He looks at her longer than he should, like he's trying to memorize this moment forever.

Lilly feels it. And she doesn't know how to feel about feeling it.

Her stomach does something uncomfortable. Or maybe... very comfortable.

"You, uh..." Oak starts, voice lower than usual. "You look sharp."

It comes out like a quiet revelation—something he hadn't meant to say out loud.

Lilly turns to him, caught off guard by how serious he looks. There's something in his eyes—not teasing, not awkward. Just... honest.

Before she can figure out what to say back, the Royal Family enters.

The Queen and her two daughters. The heirs to the throne.

And the whole room shifts.

Not with noise—but with stillness.

Like every thought freezes mid-sentence.

The Queen moves through the center like the floor was made for her footsteps. Her robes flow midnight-blue, edged in silver like threads pulled from moonlight. Her crown is delicate—just enough to remind everyone who she is. But the way she carries it... That's everything.

No speech. Just presence.

She looks out over the hall, chin high, eyes steady. And somehow, that one look says it all:

*We're not broken. Not yet.*

No one cheers. But they straighten. Shoulders lift. Spines align. Feet spread.

The whispers stop. The murmurs quiet. Pride and fear stand shoulder to shoulder—and for now, pride is winning.

The Queen ascends to the head of the table, framed by her daughters like a living portrait. Her posture alone seems to hold the structure of the moment together.

At her left sits a young princess—blond, blue-eyed, a miniature queen. And for a second, nothing seems out of place.

Until they look again.

There, seated on the Queen's other side, dressed in a breathtaking white gown woven with threads of gold—

—sits Riz.

Not Riz the mechanic.

Not Riz in smeared jeans and a stretched-out T-shirt.

No—this is someone else entirely.

# Chapter 143

## Meet the Royal Family

Riz's radiant blond hair is braided back in elegant coils, laced with golden ribbon that shimmers beneath the lights. Her face—usually streaked with oil or half-hidden behind goggles—is clear, calm, and glowing.

She looks... royal.

Zak's jaw drops.

Without even looking, Lilly reaches over and gently pushes it closed.

He doesn't speak. Just keeps staring, stunned, like the floor has vanished under his feet.

Riz doesn't notice. She sits tall, graceful—but when a young girl across the room gives her a small wave, Riz returns it with a wink. Casual. Friendly. Like this entire royal ceremony is just another stop between repair jobs.

Oak barely reacts. He blinks once, then turns his attention back to Lilly, like she's still the most surprising thing in the room. The noise and elegance don't distract him—not really.

There's something about his silence—not distant, but present. Focused. Like he's trying to solve something without knowing what the question is.

Zak finally whispers, still blinking, "She's—Princess Rizuko?"

Lilly doesn't answer. She's surprised, yes—but she keeps watching the crowd, waiting for why they're here. "Stay focused. Keep an eye out for Terco."

"I am looking," Kwi-Li's voice answers in her mind.

"Not you—the boys," Lilly mutters, correcting the invisible gati.

"What?" Zak says, confused.

Lilly just shakes her head, trying to reset her focus.

After the feast, the atmosphere in the ballroom softens. The heavy tension of the ceremony gives way to conversation, low laughter, and the soft clink of glass against glass.

Near one of the grand columns, Lilly, Zak, and Oak stand speaking with a few members of the Royal Gesh. The conversation is light, respectful—though the air still buzzes with formality.

Then the Queen approaches, princesses in tow. They move without announcement, but every Royal Gesh nearby instinctively steps aside—whether out of habit, reverence, or something deeper in their training.

The circle parts.

Suddenly, the three teens are standing in open view, very aware of themselves.

Lilly doesn't hesitate.

Her mind flashes back to something Zak once told her—about the old ways of the Ohmuno, before the pageantry, before the politics. She steps forward and bows, hands pressed together.

"Namaste," she says.

The Queen pauses, a flicker of warmth crossing her otherwise composed face. "Namaste," she echoes, rolling the word gently in her mouth. Then she adds softly, "The ancient greeting of the Noahs... I am flattered by your humility and respect."

She and her two daughters bow in return—graceful. Sincere.

"Namaste, Lilly. Royal Gesh. I much prefer the ancient greetings over all this royalty business."

Zak and Oak stand frozen, stiff-backed.

Zak especially—caught between awe and confusion. Before he can think too hard, the Queen's gaze shifts, warm but sharp, toward Riz.

"I want to thank you," she says, "for protecting the Princess of Seairland." Her tone lifts—half proud, half exasperated. "Though I do wish she would act more like a princess of her world... rather than a princess of *grease*."

Riz groans. "Mom," she mutters, dragging the word out like it physically hurts to say.

Zak blinks, eyes flicking between the Queen and Rizuko. "Uhm... Your Highness... Riz... I mean..."

He gives up, bows stiffly to both like someone trying not to break expensive glass.

Riz rolls her eyes, leans in, and socks him lightly on the shoulder. "Hey, Zap-man," she whispers. "Call me Riz."

Zak turns beet red.

The Queen looks at her daughter, then shakes her head in quiet disbelief—half amused, half eternally resigned.

The Royal Family continues through the crowd, paying respects, drawing people together with nothing more than presence.

Lilly keeps scanning the ballroom.

Then she sees him.

"There!" she hisses to Oak.

Terco enters—wearing a white uniform stripped of gold. His face lacks calm. His whole body moves like his suit is crawling with ants.

Oak nods once.

"Got him, Kwi-Li?"

"Got him," comes the answer in her mind.

# Chapter 144
### Let the Dance Begin

A soft chime rings out—clear and ceremonial.

The Queen and the princesses stand at the head table once more, her voice ringing with quiet authority.

"As is tradition," she announces, "the Unity Dance shall begin with a princess of Guya, and a member of the Royal Gesh."

All heads turn toward the oldest, Princess Rizuko.

Her white gown catches the light like a polished pearl. She rises slowly, unhurried, her gaze sweeping the room with just enough poise to silence the last of the whispers. Then she steps forward—and everyone expects her to choose from among the Royal Gesh lining the hall. Seasoned. Polished. Protocol-bound.

Instead, she walks straight to Oak.

No fanfare. No speech. Just Riz offering her hand to the baker's son, with a slight smile—unapologetic, effortlessly confident.

The silence in the ballroom changes color.

Lilly catches the Queen's reaction—a subtle hardening of the eyes, the tightening of her mouth. But the monarch gives a graceful nod. Allowing. Not pleased, but permitting.

Oak doesn't move at first. For a heartbeat, he looks like he might bolt. His hand twitches at his side. His jaw sets. Then, carefully, he steps forward and accepts Princess Rizuko's hand. His posture is stiff, shoulders tight in that ill-fitting suit—but he follows her lead as the music begins.

Zak looks like someone's unplugged him.

He blinks, fast. Watching Riz dance with Oak like he's still trying to catch up with reality.

Lilly can practically hear his thoughts racing.

Zak rubs the back of his neck, tries to play it cool, fails.

"Too tall. They don't match," he mutters.

Lilly doesn't know what she feels. Not exactly. Just that something twists inside her as she watches Oak and Riz move together. It isn't jealousy—not the sharp, obvious kind. It's quieter. Murkier. Like watching someone open a door you didn't realize you wanted closed.

"Yeah, she is too tall for him," Lilly agrees, flatly.

"No. Oak. *He's* too tall for *Riz*," Zak corrects, without looking at her.

Oak doesn't look at Riz the way Zak looks at her. He dances like he's just trying to survive—like his mind is somewhere else entirely.

His eyes flick—once—toward Lilly.

They linger, just a beat too long.

She feels it like warmth on her skin.

Then the Queen raises her hand again. Her voice, calm.

"The floor is open."

More music swells. The guests begin to move—dresses and boots sweeping across the mirrored floor. The Unity Dance has begun.

Zak shifts beside Lilly, half-stepping forward, then back. He glances toward her, then away.

And that's when they see him.

An overly eager boy—gangly, beaming—marching straight toward Lilly like a puppy spotting a tennis ball. His hair is too slick. His smile, too wide. His arms are already half-raised to ask her to dance.

Zak and Lilly clock him at the same time.

Their eyes meet.

Neither of them looks like they want to dance with each other.

But they don't want to dance with *him*.

Before Zak can make a move—or Lilly can come up with a polite excuse—a sharp sound snaps across the ballroom.

A guard rushes in, breathless.

"Mass whale beaching at the eastern inlet!" he shouts. "Unnatural patterns—there's portal interference. Possible Canker involvement!"

Gasps ripple through the room.

The music stops instantly.

Lilly straightens.

Zak freezes.

Oak has already released Riz's hand—his whole body turns toward the voice.

"Portal?" someone whispers.

Everyone knows what that means.

The disorientation.

The breach risk.

The possibility of an enemy foothold.

Royal Gesh are already moving—peeling away from the walls, slipping into formation with the precision of muscle memory.

Commanders bark quiet orders.

Boots strike marble in unison.

The Unity Dance ends in a breath.

Duty has called.

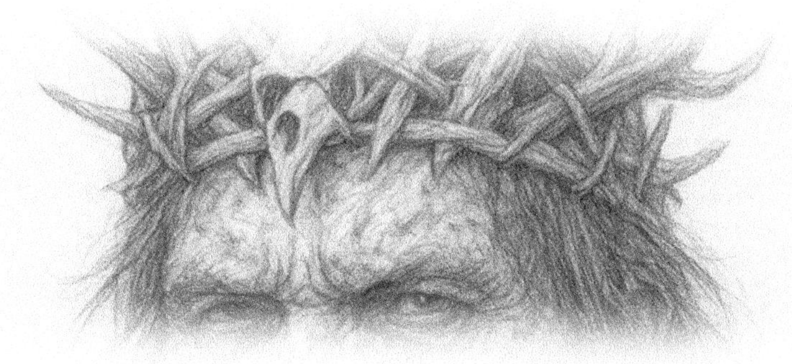

# Chapter 145

The drifting music fades into measured commotion—half-hearted dancers straighten into focused gesh. At last, they can do more than spin in circles. Idle grace snaps into rehearsed resolve. Paths clear. Positions click back into memory. It isn't chaos—it's relief. Finally, something real to do.

Lilly's navok buzzes—violently.

She glances down, expecting a Royal Gesh warning flash—maybe a quiet ping from Zak—but the display glitches, then snaps into focus with a burst of garbled audio.

A hologram erupts midair, stuttering into clarity.

It's a man who looks like he's eaten too many rats, drinks nuclear waste for fun, and thinks soap is a myth. Black stone eyes are punched deep into a rotting oatmeal bowl of a face. Fungus Face.

He grins with cracked teeth, skin peeling in sick patches around his eyes. Bones from past kills are tied into a crown across his head. His breath fogs the projection like he's practically licking the lens.

And behind him—

"Dad—!"

Her father is on his knees. Barely conscious. One eye sealed shut. Blood drips from his temple. His hands are bound behind him with metal shackles. One shoulder twisted the wrong way. He doesn't move.

Aubrin crouches beside him, gagged, eyes closed. His face is red and raw, one cheek already swelling.

Fungus Face speaks in broken syllables—a disgusting slur of sounds stitched together with hate.

"Come... alone. Bring... cube. You come... or they... die."

Her father lifts his head a little. "Lilly—don't—"

A sharp sound. He's struck. The image jitters.

Then the projection cuts.

A white-hot pulse flashes across Lilly's armband. A single directional burst. No voice. No map. Just a blinking dot and a vector.

She stares at it—at the moving dot that replaces her father's pained face. Her breath catches somewhere between her ribs and her throat.

Her stomach twists. Panic rushes in, hot and fast. Her knees threaten to drop her. She reaches for balance—fingertips brushing the edge of a chair.

Her father is hurt. Bad.

And she's just standing here.

Fear lands next—sharp, suffocating. Then anger, hot and wild, rising from her core. Her body tenses, like it needs to move, to fight, to *do* something.

She clenches her jaw. Focuses on the blinking dot moving across her screen.

There's no time to break down.

Not now.

She wipes the back of her hand across her face.

"We are coming," she says—to her father... and the ones hurting him. One sentence. Two meanings.

Then she moves.

"What does that mean?" she asks, her voice steady as she holds the wristband up, letting the hologram float for all to see.

Zak is already at her side. Eyes locked on the screen. "It's a burst-position beacon. They're not giving the full location. Just the first piece."

"Why?"

"Because they're smarter than we thought. They'll give the next direction only when you reach the current one. That way—no tracing, no planning."

"That *was* our plan!" Oak's voice tightens, like he's holding back a scream.

# Chapter 146
### The Power Thing on a Floaty Thingy

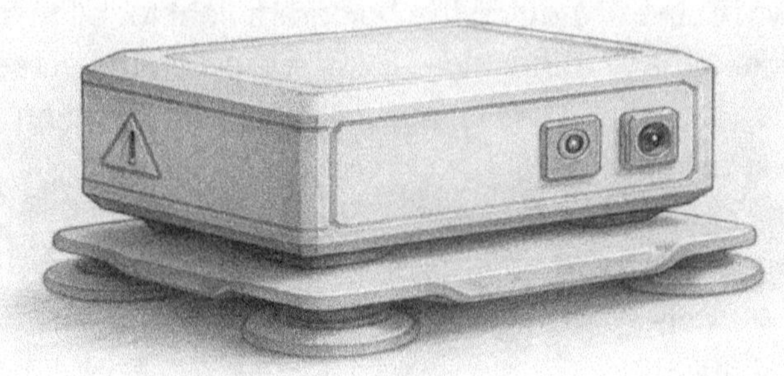

Lilly looks up from her armband, voice tight. "Then we better not lose our trace on Terco."

Zak blinks, then lifts his armband. A hologram flickers to life—a blinking red dot in a simplified line-grid world. "Oh, I've got him."

They all turn—just in time to spot Terco slipping down a side corridor. Not toward the Council chamber. Away. No hesitation. No goodbye.

"What do you bet," Lilly mutters, "Terco and I are headed to the same place?"

Oak gives her a look. "Maybe. But not certain."

Riz is already yanking her hair into a tight ponytail, crown gone, cloak swapped for a combat jacket. "I'm ready. What's the new plan?"

Lilly nods sharply. "We improvise. Then we leave with the Royal Gesh."

Nods all around.

"Zak, how many of those dragonfly hologram thingies can you rustle up?" Lilly asks.

Zak's left eye twitches at her word choice. "Lots."

Oak, can we round up all of the Warufang?"

Oak grins—far too pleased with the madness of it all. "You bet I can!"

"Riz, you said you can fly, right?"

"Better than anyone on both planets," Riz grins like someone just handed her a match and asked where the fuse was.

"Kwi-Li," Lilly says out loud—not that she needs to.

Kwi-Li materializes like smoke from the corner. "I'll keep an eye on Terco."

"No change of plans—you're with Oak."

Kwi-Li glances at Oak and nods. "Okay." Already ready before Lilly finishes the sentence.

"Alright, here's what we do..." Lilly launches into the plan.

Within minutes, Riz, Oak, and Kwi-Li lift off—mounted on their genaethers, slipping away beneath a gatiar masking field.

Lilly climbs into her own Royal Genaether, fingers tightening around the handlebars. Her eyes lift to the dome's top—to the opening Terco disappeared through.

Zak lingers beside her. "I can go. I can help."

"No. You're staying. We need you to track and observe. Give us a heads-up with whatever you see. Besides..." she smirks faintly, "you're a better geek than a flyer."

"You're a better shrimp than a geek." Zak laughs, but it sounds cracked—more panic than punchline. He nods once, serious again. "You should be able to tow the aunbis power cube with the Porto-Jo."

"The what?" The words sting her brain. Too much tech, too little time.

Zak points behind her genaether, at the anubis power supply strapped to a hovering platform. "You call them the power thing and the floaty thingy."

"Got it," Lilly nods.

He looks like he wants to say more—but doesn't.

The machine beneath her hums to life. The sound deepens into a pulse, rising through her spine like a second heartbeat.

Lilly grips the controls, stares up through the dome's open gap.

And then she's gone.

# Chapter 147
### The Canker Hide-Out

They lose Terco soon after leaving Phi Guya.

The last ping from his tracker dot shows him slicing across the frozen horizon—then nothing. It's like he steps off the map.

Communication flows in an open channel between all of them, voices layered in Lilly's mind like thoughts she didn't think herself.

"He used Geennii," Riz says, frustrated. "Where did he get the gati?"

Another surprise.

The ground rushes beneath Lilly's genaether—white to brown to green—as they fly north, toward someplace warmer. The machine hums beneath her like a coiled beast, smooth but barely contained.

"We'll assume he's sticking to the same trajectory," Oak announces, voice crisp and steady.

A long moment stretches between them—waiting, wondering, hoping.

Mountains begin to rise beneath Lilly, massive and jagged, like the ridged spine of some ancient creature half-buried in time.

Zak's voice crackles in: "I've got a blip. Tracker just came back online—probably just arriving at his destination."

"I'm being led down," Lilly says. She can't hide the fear in her voice, but it's laced with resolve. She's already made her decision.

Craggy ridges slice through the clouds ahead. Patches of mist cling to the slopes, and trees cling to rock.

Into view comes a dark cave mouth, half-hidden, isolated, and yawning like an open throat.

Lilly's genaether begins to slow. The roar drops into a purring hum. The wild vibration steadies, no longer rattling her bones—just thrumming with quiet, purposeful force.

"Sending now..." Zak's voice buzzes again. "And—yep. Signals are converging. Cave system."

"Get us there, Kwi-Li," Oak says.

Below, the world sharpens—every peak, every shadowed crevice clearer now. The cave mouth seems to pull at the light, draining it inward.

The whole region looks forsaken, like it's been waiting too long for someone to find it.

Her armband pings again. The path tells her to veer sharply into the darkness buried beneath tons of rock.

"You're both heading to the same place," Zak says.

They all know what that means.

Lilly hears it—a breath, not hers, echoed through the comms. Multiple intakes. Everyone bracing.

She tightens her grip on the controls. "Things are about to get messy. Stay alert, everyone."

# Chapter 148
### Into the Den of Danger

Kwi-Li blinks Oak and Riz onto the rock ledge just above the cave mouth.

Nods all around. Lips tight. Muscles tense.

Lilly is already there, waiting.

Zak's voice crackles through her comm. "You remember how to open it?"

"You underestimate the powers of a shrimp. Can you identify which of us here are the good guys?" Lilly throws out a little humor—like lighting a match in a hurricane. It flickers, but it's something.

"You underestimate the powers of a geek." Zak's slight, nervous laugh echoes through all their comms.

"How are you going in?" Oak asks. He already knows the answer, but asking hurts less than saying nothing.

"They'll expect me to beg," Lilly says. "I will."

Oak looks like he might punch a rock.

"She's not going in alone," Riz whispers to him. "Just in first."

The others crouch behind the rock outcroppings, just out of sight.

Kwi-Li rests a hand on Oak's shoulder. An expression is unreadable, still as glass.

Lilly takes a breath.

Beside her, the chest hovers on a low, silent trolley—sleek, rectangular, perfectly sized to match the anubis power cube. Inside, the "power thing."

She steps forward.

And enters the cave.

# Chapter 149
### New Plan in Action

The air hits her like a wet slap—sour, metallic, and stinging. The chemical reek coats her tongue.

Toxic moss clings to the canyon walls like old scars. Inside, slime stretches across the floor like spilled ink. The walls are slick with wet veins of fungus and rusted metal, fused like flesh to circuitry.

A low, constant hum vibrates through her boots. Not loud. But alive.

Light flickers from strips along the ceiling—old LED tubes barely working—casting long shadows that move when she doesn't.

She rounds the corner and sees them.

Fungus Face. Grinning.

Six Cankers. Spread wide. Weapons drawn.

Her father. Carnel. On their knees. Arms bound behind their backs.

Aubrin lies face down in the dirt. Something black clamped to the back of his head.

Lilly's voice cracks perfectly. "Here. Here's what you wanted. Just—don't hurt them anymore. I give up!"

Fungus Face sneers, stepping forward.

Lilly takes one slow step closer.

Then another.

Then—kick.

The power cube crate cracks open.

A swarm bursts out like a scream.

Wasp drones—glinting, buzzing, sharp as knives—shoot through the air like an explosion of glass.

Fungus Face recoils.

"You're not Mensch Morder," Lilly says. "But you will do!"

Then come the dragonflies—wings pulsing with light.

And then—soldiers, holograms.

Two full angs of Royal Gesh flicker into place—projected down the walls, across the floor, along the high ground. An illusion. But perfect. Shadows and all.

The cankers panic. Who wouldn't?

Zak triggers the Warufang from base—fifty-five precision wasp missiles targeting sensors and weapons.

Kwi-Li blinks Oak inside, behind the hostages.

Fungus Face turns, sees Oak.

And panics.

Oak moves like a hammer, tearing through two cankers before they can fire. He slams one into the cave wall with a blast of his vok, shatters a second's arm, and lunges straight for Carnel.

The rest of the cankers open fire—but it's chaos.

Zak amplifies the projections. More soldiers appear—more than could be real. A full battalion of ghosts.

Fungus Face grabs Carnel by the hair, dragging him toward a platform.

Lilly screams, pushes through the haze. Her thoughts flash like lightning. *Navok—override!*

Fungus Face's armband glitches. His vok goes dead.

He freezes.

That's all Oak needs.

He hits him full-force, body slamming against the wall. Fungus Face collapses.

Lilly reaches her father just as the last of the Cankers blink out—Geennii trail vanishing into the air. Fungus Face is leading the retreat.

They don't take their wounded.

But they do take a massive chest—hovering, humming, big enough to hold secrets they don't want anyone to see.

And it looks like they tried to grab two.

One is gone.

The other remains—abandoned in the confusion.

And beneath her feet, the cave starts to hum.

No one notices yet.

# Chapter 150

## That was Your Mother's

Her father looks up, blinking past a fresh bruise and blood in one eye. He's tied to a thick support pipe, hands raw from struggling, but his face breaks open with something almost too human to bear—relief.

"Lilly," he breathes, like the word itself is oxygen. "You're okay?"

Lilly drops to her knees beside him, tears already catching in the corners of her lashes. "I'm so sorry, Dad..."

But he shakes his head, straining against the shackles, as if words could break through what bonds cannot. "No. No—it's me who should be sorry. I ignored you. I let fear blind the best parts of my life. You—" his voice cracks, "—you're more important to me than anything."

Her fingers move to the small necklace resting warm against her skin, the birthday present he gave her. She holds it up, just enough for him to see.

"Thanks, Dad."

His eyes widen. "That… that was your mother's."

"I know," she says softly. "It's the best birthday gift I've ever gotten."

For a breath, the whole cave seems to pause, as if even the shadows want to give them that moment.

Then, groaning as he shifts against the restraints, he adds with a lopsided grin, "I've finally found the little green men. Didn't expect some of them to look like ogres from a children's book—or smell like the inside of an old boot."

He jerks his chin toward Carnel, who scowls back with one swollen black-and-green eye.

"Guya genus nattong neph oh flitchi flitchi oh tirth gumen gumen!" Carnel barks—gruff and guttural, like gravel being chewed.

Oak steps forward, completely straight-faced. "He says he is pleased to meet an Earthling for the first time as well."

Lilly's father gives Carnel a wary look. "Right. Sounds like he means it. Please tell him, aliens have a beautiful-sounding language. It's very poetic with the repetition, and all."

Oak's eyes catch Lilly's. His expression verges on fear.

Lilly can't help the smile tugging at the side of her mouth.

Then Mr. Dubois's eyes sweep the room—Riz in her sleeveless formal dress streaked with dust and battle, Oak in something like a half-suit, half-combat uniform, and Zak—twenty-six copies of him—lined up in silent formation, each one shimmering in a holographic.

And Lilly—standing tall in her white Royal Gesh dress-uniform, gold trim catching the cave light, like she's stepped out of someone else's story.

Her father blinks hard. "Who are all these people? And what on earth are you wearing?"

Lilly gives him a soft half-smile. "Dad, these are my alien friends. The rest..." She straightens. "I'll have to explain later."

Behind them, Aubrin slumps in his bindings, eyes glassy, a crablike clamp latched cruelly across his scalp. Carnel sits tied beside him, face rigid with silent rage.

Lilly turns to Kwi-Li, who hovers beside her shoulder like a worried shadow. "Kwi-Li, can Spot undo those locks?"

The tiny marble robot rolls forward on the gatis palm like a marble with purpose. The one eye pops up. Little arms and hands slide out of the marble and into the restraint—and with a few delicate clicks later, the locks release.

Chains thud to the floor.

Aubrin collapses into Riz's waiting arms. Carnel rolls his shoulders, flexing like a bull released from a too-small pen. A tiny green bull, though.

And Lilly's father exhales, long and full, like he's been holding that breath since the day Lilly was born.

The floor of the cave gives a shake, like they're in the belly of some monster that's beginning to wake. A sound grumbles from somewhere deep in the unexplored bowels of the cavern.

A ripple of alarm passes between their glances.

"Uhm...Riz! Can you get them all loaded on the floaty thingy?" Lilly points to their three new rescues.

Riz's brows pinch with confusion. She's ready for anything—just not quite sure what Lilly means.

Lilly shakes her head, searching for the right words. "The porto-jo."

Riz's blue eyes light with understanding, and a quiet breath escapes. "On it!"

Lilly glances over to Oak.

Oak already has his vok out and ready. No words needed.

# Chapter 151
## Too Much Left Behind

Oak and Lilly step into the depths of the rumbling cave, voks out and ready for anything.

Zak's dragonfly projection floats beside them, a flickering hologram that observes and analyzes in silence.

The cave yawns wider as they move deeper in—a gaping throat of stone that seems to inhale every sound they make. Its soot-stained walls shimmer faintly. Above, the ceiling vanishes into a blackness that feels like it could fall on them at any moment.

The deeper they go, the more the glow of their navok's fade, as if even light is afraid to continue.

Crates lean against the walls, stacked in crooked towers, slouched beneath dusty tarps like things trying to hide.

They step over broken chairs, through puddles that shimmer without light, past coils of cable snaking across the floor, like roots growing in reverse.

The air clings to their skin—thick, damp, and smelling of burnt metal and mould.

Then they see him. What's left of him.

Terco's body lies beside a small Anubis. He is collapsed like someone dropped him just to be rid of him. His limbs are bent wrong. His face twisted. Eyes open—vacant, dull, still too human. There's no breath left in him. Only the stillness of a final order followed.

Lilly stops. Her knee scrapes against stone as she kneels.

"Too late," Oak whispers.

He doesn't need to say it. She knows.

Lilly rises, her breath shallow, her voice tight. "They were tying up loose ends."

The portal beside Terco is worse than broken—it looks half-chewed. Segments are missing. Cables hang limp like torn sinew. In the dirt, a cube-shaped imprint. But no power cube.

"It is completely non-functional," Zak's hologram states. Lilly frowns, grappling with confusion. "They were still trying to repair it…"

"No…" Oak mutters. "…this doesn't make sense."

"Why take the power cube? To where, if not to use here?" All of Zak's holograms ponder. Multiple Zaks with one Zak super brain.

They stare at each other, caught in the same awful thought. That gnawing, rising certainty. That they've come too late. That they've lost.

Their glances dart back and forth—sharp, silent. Eyes full of the kind of confusion that runs ahead of grief.

Zak's hologram blinks. His brows lock, trying to wrestle with an impossible puzzle. Then he bends, scanning something in the dirt.

Oak looks at Lilly.

Lilly looks at the walls, like the cave might give her an answer.

She moves without thinking—past a half-dead campfire, past the crates slouched against the far wall. Her hand catches the edge of the biggest one and wrenches it open.

Gold.

Stacks of it. Bars piled like bricks—too perfect, too untouched. Gleaming in the dim light, like something placed there to distract.

Her voice drops. "Why would they leave this?"

A pause.

Then Zak, still crouched by the broken ring, speaks with sudden breath: "This is an imprint for a power cube. Yet their portal—"

Lilly turns, already feeling it forming in her chest. "—is broken!"

They say it together. The same words. Two mouths. One voice.

Something cracks open—not a sound, but a shift. Tension unravels. Not with relief, but with understanding.

Zak's voice is clearer now. "They couldn't use this. This was never meant to work."

"This was a trap."

"But they wanted you to bring the cube," Oak says, frowning.

"They didn't want to use it here," Zak continues, eyes narrowing. "They wanted the cube gone. Because the shield at Phi Guya runs on the anubis power cube."

Lilly's stomach drops. The cold rushes up her spine.

"Oh no…"

Oak looks at her. "It's a diversion."

"The whales. This cave. The portal. It is all a trick."

# Chapter 152
## The Bigger Plan is Revealed

"To pull everyone away from the *real* portal," Lilly whispered. "The only one that works is here at Phi Guya." Zak's hologram sputtered out the revelation.

Lilly turns—slowly, instinctively—searching the eternal darkness of the far end of the cave.

It hasn't revealed everything yet.

Smoke still hangs low there, twisting around stalagmites like it has nowhere else to go. Something pulses in the shadows. A faint clicking. Mechanical. Hungry.

And then the eyes open.

Red.

Dozens. Then hundreds. Then, thousands." Lined in rows, as far as the eye can see. Blinking. Activating. An expansive cavern of noxiar bots, standing in patient formation like they're waiting for the command.

Their matte black limbs glisten with faint residue, like they are oiled with the darkness. Each face is a smooth plate with nothing behind it but death. Each holding a powerful weapon designed for destruction.

"No…" Lilly breathes. "They're not going to stop at Phi Guya."

Zak steps backward, shaking his head. "They're going to invade Earth."

"Pull up, Haro," Lilly says, voice taut.

Oak did it. His navok buzzes and hisses. Haro's face flares into view—staticky, half there, and already shouting.

"It's a trap—EMF field—they hit us—our Gatis are down—rebooting—can't—"

"*We'll make it there first!*" Lilly shouts.

"Too dangerous—Lilly—"

The image shatters into static. Gone.

No time. No options.

They run full tilt back to the mouth of the cave.

Riz steps up, steady as ever. "Problem?"

"Countless! We gotta go. Now!"

Zak's hologram appears out of nowhere, eyes wide. His voice flares again—urgent, high-pitched, barely holding together. "The cankers are here! At Phi Guya! The shield's holding—but not for long!"

Riz's expression solidifies. "I am ready to fly. I'll take care of your dad. Of Carnel. Of Aubrin."

Lilly grips her shoulder. "You sure?"

"I know what I can do best. Go do what you do best."

"Kwi-Li," Lilly says it out loud.

Kwi-Li appears in the shadows, eyes blinking with violet light. "I can take you. I can make us faster."

She shoots Oak a glance. "We need to clear the way for Riz." She is already climbing onto a genaether.

Oak follows, slipping on the genaether beside her, already syncing his genaether with hers.

The cave behind them thrums. Machines awake. Somewhere, a deeper growl begins—something worse, still unseen.

Lilly stares into the darkness. Then into the sky ahead.

No more tricks.

No more delays.

Phi Guya is calling.

# Chapter 153

### A race to the Phi Guya

The wind outside the dome is a living thing—howling, clawing, screaming like a wounded beast across the ice plains. Snow whips sideways, a white wall of rage that scrapes the frozen ground raw. The outside of Phi Guya is death in every breath.

Inside, by contrast, is tense, humid, green, and choking in terrified silence. Families cling to each other, beneath the soft glow of artificial light. They are staring out through the reinforced shield as the end of everything moves closer.

The Cankers are already outside the dome.

Only six of them—for now—but still too many. Their plans were exposed too soon, thanks to Lilly and the others. With their secrecy shattered, the Cankers shift tactics. Eliminate Phi Guya. Silence the truth. Bury it beneath ice and ruin before it spreads.

They attack the dome like wasps attacking a glass jar. Energy blasts strike the shield in hot, pulsing bursts. Ice crusts over their armor like war paint. The six of them hammer at the protective barrier, relentless.

Kwi-Li blinks Lilly and Oak down from the sky ahead of Riz— and ahead of the swarm of death following behind. Their shields shimmer at full charge.

"We've got six on the dome!" Oak shouts over the storm's roar. "But more are coming. A lot more."

The Cankers focus on their task, unaware of Lilly and Oak's arrival. They pour fire into the dome, trying to breach the inner sanctuary before backup arrives.

"We gotta clear the garbage out of the way," Lilly says.

Oak doesn't need further explanation. His vok hisses to life in his grip.

"Hey! Fungus Face!" Lilly yells, spotting the one canker she's been aching to take down.

He stops mid-blast. Turns.

And when he sees her, his face twists into pure hatred.

"Looking for me, Ugly?" Lilly calls, her vok glowing hot in her hand.

Above them, the sky changes. Even through the blizzard, a dark mass spreads—blotting out the storm clouds. Noxiar war bots. Monster-like. Jet-propelled. They swarm the skies like a vengeance-plague.

"Where are you, Riz?" Lilly calls through her navok. "We can't hold them all. You're out of time!"

Riz's voice crackles back, strained through static and g-force. "I know! You see that black cloud of noxiars?! That's me in the middle!"

A loud *wham*.

A grunt.

"These noxiars are *not* being nice!" she growls. "Jet-powered now! Who gave them jets?!"

Then—she's there.

Riz cuts through the clouds, twisting her genaether between laser fire and incoming bots like she was born inside the cockpit. The porto-jo trails behind her, cargo box open. Inside—her three passengers—white-knuckled, barely hanging on.

On the ground, Oak is a wrecking crew. His scepter blast slams into one Canker, then another, armor shattering beneath the force of it. He takes three down by himself.

Lilly runs.

She reaches deep—into her bond with Kwi-Li, into the current of Ohmuno power humming beneath her skin—and charges straight for Fungus Face.

Surprise flickers across his face just before she drops him.

Two more cankers lunge for her.

Lilly raises her hand.

One word in her mind.

Their scepters spark, then die. Mid-air.

Fear floods their expressions. They pause. Turn. There's no shelter—just snow and sky.

They run.

The way clears—just in time.

# Chapter 154
### A Diablopero Blocking the Way

Riz dives from the storm of darkness, her craft skimming the ice like a dragonfly on a frozen lake, engines shrieking in protest. Inside her transport: a battered Carnel, an unconscious Aubrin, and Lilly's father—clinging, bruised, but alive. Behind them, a sea of noxiar machines closes in, red eyes burning from blackness in a nightmare swarm.

And then—thunder.

The diablopero.

The monster from Whale Beach. The diversion. Towering and gleaming in black gloss, it charges over the ice—followed by dozens of new cankers. They're rushing the gateway too.

"I'm not gonna make it!" Riz screams through the comms.

Oak doesn't hesitate.

He leaps onto the nearest genaether. "Learned this one from you!" he shouts to Lilly—then rams her genaether straight into the diablopero's side.

The beast tumbles. Legs flailing. Tail lashing the air like a whip. Snow explodes around its rolling mass.

Oak gets thrown, his body flailing across the ice—shoulder slamming down first, limbs cartwheeled in a blur of motion. He lands hard, snow spraying around him. Groaning, he blinks, trying to figure out which way is up.

The diablopero rises. Instinct locked on Oak. It leaps.

The dome doors hum open.

Riz skids inside—just barely—cargo safe.

"Lilly!" Zak's voice cuts in. High. Sharp.

"Kwi-Li! Now!" Lilly shouts, already sprinting toward Oak.

Kwi-Li blinks in—right at the moment Lilly grabs Oak's arm. They vanish.

The diablopero's paw swipes—

But catches only air.

The beast lands hard, snapping at nothing.

Inside the dome, a tangle of limbs hits the grass.

Kwi-Li rolls free.

Lilly finds herself flat on top of Oak.

They both freeze.

Eyes meet.

The moment holds—too long. Neither one seems to mind.

Lilly flushes. "Wow! That was close!" She scrambles to her feet.

Oak rolls up, looking a shade brighter blue. "You okay?"

"Yeah... um... never better," Lilly mutters, pushing a loose strand of hair behind her ear. Classic distraction move. Maybe it works.

Kwi-Li rushes over and hugs Lilly tightly.

Lilly hugs her little bot right back.

"We are a good team?" Kwi-Li chirps, hopeful.

"We are a *great* team! Gimme five." Lilly raises her hand.

Kwi-Li high-fives back, eyes beaming, grin wide.

But it's not over. Not yet.

# Chapter 155
### No Hope, but One

The assault begins in full.

Outside, hordes of noxiars land like flies on prey. They hammer the dome with energy guns. The diablopero stalks among them—its signals dancing like puppet strings on every warbot outside.

The dome's shield flickers.

"We've lost communication with the moon base," Zak says. "They've jammed us—some kind of signal disruption field. No reinforcements are coming."

"They're gonna break through," someone whispers.

Zak stares out at the storm. "All those noxiars... they're networked. One mind. One control. The diablopero!"

Lilly's pulse quickens. "Then take down the diablopero, and the swarm falls?"

"Yes," Zak mutters. "It should."

A long silence falls.

Lilly raises her hand and concentrates. "Off! OFF! OFF!"

Nothing changes.

"What? Nothing?" Are you doing your power-breathing thing?" Oak asked her.

Lilly gives him a sideways glance. "Yes. Of course."

The dome wall shudders—flickering with every impact. Laser blasts slash into the dome wall, relentless, searing.

"I just can't feel it! I need to get out there!" Lilly says.

"We open the dome, and we're dead."

"If we don't stop them soon, we're still dead."

Another silence stretches too long. Then—

"Wait! Kwi-Li!" Lilly turns to her little robot. "How did you get out of the dome before, undetected?"

The little gati shrugs. "Yuchii, of course. He has a tunnel under the dome. It leads out."

A flicker of hope spreads across Lilly's face.

"I can do it. Out there," she says quietly. "I can shut it down. I think... if I'm close enough, maybe... my Ohmuno thing will work."

"No," Oak snaps. "It's suicide."

"I have to."

"Then I'm coming with you."

She shakes her head. "If I fail, you'll need to protect them. All of them. That's your job now."

Oak stares at her, jaw tight. Words press behind his teeth— things he's never said. Things he knows he can't. So instead, he gives her a pained smile and says, "Go do your Ohmuno thing."

Kwi-Li grabs Lilly's hand.

A heartbeat later, they're gone.

# Chapter 156

## Yuchii's Tunnel

Beneath the dome, Yuchii leads in silence.

Lilly and Kwi-Li have to run. The ice tunnels groan above them like an old beast shifting in its sleep. Lilly's heart is racing through frozen halls until the tunnel opens onto the storm.

She surfaces in chaos.

Noxiars rocket overhead.

Energy blasts crack the sky, slamming against the dome.

The diablopero looms at the edge of the shield—like a mechanical god carved from nightmare.

Noxiars spot her and attack.

Their laser blasts slice the air—hitting only frost and mist.

Kwi-Li blinks her in and out, strobing her presence—keeping her invisible between flashes.

Lilly moves like breath through wind.

The diablopero turns.

She reaches inward, into the ancient stillness, into something deeper than fear.

She whispers to the machine, "You do not see me."

It pauses.

Confused.

She runs. Straightforward.

It lunges—blind.

She dives beneath it, sliding across the ice.

It might've been the bump of ice under her back—or her loose grip on Zak's sticky bomb—but she dropped it.

A claw slams down on her head.

She's pinned to the frozen dome ceiling.

From below, she can see the terror in everyone's faces.

Her hand scrambles through the swirling snow, searching for Zak's prize weapon.

The claw presses harder. Her vision starts to blur.

Then—

Her fingers find it. The bumpy surface of a ball.

In one swift motion, she slaps Zak's sticky EMP grenade to the beast's underbelly.

"Shut down!" she screams.

The diablopero twitches.

Zak's device triggers.

The beast convulses—every joint spasming like a cockroach doused in lightning.

Then—it collapses.

Above her, the Noxiar swarm freezes.

One by one, they fall—crashing like dead crows onto the icy dome.

Inside, silence clings, in awe.

Then the cheers erupt.

Not just celebration—but the wild, tear-streaked roar of people who nearly didn't make it.

They scream with cracked voices and broken breaths. They scream like they've just realized they are going to live.

Outside, the remaining Cankers stare—stupefied.

Some bolt in random directions.

Some drop to their knees, slapping noxiars, begging them to wake up.

Lilly approaches two.

They raise their arms in surrender.

Maybe they pee themselves before their voks clatter to the ice.

Zak's voice buzzes through the comm: "Wow! It was under swarm control. You did it!"

"You weren't sure!?" Lilly shouts back.

"Don't be such a baby," someone teases.

Moments later, the Royal Gesh drops from the sky in multitudes —precision and force wrapped in white and gold. They sweep in, capturing the dazed cankers without a fight.

Haro lands beside Lilly, shield still humming, vok out and ready. She glances at Lilly, then at the crumpled diablopero, then at the lifeless machines scattered across the snow.

"Wow," she says—low, stunned.

Then she tucks her vok away and smooths her coat. "Next time, save something for the rest of us, Ist-Kee Lilly."

She gives Lilly one of the best smiles ever.

Lilly smiles back, adrenaline still buzzing under her skin.

It's over.

# Chapter 157
## The Ring of Yishi

The air above the open amphitheater shimmers with light, as if Phi Guya itself decides to smile. Banners sway along vine-wrapped columns, their deep crimsons and golds gleaming in the midday sun.

Laughter floats up in waves.

The dome of Phi Guya stands in the distance—a shining arc behind the stage, like the secret base has been sealed away and healed.

An entire battalion of robotic ants builds this overnight, just for this moment.

It is the Royal Gesh Awards Ceremony—the first of its kind in generations. A moment meant to mark bravery. Sacrifice. Renewal.

And everyone comes.

Families press together in rows, sitting shoulder to shoulder along terraces of flowering stone.

Children wear handmade paper medals.

Older citizens clutch each other's hands. Some weep quietly.

Orriah—the girl Nafari once bullied—sits among her friends. Their faces are painted with symbols of the Ohmuno.

And in the center of it all, beneath a carved arch lined with silver lights, stands the Queen of Seairland—tall, poised, robed in ocean blue, her gown stitched with the history of her people. At her right, Princess Chico stands proud and still.

And before them, four figures wait.

They intended to place Lilly first in line.

Lilly insisted they put Kwi-Li first.

The little gati stands proud and blinking, like a loyal star fallen from the sky to stand beside her. It wears coveralls and a baseball cap. Two floating balloons—one blue, one green—bob gently from its wrist. Its other hand holds tightly to Lilly's.

Lilly stands next. Her white dress uniform glows in the sunlight—trimmed in gold, tailored crisp. The Ohmuno medallion hangs at her neck, catching the light, a golden promise of everything still to come.

Oak stands at her side. He wears the black uniform of a Burden—no gold, no badge, only quiet honor stitched into every line. His shoulders stay squared, his stance solid as stone. But his eyes lock forward, terrified of being onstage.

Beside him, Riz wears the same black. She refuses the polish. Her boots are scuffed. Her braid sits crooked. A grease stain sneaks out beneath her sleeve. She looks like she hasn't slept in two days. She looks perfect—to one person.

And Zak.

He wears no uniform. Just the respectful formal wear of a Phi Guya citizen—slightly too big in the sleeves, collar half-tucked. His dark curls refuse to behave. His fingers fidget at his sides. He tilts his head and whispers out of the side of his mouth. "Shrimp."

A smile cracks on Lilly's face. "Geek." She whispers back.

In the front row, Carnel can barely sit still. His bruised, green face is streaked with emotion and orange cheese doodle dust. He wears a leaking grin. One hand clutches a napkin, the other flails like it's giving a speech of its own.

Oak glances at Lilly's Ohmuno necklace, then leans in. His shoulder brushes hers. "You're wearing your mother's medal? You've always kept it tucked in."

Lilly leans toward him—tells herself it's just to hear him better. "It reminds me to keep searching for her… and reminds them—we're here for them. And we're just beginning."

Her other hand stays wrapped tight around Kwi-Li's.

Her father sits in the crowd, tall despite the bruises along his jaw. His hair is cut. The beard is gone. His eyes never leave her.

Aubrin floats upright in a vertical recovery chair beside the Queen. His bruises have faded to yellow and green. He looks exhausted. But defiant. His chair does not wobble.

The Queen raises a hand. The crowd falls silent.

"Today," she begins, her voice ringing like glass, "we honor not only bravery—but selflessness. Not only victory—but defiance. Please hold your applause until the end."

The crowd rumbles, barely containing its energy.

The Queen steps forward, holding a velvet-lined pillow. On top, rests a ring of crystal—pale, smooth, softly glowing.

"Lilly-D, Royal Khem Gesh. Ohmuno. For saving Phi Guya. For protecting Seairland. For defending Earth itself—I present you the highest award the Queen of Seairland can give: the first of eight sections of the Satya Vok, the Ring of Yishi."

Surprise flashes through Lilly. She glances at Oak, then at Riz, then at Zak.

Their expressions answer back: *"Oh… there it is."*

Lilly steps forward. The moment her fingers touch the ring, her hand trembles. The Queen closes her own over Lilly's. Their eyes meet.

"Thank you," the Queen whispers, just for her.

Lilly bows. Humble. Grateful.

# Chapter 158

The queen steps to them, one by one.

Oak is next.

"Oakeros, Bewhart, Nimaelle, Thassindra, Velinqua, Daroen, Elaithe, Marneth, Kessarai, Luthienn…" she begins—and just keeps going.

Lilly glances over at Oak and shoots him one of her famous *'Are you serious?'* looks.

Oak smirks and throws back his usual innocent, wordless *'What?'* face in return.

"…for unwavering strength in the face of opposition, and bravery when retreat seemed the only choice, I present to you the Royal Khem Gesh Award for Bravery."

Oak bows with military precision—sharp, exact, like he knows every rule in the book.

"Zakary Albert Peterson, for exceptional mastery in technology and innovation, and for turning obstacles into breakthroughs — I present you with the Queen's Medal for Innovation."

Zak looks stunned—frozen like someone hit pause.

"Princess Rizuko, my daughter," the queen declares loud enough for all to hear. Then, more softly, just for her, "Riz." They exchange knowing smiles. "For fearless mastery of the skies, guiding her craft through fire and fury with unwavering focus. I present to you the Royal Gesh award, Wings of Aviation."

Riz blinks. "Wait, so... does this mean I'm officially not the Grease Princess anymore?"

The queen raises an eyebrow. "Will you stop sneaking into junkyards?"

Riz snorts. "Probably not." She shrugs and smirks like it's the most obvious answer in the world.

Laughter ripples through the crowd, light and real.

The queen straightens, her voice lifting. "Then let this moment be marked by unity."

Applause erupts—not loud at first, but swelling, spreading like sunlight through storm clouds. Grateful. Aching. It rolls across the crowd and echoes long after hands fall still.

# Chapter 159
## Ohmuno!

A stillness falls.
Then—
"Ohmuno!"
It starts with a single voice.
One voice. Then two. Then the entire crowd.
"Ohmuno! Ohmuno! Ohmuno!"
It rises—a chant, a hope, a roar of belonging.
Lilly's grip tightens around Kwi-Li's hand. Her eyes flick to her father.

He's crying.

Lilly smiles, but it's small—like she doesn't want to take up more space than she already has. Pride glows in her eyes, but buried underneath is something quieter. A hope that the others are being seen too.

Aubrin smiles at her—proud, agreeing. He raises a hand toward the crowd.

Silence drops like a blanket.

He turns to Zak. "I am proud to welcome Zakary Albert Peterson as a citizen of Phi Guya. He will apprentice under our Technician, Carnel."

Carnel shrieks. Something pops. He jumps so high his chair tips.
People nearby definitely start looking nervous.

Aubrin smiles. "And today, I also announce my retirement as head of the Royal Gesh."

Gasps ripple across the audience like a sudden wind.

"I see a new era beginning. One focused on change and unity. One that needs someone youthful and open-minded. It must be one of our Royal Gesh—someone who has proven, time and again, that the Gesh are strong, effective, and necessary. Someone who holds more respect than any other Royal Gesh..."

He pauses.

"...And so, I nominate Ist-San Haro to take my place as the new Iyengar of the Royal Gesh of Seairland."

For a moment—silence.

Then thunderous applause swallows Haro's name.

She stands frozen, mouth open.

Someone gives her a push, and she stumbles toward the stage like she's forgotten how legs work.

Vishot, already halfway up, looks like someone just punched him in the gut.

He stops.

His cheeks puff like a startled frog.

He sinks back into his seat, deflated.

The queen steps forward.

"Well, if this is a time for announcements..."

Aubrin turns to her.

"...then I have one too." She smiles. "Aubrin, I ask for your hand in unity. It's about the only way I can get you to sit still."

Aubrin freezes. He blinks. Then blinks again.

"I... I would be honored."

The crowd explodes—cheers, screams, applause crashing like waves.

Zak turns to Oak. "Does this mean he's going to be king?"

Oak laughs. "I think so."

Lilly and her gang raise their fists and chant: "King Aubrin! King Aubrin!"

The crowd joins them, voices pounding like thunder across the open air.

Up high, where the branches brush the synthetic clouds, a black crow sits—watching.

It doesn't blink.

It doesn't move.

It just watches.

…to be continued…

-END OF BOOK ONE-

# Phisian Language – Alpha Letters

| Symb | Sound |
|---|---|
| п | ASK, SAT, MAD |
| Ǝ | EIGHT, FADE, MAY |
| Ɐ | ALL, HAUL, FOUGHT |
| ᗺ | BABY, HARBOR, TAB |
| 4 | CHERRY, MATCH |
| γ | DISH, READY, LID |
| ж | EGG, MET, BED |
| ıє | EAT, HEAT, SEE, MANY |
| Ⅎ | FIRE, ROUGH, BLUFF, PHASE |
| Ю | GO, BIGGER, HAG |
| Н | HAIL, AHA |
| Ɔ | IT, PIT, BILL |
| ᴐ | ICE, BILE, PIE |
| ₵ | JOKE, BADGER, BUDGE |
| Ҡ | KEEN, CAB, LACQUER, BLOCK |
| ⱴ | LESS, FOLLOW, SOIL |
| ∦ | MAIL, HEMP, STAMMER |
| ㄏ | NOW, VENT, TENOR, FUN |
| Ψ | RANG, HUNG, SWINGER |
| ⊕ | OATS, OWL, BONE, SHOW |
| Θ | HOOT, TWO, TOO |
| φ | OUT, PLOW |

| Symb | Sound |
|---|---|
| Ɵ | OYSTER, BOIL, TOY |
| π | PAL, TRAP |
| Σ | RAIL, BURN, CAR |
| ƨ | SEA, MUST, KISS |
| ц | SHOE, MACHINE, FLUSH |
| ɸ | TICK, BUTTON, BATT |
| ɥ | THIS, EITHER, MATH |
| δ | PURE, COULD, WOOD |
| ɦ | UDDER, MUTT, MUD |
| Ⴟ | VAST, FEVER, RAVE |
| Ɏ | WIN, WHALE |
| Ӿ | TAX, PACT, FAX |
| λ | YES, YELP, YUCK |
| ϟ | HAZE |

## EXAMPLES

| | |
|---|---|
| LILLY | ⱴ Ɔ ⱴ ⱴ ıє |
| ZAK | ϟ п Ҡ |
| OAK | ⊕ Ҡ |
| UNO | Ɵ ㄏ ⊕ |
| PHI | Ⅎ ᴐ |
| PAX | π п Ӿ |

# Phisian Words Used in Book 1 – Abarj to Burden

| Phisian Word | English | |
| --- | --- | --- |
| abarj | death, finish | |
| abarj-kensha | death-seeing | This is the last request a Royal Gesh can make before dying |
| aetha | fly (v) | |
| aether | flyer | term used for flying bots and vehicles |
| agu | finger | |
| ajax | hero | |
| alnahi | treason | |
| Alnahi-Soch | Treason - shame | committing treason to Seairland and Royal Gesh is considered Alnahi Soch |
| amun | queen | |
| ang | limb | also, term used in Royal Gesh - similar to the squad - 13 (2$^{nd}$ to 12$^{th}$ + Shang) Agu per Ang |
| Anubis | Passageway Portal | Large wormhole portal on Earth, Moonh, and Phi |
| ardh | half | |
| Ardhiar | half bot | a type of bot used to navigate non-Royal Gesh genaethers |
| bahu | many | |
| bahu-kwee | many-sphere | a unique, rare robot at Oak's house made up of many tiny spheres |
| Baine | Baine | a realm of Phi - Hateful, large, the cause, and epicenter of much of the turmoil and conflict on Phi |
| burden | burden | term used for a Royal Gesh in training (student) |

# Phisian Words Used in Book 1 – Canker to Gatiar

| | | |
|---|---|---|
| Canker | terrorist | terrorists typically come from the realm of Barea |
| cassii | Oat-like plant on phi | |
| Centag | 10 Millitags in 1 Centag | Term of time (1 Centag is approx. 8.19 Seconds) |
| chocfee | chocfee | a hot drink originating from the chocfee bean in Phi (tastes like a blend of chocolate and coffee) |
| daijo | Ship (large vehicle) | |
| Dekatag | 10 Tags in one Dekatag | Term of time (1 Dekatag is approx. 2.27 Earth hours) |
| Desitag | 10 Centags in 1 Desitag | Term of time (1 Desitag is approx. 1.36 Earth minutes) |
| diablo | devil | |
| Diablopero | Devil Dog | |
| dirt | dirt | |
| dirtling | dirtling | slang used for describing earthlings |
| diushi | missing | lost or missing |
| exfila | evacuate (v) | |
| fang | wasp | |
| flitchi | sneaky | |
| gati | ghost, invisible | |
| Gatiar | ghost bot | usually just called gati for ghost – unique, superior, Royal Gesh bot - undetectable cloaking abilities |

# Phisian Words Used in Book 1 – Geennii to Jaijan

| | | |
|---|---|---|
| Geennii | Self Teleportation | Gati's can disappear and reappear somewhere else using self-created worm-holes |
| gen | person | |
| genaether | person flyer | personal flying vehicles throughout Phi - looks sort of like a Flying snowmobile |
| genus | people | |
| gesh | guardian | |
| gesha | guard (v) | |
| gotress | nature | |
| guarantor | guarantor | a Royal Gesh who takes on a Burden (student) |
| gumen | anus | anatomical, used insultingly |
| guya | earth | |
| hygea | nurse (v) | |
| hygee | nurse | |
| Hygiar | nurse bot | a nurse bot used for basic first aid - silver daddy longlegs – in stasis as a silver sphere |
| hypnos | night | |
| iar | robot | term used for a robot - a person-created machine |
| iyengar | leader | term used for Uno (one, 1st) position - leader of all the Royal Gesh |
| jager | hunter | |
| jagether | Hunter-flyer | bot dragonflies used as pets and recon - look just like Earth's dragonflies |
| jaijan | good bye | |

# Phisian Words Used in Book 1 – Kensha to Nattong

| | | |
|---|---|---|
| kensha | see (v) | |
| Khem | life | |
| Khem-Geshe | Life Guardian | The official term used for Royal Gesh |
| Khemigrah | life force | The ancient way of the Ohmuno - long forgotten by the Royal Gesh |
| kinrik | royal | |
| kwan-jusalon | Circle of Judgement | A formal convening of a council to determine whether someone's actions have broken the law — a ceremonial or legal judgment. |
| Liege | Liege | 8 to 12-year-olds pledging to become a Burden |
| maa | she | |
| mett | kindness | |
| metta | kind (v) | |
| Millitag | 10 Millitag in 1 Centag | Term of time (1 Millitag is approx. 0.82 seconds) |
| mudhi | erase memory | term used for erasing one's memories of a specific event or timeline |
| naquee | pure | |
| Naquee-Hebbe | pure young | youth military party in Rein Rassig - created by Mensch Morder |
| Naquee-Rabb | pure breed | Mensch Morder influences Party of lar Bhanak (party of robot masters) to rename themselves to Naquee Rabb |
| nattong | without | |

| | | |
|---|---|---|
| navok | in | Also, the term used for the armband of the Royal Gesh - it is a receiver of the wearer's intentions |
| ne | no | |
| neph | water | |
| nikum | hate | |
| nikuma | hate (v) | |
| nityi | constant | |
| Noah | engineer | term used for the engineers who orchestrated the realms of all races on Phi |
| nox | war | |
| Noxiar | war bot | bot specifically created for war - human-like features |
| oak | brave | |
| oh | am (to be), as, are, is | |
| ohm | all | |
| ohm | all-time | |
| ohm | everything | |
| ohm | everywhere | |
| ohmuno | all-powerful | |
| pax | peace | |
| pengou | friend | |
| pero | dog | |
| Phi | Planet | Orbits Trappist-1 solar system, it is planet E, 39 light-years from Earth |
| Phi-Guya | Phi-Guya | Phi's base on earth, located in Antarctica, it has a smaller anubis |

# Phisian Words Used in Book 1 – Picus to Uno

| | | |
|---|---|---|
| picus | forest | |
| pomon | fruit | |
| porta | carry (v) | |
| porto-jo | carry vehicle | |
| pumatti | perfection | |
| Seairland | Seairland | a realm of PHI - politically neutral, keepers of Phi peace, home of the Royal Gesh |
| sho | small, mini | |
| sivagen | destroyer | |
| sivala | destroy (v) | |
| sobacco | fecal matter | |
| Sun | Sun | One 'Sun' is one Phi 'day' (1 Phi day is approx. 0.948 Earth days) |
| Tag | 10 Desitags in 1 Tag | Term of time (1 Tag is approx. 13.65 Earth minutes) |
| tirth | animal | |
| thay | teacher | |
| Tyr | great | |
| Tyr-Daijo | great-vehicle | What Phi calls Earth Moon (Noah's ship) |
| Unity | Unity | one phi annual, 100 suns (approximately equal to 94.8 earth days) |
| uno | one | One word has many definitions, (Ne Jannus - Ne abarj) (no birth - no death) (No beginning - No end) |

# Phisian Words Used in Book 1 – Uttar to Zay

| | | |
|---|---|---|
| uttar | ultimate | |
| Uttar Vok | Ultimate Out | considered to be a mythical, ultimate weapon, made up of eight pieces, each found in one of the eight realms |
| vako | later | future time |
| vesta | help (v) | |
| Vestiar | Helper bot | helper robots, come in all different shapes, sizes, and purposes, some old vestiars get re-purposed |
| vestu | helper | |
| vok | out | Also, the scepter used by Royal Gesh that is tied to their armband (netvok) |
| voka | out (v) | |
| waru | bad | |
| Warufang | Bad Wasp | 1st in Circle of Challenges (breathing awareness) |
| yishi | present, presence | |
| zay | again | repetition |

# About the Author

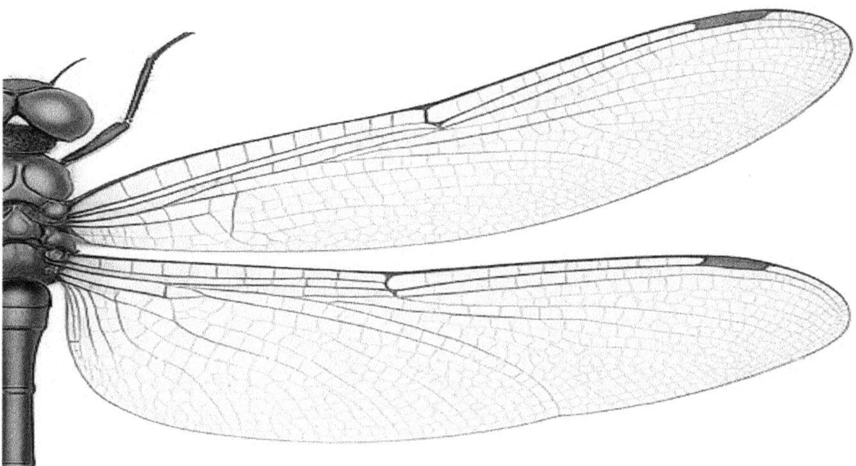

Born and raised in Canada, the author holds a university degree in sciences and has always been awe-struck by the natural world—especially the parts that don't bite. A lifelong love of science and realistic fiction sparks a passion for stories that explore the deep (and sometimes tangled) connections between people, animals, and the universe.

When not writing, the author is usually somewhere outside—hiking, canoeing, sailing, skiing, or just trying to outwalk the local mosquitoes. Home is the east coast of Canada, where the sea, sky, and forest continue to inspire new ideas and a stubborn hope for humanity.